To Yoland "O",

Thank you so much for the support,

Hope you like Atlanta

The
Last
Bad
Decision

A NOVEL

Paula Edwards

First Edition:

JUSTWRITE PUBLISHING
P.O. Box V-46
Palo Alto, CA 94304

Cover Design by Mooncheese Studios
Printed by United Graphics Inc., 2916 Marshall Avenue, P.O. Box 559, Mattoon, IL 61938

Printed in the United States of America

Acknowledgments

Thanks to ALL who have assisted me on this project. Hugs and kisses to all of you!

Acknowledgements

To every hustler in every ghetto:
You can never win the battle if your mind is too weak to fight!

The
Last
Bad
Decision

A NOVEL

1

The sound of the doorbell brought Nikki out of her trance. She got up from the sofa and scratched her head, then ran her fingers through her kinky do. Suddenly, she looked around the untidy living room confused as to why she was standing.

There it was again. DING—DONG!

The roaring bell made her sway toward the front door, kicking a McDonald's bag out of her path on the way. She thought about picking up the three stale fries that flew from the bag, but instead, decided on cleaning the entire house later, and continued toward the door. Without hesitation, she yanked it open and stared blankly at the two suited men standing before her.

"How are you, ma'am? My name is Ted Summerhill and this is Kevin Miller. We're…"

"I'm not interested," Nikki interrupted with a look of intimidation. The smell of days-old alcohol was heavy on her breath and the unwanted guests tried to be sly as they covered their noses. She stood in the doorway and held the door close to her body to keep the intruders from noticing the dingy jeans she wore. She hadn't done her laundry in weeks, and pulled the jeans from the clothes-hamper as a last resort. Then she realized her hair hadn't been attended to in days either, and rested her arm on top of her head, hoping they wouldn't notice her rivalry strands. "I swear you damn Jehovah Witnesses just won't quit, will you?" she snapped, wishing she had never opened the door.

"Ma'am, we're not..."

"And stop ma'amin' me!" Nikki interrupted again. "Shit, I know you can't tell, but I ain't that old. And anyway, do y'all know what time it is?" There was silence. Nikki glanced over at the clock on the wall. Seeing it was almost one o'clock in the morning made her wonder just who the two men really were. She studied their professional attire with caution, while trying to maintain her wobbly balance.

"Is it okay to speak now?" Kevin Miller asked, nearly jumping down Nikki's throat. Kevin had an athletic figure with a skin complexion similar to dark chocolate. He glared resentfully into her dilated pupils, intimidating her the way she tried to intimidate him.

Ted Summerhill saw the tension and hurried to step in before it escalated. "Ma'am, we're investigators. May we come in?"

"Investigators?" Nikki asked, frowning and looking Ted directly in the eye. Ted wore no facial hairs on his pale face, attaining the boyish look of a teen. He looked so young that Nikki didn't feel comfortable communicating with him on an adult level. Still frowning, she turned to Kevin and asked, "What the hell did Chancey do now? I swear that bastard stays in trouble! That's what I should'a named his ass. Trouble!" Nikki paused and swung the door open wide. "You can come in all you want. The nigga ain't here!"

"Ma'am, your son is dead," Ted murmured.

Nikki froze. She stared him down without blinking. Her mouth flew open and stayed that way for several seconds.

Ted let out a sympathetic sigh and said, "I'm sorry to give you such horrifying news..."

"Are you sure it's Chancey? Chancey Walker?" Nikki asked, voice slightly trembling. Again, Ted tried to be as sympathetic as he could while assuring her they had a positive identification. As he went on to explain the cause of Chancey's death, Nikki quickly placed her hands over her ears and cried, "No! Just stop!" as if his words were too painful to hear.

Kevin was unmoved by Nikki's emotional outburst, and was cold when he rolled his eyes and reached inside his briefcase after a pen and pad. "Ma'am, we need to ask you a few questions about your son. When was the last time you saw him?"

Nikki cleared her throat and licked the salty tears from her lips. She took in a deep breath and whispered, "About an hour ago." More tears began to stream down her cheeks. She sniffled continuously.

"Here, let me help you out," Ted told her as he went for his handkerchief.

Kevin continued. "Did he seem unusual or upset?"

Nikki closed her eyes, took another deep breath, and thought back to the violent argument they had earlier.

"Did you know of any altercations or..."

"PLEASE!" Nikki yelled at Kevin. "I can't handle no more...not right now..."

"Hey look, I'm only trying to get to the bottom of this, alright? It would make my job a lot easier if I knew what led up to this, like, was he in any kind of trouble?"

"How the hell should I know? He never told me shit!"

Ted butted in with great sincerity when he said, "I think it'll be okay to get in contact with Miss Evans a little later in the week." He pulled a couple of papers from his briefcase and handed them to Nikki. "Meanwhile," he said, "here's the number to the coroner's office where your son is."

Nikki took the information and stared at it.

"Is someone else here with you?" Ted asked. "You shouldn't be alone..."

"My daughter's in the room, sleep," Nikki irritably cut in.

"Is she old enough to understand what took place tonight?" Ted asked. "Because we can make arrangements for a counselor to come out and talk..."

"She's old enough! Thank you."

"Okay, no problem," Ted said and backed off. "Let me leave my business card with you. If there's anything I can do...*anything*...you make sure you let me know."

Nikki took Ted's business card and nodded her head, then closed the door in the investigators' faces.

"Poor lady," Ted said as they walked away. "Don't you think you were a bit hard on her tonight?"

"There you go again," Kevin said, trailing Ted closely.

"Come on, Kev, give me a break here! All I'm saying is I feel you came across kind of hard."

"Look, I've been doing this job for over five years, and you've been doing it for what, a year and a half now?"

Ted stopped in his tracks, causing Kevin to trip over his heel. "And just what is that supposed to mean?" Ted asked, slightly upset.

"It means I haven't been employed five years for nothing, Summerhill," Kevin answered in an elevated voice. "Let me put it to you this way. I'm tired of you screwing up our cases."

"I beg your pardon!"

"Every time we go out to someone's house to do an investigation, or even just to ask a few questions, you gotta get all touched and emotional to the point where we end up leaving with nothing! Just like tonight! We have nothing! 'Just get back to us when you feel better' you tell 'em. And what happens? What happens, Summerhill?! I'll tell you what happens! We never hear from them again, that's what happens! They end up avoiding us or moving out of town or something." Kevin paused and grimaced at his partner.

"I'm sorry if I have a heart, okay! Shit! The poor woman just found out she no longer has a son, for God's sake. I mean, what the fuck, man! We're gonna wake up in the morning and go on with our lives. And she…she's gonna wake up remembering nothing but this rude asshole at her door, prying on her dead son."

"You know, Summerhill, I don't think a clean-cut white boy like you can handle a job like this—not in Watts. It's nothing like Utah. Oh no! This right here is the real world, baby-boy. You know how many young men I've seen die around this camp? Murders, drive-bys, suicides, you name it, I've seen it! And every single time it's the same old shit. Parents have no idea how this could'a happened to their babies. They didn't know their son was out selling drugs every night. But, their son keeps coming up with unexplained money, cars, and jewelry. They didn't know their son was a gang member. Yet, their son has gang slogans tattooed across his neck, chest, and arms. 'I never saw any strange activities going on.' 'He never told me anything to make me think there was something wrong.' It's always,

'I didn't know!' You know why that is, Summerhill?"

Ted knew not to open his mouth. It was obvious he wasn't getting a word in.

"I'll tell you why," Kevin continued without taking a breath. "Because most of the time, the parents are so far out in left field they wouldn't know what the hell was going on with their kids if it slapped 'em in the face! Like this lady here," Kevin said, extending his arm toward Nikki's apartment. "She's so strung out, I doubt if she even remembers we were here tonight."

*   *   *

Nikki stood and looked around her dreary living room with tears flooding her eyes. Within seconds her entire face was soaked. Her eyes were bloodshot red. She could feel her knees weakening, and without warning they buckled, causing her to collapse. She laid there and thought about her one and only son who was now just a memory. "OH GOD!" she cried. She sat up on the floor in an Indian-style position and rocked her body back and forth as she tried to make sense of it all. She thought back to the words that came out of the investigators' mouths and almost lost it. She swallowed the large lump in her throat and held her breath to recoup. Then she leaned her forehead in the palm of her hand and closed her eyes—that's when she saw the image of her mother holding a four-year-old Chancey by the ear.

"Nikki, where did this boy learn all this profanity from?" she heard her mother ask. She appeared to have just gotten home from work, standing on her swollen legs in her Denny's uniform.

Nikki saw her petite self reach into the closet and grab the tightest mini skirt she could find. Her long, wavy hair was pulled up into a bun with a few curly strands dangling on each side of her face. Her golden skin was smooth and blemish-free. She was so young, so pretty, and so unconcerned. "What he say?" she heard herself casually ask.

"He called Setchi a B.I.T.C.H.," her mother told her, spelling the word "bitch" out.

Nikki frowned when she saw herself laughing.

"You think that's funny? You are so stupid sometimes, Nikole!"

"Dang, Ma, won't 'chew lighten up a lil' bit!"

"Why don't you GROW UP a little bit! You have two kids and ain't nothing but a kid your damn self! Hell, it's a good thing Niecy keeps Chancey like she does, 'cause you sure as hell ain't doing a damn thing for 'em! I feel sorry for Setchi. She don't have nobody! I try to do what I can for her, but it's hard. It's not like I'm walking around here with some time on my hands. Hell, after your father died, I had to take on two jobs just to make the house note."

"Ain't nobody making you work two jobs."

"Well, it ain't like you're helping make ends meet. When you get your county check, you're nowhere to be found. I'm doing everything by myself around here. You don't help clean up, cook, pay bills, nothing! Not a damn thing! All you do is sit around and smoke that weed shit all day, which by the way is stopping as of today. I'm tired of my house smelling like smoke all the damn time. If you wanna smoke that shit, you do it outside from now on!"

"Fine!" Nikki snapped. "Now can I get dressed please?"

"Get dressed for what? Where you think you're going at eleven o'clock at night?"

Nikki caught an attitude. "Oh, so now you don't remember me telling you I was going to Niecy's party," she said, rolling her head around.

"First of all, you are too damn young to be at Niecy's party! Second of all, you don't *tell* me shit! YOU GOT THAT! Now see, that's your problem—you think you grown! Ain't but sixteen years old and swear up and down you twenty-six. I'm tired of it! I'm tired of you disrespecting me! And I'm tired of you talking to me like I'm one of your teeny-bopper friends or something, too!"

Nikki sighed and rolled her eyes. Then she slammed her closet door. As her mother rambled on, she even yawned to show how bored she was with their conversation.

"You're not doing a damn thing in life, Nikole. Partying is all you have time for. What about these kids? You don't spend no time with them. NONE! Chancey is damn near five years old and can't even count to ten. Now if that ain't ridiculous, I don't know what is! And look at Setchi over there…"

Nikki tried to find Setchi in her thoughts. She concentrated long and hard, but couldn't seem to vision her two-year-old at all.

"Her diaper's so damn full, she can barely move," her mother jumped back into her head and added. "And I bet you haven't even fed these kids today, have you?"

Chancey butted in with large, innocent eyes and said, "No! And we hungry too, Nana!" He stood taller than the average four-year-old, and his long, wavy hair was styled with four fuzzy cornrows going to the back of his head. Nikki could see now why so many people found her son adorable. He was distinctive. One of a kind! His eyebrows were thick with a natural arch, and his eyelashes were long and full, and spread out like fans over his eyes.

Nikki started chuckling to herself, remembering his lashes being so long, she had to actually trim them with scissors. Then she corrected her memory—it was her mother who kept them trimmed. Suddenly, out of nowhere, the flashback returned. She saw her mother look at her and shake her head. She then saw herself grow defensive again. "I was gonna feed them as soon as I got dressed," she heard herself say. Her head was still rolling around, expressing mad attitude.

"We hungry now!" Chancey pouted with folded arms.

"Shut up, faggot!" Nikki snapped. "You always crying like a little sissy! Setchi don't cry as much as you do and she's a girl!"

"ENOUGH!" Nikki's mother screamed. "I'm tired of you talking to that boy like that! What'n the hell is wrong with you?"

The whole flashback scene was beginning to drive Nikki up the wall. She got up from the floor, walked in the bathroom and glanced around the tiny space, hoping to find something else to focus on. She looked over at the bathtub and discovered the dirty ring around it. The dirt stain didn't come as a surprise; it had been there for days. But to take charge of her conscious, she tried to plan out loud what she would clean first. "The bathroom or the living room?" she asked herself, forgetting about the bedroom, kitchen, dirty walls, and carpet. It wasn't long before the flashback took over her mental state of mind again. Those ever-so-promising words from her mother began to ease their way back into her ears.

"One of these days you're gonna regret everything you're doing to these kids, Nikole."

"What am I doing? God! I'm not even doing nothing to them!" the sixteen-year-old Nikki cried.

"That's exactly right! You're doing nothing to them, nothing for them, NOTHING! You're selfish! All you do is think about yourself. As long as your hair and nails are done and you got some drugs to smoke..."

"Here you go with the drug shit again."

"You watch your mouth, young lady! Who in the hell do you think you are?"

"Well, shoot, you need to stop accusing me of using drugs, then!"

"What do you think marijuana is, Nikole?"

"It's a herb!" Nikki thought she was smart.

Her mother chuckled sarcastically. She by no means found Nikki funny, but found her stupidity unbelievable! "Let me tell you what that herb is doing to your ignorant ass," she said, making quotation marks out of her fingers to quote the word "herb". "It's doing nothing but building a bridge to something stronger like crack! That's right, CRACK! You better change your ways, Nikki, or else you're gonna be sorry one of these days. Mark my word. I may be dead and gone in my grave..."

Nikki shivered at the haunting sound of her mother's voice, which echoed so loud and clear in her mind as though she had just heard it yesterday. What terrified her most was the fact that she hadn't heard or seen her mother in over three years. Then it struck her. "I don't have a mother or a son no more," she muttered, thinking back to the day of her mother's funeral.

She became disgusted with the beautiful sixteen-year-old she saw in her mind. She figured if she had taken heed to her mother's powerful advice back then, it would have saved her the pain and misery she suffered today. She stood over the sink and stared at her tear-stained face in the mirror. She immediately hated what she saw and was determined to make a change. "This time it's for good, Mama," she confessed as more tears fell from her eyes. "This time it's for good."

2

EARLY NINTIES

Chancey's eyes roamed around his surroundings constantly. He kept a firm hold on his gun, making sure his grip wasn't too tight around the trigger. He looked down at his gray Converses that were once white to make sure the laces were tied, which made him notice, then worry about his overly-sized blue jeans. "Man, I should'a wore my other jeans. These are saggin' too much, huh?"

"Nah, they cool. Just make sure your shoelaces are tied this time. You know what happened yesterday," Rondell said, immediately checking over his own apparel to make sure everything was in tack. He let his guard down and sluggishly leaned against the Security Pacific building. "I hope we get a lotta money today. I wanna get me a fat-ass medallion for my rope chain."

"Yeah, and I wanna get me some more British Knights," Chancey said.

"What happened to the white ones you just bought?"

"I still got 'em. They too clean to be wearin' everyday. I'ma wait and break 'em out the next time we go shoot some hoop at the gym,"

Chancey said.

Rondell brought his arm up toward his face to look at his watch. "I know one thing, my ass is tired of standing out here. We been out here almost thirty minutes. Don't nobody need no money today? Shit."

"What happened to all that 'you gotta be patient' bullshit you was talkin' yesterday?"

"It wasn't takin' this long yesterday…"

"Yeah, whatever…"

"Shhh, be quiet," Rondell whispered. "You hear that?"

Chancey stepped behind the building—Rondell right behind him. They listened to the car's motor as it approached. Chancey tilted his head and glimpsed around the building's corner, spying on what would be their next robbery victim, this time a Caucasian woman who appeared to be in her mid-forties.

She got out of her flawless, green Volvo and locked the doors. She removed her sunglasses, sat them on top of her head, and secured her purse underneath her arm as she walked up to the automatic teller machine. The boys watched like two hungry dogs as the unsuspecting woman pressed some numbers on the keypad, then waited for her money.

"'Ey, cuz," Chancey whispered. "She got it."

Rondell peeped around Chancey. "Where she put it?" he asked.

"In 'er purse."

"Okay, um…you don't see nobody, do you?" Rondell nervously asked.

"Just come on before she get her ass back in the car," Chancey snapped, and ran from the side of the building.

Without warning, the two frail boys were in the woman's face. Chancey aimed his gun right at her temple and cocked the hammer back. The woman became frantic and started screaming at the top of her lungs, alarming a couple of police officers who happened to be patrolling the vicinity.

"ONE-TIME!" Rondell shouted. He snatched the woman's purse and took off running across the empty parking lot. Chancey took off after him. Rondell was smooth when he jumped a brick wall that separated the bank from the residential area just seconds before the officers whipped in the parking lot after them.

Realizing the cops were hot on his trail, Chancey threw the gun over the wall before attempting to jump it, figuring being caught without a weapon would take at least a year or two off his sentence.

"FREEZE!" one of the officers hollered from behind with a raised gun. His white face was purple. His breathing was wild and out of control. "Alright, now come down from the wall. SLOWLY!" he shouted. Chancey was devastated. Feeling afraid of being shot, he eased his way down from the wall and put his hands up. The out-of-breath officer approached Chancey with caution. "GET DOWN! NOW!!!"

Chancey looked around and saw he was being surrounded by lots of men in blue uniforms with pistols pointed at his head. He immediately lay flat on his stomach, not realizing how warm it was in Los Angeles until the side of his face brushed against the fiery pavement. He quickly lifted his head, only to have an officer slam it back down. "MAN, THIS GROUND IS HOT!" he shouted.

"TOO BAD!" the officer shouted back. He pressed his knee between Chancey's shoulder blades, while other officers moved in quickly to help apprehend their suspect. "Got any sharp objects on you that might stick me?" one officer asked, patting up and down Chancey's legs.

"No," Chancey mumbled, wishing like hell that he did.

Soon, the scene was packed with crowds of people gazing in wonderment, and police cars with flashing red and blue lights. Everyone watched as the officers grabbed Chancey and brought him to his feet for questioning.

Chancey didn't notice all the chaos, and all the inquiring from law officials went in one ear and out the other. He was busy watching the officer climbing over the brick wall. He pictured him finding the gun, then pictured his prints all over it. He crossed his fingers and held his breath, hoping Rondell was smart enough to have picked the gun up. Minutes later, Chancey saw the officer return, smiling proudly as he held the firearm up for everyone to see.

"Good job, Woods!" shouted one of his colleagues.

It was all over and Chancey knew it. No more easy money. No more out-running police officers who were too slow to keep up. And no more beating cases. He let out a big sigh and choked back his tears as they escorted him to the back of one of the police cars.

*   *   *

"Well, well, well, back again, huh?" a detective asked when he entered the room and saw Chancey. "Only this time, I think you'll be staying for awhile," he said and released a monstrous giggle. The loose flab around his middle jiggled and jolted until he settled down. "Who knows though," he added at the end of his malicious cackle, "we might be able to pull some strings and get you out a lot sooner if you cooperate with us. I mean, after all, the gun *was* unloaded," he said and kneeled down beside Chancey. Chancey slid down in his chair and folded his arms. The detective continued with his bribery. "Give us the name of the guy that was with you and we'll see what we can do," he said.

Frowning, "What guy you talkin' about?" Chancey asked in a sarcastic kind of way.

"Oh, I don't know, you tell me. Was it your buddy, Kaylin? Rondell Nelson? You tell me," the detective suggested, returning the same sarcastic attitude.

"I don't know what 'chew talkin' about."

"You think I'm stupid, kid?"

Chancey stared straight ahead.

"Look, I'm sure you'd rather be at home playing Nintendo or something instead of being in a dump like this, wouldn't you?" Pausing for a second, "How old are you, kid? Ten? Eleven?" the detective asked.

"Twelve!" Chancey snapped with cockiness.

"Wow! Twelve years old! Handsome too! A pretty-boy! Smooth skin, curly hair, long eyelashes…them boys are gonna have a whole bunch of fun with you…"

Chancey cringed.

"Tell you what though. Work with me and you won't have to suffer long. You'll do a year, maybe two, but at least you'll be home before your sixteenth birthday," the detective said.

Still, Chancey showed no signs of giving in. He continued to stare straight ahead with his lips sealed.

The detective was fed up with his stubbornness. "For the last time, kid, WHO WAS THE GUY THAT RAN?!"

"And for the last time," Chancey said, "I told you, I DON'T KNOW…"

"Alright, have it your way!" the irate detective said, cutting Chancey off in mid-sentence. He got up from his kneeling position and headed toward the door. "Guess I'll see you back on the streets in about five to ten."

*   *   *

4 YEARS LATER

Chancey stood in front of the California Youth Authority building wearing blue jeans, a white T-shirt, and a pair of white PuMas. He felt like a soldier who had just been released from the Army, believing that only a real man could survive what he went through. He stood tall and confident as he ran his fingers down his peach-fuzzed goatee.

It was Friday, mid-February, and even though the sun played peek-a-boo with L.A. most of the day, the air was still hot and humid. Chancey looked up the lonely street and extended his arms to stretch. "You got the time?" he asked a security guard returning from his lunch break.

Not stopping, the security guard quickly looked down at his watch and said, "Seven-ten," before entering the building.

Chancey didn't bother to say thank you. He was a free man now, and didn't feel the need to brown-nose anymore. He wondered if he told his mother the correct time of his releasing, which he suddenly remembered that he did. "Where the fuck is she?!" he snapped to himself when he realized he'd been waiting on her for almost an hour. Just as he headed toward the phone booth to call home, a shabby, black, '76 Buick Regal with tinted windows pulled up. Chancey peered with squinted eyes as the car slowed in front of him. When he noticed the dark complexion of his best friend, Kaylin, he threw his fist up to his mouth and shouted, "Look at my boy!"

Kaylin slapped the handle in park and quickly leaped from his vehicle. "WHAT'S UP, FOOL!" he yelled, picking up Chancey and almost tossing him in mid air.

"I thought my mother was coming," Chancey said and looked for her inside the car.

"Damn! It's good to see you, too."

"I'm sayin' though, I thought my mother signed for me."

"She did, but uh…"

"But what?"

Not knowing what to say, "She had something important to do," Kaylin said.

Chancey exploded. "She had something *important* to do?! What kind'a shit is that?"

"C'mon, cuz, quit trippin'."

"Nah, fuck that! Her ass could'a picked me up!" Chancey paused for a second, thinking he was beginning to sound like a spoiled brat. "That's cool though, fuck 'er!" he mumbled and got in the car.

Chancey wasn't angry, just hurt. He wanted to use this time to make amends with his mother. Tell her how sorry he was for disrespecting her in the past, and explain how he's now a changed man. He thought back to all the times he cursed and threatened her, and wondered if she was even happy that he was coming home.

Chancey's dejected facial expression made Kaylin sick. He felt like going against the grain and telling Chancey the truth about Nikki and what she was *really* up to. But instead, he said, "Guess who had a baby?" deterring Chancey's thoughts.

"Who?"

"Rosie."

"Puerto Rican Rosie from Juniper?"

"Yep! She don't live on Juniper no more. Her parents moved back to New York. She stay in the projects now."

"The *projects*?"

"Yep! In the Jordan's," Kaylin said. "She stay over by the gym." There was silence for what seemed like forever to Kaylin. Unable to hold the gossip in a second longer, he added, "She don't go to school no more or nothing."

Chancey shook his head. "I just knew she was gon' be a doctor or a lawyer or something. Rosie used to be hella smart! I can't believe that shit, cuz," he said.

"You not gon' believe who the baby came out looking like either," Kaylin said and paused with a taunting chuckle.

Chancey waited. Then, "Tell me, nigga!" he blurted out.

"Rondell!" Kaylin said and laughed.

Chancey's face soured. "Ronnie?"

"Yep! Just like his twin," Kaylin said. He went on to tell Chancey about all the latest gossip on the streets—who died, who got locked up, and who had babies. "And remember Vic from Nickerson Gardens?" he asked. "That fool got shot six times! They found his body up at the school."

"DAMN!" Chancey shouted. "Do they know who did it?"

"You know the po-po don't give a fuck. Shit, it's just anotha' nigga dead. That's why I don't be out there in the streets no more. Shit, I'm try'na get all my credits so I can graduate next year."

"Is that right?"

"Yep," Kaylin said with a boastful nod. "I'm working now and everything, cuz!"

"That's cool, man," Chancey said, hoping he didn't sound as jealous as he felt.

"Oh, I almost forgot..." Kaylin took some folded dollars from his ashtray and said, "This right here is from Ma. I'ma give you some more when I get paid on Friday. You know I can't have my boy walkin' around broke."

"Good lookin' out," Chancey said and smiled. "So, where you work at?"

"Food 4 Less," Kaylin said, smiling from embarrassment. "I only work about fifteen hours a week, but shit, it's a job, you know?"

"Is that how you got this?" Chancey asked as his eyes roamed the interior of Kaylin's car.

"Yeah, and I know it looks like a hoopty. But don't trip, 'cause my shit runs like a Benz!" Kaylin said, causing Chancey to laugh hard. He laughed even harder when he remembered the car stalling at two stoplights.

The sight of Kaylin's car would make anyone laugh. The rust pretty much took over its color, both tail lights were covered with red tape, and the right side of the bumper was caved in, forcing the head light to hang freely from the wire it was attached to.

Kaylin knew his transportation needed work. Still, he drove it with pride, occasionally fixing it up with what little cash he had to work with. "Just wait," he said, "I already got the windows tinted. Now, all I gotta do is get some bodywork done, and get it painted. Mmm-humph...my shit gon' look brand new, watch! And after I do all that, I'ma have front-to-rear put on my shit! Watch, cuz, I'm 'bout to come through hittin' crazy switches!"

Chancey tried to visualize Kaylin's dream, but couldn't focus on nothing but the familiar scene around him as they drove across the overpass just above the 110 Freeway. Poverty grew thick in the air when they hit Imperial Highway in Watts. The Neighborhoods were filled with run-down houses, decayed churches, liquor stores covered in graffiti, and small soul food restaurants owned by big-time drug dealers.

Watts included an area of widespread projects that were divided into three groups: Nickerson Gardens, Imperial Courts, and Jordan Downs. Each housing project consisted of apartment complexes with clotheslines crossing their backyards and noise echoing throughout the units day in and day out. All the gun shots, police sirens, and loud music sounded like one big work of art.

Chancey sighed as he thought about what he was going to do with the rest of his life. He knew whatever he'd do, couldn't be done without money. He looked down and flipped through the bills in his hand.

"That's only three hundred right there, but hopefully, it'll keep you cool 'til Friday. If not, let me know and I'll get some more from my mother."

Chancey smiled. He was just about to get sentimental when Kaylin pulled in the Jordan Down Projects and said, "There go Rosie."

"Where?" Chancey asked, looking around. When he found her, he yelled out her name, then paused with a puzzled look. "Was she going to my house?"

"Nah, why you say that?" Kaylin asked, feeling and looking guilty.

Before Chancey could act on his friend's self-condemnation, Rosie was approaching the car. Her appearance hadn't changed much. She wore her lengthy spirals pulled back in a ponytail just like always, and her sexy attire was well coordinated with a denim dress, black high-heeled boots, and a pair of silver hoops hanging so low from her ears, they nearly touched her shoulders.

Ronnie, you lucky mothafucka, Chancey thought, eying her curved hips on the sly.

"Hey Chance!" Rosie said and put her arms around Chancey's

neck. She tilted her head back and stared him in the face. "Damn, boy, you don' went and got fine on me."

"Don't tell this nigga that," Kaylin said jokingly.

Rosie said, "You don't look like that same lil' knuckle-head I used to see riding around on a beach-cruiser."

Chancey smiled. His thoughts of telling Rosie how she still looked like the same young lady he had a crush on years ago, and how he was now jealous because she gave in to someone like Rondell of all people, was cut short when he looked around and noticed how unbelievably calm it was. He was used to seeing crowds of young, hardy, teenaged boys and girls hanging out on street corners, on their porches, or in parked cars. And not seeing anyone shooting dice at the neighborhood liquor stores was *very* unusual. "Why's it so quiet around here? Where everybody at?" he asked.

Rosie looked at Chancey, puzzled. "They all over…"

"Bobcat's house," Kaylin quickly butted in.

Chancey chuckled and shook his head. He knew something was up but couldn't quite pinpoint it. He grabbed his blue suitcase from the car, folded his release papers, stuck them in his pocket, and headed toward his unit. Rosie and Kaylin followed closely behind.

"So, Rosie, I hear you got a baby."

Rosie boldly responded. "Yep, a lil' girl."

"What's her name?"

"Ronda!" Kaylin hinted, looking Chancey directly in the eye.

Ronnie, Chancey thought and smiled. He rolled his eyes in Rosie's direction. "Who's the daddy?"

"Why?" she snapped. "You don't know 'em."

Chancey became occupied with the darkness coming from the front window of his apartment as they got closer to unit thirty-six. "Ain't nobody home," he said, ignoring Rosie's statement.

Kaylin said, "Oh yeah, that's right. Nikki had to pick up Setchi…"

"Pick up Setchi?" Rosie stepped in. "Where Setchi go?"

Kaylin looked at her and glared.

Chancey was confused as to why the two were acting so weird. *And why were they trailing him like two lost puppies,* he wondered as he walked up the long flight of steps. Soon as he reached his balcony, the front door gradually opened, but from what he could see, no one opened it. "What the fu…" he mumbled, immediately hardening up as he walked in.

"SURPRISE!!!" everyone, including Kaylin shouted. People ran out from all over the small apartment to hug and kiss on Chancey.

Rosie looked at Kaylin with dumbness written across her face. *My bad, I thought he knew,* her expression said.

Nikki went out of her way to throw the nicest welcome home party for her son. Her one-bedroom apartment was decorated with balloons and confetti from the living room to the bathroom. She had a huge *WELCOME HOME* banner on the living room wall, and in the kitchen, she had party wings and lasagna on the stove, along with two large bottles of liquor sitting on the counter.

"Got 'cha!" Nikki said and gave her son a tight hug. She was in a black fitted dress that hugged her petite shape all the way down to her ankles. On her head was a black cloth enfolded neatly around her cranium. Very little make-up was on her face.

Her tiny apartment was getting thick with people showing up by the minute. Guys sat around the kitchen table playing dominoes. Some squatted in a group and shot dice on the kitchen floor. Girls stood in packs, talking about which guy they wouldn't mind kicking it with, while others rolled their bodies to the music on the living room floor.

Kaylin and Chancey stood in the kitchen nibbling on chicken wings and sneaking sips from the intoxicating beverages on the counter. Chancey leaned against one of the cabinets and bobbed his head to a rap song pounding hard from the speakers. When his favorite part came up, he shouted the words with his lyrical hero, while waving his small glass of Hennessy in the air.

"'Ey!" one boy yelled from the sweaty living room. "Play number ten!" He was pumping his fist and impelling his head back and forth. A tall, lanky boy wearing dark shades handed his marijuana joint to a female standing next to him and walked over to the stereo.

"Ice Cube was hard for this shit, huh?" Kaylin asked, bouncing to the beat.

"Hell yeah! This is all I used to listen to in jail," Chancey said. He looked around the crowded living room, then quickly turned to Kaylin and asked, "Where's Setchi?"

"Damn, nigga, what I look like, Oprah?" Kaylin responded, sucking the meat off his chicken bone.

Chancey marched out the kitchen and made his way through the jammed-packed living room. He spotted his mother leaning against the wall with some teenaged hoodlum in her face. He rudely stepped in front of the lustful boy and asked the whereabouts of his sister.

"She'll be here in a minute," Nikki said. "She went to pick up your cake for me."

"Mmm. So, how you been?" Chancey asked, wondering when she was going to talk to him.

Nikki took her son's hand and led him to the bedroom. "I've been okay. How you been?"

"Cool," Chancey said. He stood in the doorway and glanced around the miniature room. It looked exactly the same, with the exception of how feminine his sister had everything. The perfume bottles on the dresser were his first eye catcher. Empty purses were all over the place. There were a couple hanging from the doorknob, and several stashed over in a corner by Setchi's twin bed. But what caught his interest the most was the pink diary sitting on her pillow. He stared at it anxiously, promising to read it the first chance he got.

"As you can see, everything is still the same," Nikki said with a sigh.

Chancey's eyes didn't let him hide the disappointment he felt when he looked at his mother. *You still in the same fuckin' predicament after four years? What the fuck you been doin'? Up here try'na dress up 'n shit! Lookin' like an African Goddess on a budget!*

"Welp, I'ma go back in here and let you get situated," Nikki said.

Chancey rolled his eyes. His lips barely moved as he mumbled, "Yeah, whatever."

Shit is already startin' off wrong, Chancey thought. His will to do right—that apologetic talk he was going to have with his mother—were all starting off wrong. He sat on his twin bed and watched a small roach race across the wall. He hated roaches! To him, roaches were the most disgusting beings that walked the face of the earth. Before, he would almost break his neck to keep them from accumulating, but now, for some reason all he could do was watch. He watched one crawl across the dresser. He winced when he spotted one above his head on the ceiling. And it took all the strength he had to keep from losing his mind when he saw a baby roach make its way across his pillow. He closed his eyes and leaned back against the wall. *Damn, I can't live like this,* he thought, opening his eyes at the sound of Setchi's voice.

"Hey big head," she said, smiling.

Chancey looked up and saw his sister standing in the doorway.

"Well, ain't 'chew gon' gimme a hug?" she asked with her arms extended.

Chancey sat still, astonished over how pretty his sister had gotten. She was tall and thin. Her permed hair was straight and long, stopping at the middle of her back. She was a shade lighter than her brother whose complexion was light caramel, and she had a pair of almond-shaped, hazel-colored eyes, which she inherited from her mother.

Chancey stared at her before focusing his attention to all her items lying around. "What's this?" he asked, trying to be funny when he picked up one of her tampons and wiggled it in the air.

Setchi was humiliated. "Oooh, I'ma kill you!" she said, quickly snatching the tampon from her brother.

He said, "Man, clean this shit up," and kicked the mate to her brown, leather sandals over to her side of the room.

"Dang, I can't get a, 'Hi!' 'How you doin'?' or nothing?" she asked. When Chancey looked up at her and smiled, she noticed his peach fuzz and added, "Oooh! Look at you, try'na get a mustache and thangs!"

Setchi sat down beside her brother and put her arm around him. "I was missing you like crazy," she said, sighing deeply. "Shoot, me and Mama haven't been gettin' along at all. She makes me sick, Chance! I be walkin' around here with no money and stuff. And my daddy be sending me some all the time, but she don't even give it to me." Setchi paused for a moment before continuing. "Talking about she gotta pay bills," she said with her lips puckered to the side. "And do you know she didn't even get me no school clothes this year?"

"Serious?"

"Yes! I had to wear the same clothes from last year," Setchi said. "I don't be having no lunch money for school or *nothing*. And it ain't like I can go in the kitchen and make a sandwich or something. Shoot, half the time it ain't even no food here."

Yep! Shit is still the same, Chancey thought, remembering all the times he starved during lunchtime.

They both sat quietly in awkward silence. Chancey felt bad for leaving his sister at the mercy of Nikki's screwed-up authority, and was beating his brains out trying to come up with some encouraging words to make her feel better. "You seen Ronnie?" was all he could produce.

Setchi smiled. "I just came from his house, but he wasn't there," she said. "He must be over Pam's."

"Who's Pam?"

"This ol' tramp from Lynwood," Setchi said. "Her legs stay open like 7-11!"

"Open like 7-11, huh?" Chancey asked, smiling at her cute slogan.

"I'm serious, shoot! I don't know what he sees in her..."

"Why you so worried about it? Shit, let's talk about you for a minute," Chancey said and crossed his arms. "Who you sleepin' around with?"

"I ain't sleepin' around with nobody, thank you *very* much!"

"Yeah, whateva," Chancey said. "Who's that nigga you writin' about in your diary?"

"Who, Curtis?" Setchi asked, then caught herself. "Why you readin' my dairy?"

Chancey laughed. "Shut up, girl. I didn't touch yo' diary...yet," he said.

Setchi leaped over to her bed and snatched her diary up. She held it close to her chest with both hands and looked around to find a place to put it.

"It's too late to hide it now. You already told on yourself," Chancey said. "I'm tellin' Ma you got a boyfriend."

"She already know! Now what?" Setchi asked immodestly. "She ain't trippin'. She met 'em before and everything! What 'chew got to say about that, butthead?"

3

The next morning, Setchi and Nikki cleaned the apartment to Betty Wright's "Tonight is the Night", while Chancey slept in. Setchi glanced through the smudged window when she heard the doorbell ring. Seeing Rondell made her grin from ear to ear.

To Setchi, Rondell was the finest man alive. His brown, muscular but slender built, gray eyes, and broad lips made her bow down every time she saw him.

"*Hiiiii*, Ronnie," she sang, blushing with fluttering eyes.

Rondell was twenty now, owned an attractive car, had plenty of money, and a cocky attitude. "What's up?" he asked nonchalantly. He walked in with a limp, wearing a plain blue T-shirt, jeans, and sneaks. When he didn't see Chancey in the living room, he walked toward the bedroom and peeked through the cracked door. "Oh, he's sleep?"

"Yeah, baby!" Nikki yelled from the kitchen as she dried off the last dish and put it in the cabinet. "It's time for him to get his ass up though." She threw her dishtowel on the counter, placed both hands on her hips, and called out, "CHANCEY!"

Rondell walked in the kitchen and leaned against the counter. "It's already the fourteenth, Nik. What's up wit' my money?" he asked.

Nikki was stuck. She looked at Rondell and started smiling.

He frowned and asked, "Do it look like I'm laughin'?"

"Boy, I'ma give you yo' damn money! Things just got a little tight, that's all," Nikki said. She pulled out the drawer filled with forks, knives, and spoons, and began to straighten them one by one.

"You said you was gon' have it for me on the first..."

"I know, Ronnie, but I had to pay Debra extra on the rent from last month."

"That ain't my problem!"

"I know it's not your pro..." Nikki stopped talking when she heard the bedroom door open. Rondell rolled his eyes and walked over to the table and sat down.

Chancey staggered from the bedroom wearing nothing but gray sweats sagging over his white boxers. He slowly walked toward the kitchen with his hands resting in the front of his pants. He tried to hold back his excitement when he saw Rondell at the table, thinking only girls got excited, and smiled as he cleared his throat to catch his attention.

When Rondell turned around, Chancey's smile turned into a muffled laughter. "What's up, my nig," he said, trying to maintain his coolness.

Rondell got up from the table and put his arm around Chancey's neck. "Damn, cuz, you startin' to look as good as me," he said. "What's up wit' that?"

Chancey ran his fingers down the fuzzy shadow above his lip and looked momentarily at his mother and sister with arrogance. His conceited grin made Setchi's stomach turn. She looked at her brother from the corner of her eye and told him, "Negro, please! You don't look that good!"

Rondell and Chancey went back to the room and kicked back on Chancey's bed. Rondell tossed his keys on the dresser and looked around. "Setchi got shit everywhere!"

"I know," Chancey said. He got up and took the panties balled up next to her bed and threw them under her sheets.

For several seconds no one said anything. Finally, Rondell broke the silence. "So, what's up, cuz? You ready to make some money?" he asked, rubbing his hands together and smiling devilishly like he always did when he was up to no good.

Chancey sat with a straight face. He knew what the question meant, but remembered the talk he and Setchi had last night, and tried to avoid answering it.

Setchi was on her brother's case all the time about the way he lived his life, but last night she really poured her heart out to him. She let him know the four years she spent without him was hard. She told him about all the times she stayed up crying because she felt alone. "All I have in the whole world is you, Chance...and I need you, man," she said as a joke, but was serious to the bone.

He and Setchi's conversation stuck in his head like a bad headache. Hell yes, he was ready to make some money, he thought, but for some reason, he couldn't fix his mouth to say it. He couldn't fix it to say no, either! "So, what 'chew been up to?" he asked, hoping to throw the conversation in another direction.

Rondell stood up and pulled out a wad of hundred-dollar bills. "Same ol'-same ol'," he said, licking the tip of his thumb. "I'm just handlin' my shit, making money, you know."

Chancey watched Rondell whisper each bill as he counted. When he reached a total of three thousand dollars, Chancey yelled, "DAMN!" and jumped up from the bed to get a closer look. "You got chips like that?"

"No, you got chips like that," Rondell said, placing the cash in Chancey's hand.

Chancey's big grin faded. His facial expression turned into a cross between showing thanks and confusion.

Rondell said, "I didn't forget, cuz. We both robbed that ol' lady, remember?"

Chancey turned his head toward the door to see if anyone was listening in. He turned back to Rondell and frowned. "How much money did 'er ass have?"

"That bitch had about forty dollars and some change."

Chancey's face soured. He looked down at the money in his hand and tried to figure out why his arithmetic wasn't adding up. "So then, where did..."

Rondell started laughing. "That's what I wanna talk to you about, cuz! Would you quit wastin' time and get dressed!"

Chancey shook his head and sighed. He played with the few hairs on his chin, then dropped his hand from his face and said, "I don't know, man..."

"You don't *what*?" Rondell asked, frowning.

"I don't know! Shit. Me and Setchi had a long-ass talk last night. A serious one! She was preachin' to me for hours—you know how Setchi can get. I promised her I would get a job and try'da do right for a change."

Rondell fell back on the bed and stared up at Chancey with his mouth open and his palm to his chest. "I *know* this ain't one of the rawest niggas on the block talkin' like a bitch right now," he said and chuckled. His eyes turned cold as he waited on a response from Chancey.

Chancey had a lot to say, but didn't know how to let it flow without sounding like the "bitch" that Rondell made him out to be. He mumbled a few things under his breath, but for the most part, was stuck for words.

Rondell got up from the bed and squared off in Chancey's face. "Nigga, what 'chew gon' do? Go work for the white man?" he asked and snickered scornfully. "Let me tell you somethin', cuz. You a nigga wit' a record. Ain't nobody gon' hire you. You don't know? Shit, you betta ask somebody!"

Chancey sighed when he saw Rondell snatch his keys from the dresser. He watched him inch his way to the door and stop. "Man, you don't understand..."

"Nah, I understand," Rondell said, turning to face Chancey. "I understand that three thousand dollars ain't shit! That's what I understand. What I *don't* understand is what the hell you gon' do when it runs out?"

Again, Chancey was stuck with no response. He had the slightest idea. He figured he would get a job. But what if Rondell was right? What if no one gave him a chance because of his criminal history? He stared at Rondell long and hard while he struggled with his conscious.

"We've been friends too long, cuz," Rondell said. "I know you like the back of my hand. How could I not? Shit, we just alike! We come from the same ol' tired-ass projects, and we both got a mama who don't give a fuck!" As Rondell spoke, he walked up to Chancey and poked him in the chest with his index finger. "You gotta be a man and provide for yourself, nigga. You know what I mean?" Chancey nodded. In his mind, he knew Rondell was right. In his heart, he believed no one cared. *What mother would let her sixteen-year-old son drink hard liquor right in front of her face,* he thought to himself, remembering all the liquor he consumed at his party last night. Painful memories began to invade his thinking, like the first time he was introduced to a bottle of whisky.

Chancey could see the lady's face clearly, but couldn't remember her name. He and Setchi were minding their business, watching an episode of "Good Times". Nikki and her company of about fifteen, both men and women, were laughing, yelling, arguing, and even fighting in the living room. The music rumbled through their small apartment as though there were speakers in every corner.

Chancey could hear the sound of Jay-Jay's voice yell, "DY-NO-MITE!" He could also hear the footsteps of the mysterious lady floundering toward their room. Suddenly, she appeared in the doorway, barely able to stand. "I hear somebody turned nine yesterday," she said.

"Yep! Chance did," Setchi said, pointing at Chancey. Chancey rolled his eyes and crawled under his covers. "He's mad 'cause he didn't get nothin'," Setchi explained with sad eyes.

The lady pulled the covers from over Chancey's head. "He didn't get nothin'?" she asked, looking at Chancey and pouting. "Let me see if I can fix that." She made her way back into the living room and returned moments later with a small, clear bottle of what looked like water to Chancey. She said, "Happy birthday," with a smile as she handed the bottle to him. "Now drink it slow, you hear?"

Setchi was tickled pink as if the gift had been given to her. "Ooooooh! I know what that is! I know what that is!" she squeaked with huge laughter.

Frowning, "Hush, girl! You don't wanna let your mama hear you," the lady warned.

"Yeah! Shut up!" Chancey ordered.

The next day, he rounded up his posse from the neighborhood and showed off his birthday present. They later crept inside one of the abandon apartments and swallowed the intoxicating beverage

like a fish. Chancey got so drunk he had to be carried home! And
though at the time it was the best feeling in the world, looking back
on things now made him see just what a disgrace he really was.
More so because it became a habit that he could no longer control.
Everything he did soon became a habit. Alcohol, stealing, lying, even
jail! From being caught with marijuana that he claimed wasn't his, to
abusing girls that were too afraid to testify, he remembered going to
Juvenile Hall so many times that even *he* couldn't keep track
anymore.

Now, four years later, he's back on the streets, still a menace, and
still, no one cared. All the painful memories raced through his mind
as Rondell's convincing words continued to jump out at him.

"Don't you wanna start havin' money again? And this time, way
more than before, nigga. I put that on the set," Rondell promised,
twirling his keys around one of his fingers.

Chancey's face remained straight, and he appeared confident
when he nodded. His body language, however, told a different
story. He sighed, fiddled with his peach fuzz, massaged his
forehead, and sighed some more.

Rondell couldn't take another second of Chancey's nervous
energy. "Man, just get dressed and meet me at the gym. Bring the
money with you, too," he said and left the room. On his way toward
the front door, he saw Nikki sitting at the kitchen table working a
crossword puzzle. He walked up to her and bent over her shoulder.
"Man, you betta pay me my money, Nik. I'm serious! You gon' need
me again, watch. Next time, I'ma tell yo' punk-ass no!" he whispered
with harshness.

"I know, Ronnie. Don't get mad. I'ma pay you. I swear!" Nikki
gently whispered back.

Rondell backed away from Nikki with evil eyes. He opened the
front door, then looked back and winked at Setchi who was sitting
on the couch watching television. Setchi's tan face reddened.

*   *   *

Chancey took a shower and brushed his teeth. He threw on his
boxers and walked into the bedroom. He gave a second thought to
everything that came to mind. *That fool just broke me off three thousand*

dollars, he reminded himself. *I gotta get me a car. A Regal! Not like that piece of shit Kay-Kay got!* He got the bottle of Cocoa Butter from the dresser and began to massage his feet, working his way up to his arms and hands. *Damn, I wonder how much them '84 Monte Carlos are.* That thought made him wonder where he put his money. His heart began to pound harder than normal as he lifted his mattress. "Yeah," he said with a sigh of relief when he saw the green paper stacked neatly in a pile. He grabbed his money and let the mattress drop. *It'll be a hell of a lot more than three thousand dollars, that's for damn sho'!*

He picked up his Levi jeans that he wore yesterday from the side of his bed and slipped them on, then pulled a plain white T-shirt from the drawer and slipped it on. "Where's my shoes?" he asked himself and walked over to the closet. He saw one of his white tennis shoes standing out like a new prize. He pulled the shoe from the closet and stuffed his foot into it. He looked it over and wondered if it was still in style. The shoes were brand new. He never had a chance to show them off.

He kneeled down at the closet and moved some shoes around to find the mate. When he didn't find it, he crawled in the closet to make sure it wasn't being overlooked. He backed out of the claustrophobic space and scratched his head as he looked around the room. "SETCHI! Where's my other BK shoe?"

"Where's what?" Setchi walked into the room and asked.

"My British Knights!" he said, pointing down at the ivory-colored tennis shoe on his foot. "I can't find the other one."

Setchi tried to keep from looking suspicious as she watched Chancey limp around the room. She saw him hobble over to the closet. When he kneeled down to crawl inside, she rushed over to her bed and pulled his shoe from underneath it.

Chancey turned around just in time to catch her in action. "What's it doin' under your bed?" he asked when he saw his shoe in her hand. When he saw the scuff mark on the side of it, he frowned. "Who the hell been wearin' my shoes?!"

Setchi smiled like a child caught in the cookie jar. "Okay, promise you won't get mad," she said.

Chancey just glared at her.

"I let Curt wear 'em…" Pausing, "But only once though!" she confessed.

"Curt! Oh, you don' lost yo' rabbit-ass mind, huh?"

"Don't nobody even wear blood killers no more!" Setchi tried to explain.

Chancey didn't want to hear it. He got up from the floor and said, "Gimme my fuckin' shoe!" as he hopped toward her.

Feeling nervous, she tossed the shoe at him before he reached her. Chancey was caught off guard and reacted solely on reflexes when he tried to catch the shoe. He fumbled it a few times as he struggled to keep it from hitting the floor. Once he secured it in his hand, he cocked it over his shoulder as if he was going to throw it at Setchi. Setchi closed her eyes, flinched, and screamed.

"CHANCEY!" Nikki yelled from the bathroom. "Leave that girl alone!"

Chancey rolled his eyes at Setchi and limped over to his bed. "I got some words for your lil' boyfriend! Just wait," he said as he sat back and wiped his shoe off.

"Little? Boy, he's older than you! Shoot, don't have me call 'em. He'll come over here and beat yo' punk-ass down!"

Chancey laughed to himself at Setchi's rough demeanor. He thought it was cute, coming from someone who hated violence. Then he thought about it. *Older than me?* He got up from the bed and walked over to his sister. "Oh, so he's older than me, huh?"

"Not for real," Setchi said, sticking out her palms to hold him off.

"How old is he, Setchi?"

"Same age as me," Setchi said. It was the guilty grin that made him doubtful.

"Keep lyin' so I can dump you on yo' head."

Setchi laughed.

"Oh, you think I'm playin'!" Chancey yelled and reached out to pick her up.

Setchi shouted, "STOAAHP! MAMA!"

Chancey covered his sister's mouth and told her to shut up as he put her in a headlock position. Then he flipped her on her bed.

"OOUUCH!" she screamed. "That hurted!"

"Good!"

Setchi put her head down and pretended to cry. "I'm telling!"

"TELL!" Chancey dared as if he really cared less. He laced up his shoes and headed for the door.

Setchi jumped up from her bed and ran after him. "Where you going?" she asked.

"To the gym," he answered, walking in the kitchen. He opened the refrigerator and stared blankly at its bareness.

"What, Jordan's Gym?" she asked, breathing down his back.

"Yep."

Setchi smacked her lips. "See, there you go, finna get in some trouble already," she whined, trailing behind him when he closed the refrigerator door and walked out the kitchen. "You know you don't have no business at Jordan's Gym. It's too dangerous up there. Plus, the cops be out like crazy, and you *know* you on probation!"

"Chill out, Setchi. I'll be right back," Chancey said as he hurried out the front door and closed it behind him.

Setchi ran up to the window and pushed it open with a pound of her fist. "Ain't been out a week and already hanging out! REMEMBER WHAT WE TALKED ABOUT!!!!" she yelled.

*   *   *

Chancey walked up 99th Place toward the gym. He glanced around his neighborhood and felt right at home all over again. The area was packed just like he'd remembered. Young, flirty girls chasing after their crushes in the streets and cars circling the blocks with bass pounding so hard from the speakers, it rattled the windows of homes nearby.

Chancey was passing by a group of kids playing football in the street when he heard an older boy call out his name. He turned his head in the direction of the voice and spotted a group of rowdy boys shooting dice on the curb. "What time did the party end last night?" one of the boys asked. He was cool, wearing a Lakers jersey, jeans, and black shades.

"C'mon, Bobcat! Quit talking and throw the dice, nigga! Shit!" shouted a dark-skinned boy with waves in his hair and a small bottle of cheap liquor in his hand.

"About four-thirty this morning," Chancey answered and crossed the street to join them. "What time you leave?"

"NINE O'CLOCK!" Dark-skinned teased. "You know this nigga got a curfew."

Chancey looked at Dark-skinned and giggled. Then he said, "Let me get some," and helped himself to the liquor before Dark-skinned had a chance to pass it.

Dark-skinned watched Chancey gulp down huge amounts at a time. "DAMN, CUZ!" he yelled, reaching for his drink. "Pass my shit back! And don't backwash in it either!"

"Shut up, busta, before I spit in it!" Chancey retorted playfully and shoved the half-empty bottle in Dark-skinned's hand.

Bobcat clicked the dice together. "Unh!" he grunted, then tossed them. The dice hit the ground, both stopping and totaling the number four. He picked the dice up and tossed them to the ground again. "Unh!" he grunted, this time popping his finger. The dice hit the ground. One stopped on the number five, the other on two.

"AH SHIT!" Dark-skinned shouted in disgust. "This nigga don' won again!"

"YEAH! Now that's what I'm talkin' about! Gimme my chips, fool!" Bobcat said and picked up the pile of one dollar bills off the ground.

"What do you expect when a nigga keep settin' the dice!" one of the other boys said, picking up the dice from the ground. He fixed his beady eyes on every inch of the dark-blue squares.

"So, now I'm settin' the dice?" Bobcat asked.

"Hell yeah, you settin' 'em! Ain't nobody stupid! All you gotta do is shake 'em like this," Beady-eyes said, shaking the dice the same way he saw Bobcat shake them.

Bobcat took ten one-dollar bills and dropped them at Beady-eyes feet. "What's up then, cuz? Throw 'em! You hit, the money's yours, but if you crap out, I get that Timex."

Beady-eyes looked down at his wrist and palmed his watch as though he would never see it again.

"Don't do it!" one boy warned.

"I'm givin' this nigga the upperhand," Bobcat explained, then turned to Beady-eyes and said, "You get to set the dice any kind'a way you want."

Beady-eyes smiled and clicked the dice together in his sweaty hand. He was just about to try his luck when Dark-skinned stepped in and said, "This nigga don't know nothin' about settin' no dice."

"Be quiet, ol' busta! You don't know what the hell I know."

"Well go 'head then, nigga, you bad!" Dark-skinned told him.

Beady-eyes smiled. He looked at the dice. Concentrated. Put the number six next to the number two. Sighed. Looked down at the black, leather band that secured his Timex watch to his wrist. Then, he grinned at Bobcat and said, "Throw in another five and I'll bet 'chew."

Bobcat studied the thin rope chain around Beady-eyes neck. "Put up that rope chain and I'll throw in a twenty."

Beady-eyes' grin turned into a broad smile. He lifted the chain from his chest and stared at it for a hot second, before glancing over at the twenty-dollar bill in Bobcat's hand. "How many tries I get?" he asked.

"One, nigga," Bobcat snapped. "This ain't no fuckin' carnival!"

Beady-eyes clicked the dice together one last time, but was hesitant on throwing them.

"Throw the dice," Chancey dared.

"Do *somethin'*!" Dark-skinned demanded. Bobcat smiled as he flashed his bait in Beady-eyes' face.

Beady-eyes took his chances and tossed the dice to the ground. Everyone watched as the dice bounced around on the concrete. One dice landed on a one. Everyone's eyes grew large as they waited for the other dice to come to a complete stop, also revealing its single, white dot.

"SNAKE-EYES!" Chancey shouted.

"*I got me a gold chain…I got me a gold chain…*" Bobcat sang as he danced around in a circle doing the cabbage-patch.

"A watch too!" Dark-skinned shouted, and laughed at Beady-eyes. Beady-eyes rolled his eyes at Dark-skinned and unbuckled the leather band to his watch.

Bobcat snatched the watch and said, "C'mon, I ain't got all day," beckoning for Beady-eyes' necklace.

Beady-eyes caught an attitude. "That's aw'ight! I ain't trippin', shit. I was 'bout to buy me another one anyway," he said, unlatching his chain.

"Don't get mad at me, nigga. Shit, I'm a hustla. Been hustlin' since birth!" Bobcat said, making everyone but Beady-eyes laugh.

*   *   *

Rondell was tired of looking up every time he heard someone coming toward him, only to find out it wasn't Chancey. He was also tired of shifting from butt cheek to butt cheek, trying to adjust to the hard element of the "Jordan Down's Housing Community" sign mounted in front of the gym.

He heard some footsteps sliding his way and prayed it was Chancey before looking up. Seeing it was, he jumped down from the sign and headed across Grape Street to his car. "Damn, cuz, took you long enough," he said as he approached the navy blue '63 Impala and chirped the alarm.

"Is this you?" Chancey asked, exposing all his teeth when he smiled.

Rondell smirked arrogantly. "Wait 'til I get my Lexus! You niggas *really* gon' be trippin' then," he said and opened the door. He got in and reached over to let Chancey in.

Wasting no time, Rondell dug down in the crouch of his jeans and pulled out a plastic sandwich bag filled with crack cocaine. "I know you know what this shit is," he said, sitting the bag on Chancey's lap.

"Yep," Chancey said as he rambled through the plastic and flicked the small rocks around. "Who got you hooked up with this?"

"This dude named Byrd. He'll be up here at two. I want you to meet him, cuz. That nigga got the hook-up on everything around here: guns, D, hoes, whatever you need! I told him about you, too. You know, told 'em you was my folks and everything, and that I wanted to pull you in the game," Rondell said, then looked at Chancey for his approval. "He got the best dope in town, too, cuz! Straight up."

Chancey became leery. A look of worry took over his facial expression. He glanced at Rondell from the corner of his eye and said, "I feel funny about this shit. I can't even lie."

"What 'chew mean you feel funny? See, nigga, there you go trippin' again," Rondell said, frowning.

"Nah, it ain't like that. I just thought we was finna go hit up somebody at the bank or somethin' real fast. I didn't know you was talkin' about this shit," Chancey said and glowered down at the bag of white rocks. "Man, I just got outta Y.A., and I *ain't* try'na go back!

Shit. Can't hit the weed, can't fuck, can't do shit!" he added with a slight chuckle.

"Ain't nothin' to sellin' this shit, cuz," Rondell said. "If I had'a known making money was this easy, my ass would'a been rich a long time ago!"

"Nigga, what makes you think it's that easy? You got one-time out here, undercovers...yeah, what about the undercovers, nigga? Shit, I might sell to a narc or somethin'."

"Cuz, I can spot a narc a mile away."

"That's you!"

"You will, too!" Rondell promised. "See, the more and more you get out here, the more and more you recognize what they look like, the cars they drive, things they say—all that! And the only black-and-white that be around here is..." Rondell got excited for this one. "Guess who patrols this area?" he asked.

"Who?"

"Busta-ass, Officer Woods!"

Chancey grimaced. "Cuz, don't even bring up that fool's name right about now."

"Chance! You don't hear me. Niggas be gettin' away wit' murder, having his big, dumb-ass around! He *still* dumb, cuz. He just got lucky when he caught you. That was your fault though. Shit. You should'a told me you was gon' throw the gun."

"Yeah, I know. I wasn't thinkin'."

"I'm telling you, cuz, I been selling this shit for about a year now and I ain't got caught yet! Woody's faggot-ass be rollin' up and down here like he's doin' something...that nigga never say shit to me! Matter fact, his punk-ass don't even look my way! He bet' not!"

"Oh, so you ain't snatchin' purses no more?" Chancey looked at Rondell and asked.

"HELL NAH! I don't get down like that no more, cuz. Shit, it's all about the "come up"! And trust me, nigga, you ain't comin' up from snatchin' a bitch's purse who prolly only got about forty bucks, *if that*!"

Rondell stopped talking when he noticed an older man approaching the gym. The man looked around constantly as though he was being followed. "YO', STAN!" Rondell yelled. Then he grabbed his bag of rocks from Chancey's lap.

Stan saw the beckon of Rondell's hand and immediately rushed over to his car. "Hey, buddy," he said out of breath. He quickly glanced over his shoulder before leaning inside the window to drop a fifty in Rondell's lap. He looked over at Chancey and spied him nervously.

This nigga's paranoid, Chancey thought.

"Here you go, homie," Rondell said, slipping one of his biggest rocks in the man's hand as he pretended to shake it. The man latched onto the rock and dashed away.

Rondell bundled up his bag of drugs and shoved it back down in the crouch of his jeans. He stuck the fifty-dollar bill in his pocket.

"That nigga was gone," Chancey said.

"No, he was tweakin'! Did you see his eyes?"

"Yeah, they looked like they was finna pop out his fuckin' head!" Chancey said and laughed.

"You can tell when they gone, 'cause they be like zombies 'n shit, out of it like this…" Rondell said, demonstrating someone who's half awake.

Chancey studied the man as he walked up Grape. "He's *rushin'* home, too! Look at 'em!"

"That's how they be when they on this shit. Real hyper! And sometimes I don't be in the mood for all that shit, either," Rondell said. "Cuz, I had to sock this one bitch in 'er jaw."

"YOU LYIN'!" Chancey shouted.

"I'm serious, shit! She was making me nervous, pacin' back and forth 'n shit. She kept laughin' and playin', tappin' all on me 'n shit."

"So, you hit 'er, nigga?"

"I knocked the fuck out 'er ass!"

Chancey laughed out loud. "What she do?"

"She calmed the fuck down. What 'chew think she did? Nigga, you gotta establish who's boss out here, 'cause if you don't, them dope fiends will run all over yo' ass."

"Did she ever come back?"

"Nah, she didn't fuck wit' me no more after that, but I ain't trippin'. Shit, she wasn't spendin' no money no way. She would come to me wit' ten dollars here, fifteen dollars there. One time, the bitch came up here wit' five dollars worth'a change!" Rondell said. "Now, dude that just left…he be spending a grip, nigga, you hear me? His ass be up here all the time, spending fifty dollars a whop! He's the one that bought me this car," he added with a smile.

"Man, you stupid as hell," Chancey said, looking around the area. "So, is this where you be at?"

"Everyday! I be right there, posted," Rondell said, pointing over at some bushes in a secluded area on the side of the gym. "This the best spot up here. I mean, it's boomin' up at the liquor stores, too—'specially Grape Market. But now, it don't get no more convenient than this shit right here. Whenever I need to use the phone, piss, whatever, Jackie don't say shit. I just walk in the gym and handle my business."

"Oh, Jackie still work at the gym?"

"Yep. She work the front desk on Fridays and Saturdays. And when she ain't there, I go over Rosie's. You know Rosie stay in the Downs now."

"Yeah, I heard," Chancey said and smiled. "What building she stay in?"

"Right there," Rondell said, pointing over at building thirty-eight, which sat directly across from the gym. "All I gotta do is give Rosie a few dollahs and she'll let me blow her spot up. Sometimes I chill over her house all day, doing nothin' but serving fiends."

"Yeah, you been chillin' over Rosie's quite a bit, huh, nigga?" Chancey asked, giving Rondell an I-know-everything type of look.

Smirking, "Why you say that?" Rondell asked, unable to hide his guilt.

"Don't trip."

"Nah, nigga, tell me!" Rondell demanded, but Chancey said nothing. He just looked at him and laughed in his face. "You know Rosie got a baby, right?" Rondell said after a moment.

Chancey looked at Rondell and glared. "Mmm-humph."

"What, you heard it was mine?"

"Is it?" Chancey asked, smiling.

Rondell took a deep breath and shrugged his shoulders. "Could be."

"Damn! Ronnie got a baby by my wife," Chancey said, shaking his head.

"I said it *could* be!"

"How long y'all been creepin'?"

"C'mon cuz, let that shit go. It ain't even like that."

"What's it like, then?"

"I told you! She just help a nigga get his paper, that's all. For real! I just go to her house, sell my shit, go home, that's it. That is it!"

Puzzled, "Rosie don't be trippin' off you sellin' drugs out her house like that?" Chancey asked.

Rondell's face soured. "Trippin'? She sold the shit for me before!"

"ROSIE?" Chancey shouted. He couldn't believe his ears.

"I showed 'er how to cut it up and everything! Shit, she cut it up better than me." Rondell stopped and chuckled conceitedly. "Cuz, Rosie do whatever I say. I'm try'na get her to get this cell phone cut on for me. I got me one of those cell phones everybody be havin'...the kind that flip down," Rondell said and waited on a response from Chancey.

Chancey was thunderstruck. He knew Rondell couldn't be talking about the same girl that got straight A's in school. No, not the same girl that graduated at the top of her class. And what about the speech she gave on the last day of school? It was so powerful, it made the newspapers!

Chancey remembered that day all so well as he thought back. "Good Morning. My name is Rosita Lopez," Rosie said, introducing herself to the staff, students, and visitors. Her velvet dress was stunning. Her long curls blew freely in the wind. Her voice captured the attention of every teacher and every student that sat patiently in the bleachers.

"I know this is just the beginning," she told the huge crowd. "I have an even bigger challenge ahead when I get to high school. But I'm determined to stay focused so I can continue to make excellent grades and make my parents proud." Loud claps roared from the stands. "Let's show everybody that the young generation can and will make a difference! Let's stay in school! Let's say no to teenage pregnancy! And most importantly, let's say no to drugs!"

And now look at 'er...an eighteen-year-old drug dealer on welfare, Chancey thought and laughed quietly to himself. He was so enfolded in his thoughts, he didn't hear the sound of Rondell's voice.

"CHANCEY!"

"Huh? What?"

"Damn, nigga, did you hear what I said?"

"Nah, what 'chew say?"

"I said it only happened once. A long time ago."

"What only happened once?"

"ME AND ROSIE!" Rondell yelled, frustrated that he had to explain everything again. "We got drunk one night and shit just happened. Next thing I know, she's pregnant. Shit, she even had a boyfriend at the time! How do I know it ain't that nigga's?"

"Who the baby come out looking like though?" Chancey asked, being sarcastic.

"So what, nigga! What that mean? Shit, you know we all look alike."

"Whatever," Chancey said, looking down at his watch. It was almost two-thirty. "Thought dude was comin' at two."

"Man, chill, he'll be here."

The longer Byrd took, the more time Chancey had to wrestle with his guilty feelings. He slouched down in his seat and stared unemotionally out the windshield. *He's been selling this shit for a year now and he ain't got caught yet,* he thought, trying to assure himself that he wouldn't get caught either.

His train of thought was broken when a dark blue Monte Carlo zoomed passed, thumping Marvin Gaye's "Give It Up." Chancey's eyes followed the car like they were magnetized to it. "That shit was tight!"

Rondell smacked his lips. "My shit is bumpin' *way* harder! Listen," he said and turned up the volume on his Alpine tape deck. The bass almost knocked the wind out of Chancey. "What 'chew got, some fifteens?" he asked, looking in the back of the car. That's when he noticed the white '77 Chevy El Camino vibrating in the rear window. "Is this Byrd pullin' up?"

Rondell turned his stereo down and looked out his side view mirror. "Yep, that's him."

"You made it sound like that nigga was ballin'," Chancey said disappointed.

"He is!"

"Pullin' up in a El Camino?!"

Rondell laughed. "Man, that fool got a Benz, a BMW, *and* he got two houses!" he said, feeling proud of Byrd.

Chancey watched the husky six-foot-four man approach the car.

Rondell opened his door and lifted up his seat. Byrd climbed in the back and looked around to check his surroundings. Then he stuck out his fist to Chancey and said, "What's up, cuz? Byrd."

"What's up?" Chancey said, tapping Byrd's fist with his.

Byrd pulled a small, brown paper bag from his pocket and handed it to Chancey.

Not really knowing what to say or do, Chancey took a quick look inside, then passed the bag to Rondell. He watched closely as Rondell took the large substance from the bag and examined it. "Oh yeah, this is him right here," he said. "You lettin' it go for two G's, right?"

"Yeah, yeah, that'll work," Byrd said.

Chancey slipped a thick stack of folded hundreds to Byrd. Byrd spread them like a deck of cards, then almost immediately pushed them back together. "Alright, lil' homie," he said, sticking out his fist to Chancey once more.

The deal was solid. Chancey studied the cocaine long and hard as Rondell let Byrd out.

Rondell started his car and drove around to the other side of the Jordan Down Projects, which sat on 103rd. "I'm 'bout to show you how'da come up, cuz. You gon' profit 'bout," pausing as he thought, "eighteen hundred off that."

4

Rondell walked in and gestured for Chancey to have a seat. He tossed his money and drugs on the coffee table, then walked into the bathroom.

"Moms ain't here?" Chancey asked, wondering why Rondell was so open with his illegal occupation.

"Man, she cut out about a year ago. Last I heard, she was living with some nigga in Norwalk," Rondell yelled from the bathroom.

Chancey waited for him to return. "She just bounced on you like that?" he asked, puzzled.

"Left a nigga for dead," Rondell explained. "When I turned eighteen, she was like, 'you on your own', and that was that."

Chancey put his head down and shook it. "Damn."

"Oh, don't get me wrong, I ain't trippin'. Fuck 'er! I don't need 'er ass, cuz. I got the place to myself, and Debra said I can stay here as long as I pay rent." Rondell stretched his arms out and nodded his head haughtily as he glanced around his living room. "Now tell me, do it look like I can't pay my rent?" he asked, smiling and feeling like "the man".

Chancey cased the apartment. Everything looked brand-new, and there wasn't a roach in sight. He saw the gray carpet was stainless, and the black leather furniture was the first thing that caught his attention when he walked through the door. "Cuz, yo' shit look like it should be up in Beverly Hills somewhere!" he said as he got up and walked down the hall toward the bedroom. "LOOK AT THIS SHIT! This is some pimp shit, nigga!"

Rondell laughed and stood in the doorway, watching as Chancey went crazy over his room. It was decorated with black art, just like the living room. Everything was black, from the dressers to the satin comforter spread across his Sealy mattress. Chancey grabbed one of the pillows and threw his body on the bed. He looked up and admired himself in the mirror on the ceiling. His thoughts went wild. "Yeah, nigga, I know you gon' let me handle my business up in here one night," he said, cracking a devious smile.

Rondell was smiling, too. "I'll think about it," he said jokingly, and then walked into the kitchen. He took an old razor blade that he kept stashed in the drawer and grabbed the plastic bag from the counter. He walked in the living room and sat down on the couch. Chancey sat down beside him and watched as he sliced off tiny portions of the crack cocaine at a time. "The key to selling this shit is to never smoke it," Rondell said seriously. "Nigga, don't even try it! This is some powerful-ass shit, and you'll fuck around and get hooked, dippin' and dabbin'! Believe that! I seen it happen too many times…niggas try'na sell this shit and smoke it, too. That shit never works. I mean, think about it, how the hell can you get rich off the product if you constantly smoking it up? You know what I'm sayin'?"

"Yeah, I feel you."

"Another thing," Rondell said, sitting back on the couch and getting comfortable, "you gotta be careful out there on the streets. It ain't like it used to be, cuz. Fools be robbin' niggas and settin' niggas up 'n shit. Just the other day, Lil'…remember Lil' Man? He used to bang on eleven-duce 'n Hoover…"

"I think so, why? What happened?" Chancey asked, sitting back next to him.

"That nigga got jacked, that's what happened! Right up here on 103rd 'n Compton. Broad daylight, too!"

"Damn, like that?"

"Yep! Some niggas rolled up and pulled him outta his shit."

Frowning, "He let 'em take it just like that?" Chancey asked, feeling like Lil' Man was a coward.

"If you got four or five niggas runnin' up on you with a gun, what the hell would you do?! Hell, you'll give up yo' shit, too, trust me!" Rondell said. "That's why I keep my heat with me at all times. I will blow a mothafucka away, nigga, you hear me!"

"Damn!" Chancey said and shook his head. "I keep try'na tell Kaylin to lock both locks on his door, but he don't wanna listen. He never locks the top lock! Ever! I keep tellin' 'em somebody's gon' catch him slippin' one day."

"Yep," Rondell said and scooted up close to the coffee table to finish cutting up the cocaine. "You gotta be careful. Like with this shit here...you got some niggas selling it just to get by. You know, pay some bills or maybe buy some herb or something. Those niggas are the ones you gotta watch out for. They be jealous 'cause you havin' thangs and they ain't. And them be the main ones up in your face 'n shit, you feel me?"

"Yeah," Chancey said, scooting up, too.

"Then you got some that are makin' *alright* money," Rondell said while chuckling. "They be ridin' around in their low-riders all day, flossin' like they just the shit! They be up in the gym, countin' their chips all out in the open. I just sit back and look at them fools. Niggas like that is what you call wanna-be-ballers. See, a true baller will never let you know what he got. Like Byrd! That nigga got a gang of shit, and you see what he pulled up in." Rondell paused and looked Chancey in the face. "Alright, let me ask you a question. If you knew Nikki was on this shit, would you sell it to her? Be honest!"

Chancey fixed his eyes on the ceiling to think. He took in a deep breath, stroked his chin a few times, exhaled, then looked at Rondell and said, "I don't know."

"Now see, that's your first mistake right there. If you can't answer *that* question, you in the wrong business. See, me, I'll sell to my grandmother if I had to, nigga. This shit don't discriminate!"

"Aw," Chancey said in a chuckle, "that's fucked up, cuz."

"That ain't fucked up. That's real! I'm wholehearted at this shit, nigga. I gotta be! The streets is all I know, just like you, and if I don't get out there and get my hustle on, I don't eat. Simple as that! Now, tell me you don't feel the same way." There was silence. "That's what I thought!" Rondell said as he scooped the cocaine into the plastic bag and handed it to Chancey. "Cuz, you looked out for me when you went to Y.A. You could'a sold me out and had us both locked up, but you didn't. You held shit down, and I love you for that. That's on everything! I couldn't wait for you to come home. I don't be kickin' it wit' nobody around here. You can't trust 'em. You the only person I really trust," he said, then paused and looked Chancey in the face once more, this time with warmer, sincere eyes. "I need somebody like you on my team. I can't lie. And I mean, I think we want..." stopping to correct himself, "no, fuck that, I KNOW we want the same things in life," he said. "Shit, I can see me and you comin' up together with no problems, nigga. Give us about a year. We gon' have at least a million! I'M SERIOUS!" Rondell shouted when he noticed the cynical look on Chancey's face. "Cuz, I'm tellin' you, once your money start rollin' in, we can take about seven G's a piece and go buy a kilo. Then after that, we can take seven more G's and go buy another one, then another one...see how it works? We can get out there and hustle early. Some of my best customers come through in the morning. We can meet up at the gym around nine or ten. I'ma teach you everything there is to know about this shit. You hear me?"

Chancey heard him, but his conscious wouldn't let him interact. He hadn't planned on making a career out of selling drugs.

"Cuz, this shit ain't for everybody. So, if you feel you can't handle it, fine! But when I come through in my Lexus, you gon' be lookin' real stupid on the curb."

Chancey laughed. "Oh, so I can't roll in the Lex? That's fucked up," he said.

The time spent at Rondell's house was exhausting, yet at the same time, stimulating. Knowing he had money in his pocket and drugs that would make him even more money made Chancey's adrenaline turn on him. He laid his head back against the couch, then almost immediately jumped to his feet and walked in the kitchen. "What 'chew got to drink?" he asked, swinging the refrigerator door open. Before Rondell could answer, he slammed the door shut and walked back in the living room. "I need a drank!"

Rondell started laughing. "Cuz, quit stressin'," he said. Chancey was now rubbing his hands together and pacing the floor. "C'mon, let's go hit some corners."

They drove around town visiting those who didn't make it to Chancey's party. They ended up at the Foxhill Mall, where Chancey bought three pairs of jeans and three shirts to match, two pairs of tennis shoes, all black Nike Air Jordan's and some blue and white FILA's, a gold link chain with the bracelet to match, and a black pager, which he had activated on site.

The Foxhill Mall was known for being filled with young, lustful boys and girls who came specifically to find their soulmates. Chancey and Rondell walked around the mall laughing and cracking jokes about each other's mother, something they often did back in the days. They were totally oblivious to the world around them as they walked pass two young ladies leaning up against a bench, showing off their daisy dukes.

"Oooh, Kim, look," one of the young ladies said, pointing at Chancey and Rondell. Kim turned to get a quick glimpse.

"They was fine, huh?"

"I can't really see 'em," Kim said, searching through the swarm of people in front of her.

"Watch this," Kim's friend said and pulled her by the arm. She pushed her way through the crowd in a hurriedly fashion, almost dragging Kim alongside. When she made it behind Chancey and Rondell, she halted her and Kim's pace, reducing it to the same speed as theirs. "Excuse me," she said, yanking on Chancey's sleeve, "my name is Renee and this is my girlfriend, Kim."

Renee was bright-skinned and had a tiny waist with widespread hips. She stood before Chancey with her chest stuck out, hoping he'd notice her pert breast through her skimpy tank top. Her legs were slightly opened, suggestively. Chancey's eyes occasionally roamed between them. "Do you have a girlfriend?" she asked.

Chancey said, "Nah."

"Well, can I have your number, then?" Renee asked, smiling a seductive smile to fit her appearance. When Chancey said yes, she arrogantly flipped her eyes in Kim's direction. Kim wasn't studying Renee though. She was all into Rondell, cooing over his gray eyes.

"Here, let me give you mine, too," Renee said. "It's eight four seven…"

"Hold up," Chancey interrupted and tore off a piece of the MACY'S bag he carried. "Write it on this."

Renee rambled through her fake designer purse for a pen. She wrote her number out and eased it down Chancey's pocket. "You better call me, too," she retorted playfully.

*   *   *

Is that Chancey? Tia asked herself as she and her mother headed toward Chancey, Rondell, and the two underdressed females. *Oh my God, that is him! So it's true…he did get out. And look at 'em all up in that skeeza's face. He ain't changed a bit.*

Tia reached down and picked up the bottom of the plastic that protected a dress she caught on sale. She tied it around the hook of the hanger and held it up to block her face as she and her mother passed the group by. *Oooh, please don't let him see me, Lord,* she begged. *I do not want his ass up in my face!*

Tia didn't hate Chancey. She didn't like him either. At least that's what she forced herself to believe. She lived right across from the Jordan Down Projects and could never seem to avoid him. Not even if her life depended on it. He harassed her constantly. The more she ignored him, the more he pestered her. She paid no attention to him back in elementary when he made fun of her and pulled her ponytails in class, and although flattered to no avail, she still turned him down when he asked her to be his girlfriend on the first day of Jr. High.

Seeing Chancey gave her butterflies and little crush feelings that she would never admit to. Her insides felt like they were going to burst right out of her body as she nervously bypassed him. All she could think about was finding the exit. And when she did, she rushed her mother out of it, believing he was sure to bump into her today, of all days, since she had on a tacky outfit and no makeup.

*   *   *

After being at the mall for well over five hours, Chancey and

Rondell headed back to Rondell's place. Besides, it was eight o'clock and the mall would be closing in an hour. Rondell went into his bedroom and returned with a tiny bag of marijuana and his black, cordless phone. He took the crushed leaves and separated them on the coffee table. "Here, roll this up for me while I make this phone call."

"Where's the zigzags?" Chancey asked.

"Look on the fridge...Hello? What's up, baby?"

Chancey found the zigzags on top of the refrigerator. He went back to the living room, sat on the couch, and rolled three marijuana joints. He periodically shot a look of amusement in Rondell's direction, and smiled at the things he said to the girl on the other end of the phone.

"C'mon, Pam, quit trippin'! Why you won't let me hit it no more?" Rondell asked her. "Well, I can't help it if my shit is big!" He glanced over at Chancey and smiled.

Chancey shook his head. "You stupid, nigga," he said and laughed.

"Come through. Oh, and bring yo' patna for my homeboy," Rondell said and hung up the telephone. "We finna kick it, nigga!"

Chancey took a puff of the joint and held the smoke in for as long as he could stand it. Finally, he exhaled with a dramatic cough. "Who's Pam?" he asked once he gained his composure.

"That was one of my hoes. She fine as hell, too! Watch! When you see 'er, you gon' be like, DAMN! She look better than light skin baby at the mall," Rondell said. He got up and turned on the radio, tuning it to a local oldies station.

Oh yeah, the legs open like 7-11 girl. Chancey took another puff from the joint and passed it to Rondell. "And what about her patna?"

"She's cool, too! Do you honestly think I'ma hook you up wit' a ugly bitch?" Rondell paused. "*Shid*...nigga, I don't even know a ugly bitch," he said.

Chancey laughed.

They both reminisced about the good ol' days while they waited on the females to arrive. They talked about everything from how they used to slap-box to who got the most girls. Rondell smirked as he looked Chancey up and down. "Listen at this lil' youngsta'..."

"What?" Chancey asked, laughing. "I did get the most hoes!"

*   *   *

Pam arrived with one of her closest girlfriends in exactly one hour. Rondell was right about Pam. Pam *was* fine! The diamond stud earrings glistening through her highlighted shoulder-length hair gave her a ritzy appeal. Chancey stared boldly in her face as she walked through the door. Everything down to her glowing, green eyes was appealing to him. He prayed that she was Pam's friend and not Pam. Seconds later, Pam walked through the door, so he hoped.

"Rondell, you remember Tomika, right?" Pam asked.

Fuck! Chancey snapped.

"Yeah, I remember that chickenhead."

"Don't start, nigga!" Tomika warned with her hand on one of her healthy hips.

To Chancey, Tomika was just O.K. There was nothing spectacular about her other than her well-proportioned body. She was kind of flat in the chest area, but the fullness in the hip area and the roundness in the back area made up for that. Her head was full of big, long braids pulled up into a ponytail that dangled to her shoulders. Chancey thought her hairdo was a turnoff. However, when he got a good look at Tomika's backside when she pulled off her jacket, the braids didn't look so bad all of a sudden.

"Go on, sit down. What 'chew standin' around lookin' stupid for?" Rondell said before alerting Chancey and gesturing for him to come to the room. They walked up the hall with Rondell leading. Rondell leaped through his bedroom door, then turned and smiled at Chancey. "So, is she cool or what?"

"Hell yeah," Chancey said, cheesing and fantasizing. "She got some sexy-ass eyes."

"Nigga, I'm talking about Tomika!"

Chancey's nose curled. "She aw'ight. She kind'a dark though," he said, frowning.

"What, you don't like dark women? Black is beautiful."

"I know, but damn! She so damn black, I could barely see that tattoo on her arm," Chancey whined. "Walkin' around wit' all that shit in 'er head!"

Rondell laughed. "I ain't try'na scare you, cuz, but she had braids the first time I met 'er, too."

"Yeah, that's 'cause the bitch is prolly baldheaded!" Chancey said, disappointed.

Rondell stood back and gave Chancey a persuasive smile. "Yeah, but she's thick as hell! And plus, nigga, it ain't like you try'na marry 'er, damn! We just try'na have some fun amongst other things," he said, turning his persuasive smile into a devilish one.

Chancey cracked half a smile. Tomika didn't look all that bad, he thought. She just didn't look like Pam. Then, a full smile appeared on his face. Pam's body didn't look like Tomika's either.

*   *   *

Pam looked at Tomika, took a sip of her Snapple, and screwed the top back on. "Sooo…" she said, gesturing for Tomika to spill her guts.

Before Tomika could gather her thoughts, she held her sweaty hands together, pulled them close to her chest, and squeezed as tight as she could. She was cheesing so hard that her eyes closed.

Tomika's thrilled response hit Pam like a thousand watts. She began to bounce up and down like she had just won the lottery. She grabbed Tomika's arm and they both looked at each other and giggled like two excited little girls.

Tomika took a couple of deep breaths and nervously shook her hands. "*Girrrl…*" she purred. "He is *so* cute!"

"Yeah, and he got some big feet, too," Pam confessed, raising her eyebrows twice.

Tomika calmed down and said, "I wonder how old he is."

"He look young, huh?" Pam asked. Then she laughed out loud and said, "Girl, you gon' have his young ass sprung!"

5

Nikki was awakened by the sunlight's glare peeking through the curtains. She rubbed her eyes and flexed her body to stretch. Being hit with a strong urge to urinate made her get up from the couch. She took one step and stumbled over Chancey's body.

"DANG!" he yelled. "Watch where you goin'!"

"Well, nigga, I didn't see you there!" she said. Nikki's urge for the restroom went away. "What time you come in this morning?"

Not lifting his head or opening his eyes, "I don't remember," he said.

"Where you been?"

"Over Ronnie's."

"All day?"

"Yep," he lied.

Nikki gave her son a look of doubt. "So, what 'chew saying is, you didn't meet up with Byrd at the gym?"

Chancey looked up and smiled at his mother. He was speechless, and wondered how she knew Byrd.

"You sellin' drugs, boy?"

Chancey shook his head. "Nah."

Nikki smiled and put her hands on her hips. "Let me try this again. Did you buy some drugs from Byrd yesterday?"

"How you know Byrd?" Chancey asked, avoiding the question.

"Don't worry about all that. Just answer my question!" she demanded.

Chancey laid his head back down and closed his eyes.

Setchi came sluggishly walking from the bedroom, yawning, eyes barely open when she heard all the commotion. Her intentions were to tell Chancey off for not coming back like he promised. And the fact that he thought he was slick by not coming in the room when he got home, only made matters worse. "Why you layin' in here?" she asked, ready to explode.

"I didn't wanna wake…"

"I *know* you didn't wanna wake me, 'cause you know you was wrong!" Setchi said, outtalking her brother. She was getting ready to tear him a new asshole. She turned to take a seat in the chair across from the couch so she could be comfortable while doing it. But when she spotted the MACY'S, CHAMPS Sports, and FOOTLOCKER bags stashed in the corner, she ran toward them and said, "Oooh, who been shoppin'?"

Chancey lifted his head and frowned. "Leave my shit alone, Setchi!" he snapped.

"Where you get money from?" Nikki questioned when her eyes followed Setchi over to the bags of merchandise.

"Yeah!" Setchi interjected. Nikki walked over to Chancey and began patting on his pockets.

"What 'chew doin'!" he yelled and pushed her hands away.

"Gimme some money," Nikki said.

"I don't have none."

"Well, where did all that stuff come from, then?"

"Yeah!" Setchi yelled, still rambling through his bags.

Chancey took a deep breath and used all the strength he had to get up from the floor. He had been up all night and was dead tired. He wobbled in his stance as he stretched, and then staggered toward the bathroom. Setchi and Nikki both rushed and surrounded him like two groupies.

"Gimme twenty dollars!" Nikki begged.

"I don't have twenty dollars!"

"Yeah, right!" Setchi snapped, while trying to ram her hand down one of his pockets.

Nikki barged her way in front of Setchi and grabbed a hold of her son's arms. "Just twenty dollars, Chance! Please! It ain't like I won't give it back. GOD!"

"Nikki! I do not have twenty dollars! Stop askin' me for money. Damn!" he angrily said, jerking his arms away.

"Don't believe 'em, Mama! I felt something in his pocket," Setchi said with a keyed-up smile. Chancey looked at his sister with brutal eyes.

Nikki shifted her body to one side and crossed her arms. "You gon' be stingy like that, nigga?" she asked with an attitude.

"Ma, I need this for something."

"I'ma give it back!"

"Oh my God! I swear!" Chancey huffed as he pulled a crumbled-up twenty-dollar bill from his pocket and shoved it in Nikki's hand. When he glanced over at Setchi and saw her puppy-dog eyes, he smacked his lips and dug in his pocket again. "HERE!" he yelled and tossed a twenty her way.

"Oooh, thank you, thank you, thank you! Now I can get my nails done," Setchi said, prancing back to the room, smiling.

Nikki wasn't finished yet though. It was obvious he had more money. She could tell by the way he fiddled around in his pockets. "Gimme forty," she said bluntly.

"What?! HELL NO!"

"Okay, thirty! Just ten more, Chance. Please!" Nikki whined.

Chancey sighed and rolled his eyes at his mother. All of her imploring was making his head hurt. He pushed his way past her and went into the bathroom to calm his nerves. *I gotta get the fuck up outta here!*

After showering, dressing, and grabbing a bite to eat, Chancey stepped out on the balcony and eyed his slump of a neighborhood. The weather was scorching hot. He looked down at his jeans and debated on whether to put on some shorts. "Fuck it," he said and headed toward Kaylin's unit.

*   *   *

Kaylin was startled. He jumped up and sat in his bed.

Knock, knock, knock.

Once it dawned on him that someone was at the door, he leaned back and rested his body on his elbows, then glanced over at the clock on his nightstand. *Who the hell is this at eight o'clock in the fuckin' morning?* He laid there annoyed, listening as the knocks grew stronger. "HOLD ON!" he yelled, hauling himself out of bed. He moved slowly toward the front window and yanked the curtain to the side. When he saw Chancey, he frowned. He stomped toward the door to open it. Chancey walked past Kaylin and plopped down on the couch like he lived there.

"Me and Janet Jackson was just about to get busy, then here yo' ass come!" Kaylin told him and slammed the door.

"Don't trip, you didn't miss nothin'."

"What?" Kaylin asked, puzzled.

"Nigga, I already wore that ass out about two hours ago," Chancey said, smiling a cheery, bright smile.

Kaylin thought the joke was funny, but was too tired to laugh. He cracked half a smile as he staggered over to the couch and sat down. Chancey said, "You still don't be lockin' yo' shit up!" and went over to the front door to fasten the top bolt. "Somebody's gon' run up in here one day, watch!"

"Ain't nobody comin' up in here. That's just your paranoid ass!"

"*Okay...*" Chancey warned and shook his head. "You can keep thinkin' that if you want to."

"Cuz, it's too damn early in the morning to be trippin' with you! Shit, I'm finna go back to sleep while my mother's gone."

"Where Moms at?" Chancey asked.

"She went to the store. I'm surprise you didn't run into her, 'cause she just left," Kaylin said. "What 'chew doing up so early?"

"Man, I can't sleep at my house. They stressin' me the fuck out over there!"

"Come lay down, then," Kaylin said, rising to his feet. He arched his back, and then headed to his room.

Chancey got up and followed. "Nah, I bet' not," he said, looking down at his watch.

Kaylin stretched out across his bed. "Where you goin'?"

Chancey gave him one of those I-wonder-should-I-tell looks. He waited a minute, then said, "I got something to do."

"This early?"

"Yeah! I gotta go meet…I'm supposed to be…put it like this, I'm about to start havin' crazy money. Cash flow! Chips, nigga!"

"Doing what?" Kaylin asked eagerly.

Chancey bit down on his bottom lip and looked around nervously although he knew he and Kaylin were the only ones home. Kaylin had no brothers or sisters, and his father died when he was five.

Chancey looked at Kaylin long and hard before sitting at the foot of the bed. He pulled the sack of white rocks from his pocket and said, "Check this out!"

Kaylin jumped up, eyes wide open. He snatched the bag from Chancey's hand, spilling a few of the rocks on the floor.

"Damn, cuz, watch what 'chew doin'!"

"Ooops! My bad. Give 'em here," Kaylin said and held out his palm. Chancey picked the rocks up from the floor and dropped them in Kaylin's hand.

"Who gave you this? Ronnie?"

"He gave me the money and I bought it myself."

"How much he give you?"

Smiling, "Three G's," Chancey boasted.

Kaylin's mouth flew open. "HE GAVE YOU THREE THOUSAND DOLLARS?! His ass always wanna act broke when he around me. That's cool though."

"Look! I got a beeper, too," Chancey said, unclamping the pager from his pocket. He took a pen from the dresser and tore off a tiny corner of a page in Kaylin's Right On! Magazine. "We went to Foxhill yesterday," he added as he wrote his pager number down.

"Who, you and Ronnie?" Kaylin asked.

Chancey nodded.

"You didn't have to ask me to go, punk!"

"Oh, I didn't even trip…"

"Yeah, whatever! Me and Moms came by yesterday, too…"

"Oh, for real?"

"Yeah. She wanted to see you. Setchi said you went to the gym."

"I did…for a minute. Then we went to the mall. I got me some gear…and look at this…" Chancey pulled the gold chain from underneath his T-shirt.

"You got the bracelet to match, too, huh?" Kaylin said, noticing the link around Chancey's wrist.

"Yep! *And* I got these," Chancey said, twirling his foot around to show off his Air Jordans.

Kaylin tried hard not to stare at the tennis shoes, but they were the latest additions—the ones he wanted, but couldn't afford.

"'Ey, these the bomb, huh? They just came out."

Kaylin curled his nose. "They aw'ight," he mumbled, wondering what the penalty would be if he broke the foot off that was wiggling in his face.

"Wait 'til I get my car! I already know what kind I want, too."

DAMN, A CAR, TOO! "What kind?" Kaylin asked, feeling the onset of a jealous rage.

"I'ma flip me a Monte Carlo. Have a candy paint thrown on it...I don't know what color yet though. I'ma have it sittin' on some Daytons." Chancey closed his eyes and smiled at the car he painted in his mind. Then he looked down at Kaylin, who was staring at his shoes. Chancey grabbed one of the pillows, fluffed it up, and dove across the bed. "Man, I can't wait!"

Kaylin pictured his Regal and sighed. He looked down at the sack of rocks and forgot about all the times his mother preached on not selling drugs. She would always say, "That's dangerous money." He sat quietly while her words penetrated. Then he looked over his shoulder at Chancey. *Man, I wanna sell, too,* was what he thought. "Man, I'm sick of my job," was what he said. "The manager's a fat-ass redneck, and..."

"Least you got a job." It went right over Chancey's head.

"I wanna make some money, too," Kaylin said, feeling the need to be straightforward.

I know that's not what I heard! Chancey lifted his body from the bed and looked at Kaylin as though his eyes could hear.

"I'm serious, cuz, hook me up!"

Chancey was stunned. "You playin', right?"

"Do it look like it?" Kaylin's face was expressionless.

"Are you crazy?! Man, Moms'll whoop yo' ass!" Chancey said, pronouncing every syllable.

Kaylin smacked his lips. "Man, she don't haf' to know! I can just sell a lil' on the side…after I get outta school."

"What about work?"

"I don't work seven days a week, fool!"

Chancey had to stop and think. He looked at Kaylin without blinking, almost staring clear through him. He and his best friend rich together. Both driving fancy cars, wearing the finest clothes, and catching the prettiest girls together. Chancey couldn't imagine having all those things without Kaylin. He knew Kaylin wouldn't have them without him. Kaylin was the reason he didn't go hungry most of the time in school. And what about the time Kaylin let him wear his brand new Converse All Stars just to impress one of the girls in his class? *And the toys*, Chancey thought and smiled. He could still hear Kaylin's little five-year-old voice inside of Toys R Us. "Mommy, can Chancey have one, too?"

Chancey blinked right out of his thoughts and brought Kaylin back into view. "Whatever," he said, not happy at all that he didn't try and talk Kaylin out of his decision, "but if Moms find out, you on your own, 'cause I'ma act like I don't know nothing."

"Cuz, quit trippin'! She don't know everything I do. Shit, I'm grown," Kaylin said as he grabbed the other pillow and laid back.

*   *   *

Niecy walked in and sat her groceries on the kitchen table. "What time is it?" she asked herself, and then took a quick glance over at the clock on the stove. "Eleven-fifteen already? Boy, time ain't waiting on nobody." She began pulling groceries from one of the bags, and called out for Kaylin to come and help. When he didn't answer, "I know this boy is not still sleep," she mumbled and walked back to Kaylin's room. "Kaylin Rogers!" she called again and pushed his bedroom door open. To her surprise, Kaylin and Chancey were lying across the bed asleep. She stood in the doorway and laughed silently to herself at the boys. They'd been best friends for so long that Chancey was just like her son, too. And for a long time, people actually thought he was. Everywhere she took Kaylin, she took Chancey. They were inseparable. She stared at him and wondered how he turned out to be so bad.

She walked in the room, stood over the boys, and whispered,

"Sleepy heads."

They didn't budge.

"Hey, sleepy heads!" she said.

They both stretched, moaned, yawned, flexed. She stood and waited for one of them to notice her. Kaylin opened his eyes first and looked up at his mother. He shoved Chancey's shoulder and gestured for him to do the same.

Chancey looked up at Niecy and smiled. She hadn't changed much, only a tad bit grayer. He adored her. She was everything a mother should be—everything his mother wasn't. She always had dinner on the table. Was always active in Kaylin's little league baseball games. And her beauty…to Chancey, Niecy had a beauty that stood out. She had high cheekbones, and dark, blemish-free skin, with sparkling, tight eyes and white teeth. It wasn't a mystery why Kaylin always had some girl or another chasing after him. He was the spitting image of his mother.

"Get up, boy, and give me some suga!" Niecy said, holding out her arms. Chancey got up and kissed her on the cheek. "Look at you! You really have grown. You're about what, six-feet now?" she looked up at him and asked.

"Almost."

"Oh, okay," Niecy said and nodded. "We came by yesterday, but you were gone."

"I told 'em, Ma," Kaylin said.

"Oh, you did? Okay." Niecy looked at Chancey for a minute, then asked, "Well, you staying outta trouble this time?"

"Yeah," Chancey lied and looked back at Kaylin. Kaylin put his head down.

Niecy gave her son a proud smile. "My baby is doing so good…he's going to school *and* working."

"C'mon, Ma…" Kaylin said, rolling his eyes.

"Well, I can't help it if I'm proud of you," she said, then looked at Chancey and palmed his cheeks. "I wanna be proud of you, too, but you just won't let me, will you? You just keep insisting on doing all the wrong things in life. Why?"

Chancey dropped his head in shame.

"Dang, Ma!" Kaylin snapped with a soured face.

"Oh, I still love you," Niecy assured Chancey. "I just want you to do something right for a change. Okay? I taught you better than that. I have always told you *and* Kay-Kay that if you want something, just ask. Don't steal! Because what goes around comes around. You steal from one person, another person comes and steals from you. Didn't I tell you guys that? I also said if you ever go to jail, don't look for me to come visit. I haven't seen you in four years...thought I was playing, huh?" Niecy asked, looking at Chancey with a pair of I-told-you-so eyes. "Now that you're home, you really need to straighten up and fly right, Chancey. Go to school and get an education. I'm telling you, baby, now-a-days you can't make it without one. You better listen to me, Chancey. These streets will get you in a world of trouble. Trust me, I know. I've been there..."

Sighing, "Done that! Yeah, yeah, Ma, we know!" Kaylin said.

ASSHOLE! Niecy silently called her son and rolled her eyes at him. "Anyway," she said, focusing her attention back to Chancey. "Please, Chance, get yourself together, baby. I can't keep worrying about you like this."

"You ain't gotta worry about me."

"Why I don't?" Niecy asked, but Chancey just stared at her. "You can't tell me, can you?"

"Because you just don't!"

"Tell me why, then, Chancey?" Niecy demanded.

Chancey put his head down and massaged his forehead. He felt the headache from earlier coming on again. "Because Ma, I'ma do right this time, okay?" he said, using everything he had to keep his attitude in check.

"You promise?"

"Mmm-humph."

"That doesn't sound promising to me."

"I PROMISE! You happy?"

"That's better! And boy, don't get smart with me," Niecy said. "Now go on and wash your hands. I'm making some breakfast this morning."

Kaylin watched his mother leave the room. "I know she was gettin' on your nerves. Imagine hearing that shit everyday," he whispered.

"Yeah, but she's right though."

"She's right?" Kaylin asked, frowning. "So, you not..."

"Man, I gotta do what I gotta do. Fuck that! I gotta make me some money," Chancey interrupted.

"Yeah, me too."

"What 'chew mean, you too? Nigga, please!" Chancey held out his arms and looked around Kaylin's room. "Nigga, look how you livin'."

Kaylin's large room was that of a spoiled child's, with his Sony PlayStation attached to his 25-inch TV and the thirty-or-so games scattered around it. One couldn't tell just how big the room really was due to the king-size bed taking up most of the space.

"Me and you…we different, Kay. You got everything you can ask for. Why you wanna get out there and sell this shit?"

"'Cause, nigga! Shit. I'm try'na get my car fixed and my job ain't payin' me enough."

Chancey smacked his lips. "Man, just keep savin' your money like you been doin'. Shit, it ain't like you payin' rent."

Kaylin got defensive. "Nigga, I do pay rent! What 'chew talkin' about?"

"How much you pay a month? Two…three hundred, what?"

"Hell nah! Shit, I barely make two hundred. I pay about forty bucks a month. Sometimes fifty."

Chancey shook his head and giggled. "See what I mean? What the fuck is forty dollars."

"That's all she ask for!"

"That's 'cause she care, dumb-ass! She know you don't make that much money, so she ain't try'na take you all in. She's just try'na make you be responsible. Now, my mother…that bitch will beg for every dime I got until she breaks me! Why you think I left this morning? Her and Setchi's ass beggin' me for money already and I ain't even started makin' none yet."

"You told Nik you sell drugs?"

"No, but I will eventually. Shit. She don't give a damn! When she found out we was snatchin' purses up at the bank, she used to tell me and Ronnie to give her some money or she was turnin' us in. Ain't that some shit?" Chancey chuckled.

Kaylin laughed. "Man, Nikki ain't right."

"I know she ain't! And, nigga, one time, Setchi stole some nail polish from Savon's and Nikki found out. Do you know she made

Setchi walk all the way back to Savon's and steal her one, too!"

Kaylin laughed out loud. "Nikki's a fool, cuz!"

"Yeah, mmm-humph, she's a fool alright! She just betta' gimme my twenty dollars back, that's all I know."

"Oh, you gave 'er twenty dollars?"

"She wanted forty!"

Kaylin got up and squared off in Chancey's face. "Like you told me, nigga, what the fuck is forty dollars!"

"All I had was sixty! Shit, after I gave her twenty, I turned around and gave Setchi's ass twenty. Now all I got is twenty left, and I'm using that to get me something to eat. And anyway, nigga, I would live on the streets first before I pay my mother rent. Shit. Ain't never got no food! And the house STAY dirty! Man, you should'a seen that room when I first came home! Setchi had shit all over the fuckin' place! And roaches was EVERYWHERE! I walked in the room and saw a roach chillin' on the side of my bed...he had his feet all propped up 'n shit! He looked at me and said, 'What up, loc?'"

Kaylin laughed hard.

"Nigga, he had a blue rag on his head and a joint in his mouth. He passed it to me, but I was like, 'Nah, I'm cool.'"

Kaylin gripped his stomach and laughed so hard that tears flooded his eyes.

"I'm serious! Shit. Man, you got it good and don't even know it. Don't get caught up out here on the streets like me. You'll fuck around and lose everything. You do wanna graduate, don't you?"

Smacking his lips, "Nigga, I *am* graduatin'. Trust me!" Kaylin promised.

"Not out here taking penitentiary chances!" Chancey said, returning the same promising attitude. "Once you catch a case, that's it. That shit'll hunt you for the rest of your life, cuz. I would give anything to have a clean record again. Just to start all over again, you know? I would do things way different. I would be graduating right along with you, Kay. I'm tellin' you this shit because I care about you."

Kaylin smacked his lips again. "Man, you don't care about me."

"Shut up, punk! I do."

"Then why was you sittin' up there throwin' all yo' shit in my face?" Kaylin asked, evil-eyeing Chancey's shoes.

Chancey laughed. "Man, no, I wasn't."

Frowning, "Yes, you was!" Kaylin shouted. "'Look what I got, Kay-Kay! And look at my new Air Jordans. They just came out'," he added, marking Chancey. "I used to never do yo' broke ass like that, but it's cool though."

"C'mon, cuz, you know it ain't even like that," Chancey said, trying hard not to laugh at Kaylin's immaturity. "After I make a few sales, I'ma buy you some shit, too. And when I *really* start makin' money, I'ma help you get another car. Watch! I'ma take care of you. You took care of me! 'Member back when we was in school?"

Kaylin giggled. "Yeah, I remember you was always broke. Nigga, I ain't never seen nobody as broke as you was. You NEVER had money! Toys either! Rocks was yo' toys. 'Member you used to collect 'em? You used to use 'em for marbles," Kaylin said and laughed. "Nigga, I remember you used to stare at people while they was eatin' lunch. 'Member that?" Kaylin was roaring with laughter.

Chancey held a straight face and just looked at Kaylin, which made him laugh even harder. "That shit ain't funny, punk!"

"It is to me," Kaylin said, now in tears.

"Yeah, but that's okay. At least I wasn't gettin' pimped."

Kaylin's laughter faded. "Gettin' pimped? Fool, what 'chew talkin' about?"

"Oh, don't act like you don't know. You used to buy my lunch everyday. And you used to give me half yo' allowance. Yeah, nigga! What!"

"I only did it 'cause I felt sorry for you."

"Nah, you did it 'cause you knew I would beat that ass!"

Kaylin had to laugh at that one. "Nigga, please! You ain't never beat me at shit: fightin', football, baseball, basketball, NOTHING!"

"Whatever."

"I know whatever! Get it straight."

"Shut up and go brush your teeth. Breath smell like wet dog fur!" Chancey took Kaylin's words personal and tried to say anything to shut him up.

It worked. Kaylin tackled Chancey, held him down, and blew his breath in his face.

"UGH! NIGGA, GET OFF ME!"

Kaylin laughed. "Say somethin' else!"

*   *   *

Niecy was busy in the kitchen. She turned her dishwater off when she heard all the fuss in the back. "Alright you guys! Watch the language back there!" she yelled, then hurried to take her bacon out the skillet before it burned. She looked at her golden pancakes and patted herself on the back. The scrambled eggs were simmering perfectly, and the grits were just about done. She took the orange juice from the refrigerator, poured two large glasses, and set them on the table.

*   *   *

Four loud beeps sounded. Chancey looked down at his belt buckle, but didn't see his pager.

"It must'a fell off," Kaylin said, looking down on the floor, under the dresser, then on his bed.

"Here it is," Chancey said, making his way over to the other side of the room. He picked his pager up and tried to figure out who the number belonged to. He stared at the digits with a frown for a minute. "Oh, this must be baby I met at the mall yesterday," he finally said. Then he smacked his lips and said, "Or Tomika. Where's the phone?"

Kaylin pointed at his nightstand. "I'm 'bout to go grub," he said and jogged to the kitchen.

Chancey dialed the number and waited for a female to answer. "Ronnie?" he asked, puzzled by the sound of the familiar voice on the other end.

"Yeah, cuz. Where you at?"

"Over Kaylin's. What time is it?"

"Almost twelve-thirty!"

"Where you at?" Chancey asked.

"At the gym waitin' on you, remember?!" Rondell answered with an attitude.

"Alright, I'm leavin' right now," Chancey said and hung up the phone. He walked to the living room, then followed his nose to the kitchen.

Kaylin was sitting at the table, stuffing his face as though the food would jump up and run away from him. "You gotta make your own plate," he managed to mumble.

"What I tell you about talking with your mouth full?" Niecy asked her son.

Chancey picked the glass of orange juice up from the table and downed it in four swallows. He walked over to the stove, took a piece of bacon from the aluminum pie pan, and stuffed it in his mouth. He was just about to go for another piece when Niecy snatched a plate from the cabinet.

"Boy, take this plate and go sit at the table like you got some sense," she said, shoving the plate in Chancey's hand.

Chancey hesitantly filled his plate with tiny portions of grits, bacon, and eggs. He was starving, but knew he didn't have time to eat. After a moment or two of debating, he could no longer resist the perfectly shaped pancakes that were staring up at him. He threw two on his plate and rushed over to the table.

Frowning, "You in a hurry or something?" Niecy asked.

BEEP! BEEP!

"Oh shit!" Chancey mumbled and quickly turned the pager to silent mode. He glanced over at Niecy out the corner of his eye and prayed she didn't hear it. She did.

"Is that a beeper?" she asked. "Chancey, what are you doing walking around with a beeper?"

Here she go, Chancey thought, rolling his eyes. Kaylin giggled and stuffed more eggs in his mouth.

"You're messing up already," she said.

Chancey frowned. "By havin' a beeper?!"

"Boy, what makes you so damn important that people can't wait for you to get home to talk to you?"

Chancey sighed and mumbled a few smart words under his breath.

"And is Nikki enrolling you back in school tomorrow?"

"Huh?" Chancey asked, still frowning. He had enough of Niecy and wanted her to leave him alone.

"You heard me! Are you enrolling back in school tomorrow?"

"Yeah," he lied, flinching when he felt his hip vibrate.

When Niecy turned her back, he quickly stuffed both pieces of bacon in his mouth at once, then scooped up a spoonful of eggs and stuffed them in his mouth, too. He scooped up some of the grits when Niecy turned around.

"CHANCE!" she shouted. "Slow down before you mess around and choke, fool!" She took her apron off and threw it on the counter. "Boy, boy, boy," she mumbled, "you kids are a damn pain in the ass!"

After Niecy left the kitchen, Chancey took the remainder of his food and raked it onto Kaylin's plate. "'Ey, I gotta go," he whispered. "I'll be back later on to show you how much money I made."

"I get off work at nine tonight."

"Beep me when you get home," Chancey said. Then he turned his pager from silent mode as he crept out the door.

6

Chancey left Kaylin's house and headed toward the gym, which was diagonally across from Kaylin's unit. He crossed 99th Place and looked around for Rondell, but didn't see him.

BEEP! BEEP! BEEP! BEEP!

He looked down at his pager and saw the number to the gym again. He immediately rushed over to the gym and pushed its doors open. There was Rondell, hovering over the reception's desk, quickly punching in some numbers on the phone. Then all of a sudden...

BEEP! BEEP! BEEP! BEEP!

Rondell turned around at the sound of the echoing noise and saw Chancey lounging in the doorway, frowning down at his pager. "I see a nigga gotta page you fifty million times just to get you to show up!" he snapped.

"Man, I said I was comin'!" Chancey snapped back before being alerted by his pager again.

Smiling, "That's me," Rondell confessed with a touch of embarrassment in his voice.

"GODDAMN!" Chancey shouted. "How many times you page

me?!"

Rondell couldn't believe Chancey's nerves. "How many times did I page you?" he asked. "Nigga, first of all, you two hours late! Second of all, you..." Rondell stopped, sniffed, then leaned in closer and sniffed around Chancey's chest area. "You smell like bacon and eggs."

Chancey's smile pissed Rondell off. He chewed Chancey out about being late, and reminded him that most of his customers came either early in the morning or late in the evening, and how *he* was up early, ready to take care of business and Chancey was somewhere else, kicking back eating breakfast. "You ain't right," Rondell told him.

Sighing, "Miss me wit' all that, cuz," Chancey said, looking around the empty gym to direct his attention to other things. "Where's Jackie?" he asked.

Rondell just looked at him. He then flagged toward the women's restroom with a jerk of his hand and walked off.

Chancey headed straight for the women's bathroom without looking back. He eased the door open and peeped around before tiptoeing in. He held on to the handle and eased the door shut.

Jackie was humming a tune that was stuck in her head from the radio on her desk. She looked in the mirror and frowned. Mainly at her hair. It was in four braids, two in the front, two in the back. The braids had been up for a while and were matted to her head. "I need to get this shit done," she told herself in a whisper as she combed out her wig, which was similar to that of Halle Berry's short hairdo.

"You need to *hurry up* and get it done, damn it!" Chancey boldly, but playfully stated.

Jackie jumped at the sound of his voice. Chancey started laughing. He got a real kick out of the fact that he nearly knocked her socks off. Jackie sighed in relief when she realized she wasn't encountering with a ghost. Traumatized, she patted her chest a few times and took in a couple of deep breaths as she made her way to Chancey. Before welcoming him into her arms, she looked at him and smiled. Her eyes told him how lucky he was that she couldn't get to her weapon fast enough.

"Don't be sneaking up on me like that, stupid! You almost got cut up!" she warned, still smiling.

Jackie only intimidated those who didn't know her. Everyone that knew her knew her bark was usually louder than her bite, and therefore, never took her threats serious. In fact, Jackie was a well-respected young lady. She was in her late twenties and had a two-bedroom apartment in the Jordan Down Projects, where she and her eleven-year-old daughter stayed. Refusing to be on welfare, she worked two jobs to pay her rent, car note, and the rest of her bills. At the same time, she tried desperately to keep close tabs on her boy-crazed daughter. Jackie, unlike many others, set a good example for all the young women living in the projects, and everyone admired her for that.

Jackie and Chancey got reacquainted with each other. She updated him on a lot of the same things that Kaylin did with the exception of how her daughter was doing. She had another conference with one of the school's counselors last week and told Chancey about it. She started with, "Yolanda is fucking up big time," and continued by explaining how her daughter had a problem going to school. "She keeps cutting her classes," Jackie said, shaking her head in disgust. "Sneaking off with all these no-good, hardhead boys! It's so bad, I can't take a shit without some nappy-head nigga calling my house. And what makes it even worst is these be grown-ass men!" Jackie took in a deep breath, held it, and sighed. "I don't know what I'm going to do with that girl, Chancey," she said seriously. "She's driving me crazy. Look at all these gray hairs I got now!" Jackie lifted her wig and started to laugh. "I just don't want her to end up like me…stuck with a baby at fifteen. And it's worse now! At least back then I didn't have to worry 'bout that AIDS shit!"

"I feel you, Jackie. Setchi is fourteen now and my mother lets her do whatever the fuck she wanna do. She's into boys and shit, too. I think she messin' with a nigga that's older than me!"

"You lyin'!" Jackie said with large eyes.

"Nope. And my mother knows all about it!"

"Nikki needs to be ashamed of herself. Now you know that don't make no sense," Jackie said, wishing she could give Nikki a couple of good slaps to the face.

"I know! She ain't teachin' Setchi shit! Setchi's lazy, dirty, just…just fuckin' nasty! You know what I'm sayin'? It's all good though, 'cause I'm puttin' a stop to all that shit! Watch me."

"Yeah," Jackie said with a nod of understanding. "It's hard though. Once they get out there, you can't tell 'em a damn thang. They know everything. They know so damn much, they try'da tell you how to run your life." Jackie chuckled a little, then said, "I'm on her ass though...on 'er like a fly to shit. And I'm gon' stay on that ass for seven more years. Once she turns eighteen, she gotta get the hell outta my house."

*   *   *

Rondell was standing outside the gym thinking. Thinking about Chancey and wondering if he was really ready for his new line of work. And then thinking about how he could *make* him ready. He silently went over all the things he was going to do to prepare him.

The sun was starting to release its warmth, and the Jordan Downs were beginning to come to life with people emerging from their units. Young boys were running in and out of the gym, either chasing or being chased by promiscuous girls. Kids were moving about up and down the sidewalks on their skates and bikes.

A loud, rattling muffler was just one of the many sounds that drew Rondell's attention for a second. As the rattle got louder, Rondell became more interested in seeing who it was. Although his customers had slacked off a little, he knew it was a good chance that he would still get a sprinkle here and there, so he decided to hang out just a little while longer.

The trembling got closer, stronger, and unbearable. That's when Rondell noticed the two ladies as they pulled up in a white '85 Dodge Ram. He approached the passenger's side of the worn-down pick-up and said, "What's up," to the two familiar faces.

The driver leaned forward to look at Rondell. Her thin line between kinky and permed hair, to her broken off, unpolished fingernails made her look a complete mess. The passenger looked even worse.

"Hey now!" the driver chanted, smiling and showing all of her four front teeth. "Hook us up with something decent today," she told Rondell, flashing a hundred-dollar bill.

"Alright, hold up," he said and walked inside the gym.

*   *   *

Jackie took the hairpin from between her lips and pinned the last section of her wig down. "How does it look?" she asked Chancey, knowing that if anyone would tell the truth, he would.

"It's cool."

She turned her back to him and asked, "Can you see my hair underneath?"

"Nah, it's cool."

"You sure, Chance? Look real good."

"It's cool, girl!" he snapped, thankful to be a male.

*   *   *

BOMP! BOMP! BOMP!

"Chance! You still in there?" Rondell yelled through the bathroom door. He stuck his head in and looked around. "What the hell y'all doin' in here?"

"Don't come up in here yelling at nobody, ugly!" Jackie told him. She knew Rondell was far from ugly, and he knew that she knew it by the way she would always flirt with him. Even now, she was hoping to start another one of her flirty arguments, but again, he didn't feed into it.

Instead, "C'mon, cuz, it's money out here," he said, grabbing Chancey by the arm.

They walked outside the gym and were ready to approach their clients. Chancey got nervous. As he got closer, he got excited. Then he got nervous again. Nervous. More nervous. "What's up?" he asked and bent down to make eye contact with the two females.

The driver gave her commuter a no-he-didn't expression before turning to make eye contact with Chancey. She raised her wild, unarched eyebrows at him, and in her snootiest voice asked, "Who are you?"

"Who am *I*? Don't worry 'bout all that," Chancey said, nervously stuck for words.

"Whatever!" the driver said, and threw up her palm. She maneuvered her eyes around Chancey and called out to Rondell. "Who is he?" she asked, confused and somewhat upset.

Rondell stepped up to the truck with one big leap. "This is my lil' homie, Connie," he assured. "I'm just introducin' him to these streets…"

"That's cool and everything, but uh, I don't feel like dealing with no new-booties right now. I want some good shit!"

"Yeah, Ronnie!" the passenger said before snobbishly flipping her eyes over at Chancey.

"Connie! Come on, now! Would I lie to you?" Rondell asked in a strained whisper. "I'm try'na tell you he got the same shit I got!"

Connie and her passenger both frowned as they looked Chancey up and down. Connie sucked her teeth and mumbled something to the effect of how she didn't want to be a guinea pig, followed up with an "I know!" from her passenger.

Rondell was just about to do some more explaining to try and put their minds at ease, but Chancey had too much pride. "Man, fuck these bitches," he grumbled and turned to walk away.

Rondell's reflexes were quick and spontaneous when he grabbed Chancey's arm and turned him back around. "C'mon, cuz, quit trippin' and give 'em the shit so they can get the fuck on."

Chancey hesitated. Then he shoved his hand down his pocket after his sack of rocks. He leaned with force, almost throwing himself inside the passenger's window, and unwillingly showed the ladies what he had. Rondell backed away and looked around.

The passenger smirked, intrigued by what she saw. Connie tossed her hundred-dollar bill in her passenger's lap and rolled her eyes away as if Chancey wasn't good enough to deal with directly. The passenger's smirk turned into a full-fledged smile, knowing her long-awaited prize was about to be awarded as she placed the money in Chancey's hand.

Everything was going smooth, until Chancey said, "Hold up. Let me get some change."

"What?!" the two ladies looked at each other and asked.

Rondell palmed his forehead and shook his head. He walked up to Chancey and led him back to the truck. Chancey followed in confusion. Rondell knelt down at the passenger's window and beckoned for his unskilled student to do the same. "Give 'em five rocks," he told Chancey in a soft, but dogmatic tone. His tolerance was fading.

"Five?!" Chancey shouted. He didn't mean to be so loud and obnoxious, but before he knew it, his mouth just flew open and his vocal cord erupted. He looked around awkwardly, embarrassed by what he'd done.

"Yeah, idiot, c'mon! Five big ones!" Connie demanded, banging her fist against the steering wheel as she spoke. She was so teed off, her nose flared. Chancey took five rocks from his sack and dropped them in the passenger's palm.

Connie glared over at Rondell. "Your boyfriend, here, better be giving us some good shit," she threatened.

"BOYFRIEND?!" Chancey roared. He snatched as many rocks as he could out the passenger's hand and said, "Fuck you, bitch!" to Connie. He was hot.

"Bitch? I'll get out this truck and show you who the *real* bitch is!"

Chancey raised one of his eyebrows and grinned at the woman. "Oh, you will, huh? You will? You sure about that?" he asked, hoping to urge his rival into doing something *she* would regret later.

Chancey was short tempered, somewhat like a time bomb waiting to ignite. He had a mean streak that ran deep. No one could explain it, and would often excuse his resentment by believing he just had a lot of anger built up inside of him for some reason or another.

Rondell looked at Chancey and saw his ruthless, cold eyes. He studied Chancey's facial expressions for years and was very familiar with what reactions went with what, which is why he suddenly became apprehensive about the whole situation as the arguing escalated.

"Bitch, I will beat the hell outta yo' ass!" Chancey told Connie. He held a straight face and was firm.

"I'll make you *kiss* my ass, you punk!" she retorted and opened her door, but didn't get out.

Chancey aggressively made his way around to her side of the truck.

Rondell stepped in. "C'mon, cuz! It's not that serious," he said, trailing closely behind Chancey as he spied on the multiplying onlookers. But Chancey continued to pursue her.

Connie slammed the door and locked it. "You know what…I don't need this shit! Just gimme back my fuckin' money!" she screamed through the window.

"I ain't giving you shit!" Chancey said, pulling on the door handle.

All the "Ooohs" and "Ahhs" were growing louder as the horde of unwanted guests grew thicker and rowdier. One of the boys from the audience yelled, "Bust 'er window out!"

Rondell knew Chancey's first day would be a challenge, but he never expected this. He stepped in front of Chancey and opened his arms wide to keep him from passing.

Chancey leaned into Rondell and shoved him with his shoulder. "Move, nigga!" he said, forcing him to step back.

Rondell stumbled back a step or two, then sprung forward and squared off in Chancey's face, but Chancey kept shoving and pushing, trying to maneuver his way around Rondell.

"Chancey! CUZ!" Rondell yelled as he struggled to hold Chancey off. "You need to chill! I'm serious!"

Chancey backed off, huffing and panting like a pouting child. "Man, tell that bitch to quit talkin' crazy, then!"

"YOU TALKIN' CRAZY TO ME!" Connie yelled through her window.

"YEAH!" the passenger yelled, siding with her friend.

Rondell tried to keep the peace by sympathizing with everyone. He made individual eye contact with all three defendants when he said, "Everybody just calm the fuck down."

Rondell gripped Chancey by the shoulders and pushed him off to the side. He looked him directly in the eye and said, "Cuz, you drawin' too much attention! Now, c'mon now…give 'em the shit so they can get the fuck up outta here!"

"You give it to 'em!" Chancey snapped and dropped what rocks he managed to snatch from the passenger into Rondell's hand.

Rondell let out a conquering sigh and looked out for police before he approached the truck for what he hoped would be the last time. Chancey went over and stood in the doorway of the gym. Some of the nosy witnesses rushed over to see what they could pry out of him.

"Sorry 'bout that, Connie," Rondell said sympathetically as he leaned inside the driver's window. "That nigga got a temper," he added and grimaced over at Chancey. "Don't sweat it though."

"Don't sweat it?! I heard that! It's way too many dealers around here to be..."

"Don't get us wrong, we like dealing with you," the passenger butted in. "You always hook us up with some good shit, but we just don't wanna get..."

"We ain't try'na get our asses busted out here, fucking around with that over there!" Connie said, flipping her hand toward Chancey.

"Connie! You trust me, right?" Rondell asked.

"Yeah, I trust you, but..."

"Do you trust me, Connie?"

"Yeah!"

"Alright then! Don't sweat it! This won't happen again. Matter fact, here you go," Rondell said, quickly sneaking another rock from the crouch of his pants. "This one's on me."

That made both Connie and her passenger smile. "Thank you, baby," the passenger said.

"Alright, you ladies be safe...and come again!" Rondell urged, smirking as he backed away from the truck.

"We will," they both promised. Connie started her ignition, and as she pulled off, she and her passenger rolled their eyes at Chancey once more.

Rondell shook his head as he walked over to Chancey. He stared at him in silence. Chancey didn't say a word either. Then Rondell grimaced around his surroundings, threatening the observers with his eyes. They all began to scramble and disappear. Rondell looked back at Chancey and told him that he needed to control his temper.

"What?! Fuck them crackhead bitches!" Chancey snapped.

"You need them crackhead bitches if you wanna get paid. Remember that! You do wanna get paid, right?"

"Yeah, but I ain't no punk though!"

"It ain't about being a punk! It's about us, crackheads, money, and jail! In order for us to get paid, we need them crackheads. You follow me? 'Cause without them, we ain't got shit! And in order for us to stay outta jail, we gotta have a plan...a strategy! A transaction should never be more than a minute. One minute! All that arguing 'n shit could'a got us fucked up! You gotta be quick. Oh, and discrete, too, nigga! You all loud 'n shit, talking about you gotta get change," Rondell said and chuckled a little.

Chancey eased up a bit and smirked. He could feel his tensed body relax. He then thought about how stupid he must have looked and glanced at Rondell with a silly grin. "A hundred dollars though?" he asked, surprised that anyone could spend that much money on something that would be gone in a matter of minutes.

"That's right! We don't give change. If they don't come with the exact amount, they don't get served. Period. This ain't no joke. This shit is real. Sometimes I pull in over a thousand dollars a night! I'm telling you, cuz, it's money to be made out here! All we gotta do is make it! Fuck who they are! Fuck what they look like! Fuck what they talkin' bout! Let's just make this money, nigga!"

7

The weather in Los Angeles was nice and vivid. The sun was blazing hot with a cool breeze to tease everyone from time to time.

Jordan's Gym was filling up fast. Sounds of bouncing basketballs became more apparent as fathers taught their eager little boys how to aim and shoot, and teenaged boys showed off for one another as they zoomed up and down the basketball court, dribbling their balls in a fancy fashion. Most of the girls stood off to the side chanting like cheerleaders, especially when the boys would run up to the basket, jump, and slam the ball through the hoop.

Jackie was heard all the way outside, yelling a few times at some of the boys when she thought they were getting too far out of hand or in her office crowding her space.

"Damn she got a big-ass mouth!" Rondell said, referring to Jackie, but talking to no one in particular. He and Chancey stood outside most of the time and held their positions, providing excellent customer service to their clients.

"Let me see you dunk it this time," Chancey heard one girl bellow out to her boyfriend. He hurried inside the gym to catch a glimpse of the tall, baldhead fellow as he arrogantly muscled his way down the court in his Lakers short set.

The fellow jumped up, cocked his bony arms back, and slammed his basketball through the net. Hard! Loud cheers echoed from the sidelines as the boy dangled from the rim, posing his lanky, dark frame for his fans.

Chancey beamed at the basketball star for a second, which would have been longer if Rondell hadn't called him back outside. "You got a customer," Rondell told him.

After Chancey took care of his customer, he lazily walked back over to the gym and said, "It's startin' to slow down," to Rondell who was squatted, counting money behind a bush on the side of the gym.

"I told you it usually does about this time. In the morning and at night though," Rondell rose to his feet and climbed out from behind the bush, "I make so much money, seems like fifty-dollar bills be fallin' out the sky," he said with exhilaration as he dusted himself off with one hand, while clutching a stack of money in the other.

"How much is that so far?" Chancey asked.

"Four hundred and fifty-six dollars," Rondell said. "Are your pockets empty?"

"This one is, I think," Chancey said, scrunching his right pocket in his hand. "Why?"

Rondell didn't answer. He folded the money and slid it down Chancey's right pocket.

Chancey's face lit up.

Rondell's face was firm. He stalled for almost thirty minutes, speaking on insignificant subjects, then he asked, "How much money you got?"

"Um," Chancey thought out loud as he patted both his pockets.

"No, how much money's in that pocket?" Rondell asked, pointing down at Chancey's right side.

"Oh. Four hundred and fifty-somethin' dollars," Chancey boasted before looking at Rondell like he was crazy for forgetting that fast.

"You sure?"

Chancey smacked his lips. "That's what you said, right?! You said it was four hundred and..." Chancey stopped talking and willingly reached in after his riches. "Let me see what the hell is goin' on around here!" he continued in a playful tone, and began to count out his wealth. "One hundred, hundred and twenty…"

"Yeah, you do that," Rondell said seriously.

"…Three hundred." Chancey licked the tip of his thumb and continued. "Three hundred and twenty, three hundred and forty, forty-one, forty-two…*FORTY-TWO?!* Three hundred and forty-two dollars?! Ah, that's fucked up! You got me," Chancey said, voice full of disappointment.

"Yep. And you see how easy it was?" Rondell asked scornfully. "Always, ALWAYS count yo' shit!"

Chancey felt like a fool. He gave Rondell a look that was mixed with a frown *and* a smirk before reprehensibly turning away.

"Don't trip—just be careful, that's all. I don't expect you to get out here and learn this shit over night. It takes time. But if you don't be careful, what's the point? A careless nigga, especially a careless-wit'-his-money-ass nigga, is a what? A BROKE NIGGA, that's what!" Rondell explained, noticing a paper-thin man approaching in their direction, wearing a white, outdated windbreaker jacket and a pair of dusty stonewashed jeans.

What caught Chancey's attention was how the sleeves of the man's jacket stopped midway above his wrist, and his pants appeared to be two sizes too small. He cracked a quick joke to Rondell about it, then openly stepped to his buyer. Rondell reminded him to be discrete.

The antsy man said a simple, "Hey," to Chancey as he rambled through one of his pockets.

"What's up," Chancey replied and waited patiently. He was cool, calm, and collected.

Mr. Antsy gave Chancey five dollars and asked what he could get with it. Chancey threw his head back to look at Rondell with a twisted lip before stepping behind a tree nearby. He poured a few crumbs in his hand like Rondell told him to, looked around, then secretly passed them on to Antsy.

Antsy dashed away all happy just like Rondell said. "Crumbs are important, too. *Shid…*you'll be surprised what a fiend'll do for some crumbs!" Chancey remembered him saying. He headed back toward the gym feeling lazier than before. His stomach was growling hungrily, followed by hunger pains that radiated from his belly to his forehead. He'd been out there all day, making one drug sell after another. Whenever he tried to settle down and relax for a minute, up popped a keen customer.

Rondell smiled pleasingly as Chancey stepped up. "That was good," he said with a nod of approval. "You gettin' better. Next time though, stay over where I can see you."

"Yeah, whatever," Chancey mumbled in a sigh, rolling his eyes away. He knew he was making a great deal of progress and felt good about it. He would feel even better if he could kick back, stretch, grab a quick bite to eat, or just have a little space to breathe for once without being smothered to death. With every move he made, Rondell came questioning him or making some kind of remark about it.

Earlier, when Chancey made an attempt to buy some chips from one of the vending machines inside the gym, Rondell had a fit. Preached for almost thirty minutes straight about how Chancey would miss all the customers if he kept walking away. "And you remember what I told you: no fiends, no moo-lah!"

Chancey yawned, scratched his damp, sweaty head, and rested his body against the wall. He grabbed the back of his neck and rotated his head from side to side.

"So how much you get?" Rondell questioned.

Chancey slowly slid down the wall and plopped to the ground. He let out a dramatic yawn. With it came, "All he had was five dollars."

"Did you do what I said?"

"Yeah! Why you think I went behind the tree?!" Chancey paused to chuckle before adding, "That fool was all happy 'n shit just like you said, too."

Rondell smiled and said, "*Seeeeeee...*" in an I-told-you-so tone.

"Yeah, yeah..." Chancey moaned, unenthused. He held his breath to prepare for the hunger pain he felt building up in his stomach. After it passed, he let out a relaxing sigh.

"I know you ain't gettin' tired on me, are you?"

Chancey looked at Rondell and yelled, "I'm tired! Starvin'! And bored! Shit!" but only to himself though. He made all of his troubles known to Rondell over two hours ago, and...

"Think money! 'Member what I told you? Mind over matter!

'Member? All you been doin' since you got out here is complaining, talkin' 'bout 'it's hot', 'I wish I was shootin' some hoop', 'I'm hungry', 'I'm tired', I'm this, I'm that! Damn, nigga, quit actin' like a bitch and be a man!" is what Rondell told him.

So, with that said, Chancey held all his frustrations in and took his stomachaches, headaches, and any other ache that had the guts to challenge his will, like a man. He started feeling like one, too. Rondell knew what he was talking about. Mind over matter! *Shit works*, Chancey thought as each ache became more and more bearable with time. Eventually, he became numb, feeling no pains at all. Emotions either. All he felt was his urge to have money. Lots of money! Enough money to buy the world if he could!

Feeling this way got Chancey stoked when he saw the black BMW rolling his way on chrome rims. He couldn't really see the driver through the tinted widows, but could tell it was a dude from the outline of his strong facial features and tapered haircut. The BMW cruised at a snail's pace down Grape Street. "That shit is tight! Who is that?" he asked Rondell.

"I don't know," Rondell answered, watching and wondering who the slow traveler was looking for. "I see 'em passin' through here all the time though."

*   *   *

Kaylin picked his ID badge up from the dresser, grabbed his car keys from the bed, and yelled, "I'm gone, Ma," as he headed for the door.

"Have a good day at work, honey!" Niecy yelled back from her room.

Kaylin walked over to his car, got in, and attempted to start it. The weak motor revved up for no more than a second before it conked out. He pressed the gas pedal a couple of times before making the second attempt. His car revved for a hot second, then conked out again. After the third attempt, he slammed his foot on the brake, threw the car in reverse, and backed onto 99th Place with force.

Chancey heard the familiar noise of the overworked engine. *Kaylin*, he thought and smiled. He walked out in the middle of the street and stood with his arms folded, legs spread apart, and daring

Kaylin to hit him.

Kaylin smiled and slowed down, but didn't stop. Chancey laughed and put his hands on the hood as he backed up to keep from being run over. Kaylin came to a complete stop and the car began to shake real, real hard.

"Damn, this piece of shit sounds like it's about to fall apart!" Chancey said as he walked around to the passenger's side. Rondell laughed from the doorway of the gym.

Chancey wiggled the door handle and said, "Take me to Jack in the Box real quick."

"Walk!" Kaylin taunted, but then unlocked the door.

Smiling, "Oh, you got jokes," Chancey said. "Wait 'til I get my shit. I already made over six hun' today, fool!" he bragged, hopping in just as blasé as always.

Rondell walked up to the car and asked Chancey where he was going.

"Jack in the Box!" Chancey snapped with large, ready-to-argue eyes. Kaylin looked over at him as if to say, *not in my car!*

"Bring me back something," Rondell said, reaching into his pocket for some single dollars.

"What! I heard the hell outta that!" Kaylin barked. "I couldn't even get twenty dollars from you the other day!"

"I don't remember you askin' me for no twenty dollars," Rondell said. He was calm.

"Oh, so now yo' funny-style ass wanna act like you don't remember, right?" Kaylin questioned with hurt feelings.

"Cuz, if you asked me for some money, I would'a gave it to…"

"Nah, cuz," Kaylin butted in. "Raise up outta here!"

*   *   *

Setchi strutted her stuff toward the gym in a baby blue tank top and a pair of denim shorts that were so short, her butt cheeks were exposed as she extended each leg to walk. She felt vibrant and pretty in her cherry-red lipstick that her mother showed her how to put on with no flaws. She was excited and overly anxious to show her sexy self off to her companion. She sped up, then slowed—almost stopping when she saw Rondell arguing with Kaylin, and the back of her brother's head in Kaylin's passenger seat. She immediately quickened her pace in the opposite direction, cut through all the units of the housing project, and finally reached the corner of Grape and 103rd.

*   *   *

"Nope!" Kaylin was persistent.

"I was talkin' to Chance!"

"Whose car you see Chance in?"

Rondell snarled at Kaylin. "Nigga, what I look like, Bank of Ronnie?!"

"Well, that's the only way I'm bringin' you something back!"

Rondell said a few curse words under his breath about Kaylin, his worn-out car, and about Chancey, too, since he found everything to be so funny. He pulled ten ones from his pocket and shoved it in Kaylin's face. "Bring me a number one with a Sprite. Super-size it!" Rondell said and turned to walk away.

Kaylin laughed and yelled, "Can I have mines super-sized, too?"

Still walking, "Whatever!" Rondell said and threw up his hand. Then a thought stopped him in his tracks. He turned to approach Kaylin's car again, and Kaylin, still laughing, yelled, "Okay! Okay! I don't haf' to have it super-sized!"

Rondell passed Kaylin up and made his way around to Chancey. He bent down and said, "Gimme the sack. You don't *ever* wanna ride dirty unless you haf' to."

Chancey pulled his sack from his pocket. Kaylin watched with inspecting eyes as if he would miss something if he blinked. Rondell cracked an admiring smile when he saw Chancey count his rocks. He felt proud knowing he taught him well.

Chancey's smile was more egotistical and boastful when he said, "Don't take it personal," and handed over his sack.

*   *   *

Kaylin toured around to check out the neighborhood before going to Jack in the Box. Chancey needed the break. Kaylin could tell by the way Chancey talked his ears off, venting about Rondell and how he was driving him crazy. "I can't take a piss without that nigga lookin' for me!"

Chancey told Kaylin all about his day, who he met, who he saw, and how much money he made. "Here you go, cuz," he said, placing five folded twenty-dollar bills in Kaylin's ashtray. He promised Kaylin there would be plenty more where that came from.

The two covered just about every block in Watts before Kaylin zoomed up 103rd and swerved his Buick in the parking lot of Jack in the Box.

"Look at Tia!" Chancey yelled, staring her down as she and a chunky girl strolled in the fast-food eatery out of his sight. He rose a bit to try and bring her back into his view, but Jack in the Box was crowded, making it difficult to spot her. Just as he caught a quick glimpse of the pink summer dress she had on, Kaylin was the next in line to pull up and place his order. "Ah, man!" Chancey cried, feeling like he would never see her again.

Kaylin told the intercom what he, Chancey, and Rondell wanted, then pulled up to the window to pay. "You still in love with Tia?"

"Fool, I'm a playa'! Playa's don't fall in love!" Chancey snapped.

Kaylin giggled and said, "Yeah, okay Ronnie," finding it humorous that Rondell's self-centered ways were already starting to rub off on his friend.

Chancey begged Kaylin to hang out in the parking lot for a little while. "Just 'til she come back out," he said, but Kaylin sped off, explaining how late for work he was.

All four of Kaylin's tires screeched as he spun onto 99th Place and stopped in front of the gym. Rondell stepped outside, frowning. "What the hell took you so long?"

Chancey got out and slammed Kaylin's door. He leaned inside the window with a flustered face. "See what I mean?"

Kaylin laughed.

"Take me to work with you," Chancey said.

"I need to be comin' to work with you. Shit, Food 4 Less ain't payin' no six hundred a day!"

"Yeah, but at least you don't have to worry 'bout this nigga stressin' you out," Chancey said, nodding his head toward the gym. He checked his bags to make sure he had everything. "I'm serious though," he said, leaning down to Kaylin's eye level again. "Bring me back an application."

"For what? It ain't like you gon' fill it out."

"Don't tell me what I'ma do!" Chancey snapped. "I don't plan on being out here too long. Two months, max! Just long enough to get my transpo' and stack me some chips."

Kaylin took the last bite from his Jumbo Jack, crumbled up the wrapper, and threw it to the side. As he took a long swig from his root beer, he observed Chancey with somewhat convinced eyes for a second or two, then said, "Yeah, whatever," and put his car in reverse.

"'Ey! You almost ran over my foot!"

8

"I don't know why you trippin', cuz. She ain't even worth it! And anyway, you don't even know if it's true," Rondell explained, but in the back of his mind, he knew the rumor had come from too many valuable sources for it not to be.

Chancey was fuming mad. "It bet' not be! 'Cause if it is...I'm tellin' you..." He took a deep breath and said, "I'm servin' her ass with a black eye! Watch me!"

"Chance," Rondell said, sitting down beside him, "listen, cuz, you don't wanna get locked up over no bitch. Shit is just startin' to take off right now. You hear me?"

Chancey didn't. The only thing he heard was his conscious telling him to hurt Tomika bad if she confessed to the dreadful allegation that she was being accused of. He rubbed his hands together slowly before briefly palming his face.

Rondell looked at Chancey and pitied his sorrow. He rolled his eyes away and snatched the plastic off the cigar he bought from Grape Supermarket earlier. He carefully pulled the cigar apart and dumped the tobacco on the coffee table. Then he opened the tiny ziplocked bag filled with some fresh marijuana, sprinkled the green leaves inside, and rolled the cigar back together. Smiling boastfully, "I'm 'bout to get faded off this Indo, nigga," he bragged, sliding the cigar he created under his nose with one hand and patting his pockets with the other. "You see my lighter?" he asked.

Chancey didn't answer.

"I don't know why you trippin' so hard. Shit, it ain't like you never fucked around on her."

Chancey jumped up from the couch and shouted, "She tried to fuck one of my homeboys! My home — boy!"

Chancey grabbed his head and angrily paced back and forth, then glanced over at the time on Rondell's VCR. "Just wait 'til she get here," he warned. "I'm just gon' ask 'er straight out—Tomika, did you try to get wit' Bobcat last night? And if the bitch say yeah, or even look like she wanna say yeah, I'm sockin' 'er in her fuckin' jaw!"

Rondell laughed and said, "See, that's why I don't fall in love with these hoes."

"Oh, I ain't in love! It's just the principle..."

"Whudeva," Rondell said and snobbishly threw his eyes up at the ceiling.

How the fuck did I let myself get caught up with this bitch like this? Chancey asked himself, reliving the painful moment Bobcat came and disintegrated his heart.

It was almost three in the morning when Nikki heard the calm taps at the door. "Who is it?!" she yelled. She heard a faint, "Bobcat," then called out Chancey's name as she went over to the door and opened it. "Lil' Bobby's here!"

Chancey could barely stand, let alone walk to the door. He, Rondell, Kaylin, and a few others from the area had hung out at Rondell's place most of the night, drinking and getting high, and he had just made it home and into bed. "What's up?" he mumbled, leaning against the wall in the hallway. Nikki got back on the comfort of the couch and flung the covers over her head.

Speechless, Bobcat stood on the porch. It took a minute for Chancey to become aware of the seriousness of Bobcat's visit. He was careful not to fall as he gradually moved his drunken, half-asleep body to the door. A whiff of the tainted air hit him in the face, completely waking him. He looked at Bobcat, fully alert, and asked again, "What's up, cuz?"

Bobcat started out by saying, "I'm tellin' you this 'cause we boys..."

*   *   *

Rondell tried to get Chancey's attention by turning up the radio when he heard one of his favorite songs, but Chancey was so engaged in last night's experience with Bobcat that not even the aroma from the weed Rondell blew out got his attention. Rondell inhaled the smolder for a good twenty seconds, then blew a cloud of smoke in Chancey's frowned-up face. Chancey didn't budge. They sat in silence for a minute or two, contemplating, before Rondell callously looked at Chancey. He started to say something, but then thought, *to hell with it!* And instead, spitefully turned his back to him and enjoyed the rest of his high by himself. Rondell wanted to tell Chancey off for being so naïve, feeling all the unnecessary turmoil should have never taken place since he warned him time and time again about materialistic girls like Tomika. But all Chancey would say was, "Yeah, I know, but 'Mika was wit' me before I got all this shit," referring to his substantial amounts of cash, clothes, jewelry—more so his silver Rolex with the blue face trimmed in diamonds.

The number of dollars Chancey secretly accumulated per week was extremely high and constantly climbing as each week progressed. Part of the reason he tried keeping his success hidden was because of those he feared might beg him or even rob him of his riches. The other was so he wouldn't draw too much attention from police and money-hungry females that Rondell armed him with information about.

Tomika also did her share of advising Chancey when it came to females. "You betta' keep 'em out of your mothafuckin' face!" she would always warn.

She was extremely jealous and hated for anyone, especially females, to take up too much of Chancey's time. It was bad enough her time with him was limited due to his everyday hustle, and she'd be damned if the next female came taking what little she did have.

Chancey couldn't leave Tomika's side for five minutes without her getting all green-eyed, feeling that if he wasn't with her, he was with another girl. It was always the same old scenario—she would hunt him down and jam him up about sexing some girl or another.

Chancey soon grew tired of Tomika's abuse and called himself leaving her for two whole days. But when she cried, begged, and promised, he gave in and went back to her *and* her same old, jealous ways.

Tomika wished she could stop her obsession with Chancey. It had to stop before it killed her. Or she killed him. Many nights she sat at home, drained from crying because he hadn't been home all night. Usually, crying nights like these occurred after she searched the entire neighborhood looking for Chancey, only to return home hours later empty-handed.

All night, she would page him back to back, worried sick that he was laid up somewhere with a girl snuggled under his armpit. The next day, she'd finally catch up to him and break all hell loose. She'd hit him over the head with pots, irons, and anything else she could get her hands on. Once, she even chased him down the block with a butcher knife, threatening to stab him to death if she caught him.

Chancey caused Tomika all sorts of pain, mentally and physically, but for some odd reason, she chose to still stay with him and suffer the consequences. Most of the time, she was left lonely and craving for his affection. When the loneliness became too much for her to bear, she became desperate and did whatever she saw necessary to get his attention. Even if it meant switching her big butt extra hard in front of his friends when she saw them looking. Even if it meant lying and saying they made a pass at her when they really didn't. And if Chancey got mad, "What 'chew gettin' mad for? Shit, I should'a went out with 'em! Ain't like your sorry ass is spendin' time wit' me!" she would hit him with.

After hearing a few statements like that, Chancey would pacify her with something he believed she loved more than his time. Something he thought attracted her to him in the first place. Money!

Chancey bought Tomika's happiness so he could be happy. He kept her draped in gold and whatever else she wanted, just so she would stay off his back. She'd prance throughout the projects, flashing the jewelry that he bought, talking Chancey this and

Chancey that, dressed in every piece of clothing he owned to let everyone know he belonged to her. And if that wasn't enough to let all the girls know Chancey was off limits, she sported his initials on her necklace, nails, and toes.

Being given gifts didn't necessarily make Tomika happy though, just satisfied. Sure, she wanted more. She wanted Chancey. And in the beginning, she did love him for who he was, but here lately, she found herself loving him more and more for what he had.

Tomika also found satisfaction in bragging about the things Chancey had. She felt proud to be the lady of a baller, which everyone labeled Chancey after he bought her a huge ring filled with diamond chips.

It wasn't until the day he boldly rolled up at the Jordan Down Projects in his brand new Jeep Cherokee, the Limited Edition, that many learned his true wealthy status. When he pulled up on the scene, everybody lost their minds and surrounded him like he was a superstar.

Chancey's jeep was pitch black, fully loaded with black leather seats, and sat on a set of chromed, Dayton Wire rims. All the attention he received didn't boost his ego though. He was actually content with his 1973 Monte Carlo, and wouldn't have even bothered with the extra set of wheels if Rondell hadn't went out and surprised the entire neighborhood, returning in a dark blue, pristine Lexus—the LS 400 model with ten miles on it!

Once out of the closet, Chancey spent money like it grew on trees, soon forgetting all the promises he made to Setchi, Niecy, and Kaylin. In the beginning, Kaylin would slip in a few daunting words to try and scare Chancey off the streets and into a legitimate lifestyle, but soon as Chancey changed Kaylin's Buick into the powerful, unblemished, gold-colored '64 Chevy Impala he spotted down at one of the local car dealers, Kaylin defended Chancey on everything as if he could do no wrong.

Niecy sensed something was fishy when her two sons suddenly popped up with new vehicles and whatever else they had the audacity to showboat. She confronted them one day with plans of grilling the truth out them, but they had an alibi for sell—Kaylin got a promotion at Food 4 Less, and Chancey was hired at some shipping and receiving company out in Compton. Amazingly, she bought it.

It didn't take long before selling drugs became Chancey's nine to five, or more like twenty-four-seven. He hustled alongside Rondell all night, sometimes bringing in no less than a thousand dollars, which he kept, along with his leftover drugs, wrapped in foil and stored away in Rondell's freezer. He didn't like the idea of letting his assets out of his sight for one minute, let alone all night. But after several times of learning the hard way, Rondell was the only one he fully trusted.

Each time he came up short, no one said anything. For one, the thief didn't want to blow their cover. And two, Chancey didn't want to blow his. And so, on many occasions, he was left dumbfounded, thinking maybe he didn't have as much as he thought he had, and simply took it as a lost. Then one day, the unsolved mystery came to light.

There was nothing peculiar about that night—the night he came home and saw Nikki stretched out as usual across their scruffy, old couch. He walked passed her, just as he always did, and headed straight for his room. "You ain't speaking today?" she asked him. Now that caught him off guard since she was always sleep when he got home, or so he thought.

He stopped, backed up a step or two, and looked at his mother, puzzled. "You still up?" he asked.

"Yeah, it's too hot to sleep," Nikki answered.

Chancey saw no reason to oppose and headed back to his room. It was truly hot. Eleven o'clock at night, and still, the muggy weather in Los Angeles lingered ferociously, which is why he and Rondell opted to turn in early.

He sat on his bed and quickly counted out ones, fives, tens, twenties, and fifties, totaling almost seven hundred dollars. He popped the top off the small 35mm film container, saw he had two rocks left, then almost immediately jumped out of his pants when he heard the sound of the crackling floor in the hallway. He tensely fumbled his belongings before rapidly tossing them under his pillow.

"Hurry up and bring yo' ass out that bathroom! Shit!" Chancey heard his mother yell as she banged on the bathroom door.

"Setchi?" he whispered, then rushed over to Setchi's bed and yanked her blankets back. He was surprised when he discovered the empty cot. He was so used to routinely coming home and finding his sister fast asleep in her bed before he began counting and securing his profits, and tonight, saw no reason to question the way her covers were positioned, giving the false impression of a bodily image. "Where's Setchi? In the bathroom?"

"Yeah! She's been in there for damn near fo' hours!" Nikki said, entering the room. She stood and restlessly threw her eyes around, but only around Chancey's side.

"Wassup?" he asked, feeling even more tensed, but Nikki just smirked and made some kind of sarcastic grunt before walking out.

She stepped out on the porch and lit a cigarette. She grinned at all the kids playing with water balloons and whatnot to stay cool. She yelled, "Get 'em, girl!" when she saw one of her girlfriends chasing her five-year-old with a water gun. Nikki's girlfriend then swiftly turned the water gun on her, sending her back inside screaming.

Tensed and now frustrated, Chancey tossed his belongings back under his pillow and raced in the living room to see what was going on.

"Get back!" Nikki hollered, laughing and hiding behind the front door. "Gail's got a water gun!"

Chancey smacked his lips, and once again, headed back to his room, this time with swearing words seeping from his mouth. He plopped down on his bed, exhausted, and rested his face in the palm of his hand for a minute. When he heard his mother thrust back outside, he went for his possessions and told himself to make it quick. He poured the two rocks in his hand and slowly counted them with concentration. There had been some funny stuff going on lately, and he wanted to make sure he had what he *knew* he had.

Just as he was about to place them back in their holder, a lively Setchi came flouncing from the bathroom. "Oooooh..." Her lips parted like the Red Sea when she caught a glimpse of her brother frantically trying to hide his things. "I'm telling!" she squealed, and took off running to the living room. Chancey hurried after her. She looked back and let out a nervous giggle when she saw him hot on her tail. She swooped in the kitchen, looking for Nikki. He swooped in after her. She kept running, latching out at the doorknob when she reached the front door, but Chancey was too fast and pushed it shut just as she'd opened it.

"MAMA!!!" Setchi screamed at the top of her lungs, laughing

hysterically. Chancey grabbed Setchi and scooped her up like she was a toddler.

Nikki and her girlfriend stood outside talking and enjoying some fresh air. She heard the familiar cry reverberating from her apartment and yelled, "Boy, what'n the hell are you doing to that girl now?!" before she turned to her friend and said, "Girl, they fight like some damn cats and dogs!"

Setchi kicked, squirmed, and pulled, but couldn't break loose as Chancey dragged her back to their room. He angrily threw her across her bed and stood over her, daring her to make a move. "I'm telling," she whimpered, gripping her lower back.

"You play too much, Setchi," Chancey scolded. "And you need to stop tellin' so fuckin' much!"

"Well, you got drugs…"

"Shut up! You don't know what the fuck I got!"

"Uh-huh! I saw it! I ain't dumb! You either selling 'em or using 'em…"

"Would you shut the hell up? Damn!" Chancey snapped, backing up and sitting down on his bed. He sat in a state of confusion as irritating thoughts jumped out at him left and right. *Setchi never had a clue that I was sellin' this shit. And she didn't know it was under my mattress either.* Chancey looked at his sister and studied her. *Did she?* he wondered before asking, "Setchi, you didn't know this stuff was under my bed? And don't lie either!"

"NO!" Setchi snapped seriously, with extremely large eyes gazing at her brother like she no longer knew him.

Suddenly, *NIKKI!* he heatedly suspected, convinced that she was the one stealing from him all along. His money, drugs, jewelry, knickknacks, everything. "Ain't this a bitch!" he bellowed out while collecting his thoughts. His eyes wandered pass Setchi and did a double take when he noticed her still large eyes plastered on him. He felt bad for snapping at her. "Setchi," he said as he shifted from his bed to hers and placed his arm around her shoulders, "I'm sorry."

Setchi rolled her eyes around and curled her lips to the side. "For what?" she asked, on the borderline of crying. "Gettin' busted with drugs or almost breaking my back?"

Chancey noticed the water forming in his sister's eyes and quickly embraced her, hoping to stop it from turning into heartbreaking tears.

"Don't cry, Setchi," he said when he saw a tear burst from one of her eyes. He watched the bead of moisture stream down her cheek and hang from her chin before he finally wiped it away. Then he laid his head on her shoulder and comforted her until she stopped weeping. "You mad at me?" he asked.

"No!" she lied.

"Setchi, I didn't mean to throw you…look, I'm sorry, alright? And about the…me sellin' drugs…look, you need to understand…look, I'm doing this for me *and* you!"

Setchi got mad. She pushed Chancey's arm from around her, got up, and squared off in front of him. "How's that?!" she asked, feeling recharged and twisting her neck with each word. "What are you, stupid?! You gon' end up going back to jail in a minute, watch! All you did was sit up here and lie, talking about how you changed! You ain't changed! You still the same! And I swear, I can't stand you! I'm not talking to you no more! I don't even want nothing else to do wit' 'chew!! You don't care about me or Ma! You just caught up in the game, doin' dumb stuff! How stupid! UGH! You get on my nerves!"

Chancey got up in the haze of Setchi's outbreak and peeped in the living room to see Nikki's whereabouts. He turned around only to find his outraged sibling in his face again, looking like she was ready to fight. "Okay, Setch, sit down. Let's talk…"

"Nah, forget that! I don't wanna talk to you! I don't even know you! Matter fact, I'm goin' to get Ma…"

Chancey conquered a hand full of Setchi's free-flowing hair and tugged, bringing her paddling feet to a halt. "You see what I mean? There you go again!" Chancey fumed. "That's why I never tell you shit! Always runnin' to Ma like a lil'-ass kid!" He thought about slamming her again, this time on the floor, but relaxed when he saw her surrendering gestures. "Now, you gon' let me talk to you or not?!" he asked, feeling undefeated.

"I said okay!"

Chancey unleashed Setchi's hair and gently pushed her down on his bed by her shoulders. He didn't know where to begin or what to say even. But he knew the long-awaited discussion would bring strong modification into their lives, and was cautious not to scare her. "Look, Setchi," he said, thinking of what to say next. "I'm your big brother. I might not always do the right things, but I do try to look after you the best way I can. That's why I'm always on you about gettin' up in the morning for school and shit like that. See, you be thinkin' I'm being mean, but Setchi, think about it. If I wasn't around, you'd still be in the same position you was in last year...fucked up! Right or wrong?" There was a brief moment of silence before Chancey proceeded with his declaration. As he carried on, the words flowed with less effort. "I'm the one takin' care of you!" he exclaimed. "When's the last time you talked to Amir? That fool ain't called you in months! Shit, I'm your mothafuckin' daddy! I'm the one buyin' you school clothes, books, paper, pencils—all that shit! Where you think the shit is coming from? It sho' ain't comin' from Ma! Shit. Her ass is too busy runnin' 'round gettin' high—and I'm not talking about weed either!"

Up until that point, Setchi sat quietly, mesmerized by the truth Chancey spoke. And during most of his talk, she periodically looked him in the eyes and gave him an understanding nod. His words captivated her, making her realize how lucky she was to have him.

She was just about to give another nod of agreement, but shook it off after hearing the getting high and not from weed statement. She stared at Chancey deeply and spoke to him with her stunned eyes first before asking, "High off what, then?"

Chancey went on to tell her about his missing drugs and money. "And you *claim* you..."

Interjecting, "I didn't!" Setchi snapped. "Chance, if I knew you had all that money and *drugs*, at that, I would'a said something a long time ago," she added with earnest.

"Well then, Ma's the one..."

"How you know? I mean, who's to say you didn't misplace it?"

Chancey caught an attitude. "Setchi! Every other night?! I don't think so! Forty dollars here. Twenty dollars there. Hell, one time, three of my rocks even came up missin'. Three! Trust me, Setchi, I don't lose shit like that, alright!" He stopped and thought about the way Nikki entered the room and stood before him, spying his area. "She must'a seen me hide it one night. She had to! How else would she know...unless she came in here when I was gone. No, 'cause I always take my shit with me when I leave." Chancey thought some more. "Unless she snuck in here when I went to the bathroom. That's exactly what 'er punk-ass did! I bet she's been bringing 'er ass in here when I go take a shower, Setch! I bet 'chew!" he added, encouraging her to believe, while hitting his fist against his palm. "Sneaky bitch! I should go out there and say somethin'!"

Setchi sat overwhelmed with upsetting questions racing back and forth in her head. Nikki using drugs? She tried picturing it, but couldn't imagine her mother even so much as encountering with the addictive product.

Chancey was just as bogged down as Setchi with antagonizing thoughts beating against his brain. "Now that I think about it..." he said, putting two and two together, "that night she went to the store for some food...I gave her like, thirty-somethin'-dollars...my last! Remember?"

Setchi nodded.

"We sat up here all night, starvin' and waitin' on her! Remember? She came back talkin' about she got robbed or some shit like that? Remember that?"

Setchi remembered it so well, she could still feel her stomach aching. She could still hear herself praying with tears for her mother's return. She could still see herself searching the cabinets and scrounging up some moldy bread to nibble on. If it hadn't been for Rondell coming to their rescue, they would have both gone to bed hungry—again.

Chancey really didn't want to ask Rondell for his help at first, too embarrassed about his mother's situation, but seeing Setchi's miserable self curled up on her bed, fighting off hunger pains, made him pick up the phone. He had no other choice. He had already checked all his options, even searched the pockets of all the jeans he wore earlier in the week. Realizing two dollars and three cents wouldn't cut it, he picked up the phone.

As Chancey dialed Rondell's number, he told himself to just ask for a loan until the next day, after he made a few drug sells. That way, he wouldn't have to go into the whole humiliating state about his mother. But when Rondell asked why he was broke, remembering the few bucks he had before they turned in, Chancey was left feeling forced to explain something that, astonishingly, Rondell already knew.

*   *   *

Rondell finished his Indo and was feeling good. Talkative too! He said, "I told you from the get-go to kick that bitch to the curb. Let that hoe buy her own shit! Shit. She knew you had money and was basically try'na use you. I tried to tell you, but nah…you didn't wanna listen to a nigga." Rondell paused and shook his head. He didn't want to laugh at Chancey's stupidity, not out loud anyway, although a faint giggle slipped out when he grunted, "Mm, mm, mm! She was depending on yo' ass for *everything*! Rides, money, clothes…"

"My dumb ass couldn't see it, cuz," Chancey cut in, feeling like he contributed more than his share to their relationship.

"Well, yeah, but I didn't wanna be the one to say it," Rondell said and broke out laughing.

Chancey wasn't bothered. He figured Rondell was just buzzed off all the marijuana stench he took in, and ignored him as he silently wondered why Tomika would do something like that to him.

True, he's cheated on her many times before. He knew that. So did she. But that was months ago. He thought they had wiped the slate clean when they both sat down one night and confessed all their wrongdoings, vowing to be faithful to one another from that point on. A burst of anger shot throughout him when he realized he was the only one who kept their vow.

During the moment of silence, Rondell glanced at Chancey's perplexed face and could almost hear him thinking. "Chance," he said, suddenly feeling somewhat sorry, "you got a lotta hoes, man. Shit, you almost got more than my black ass!" He called himself joking, but Chancey didn't laugh. "All jokes to the side though, don't let a bitch make you lose focus. 'Specially a bitch like 'Mika."

The doorbell rang.

All in the same flurry, Chancey rushed over to the door and yanked it open.

There was Tomika, looking all confused when she saw Chancey's angry eyes staring her down. Chancey didn't know what pissed him off more—the fact that she came on to his homeboy or the fact that she looked extra appealing in her tight, Guess overall jeans.

"What's wrong with you?" Tomika asked Chancey.

Rondell stepped in between them and pulled Tomika by the arm. "Y'all need to take this shit to the back," he said, leading Tomika to his room.

Chancey slammed the door and huffed behind them.

Tomika walked over and sat on the edge of Rondell's bed. She looked up at Rondell, then Chancey. Fear quivered her voice when she asked, "What?"

"That's between you and this nigga right here," Rondell said, snickering as he walked out.

Chancey got up in Tomika's face and pointed his finger right at her nose. "Now Tomika," he said, "I'ma ask you this, and I'm only gon' ask you once. What did you say to Bobcat last night?"

Tomika began to think out loud. "Um..." She could feel the regular pumps of her heart turn into hard, erratic ones. The reflexes in her throat were acting as if they had a mind of their own, forcing her to swallow repeatedly, not swallowing anything in particular, just the large lump that wouldn't stay down. She looked into Chancey's eyes, saw their bleakness, and quickly turned away.

"Look at me!" he yelled, grasping her face hard with one hand.

Tomika's jaws burned from the pain inflicted by his fingers digging holes in her cheeks. "Ouch!" she cried.

Still gripping Tomika's face, "Did 'ju try'da get at Bobcat last night, 'Mika?" Chancey asked.

Tomika opened her mouth and stuttered some scrambled words.

"Bitch, you better answer me! Did 'ju, yes or no?!"

In the beginning, Tomika was only a little afraid, thinking Chancey would curse her out real good and be through with it. But now, however, the never-before-seen look to kill written all over his face made her downright terrified. "YES!" she shrieked. "But I was only play..."

Chancey's eyes tightened. One of his eyebrows almost rose to his hairline. He drew his arm back, and with all his might, swung forward and struck Tomika in the face with a closed fist. His blow sent her soaring from the bed, first hitting the wall before she tumbled to the floor. She saw a trillion stars, and in the mist of the twinkles, she saw Chancey charging her again.

She covered her face and started kicking and screaming as fast and as hard as she could to hold him off. He was blazing though, and felt nothing as he confiscated her legs, then braids like it was nothing to it. He yanked her head back to get a clear shot at his target before he slapped the living daylight out of her.

Still kicking and screaming, Tomika landed a lucky boot dead center between Chancey's thighs, backing him up for a minute. But *only* for a minute as he almost immediately clutched a hold of her neck and started jerking her around like a vicious pit bull.

Her kicking and screaming stopped, giving Chancey more ammunition as he shook her limp body around by her neck. She was gasping for air. The room was darkening. Amazingly, she was able to yell out for Rondell with her last breath before blacking out.

9

Sweat was gushing from Rosie's pores; she was sweating like she'd just run a marathon in a hundred degree weather as she ran the vacuum cleaner over the last section of the carpet in her compact living room.

It's a wonder Rosie hadn't dropped dead from all the restless days and sleepless nights she had in the past week. She'd been on the go constantly, from club-hopping with the girls to drug-running for the boys.

It was now Saturday, three o'clock in the afternoon. Rosie was supposed to have her house cleaned on Thursday, since her weekends were usually tied up with a dude in her ear at one of her many party spots. Tonight, she and her girls were visiting a new joint that just opened on Wilshire Boulevard.

She shut the vacuum cleaner off. A Sprite commercial was screaming through the speakers of her boombox radio. Her ears could barely stand it as she moved in close to change the station. Quickly and aggressively, she hit the button programmed to an R&B station. The sweet melodies of Mariah Carey flowed over the airwaves. "You got me feeling emotions..." Rosie sang as she danced her way over to the vacuum. She reached down, grabbed the cord, and started to wind. When she finished, she rolled the machine to the hall closet and shoved it inside.

Everything was done, she thought, going over every aspect of her one-bedroom apartment. "Shit, I gotta find somebody to keep Ronda," she remembered, picking up her phone. "Hello. Can I speak to Sonya?" She waited. "Hey," she said and went over to the couch. "What are you doing tonight?" She waited. "Oh, you are? Damn. I was calling to see if you would keep Ronda for me," Rosie said, then listened to Sonya explain how she couldn't. "No, I understand. Talk to you later. Bye." Rosie hung up, disappointed. This would make the fourth turndown tonight. She grabbed her purse, took out her organizer, and skimmed through it. She flipped page after page after page, then stopped when she felt the tap on her shoulder. "Get back in your room, Ronda. Right now!"

That wasn't right, Rosie, she thought, chuckling over the way Ronda dashed back to her room. Oh well, being a mother was far from her mind in the first place. She was too young for that, she thought. And although she wasn't totally free, with her baby and all, she was still settled on living her life the way *she* wanted to live it for a change. She was tired of doing what everyone else thought she should do. She had enough of all that torture in school. From grade to grade, she was labeled the "teacher's pet". She was called that so much that she was beginning to wonder if there was an imaginary sign pinned to her forehead that read: Teacher's Pet Here.

Rosie was an A-student, true enough, but paid the price dearly by having absolutely no friends at all. Her classmates hated her. They thought she was stuck-up and snooty. On the same token, Rosie had several boys to worship the ground she walked on. They thought her off-white skin, long spiral curls, and above all, Puerto Rican accent was flyy.

She was fresh out of Yonkers, New York, and was considered "new meat" to the watering-mouth, sexually active boys at her school. They would hound her, write her corny love notes, and beg to carry her books home from school. Some would even try to impress her by swiping a few roses out the yards of neighbors on the way.

The attention Rosie received was enormous and she loved it. Only problem was, if she liked a boy and her parents didn't, that boy was history, no questions asked. Bottom line, like friends, Rosie had no boyfriends either.

For a long time she was miserable. She finally got her big break when her parents announced they would be moving back to Yonkers due to her father's job relocation. She convinced them into letting her stay with her mother's sister in Lynwood by making them believe taking her out of school in the middle of the semester would have a damaging affect on her grades. And at the age of fifteen, with nothing but luck on Rosie's side, her parents, their nagging ways, and her younger sister were off to New York, leaving Rosie to move in with her aunt, Maria, who was nine years younger than her mother, and just ten years older than she was.

Maria was single with five children. But only by choice, she'll have you know. Her explanation, "I don't believe in abortions," made so many wonder why she didn't believe in using protection since all five of her kids had different fathers.

Maria didn't consider herself a deadbeat mom though. And, "I'll work day and night if that's what it takes to keep a roof over my kids' head," is what she swore by, yet thanked God her welfare check was enough to handle everything.

Maria's three-bedroom house wasn't big enough for her, Rosie, and her kids, but they made due. Her two boys shared a room, her three daughters shared another, and Maria and Rosie bunked in the other. Things were super tight, but to Rosie, they couldn't have been better.

For the first time in her life, she got to run wild, be free, and stay out past curfew. She partied. She had friends to hang out with, laugh with, and share stories with. Her main acquaintance, Angela Johnson from Watts, the one she ran with most, the one who showed her the ropes, taught her about life, told her what to do and what not to do, was the teenager from hell to many. She did it all and had seen it all.

Angela's complexion was that of a sunburned tan. She wore her bleached-blonde, color-treated hair straight down with pieces of add-in hair to make her crop come at least to her shoulders when she flipped the ends. She wasn't too appealing face-wise, which is why many assumed she combed a portion of her hair swooped over one of her eyes. On the flip side though, Angela never had a problem catching a man. She was shapely, with a dime-thin belly to work in her favor. And for the most part, she was very, very easy.

Rosie, however, was a virgin between her legs. But with the help of Angela, she had a fiery sex drive waiting to be unleashed. She learned from Angela how to twirl it, squeeze it, and everything else associated with it. "No! You doing it wrong," Angela said, snatching the cucumber from Rosie. "You 'spose to put it in your mouth like this."

Life for Rosie was copasetic until her grades started to drop—until Maria promised to send her back to New York if she didn't clean up her act. Deep down, Maria didn't want to do it. She loved having her niece around. Rosie was a lot of fun and helped out a great deal with the kids and the household chores. It was just that Maria knew Rosie was ideal in her parents' eyes and didn't want them thinking she was the cause of their daughter to fail. When she made that clear to Rosie one night, she had no idea there would be a huge can of worms waiting to be opened.

Rosie was understanding of Maria's concerns, and paid close attention to every bit of her advice. Then Maria had to bring Angela into the conversation, as she always did, taking things on a turn for the worse. "I know I'm only twenty-five, Rosie. I dropped out of school at an early age. Got five kids. And you're probably thinking what do I know, right? But it don't take a rocket scientist to see that Angie is bringing you down. She's nothing but a bad influence. She don't go to school…and don't even try'da lie for her, 'cause I know! I got my connections. And if it wasn't for abortions, that slut would have more kids than I got," Maria said. Rosie's look of interest immediately turned into a look of worry, and Maria could see it. In the pause that followed, she examined Rosie's face to make certain her eyes weren't playing tricks on her. Sure enough, there it was, the puckered eyebrows spelling out trouble. "Why you look like that?" Maria asked her niece.

Rosie's look turned even more fretful.

"Okay…" Maria groaned as she rocked her body forward and rose to her feet from the sofa. Rosie remained seated in the reclining chair across from the sofa, still wearing her same uneasy mug shot.

Maria brought her little ones together and sent them to their rooms. She listened to them whine and fuss as they tentatively escorted one another to the back. Maria shouted, "Ándale!" and stood in the hall to make sure they hurried along as they were told. Once the coast was clear, "Okay Mama, talk to me," she said, walking up to Rosie. She kneeled down and placed her hand on one of Rosie's thighs.

Mama? Rosie had to laugh at that one, believing the word couldn't have been used at a better time. She looked at her aunt with a vague grin and couldn't take her eyes away.

"What is it, Rosario?" Maria asked, staring at Rosie, hoping some sort of psychic ability she never knew she had would take presence over her mangled thinking. "Don't tell me you been to the abortion clinic," Maria said out of nowhere. Her accented voice was filled with distress.

"NO!" Rosie snapped, raising her upper torso to sit up straight in a combat position. "Well..." she then sighed and slouched over again.

"Well, what? You went with Angie again?"

Rosie sat still.

"Spit it out, Mama! I already know you had sex before. And I *know* miss thing can't keep her legs closed to save her life, and..." Suddenly, she paused. "You pregnant?" she asked, afraid of the answer she was about to hear.

*   *   *

Rosie shooed Ronda away, feeling no remorse when she returned to the living room for a second time. She turned the stereo up to tune out her daughter's whimpering. The louder Ronda cried, the louder the stereo went. When the stereo reached its maximum capacity, Rosie got irritated. Very irritated! "I'm sick of this shit," she complained, turning the volume down with one big twist. She barged into the room like one of Satan's chief warriors and asked, "What is it, Ronda?! What?!"

Ronda's little body shook wildly as she looked up at her mother, bawling uncontrollably. Her room had been ransacked. Toys, crayons, books, and paper were scattered all over. "Mommy," she sniveled, bracing herself on the edge of her Barbie toddler bed.

"Don't call me no more, Ronda!" Rosie yelled, preparing to close the door.

Ronda's crying escalated. Her head full of pigtails vibrated harder as her spasms grew more intense. "Can I come in there wit' 'chew?" she asked, catching the door just before it closed.

Rosie thought about giving in to her little one since she was incapable of tuning out her holler, but when she threw her eyes around at all the rummage, she yelled, "No! You clean this room up! And if you come out before it's done, I'm tearin' your ass up!" Then she slammed the door.

She marched away feeling close to a nervous breakdown. She found her purse, which she threw under one of the end tables, and rambled through it after her cigarettes and lighter.

She flicked and flicked, then shook the cigarette lighter and flicked again before tossing it on the coffee table. On her way to the kitchen, she glared at Ronda's bedroom door and swore she needed a vacation.

Rosie told Maria before Ronda was even born that she didn't want any kids. Said she was too young and could barely take care of herself.

"I was two years younger than you when I had my first kid," Maria implied, throwing Rosie for a loop. "I'm not letting you get no abortion, Rosario, so don't even think about it!"

When Maria found out Rosie snuck and terminated her pregnancy anyway, she threw Rosie out. And to make matters worse, when Rosie's parents found out she was even pregnant, they did away with her *and* Maria.

After being kicked out on the streets, Rosie moved in with Angela and her mother across the street from the Jordan Down Projects. They became her new family, since her biological one appeared to have done away with her.

Rosie started slacking off in school, eventually dropping out all together. And it wasn't long before she found herself packed with a growing organism in her belly again. However, with money from the young men she had slept with, and Angela's mother's signature to authorize it, getting an abortion was a cinch. Rosie's luck ran out after her fourth pregnancy when the father-to-be gave her no money. With no money, Angela's mom gave her no support. It was then

Rosie thought it was time to pay a visit to her pro-life auntie.

She started out by apologizing. Then she explained her situation before popping the question. And once Maria made it clear that she would, under no circumstances, pay for Rosie's abortion, she begged. Even swore she'd go back to school if Maria would only understand how impossible school would be with a baby. In the end, she put it in plain words for her aunt: she did not want any kids.

Eight months later, Rosie gave birth to a brown baby with gray eyes and full lips, and named her Ronda Lopez.

*   *   *

The phone rang just as Rosie was about to draw in some smoke from her cigarette. She picked the handset up from its holder on the kitchen wall and heard the raspy voice on the other end. "Que Paso? Where you at?" she asked, tapping some ashes from her cigarette into the sink.

"Grape Supermarket," Chancey answered. He pulled his jeep up and parked it in one of the parking spaces. He got out, but left the motor running, turned up his CD player, which had an Ice Cube CD in rotation, and closed the door. He threw up his fist and nodded his head at some of the guys loitering out front as he walked in. He asked Rosie if she wanted him to bring her something back, and on his way to the beer section, per her request, he picked up a Kit-Kat bar from one of the racks and tossed it on the counter. "After I leave here, I'm on my way," he told her. "Is the food ready?"

"Yeah, almost," Rosie fibbed with her cigarette flapping between her lips and the earpiece sandwiched between her head and shoulder. She pulled open the drawer of loose utensils, where she kept her razor blades hidden.

"Almost?!" Chancey snapped. He snatched one of the 40oz. Old English beers from the cooler. "I can't be waitin' on you, Rosie. I got thangs to do," he said as he made his way to the counter.

"Let me hang up, then, so I can hurry up and finish," Rosie said, knowing she was nowhere near finished.

Chancey clicked Rosie off without saying goodbye. He looked at the cashier, an Arab fellow, looking all of sixteen or seventeen years old, and watched him expressionlessly as he rung up the customer's items in front of him. He wasn't thinking about much; his mind was rather blank with Rosie popping in and out of it. He hoped she'd have his drugs ready so he wouldn't have to wait on her like he did the last time and the ten other times before that. He looked down at his watch, and then glanced out the door, looking for nothing or no one in particular, just checking. Things were the same on the scene. His radio was still bumping his favorite rapper. People were still hanging out in front. Some selling drugs, some shooting dice, some were just standing around watching.

The time was now four-ten. Chancey knew he had a good forty-five minutes or so to kill since he told Rondell he'd meet up with him around five-thirty. He figured he'd hang out for a minute, see what everybody was up to.

When the customer in front of Chancey grabbed his bags, Chancey yelled, "'Bout time!" along with a few other things, joking around to get a quick laugh in. The young boy smiled and joked back as he walked outside.

"What's up, Hasan?" Chancey asked, contemplating on buying one of the packs of gum next to the counter. "Pop's got you working today, huh?"

"Yeah," Hasan said in a huff, then told Chancey how he wished he were somewhere else.

"I feel you, cuz," Chancey said, tossing a pack of Wrigley's Doublemint gum on the counter. "Add this up, too."

*　　*　　*

Tia could kick herself in the butt for not going to the store earlier. Everybody knew that in the middle of the day, the sun beamed down over Los Angeles like a fierce animal viewing its prey in the summertime. It was four-thirty in the afternoon and was blazing hot. The temperature was ninety degrees. Tia usually withstood days like these, but today was unbearable. The sweat was running down her back, making her Adidas T-shirt stick to her like glue, and it felt as if the heat was burning straight through her bell-bottomed jeans. She was glad she thought to pull her hair back in a scrungie once she felt the sweat drip down the sides of her face. Her hair hadn't been permed in over three months, and if wet, her new growth would poof out like a swollen thumb.

She speedwalked to Grape Supermarket, which she couldn't stand going to. It was always surrounded by gang bangers, drug dealers, and untamed females. Tia always felt out of place whenever she stepped foot on the premises. And after the shooting incident last week, she swore she'd never go there again. She only made an exception today because they ran out of soda at her house, and she hated water.

She couldn't get to the store fast enough. The smog was heavy and thick, and it was hard for her to breathe. She felt relieved when she saw her destination was finally within arms reach, but by then, her entire body was almost saturated. There were big, damp circles under the armpits of her T-shirt—that, she could deal with. The wet streak underneath each of her breast though, was embarrassing.

She hurried pass a group of young men standing against the wall, dodged a crazed kid as he zipped down the walkway on his ten-speed, and liked to have died when she saw Chancey looking shockingly handsome, alongside five other guys standing near the entrance way. He was topless, wearing only a pair of jeans sagging over some blue boxers and a pair of blue and white FILA's on his feet.

For a second, Tia's heart stopped. She slowed down a bit and actually thought about turning around, thinking, as always, she didn't look good enough to be seen by him. Just as she made an attempt to follow her mind, their eyes met.

*   *   *

For the first time in a long time, Rosie had everything ready for Chancey before he made it to her house. She was surprised he hadn't shown up yet. She had expected him to pound on her door at any minute, ranting and raving because she didn't have his stuff ready.

She finished up in the kitchen and walked back to the room to check on Ronda, who had fallen asleep at her play table. She was slumped over the tabletop, drooling and still gripping one of the teacups from her dish set.

Rosie didn't bother to make her daughter comfortable. She just didn't feel like it. Instead, she closed the door and headed back to the living room. She stood, looked around, looked out the window, and then went back to the kitchen.

She licked her lips at the tiny rock she set aside for herself before diving in to have some fun. It wasn't but as wide as a dime in width. She was scared to take any more than that.

Rosie cut her rock down until she got a size small enough to fit in her broken antenna. She flicked her lighter; it was time for blast off! All of a sudden, she started to float. She walked back to the living room in ecstasy and nestled on her daybed where she waited patiently on Chancey to arrive.

*   *   *

Chancey couldn't believe his eyes when he glanced to the right and saw his wife coming toward him. Wishful thinking, maybe, but the thought sure made him feel good. He took one look at Tia and flashed his pearly whites. Tia took one look at Chancey and quickly turned her eyes away as she headed for the door. Chancey darted out in front of her, stopping her just before she made entrance. "What's up, Tia?" he asked, standing in her face as nonchalant and bold as ever.

Tia didn't realize Chancey was as tall as he was until she observed his body towering over hers. She remembered him looking shorter the last time she saw him at the Foxhill Mall. "Hi," she simply said and moved around him nervously.

OH GOD, NO! Tia thought, sweating boulders when he came trailing behind her. Lord knows she tried to restrain herself from this gorgeous man, and like so many times before, she was left hoping she looked good enough to compete with all the pretty girls he accompanied.

She could feel his eyes x-raying up and down her body, and questioned whether she looked funny from behind. She became incredibly weak to the point where she didn't think she'd be able to take another step; her legs were trembling just that bad. And her arm, for some reason, wouldn't move. She had to force it up after the two-liter Coca Cola bottle on the shelf. *Why is he torturing me like this,* she wondered, wanting to cry.

Chancey, on the other hand, was wondering why he was

torturing himself. *I don't know why I'm followin' this girl. All she gon' do is dis' a nigga,* he figured. Still, he kept on trucking behind her. *Wit 'er skinny ass,* he thought, smiling as he checked her out. He liked the way her booty twitched when she walked, feeling certain she was putting the extra bounce in her hips because he was watching. And watching is what he did, almost hard enough to envision what things looked like underneath her clothes. Her loose-fitting T-shirt made it hard for him to size up her breast, but Chancey was a "butt" man, and thanked the heavens above that her shirt stopped just above the top of her jeans, exposing the way her rear protruded outward from her diminutive frame.

Chancey was suddenly puzzled when he saw her attempting to reach for the Coke bottle on the shelf. He didn't know if she was reaching for it or deciding on something else. Whatever the case, she looked like she was having a hard time, so he thought he'd help her out by reaching from behind her and grabbing the soda before she did.

Tia felt Chancey's chest press against her back and almost lost control of herself. Before she knew it, she had turned around and was in his face yelling, "Boy, what are you doing!"

Scared Chancey! He looked at her for a minute, then smiled, thinking her little flare-up was cute. Made him feel all mushy inside. "This is what you wanted, right?" he asked, grinning from ear to ear and staring in her average-looking eyes with his illustrious ones.

Shocked Tia! She was positive the explosion of her voice would get rid of him for good. She saw his pretty eyes staring her down. His white teeth were sparkling from every angle. She wondered how in the world could somebody be that fine. And why somebody that fine would want her. Just then, she found herself terribly wanting him, too. She wished she could spark up some sort of conversation to keep him in her face, but was too spellbound and fearfully stuck for words, not to mention, sweaty, ugly, and in Tia's mind, the list went on and on.

Chancey had a hard time figuring Tia out. All he asked her was a simple question, and instead of getting a simple yes or no answer, he got the silent treatment. Still not ready to be defeated, he got silent right along with her and waited to see what she would do next.

"Can I have my soda, please?" Tia asked after the drawn-out

moment of silence, wanting to hurry up and put an end to his torturing.

"Why you always so mean to me?" Chancey curiously asked, but of course, she ignored him. Unintentionally though, which was why she couldn't help feeling like a freak.

If only she had the guts to tell him how badly she wanted to loosen up, exchange a few love taps as they playfully tussled over the soda. Chancey's presence made her emotions go nuts though, and just the *thought* of telling him how she felt made her inner voice stutter.

Chancey was tired of making a fool out of himself. In his opinion, she obviously hated him. His ego hadn't been this shattered since the altercation that tore him and Tomika apart. Tia saw the bleakness written all over his face, and she hated herself for not doing something about it. She was that close to putting up a playful fight to break the ice, but when Chancey turned from her and walked her drink to the counter, she quietly followed, feeling stupid.

Chancey pulled a twenty-dollar bill from his pocket and asked Hasan to ring the soda up. As he waited, he occasionally looked over his shoulder at Tia, only to have her roll her eyes away.

Feeling helpless, Tia watched Chancey pay for her soda with her eyes periodically scrolling across his bareness. *My, my, my,* she thought, feeling herself getting turned on by the bad-boy image his tattoos portrayed. She examined the panther stretched out on his back, then suddenly remembered something being tattooed on his chest and thought to sneak a peek when he turned around. But when Chancey turned to pass Tia her bag, again, she panicked, snatching it from him and jetting for the door before he could even blink.

"Where you goin'?" he asked, feeling cheated.

"HOME!" Tia yelled without looking back.

Chancey followed her outside and said, "C'mere for a second," but she acted as if she didn't hear him and kept going. "C'mere!" he repeated, only this time, lightly tugging at her ponytail.

The pulling of the ponytail brought Tia old memories of how he used to pull her tresses in school. Reluctantly, she stopped and turned to face him. She wanted to ask him what the connection was between him and her hair—why he felt the need to always put his hands in it. But needless to say, her lips were jammed.

"So, when can I take you out, Tia?" Chancey had the nerve to ask.

"Who said you can take me out?" she responded playfully, wondering where her all-of-a-sudden-braveness came from.

"Oh, you got jokes," he said and gave Tia a smile she would remember for days. He reached to grip her chin, but she slapped his hand away, still refusing to let her guard down.

Tia knew Chancey was definitely charming, and there was no way she was falling victim to his infidelity, becoming another statistic like all the other females he encountered with. Speaking of which, "What happened to the girl you was talking to at the mall? Why you ain't takin' her out no more?" Tia asked, trying to be funny.

Chancey was drawing a blank. "What girl?"

"The big booty girl in the daisy dukes."

"Daisy dukes?"

"Quit acting like you don't remember," Tia said, forgetting all about her hideous appearance. She waited for him to fess up, before throwing out another hint. "The Foxhill Mall!" When Chancey didn't respond as fast as she thought he should have, she said, "Yeah, that's what I thought," and backed away from him.

Honestly, Chancey didn't know who Tia was talking about. He called off a couple of names in his head as he tried to work with her silly conduct. Quite naturally, Tomika's name popped up first since that was his girlfriend and she had a thick rear end. One problem though, he and Tomika had never been to the Foxhill Mall together, or any mall for that matter. Another female popped up shortly thereafter, but he couldn't remember her name. He remembered her being thick, too. He remembered meeting her at the Foxhill Mall, along with the other three females he met there.

Tia backed up, almost out of Chancey's reach before he grabbed one of her arms and pulled her to him. She immediately brought her free arm up to her chest to keep her body from brushing up against his.

"So, it's like that, Tia?"

"*Well*, shoot, I don't want you huggin' on me," she lied, eyeing the slogan "Grape Street All Day" tattooed on the right side of his chest. *Gang banger,* she thought. The name "Setchi" tattooed on the left made her wonder.

"Who said I was finna hug you?" Chancey asked, bringing her eyes back up to his.

"Well, let me go, then."

"Gimme a kiss first," he told her, acquiring a playful yet naughty expression.

"Boy, you better let me go!" she yelled, jerking away from his embrace, but craving for him to pull on her again. She secretly loved the way he aggressively handled her.

"I can't get a kiss—just one lil' peck like this…" Chancey blew Tia a kiss, and she nearly passed out!

Smiling, "No," she teased.

Tia's smile reassured Chancey's ego. "Well, let me call you sometime," he was able to suggest with ease.

"Hmmm…" Tia thought out loud before saying, "No," followed with a slight giggle.

Chancey sighed loud and hard. He thought Tia was childish and a little less adorable. Here he was trying to be serious, and she was acting like a kid.

Tia knew she was acting a bit silly, but couldn't control it. She didn't know how to act or what to say. And when Chancey's cell phone rang, she thought to get the hell out of dodge before she *really* made a fool out of herself. Furthermore, if she stayed until he finished his phone call, he would know she was interested, and she certainly didn't want that.

Chancey answered his phone after the first ring. He had an idea who the caller was when he looked at his watch and saw it was five-forty. He held his phone with one hand and put the other around Tia's waist as soon as her legs started to shuffle. When she wiggled, he held her tight so she couldn't move.

Tia loved it. It felt right being in his arm, and amazingly, she stopped resisting, which is why she couldn't understand the loosening of his grip. Didn't he realize she was letting him hold her? Right then, Tia thought Chancey was brainless.

"Alright. Alright. Alright! I'm on my way," Chancey told the person on the other end.

Tia immediately caught an attitude. "Well, I guess I better let you go," she said after he disconnected the call. "I don't want her to get mad."

"Can I take you home?" Chancey asked, ignoring Tia's sarcasm.

"No, I can walk, thank you."

"C'mon, Tia, pleeeeze!"

"Noooo," she sang in a high-pitched voice, laughing and marking him.

Chancey looked down at his watch and saw the time ticking away. "'Ey, I gotta go…"

"BYE!" Tia snapped right in the middle of his sentence. Chancey smacked his lips and gave her a grave look. Tia laughed and said, "Nah, I'm just playing."

"You so cute to me, you know that?"

"Yeah, right!"

"Yeah, right?" Chancey asked, confused. "Alright, you to the curb, then," he said.

Tia broke out laughing. "Boy, you so crazy!"

"I know. Crazy about you," he said and smiled.

Tia broke out laughing again, this time, not really understanding why. She stopped herself to gain control, but couldn't get rid of the grin smeared across her face. The more Chancey looked at her, the more she smiled, eventually snickering again.

Chancey's phone started to ring again. "Here, I want you to remember this number," he told her, then called out seven digits. "That's the number to my cell. Hit me later, alright?"

"If I can remember it," Tia said, trying to stall him as long as she could. She didn't want him to leave and was pissed at herself for not enjoying his company a lot sooner.

Chancey whistled over at the boys against the wall and yelled, "'Ey, somebody throw me a pen real quick!" Within seconds, a pen was being tossed his way. "Now you don't have an excuse," he said as he grabbed Tia's hand and wrote his cell number and his home number in her palm. When he finished, he looked up and was right in her face. He held on to her hand, with his eyes traveling across her features and stopping at her mouth. He leaned in to kiss her and laughed when he felt the gentle slap on his cheek.

"Boy, you better let…"

"Boy, you better let me go," Chancey said, copying Tia's voice as best as he could. "Be quiet."

"You be quiet!" she said, cheesing.

Chancey started to back up, one foot after the other as he stared in her face. Without stopping, he said, "Call me tonight," and gave her another one of those alluring smiles.

"I'll think about it," she said, smiling more of a smitten one.

10

Tia walked home wondering if Chancey really did like her. He seemed sincere, and after all, he did pay for her drink. She looked down at her bag and treasured it as if it were an autograph from her favorite performer. When her mind began to wonder about Chancey some more, she embraced it in her arms, the way he did her. She laughed at his persistency, still able to hear his voice begging her over and over again. She knew she wouldn't sleep a wink tonight. She was too overwhelmed with her new sense of self, feeling like the most highest being in her gender. Chancey did that to her. Everything she thought she lacked, from thickness to bigger boobs, was suddenly given to her by word of his mouth. His voice sang to her, with *you so cute to me* replaying in her head. He made her feel prettier than the "big booty girl" he couldn't take his eyes off of at the mall.

Tia walked up 103rd and made a right on Kalmia Street. She saw three boys whiz past her on their bikes, laughing hysterically. She looked back and watched them hook a left on 103rd, almost immediately turning around at the sound of her neighbor yelling, cursing, and running her way with a bucket of water. Her chunky body moved about like she was nothing but skin and bones. She was fast, but not fast enough to catch her enemies. She stopped midway past Tia and made a U-turn.

"Who you yellin' at, Carla?" Tia asked as if it wasn't noticeable.

"Those stupid-asses!" Carla yelled, holding her bucket out at 103rd. Tia saw that Carla was wet and asked what happened. That's when Carla went off. "They was throwin' fuckin' water balloons at me!" she explained, frowning and lugging her pail back to her house.

She poured the water out on the lawn and walked up the steps to sit on her porch. Tia didn't want to tease Carla since it was clear she didn't find anything funny, but seeing the extensive spot of moisture covering her from the back of her head down to the back of her black spandex pants made Tia fall out with laughter. "Don't get mad...I can't help it...oooh, God..." She paused to take a breath. "You look hecka crazy!" she said, gasping for air. "How did they get you in the back?"

"They threw 'em when my back was turned! I was on my way in the house! Lil' bastards!"

Tia sat down beside Carla, still laughing. "I'm sorry, girl..." she said, teary-eyed and barely able to speak.

"Don't laugh! Shoot," Carla said, almost smirking, and playfully nudged her shoulder up against Tia's. She was mad, but knew Tia had a good reason to laugh. She looked funny. She looked funny running up the street with her gigantic bucket of water that she could hardly carry, spilling water everywhere. And she was sure her humungous breasts were bouncing all over the place, making her look even funnier. "Girl, look at my hair!" she cried out, trying to pat her once, mushroomed bob back in place.

Tia didn't look up. She smiled and heaved a sigh, thinking how wonderful life was as she gazed down at her soda.

Carla asked Tia if she was coming from the store when she saw her snake her arms around her grocery bag.

"Yep! Grape Supermarket," Tia said, still smiling. "I came to see if you wanted to walk with me, but you wasn't here."

"I know. I had to take my lil' sister to my grandmother's house."

"I know. Your mother told me." Tia's smile turned into a moan of passion. She turned to Carla with bright, eager eyes and said, "Girl, guess who was up there?"

"Who?"

"You know!"

"Chancey," Carla said. She and Tia laughed.

"Something told me he was gon' be up there, and he was! Girl, you should'a seen him..." Tia was animated when she described Chancey's appearance. "He was naked! All this was out!" she said, feeling from her shoulders to her waistline. "Girl, he must'a followed me all *over* that store! And then after I bought...no, *he* bought my soda, he followed me outside! Girl, he was try'na kiss all on me...begging for my number...I kept saying boy, leave me alone..." Tia paused again to chuckle, then she screamed, "Girl, he was drivin' me crazy!"

Carla listened to Tia ramble on about Chancey as she did many times before. When she saw her chance to get a word in, she smiled and said, "He just love his little Ti-Ti, that's all!"

*   *   *

Tomika had to get out and into something today. She hadn't been out the house in almost a week and it was starting to feel like the walls were caving in on her. She went by Pam's house, who was accompanied by one of her many men-friends, and not wanting to be a third wheel, she left without accepting Pam's offer to come in.

Before, when she and Chancey were together, she would kick back at home and wait on him to come through and raise her spirits with his funniness. He was always laughing and joking about something. She really did miss him. Especially the way he used to pop in on her whenever he got a break from the madness of his day job and surprise her with gifts or her favorite food; she loved the burrito supreme with extra sour cream from Taco Bell.

When Chancey broke up with Tomika, the night at Rondell's house, he told her he hated her and never wanted to see her again. And if it hadn't been for Rondell prying his hands from around her neck, the last place *anyone* would have seen her was at her funeral.

Chancey beat Tomika up pretty bad that night. Her left eye was swollen shut. There was a painful knot on the right side of her temple, which she believed happened when her head hit the wall. And her neck was so tender, it hurt to turn her head for days.

She left Rondell's house feeling remote, more like regretful, like this time it was really over between them. But just in case there was a small chance they'd make up, she held off on calling the police.

She and Chancey didn't so much as talk to one another for two days—two days seemed to always be the limit to their loathing, which is why on the third day when he called her, she believed his love for her had resurfaced. She sexed him like never before on that day, rotating her hips up, down, around, hard, fast, slow. Chancey was loving it. His moans were the proof. It was intense the way he penetrated her. His hips matching hers move for move. She was positive she had him hooked by the way he grabbed every last one of her braids and pulled hard as he climaxed.

Nearly a month had gone by when they saw each other again—when they had another one of their provocative episodes. Tomika knew what was up. She told Chancey her mother didn't raise no fools after accusing him of just wanting her for sex. Nonetheless, it didn't stop her from spreading her legs and whipping her stuff on him whenever given the opportunity—so long as he knew she was doing it for herself and not him.

The only thing Tomika was sorry for throughout her Chancey experience was the fact that she let him run her life. And now that he was out of it, she didn't know what to do with herself. One thing's for certain, she wished she hadn't pushed Pam away when her relations with Chancey began to get serious. If only she'd listened to the older people when they told her to never give up her friends for a man.

Pam and Tomika were still close, but definitely not the way they used to be. They were indivisible until Chancey came along declaring how he thought Pam was no good, and how he didn't want his woman around her. What a fool she was for despising her friend, is what she thought now as she crossed over the railroad tracks and made her way towards Kalmia Street to visit Carla, her mediocre friend.

Really, Tomika saw Carla as homely, a nobody, just a girl to shoot the breeze with when all else failed on boring days like this one. Tomika knew Carla was always available, and enjoyed hanging around her to pick up the leftover men she didn't want—chasing the boys was their main forte'. They really didn't have much else in common. And Carla, unlike Pam, had easy access to transportation, and for the most part, always kept a few dollars in her pocket, willing to gas up the car and take Tomika wherever she needed to go.

It had been a while since Tomika visited Carla. She questioned whether or not she was still easily accessible, and called her first before making the long walk across town. Carla's mom said she was outside washing the car, which was enough for Tomika to start her route; she was desperate.

Honestly, it wasn't in Tomika's plans to walk over thirty minutes away when she left the house, but since Pam was obviously still in a funk, she figured she had no choice. Besides, what else did she have to do?

She headed up Kalmia fairly pissed at Pam for inviting her in, knowing good and well she only offered so she could show off her new boyfriend as if who cared. True, Tomika did, but Pam would never know it.

Tomika hated the fact that she didn't have a man and Pam did. And she hated that Pam did whatever to publicize it. She never did Pam that way. When Pam and Rondell's relationship hit rock bottom, Tomika dragged Pam along on all of her outings with Chancey, even welcomed her to join them on romantic movie nights. And when the word got out that Rondell left Pam, Tomika defended Pam, even lied and said it was the other way around. She believed that's what friends were for. She made Pam feel like being the third wheel was okay until Chancey, one day, came and stopped everything cold turkey. Tomika recalls that being the downfall of their friendship.

Everybody said Pam was jealous of Tomika for being with Chancey in the first place. Maybe that explains all the dirty stares Pam gave whenever she saw Tomika and Chancey smooch. And rumor had it, she even slept with Chancey when he and Tomika broke up, which she denied when a very riled-up Tomika confronted her. However, when Tomika confronted Chancey, he got mouthy and told her to get out of his face asking him about his sex life; he still had a grudge.

Not knowing the truth to the rumor kept Tomika exasperated, considering how she's busted them before flirting and eyeballing each other. So to ease her mind, as well as pay them both back for their sneaky betrayal, she slept with Rondell. Twice!

All that drama was in the past though. Everyone had forgiven and supposedly forgotten. Last Tomika heard, Rondell had three or four girlfriends. Although he would never admit to it, she suspected Chancey was also with someone by the way he appeared every blue moon, looking for nothing but sex. And Pam? She still walked around with a chip on her shoulder, making fun of Tomika's fate.

As Tomika got closer, she could see Carla sitting on her porch talking and laughing with someone who looked familiar to some extent. She focused in on Carla's ragged hair and thought she had a lot to learn about beauty. *And who would wear stretch pants, black at that, in the summertime?*

As she approached the two girls, she heard Carla saying something about being in love. "Who are you in love with now, Carla?" Tomika asked, getting in on the conversation.

"Hey, Tomika," Carla said. "We was talking about this guy, Chancey. He's in love wit' Tia," she added, smiling proudly at her neighbor. "Tia, you met Tomika before, right?"

"Yeah, we met before," Tia said, followed by a cheery greeting.

Tomika flipped her eyes up and down Tia's body a couple of times before she looked at Carla and asked, "Chancey who?"

Carla wasn't sure, and looked at Tia to see if she knew Chancey's last name. Tia smiled innocently at Tomika and said, "Walker."

Tomika shot a disdainful look at Tia, then turned to Carla and said, "I used to talk to him before—he still be all up in my face now!"

Carla frowned at Tomika, wondering why she never knew that. She then simultaneously turned to Tia with consoling eyes before glaring at Tomika again.

"I had to leave his ass alone though. Shit. All he liked to do was fuck! He used to try and tear my shit up!"

Carla quickly cut her eyes at Tia in response to Tomika's comment.

Looking disappointed, Tia said, "We never went out or anything. He just always got something…something crazy to say every time he see me, that's all."

"That's still my nigga though—him, Ronnie, Kay-Kay, all them niggas!" Tomika butted in like Tia's words weren't worth two cents. She was moving her hands around and snapping her neck to her statement.

It wasn't Tia's will to listen. She wanted to blow Tomika off the same way she had been blown off, but was too interested to do it. Embarrassingly as it seemed, she wanted Tomika to tell more...every shameful detail. She wanted to know what Chancey was *really* like. What he was like to be around. What he was like to date. Especially what he was like in bed. She tried to keep herself from imagining him begging Tomika for sex though, and was envious right off the bat, wondering when the last time their sexual encounter took place. Was it good to him? Is he sprung? Will he try and do it to her again? All of her pondering was nerve-racking as she stared helplessly at Tomika in awe, stuck on how dull she was compared to her.

Tomika's braids were long and neat, curving her oval-shaped face just right. She wore a pink bra-like halter, exposing her bellybutton, with some pink biker shorts. In her ears were a huge pair of triangular-shaped, gold earrings, and around her neck was a fat herringbone chain. The girl was definitely brassy, the total opposite of Tia.

Tia jealously eyed Tomika's full figure and thought, *another big booty!* She could see Chancey all over Tomika, touching, feeling, and begging. But her? She couldn't imagine it as she glimpsed at her thin self. Her heart was broken. Just like that, again she was robbed of her essence.

Tomika asked Carla what happened to her hair as she ran her palm down the back of her bush. Carla told her dramatic, horror story with a silly giggle every now and then. She looked at Tia, expecting an insult, but Tia was out of it, staring off to the side most of the time. She couldn't bear to witness Tomika's star appearance anymore. And she wished she would sit down and quit flaunting her big behind around in everybody's face.

Carla asked Tomika where she was coming from and where she was headed. Tomika sat down next to her and said, "Nowhere. Shit. Over here. It's so fuckin' boring today." She tilted her head to look around Carla at Tia when she asked, "What are y'all doin' today?"

Tia wasn't going to answer, but when she saw Tomika's crafty eyes fixed on her, she felt the need to answer. "Nothing."

Tomika looked at Carla's mother's car reflecting from every corner and smiled. She asked Carla if she cleaned it up and then said, "Let's go riding," all in the same breath.

Tia smiled. So did Carla. But nobody moved.

"Where y'all wanna go?" Carla said.

Tia looked at Tomika to see where her thoughts were going.

"I don't know. Let's just hit some corners. Shit, ain't nothing else to do," Tomika said.

Sounded good to Tia. She confirmed it with agreeing eyes when she looked at Carla, who was already up on her feet and on her way in the house after her mother's keys. She returned excitedly, eyeing both girls as she leaped toward the driveway, urging them to follow. Tomika candidly raced for the front seat. Tia hated her! She pushed the seat up and crawled in the back as if nothing was wrong.

"Let's ride by the Nickerson Gardens first. I wanna see if this nigga, Dame, is out there. I'ma see if he'll give us some money," Tomika said. Carla started the ignition. Tomika started punching buttons and turning knobs on the radio. "What tapes do your mama got in here?" she asked. Before Carla could open her mouth, Tomika was popping in an Al B. Sure tape. She began rocking and snapping her fingers as she crooned to the music.

Carla looked over her shoulder at Tia as she backed her mother's car in the street. Tia gave a fake smile, pissed that Carla was letting Tomika take over.

"Make a left right here," Tomika said. Carla turned on Imperial Highway.

Tia became concerned, but since Carla seemed to be having a grand of a time, she didn't want to look too uptight. She hid her frenzy well as she slowly mellowed out. Then Carla made the troubling right on Success Avenue, sending Tia a shockwave when she saw they were surrounded by barricaded housing.

Tomika stuck most of her body out the window and yelled, "DAAAME!"

Tia slapped Carla's arm and looked at her with what-in-the-hell-are-you-doing eyes when she got her attention. Carla's eyes were puzzled when she shrugged her shoulders. Before they knew it, a flashy young fellow had skipped up to the car. His attire was plain—red shirt, black dickeys. He had lots of jewelry glistering from his ears to his fingers. He leaned in the window with a face full of pimples, and both Carla and Tia looked at each other and frowned.

Tomika bluntly asked Dame for some money. He whispered something funny in her ear, because she laughed out loud, then told him, "Miss me wit' all that drag!"

"What! Blood, don't get fucked up," Dame said in a joking manner.

"Come on, Damien...I just need thirty."

"Blood, you been avoidin' a nigga for the longest. Now you try'na get paid? I don't think so, baby," Dame said, standing there punching his fist against his palm. He would occasionally throw his eyes around the car and smile at Tia and Carla before locking them back on Tomika. After minutes of playful jabbering, he asked Tomika to get out and talk to him for a split second, which she did, but for way more than a second.

Carla was patient. Tia, irritated! She sat in the back with her arms folded, frowning as her eyes traveled off with Tomika and Dame. "Where is she going?" Tia asked. "I hope she don't think we 'spose to sit here and wait on her like she's God's gift to man or something! And anyway, when did y'all get so tight?"

"We always been tight," Carla said.

"She don't go to Jordan, do she?"

"No, she's like two years older than us."

"And messing with Chancey?"

Carla turned around. "Oooh, girl, I didn't know about her and Chancey. I swear!"

"Oh, I don't care! You know how I feel about him. It ain't like we're going out. And it ain't like we ever will!" Tia snapped, rolling her head.

"Ugh. What's wrong with you?"

Tia sighed and rolled her eyes over in the direction of Tomika and Dame, even though she could no longer see them. "Nothing," she muttered.

"Then why your attitude change all of a sudden?"

"My attitude didn't change! I'm just saying...we're sittin' in the damn projects, Carla! We don't know none of these guys out here! Shoot, they might try'da take your mama's car! It's not like she got a hoopty! You're in a thunderbird—blue at that! Did you forget?"

"No," Carla answered in a groan. "Tomika know 'em, so..."

"Tomika?! You trust her judgment?! Please! Where's she at now? That's what I wanna know...walkin' around looking like a skeeza."

Carla turned all the way around in her seat with a big grin smeared across her face. Tia knew some juicy gossip was coming. "I'm not try'na talk about nobody, but...did you see how tight those biker shorts was?"

"Carla! Girl! I swear I didn't wanna say nothing, but what about her top! Is that a bra or what?!"

Tia hushed when she saw Tomika coming. Tomika approached the car with three young men at her side—Dame and two of his boys. Tia only thought one was semi-cute out the bunch, and he was on his way around to Carla's side. The one that got in her face was uglier than Dame, she thought.

"What's up, baby!" Uglier asked her.

Not you, was what Tia wanted to say, but decided to be good.

"You got a man?"

"Yes. I'm sorry."

"Y'all happy?"

First of all, nigga...correction, ugly-ass nigga...you need to get yo' nappy head, dirty-clothes-wearin', wanna-be-mack-daddy-ass, out of my face! "Yeah, we're happy," Tia said and smiled.

Carla was enjoying herself like always. She was interested in her new friend. He was cute...clean too. He wasn't as interested as she would have liked for him to be, but that was okay. She'd never had a man that handsome in her face before, ever!

"Well, we better get going," Tomika said. She looked Carla dead in the eye and winked as she said, "We gon' be late pickin' up your mother."

"YEAH!" Tia hollered from the back seat.

Carla smacked her lips and looked around for some paper. She wrote her number down, then asked her friend for his.

"I don't have one."

There was silence for a long time. Finally, Carla said, "Oh. Okay," just as pleasant. "Well, just call me when you get a chance, then."

As Carla pulled off, she stared at him out the rearview mirror, centering in on his vanilla face and long jheri curl, thinking God definitely broke the mold when he created him.

"Watch the road, Carla," Tia said.

"I am," Carla said, jerking the steering wheel when her tires hit the curb.

"He like you, girl," Tomika claimed, smiling at Carla.

"I like him, too. He was fine!"

Yeah right, Tia thought to herself, thinking light-skinned brotha's played out in the eighties.

"Y'all wanna get somethin' to eat? I got thirty-two dollars outta Dame's ugly ass," Tomika said, counting her money.

"Yeah! Shoot, come on!" Carla said.

"We can go to Jack in the Box…can you just take me to one more place though, real fast. I wanna see if I can get some weed from Ronnie…right there at the Jordan Downs…right over there by Jack in the Box," Tomika conned before looking back at Tia and smiling. "We're going to see *Chancey*."

Right then, Tia was having an anxiety attack. "I don't wanna see him!" she yelled, meaning every last word. Her hands began to tremble when Carla made the right on 103rd. She felt lightheaded when they reached Grape Street.

"Pull up in here," Tomika said. Without question, Carla drove her mother's car in one of Jordan Down's entrances. She pulled up in front of Jordan's Gym and stopped to let Tomika out. Tia squished down in her seat like a terrified pup.

Tomika said, "I like your hair, Yolanda," to a tall female standing out in front. "Who did it?"

Yolanda's energetic body wiggled up to the car. "Me!" she snapped as if Tomika should have known.

"Oh. It's cute. What color is it?"

Yolanda got eyelevel with the sideview mirror to peep at her brownish-blonde hair. "I used bleach."

"That didn't break your hair out?"

"Not yet, knock on wood," Yolanda said, knocking on the roof of the car.

"Unh. 'Ey, you seen Ronnie?"

"Yeah. Him and Chance got into it. They was just out here arguin' a minute ago."

"For real? Why?" Tomika asked.

"I don't know. Something about Chancey being late."

Tomika smacked her lips and sulked. "I'm try'na get some bud. Shit."

"Me too! What's up?" Yolanda exclaimed happily.

Tia and Carla gave each other a fleeting look, disbelieving the filth coming from Yolanda's mouth. Yolanda looked like a kid by her undeveloped body. Even her throaty voice couldn't disguise her youth.

"We gotta find Ronnie first," Tomika said.

"Hold up, let me see if he still over here," Yolanda said and darted over to building thirty-eight.

"Who lives over there?" Carla asked, watching.

"Rosie," Tomika said, then looked back at Tia, who was in a silent panic. "You happy?" she asked with a smile.

Tia frowned and asked, "Happy for what?"

"'Cause! You finna see Chancey," Tomika said.

"Where's Chancey?" Carla asked.

"I'm sure he's around here somewhere. Shit, if Ronnie's here, Chancey's close by," Tomika said.

Tia prayed that Rondell was nowhere to be found. She begged the Lord to have mercy on her soul. Wished she could snap her fingers and be in the safety of her home. And now, she found herself a nervous wreck, seeing Yolanda returning with a handsome man.

They both stepped to the car. Then, Jackie yelled out Yolanda's name, drawing her to the gym. Rondell knelt down first on Carla's side, then spotting Tomika in the passenger's seat, he headed around to her side and said, "What's up?" He looked in the back seat, saw Tia, and rolled his eyes back to Tomika. Tia could tell that he was stuck on himself, and instantly, she didn't care for him. Carla gawked openly in his face, admiring his gray eyes.

"Let me get some bud," Tomika said.

"What 'chew got?" Rondell asked with a stern face.

"Where's Chance?" she asked as she flipped through her bills.

Rondell sighed and looked out toward Grape. "He had to go make a run...him and Kay just boned out."

Tomika was just about to ask why he and Chancey were feuding, then remembered she didn't introduce her girls. "Oh, Ronnie, this is Carla..."

"What's up, Carla?" Rondell said in a simple, dispassionate voice.

"And that's Chance's girlfriend, Tia, in the back," Tomika said, smiling as she pulled a twenty from her stack.

Rondell stopped all movement. He looked at Tia from the corner of his eyes and glared at her for what felt like an eternity. He kept his non-blinking, glowering eyes magnetized to her. She was scared and felt apologetic for whatever she did to piss him off.

Just as Tomika positioned her mouth to ease the tension, Rondell said, "So, that's Tia."

11

The stoplight was showing red for the longest. Kaylin was beginning to think it was malfunctioned. He glanced to his right, then his left to examine the oncoming traffic. Chancey, from the passenger's side, sensed Kaylin's contemplation and said, "Don't even think about it! We got too much shit in here right now."

"Well, this shit betta' hurry up and..."

The light turned green.

Kaylin accelerated to the speed limit. He drove down Century Boulevard like a cautious, old man. "I hope you know this is the last time I'm doin' this."

"I know. I'm goin' to get my license next week," Chancey said.

"Yeah, right!"

"I'm serious this time. For real! I'ma prolly go Wednesday...no, Thursday, since they stay open later."

"Why you care how late they stay open? Ain't like you got shit to do all day."

"Fuck you. Go right here so I can get something to eat," Chancey said.

Kaylin pulled off Century and up to the drive-thru window of McDonalds. He ordered what Chancey wanted, along with a double cheeseburger, fries, and drink for himself.

"I hope this shit don't make me sick," Chancey said when he got his food.

Kaylin stuffed his mouth with fries as they rolled off, then mumbled something that only a person who truly knew him would understand.

Chancey said, "'Cause I was late. That fool just don't know though. He almost got dealt with! I was that close to jawin' his ass, cuz! He was talkin' to me hella crazy! Talkin' 'bout, 'Where you been?'" Chancey said, impersonating Rondell. "He was yellin'! Try'na check me like a bitch in front of the gym! I walked up on 'em like, 'Cuz, you betta' back the fuck up off me'! I said it just like that, too; I wasn't playin'!"

"What he say?"

"Man, I think his feelings was hurt, 'cause he was like, 'Oh, so now you wanna fight me? After all I done for you, you wanna fight me now?' I'm tellin' you, cuz, I don't know what he think this is, but shit, he ain't my fuckin' daddy, you know what I'm sayin'? I ain't had one of them since, shit…birth!" Chancey settled down to ponder his father's whereabouts. He missed him for a brief moment. "I don't blame his ass for bailin' out though. Shit, can't nobody put up wit' Nikki's crazy ass too long!" he said. "I don't know, cuz, I'm just tired of everybody—Ronnie! Setchi! My mother! Even you, nigga!"

Kaylin laughed and asked, "What I do?"

Inside, Chancey laughed with Kaylin, but the hurt he felt left his face without a trace of emotion. He said, "Man, I just wish things was different sometimes. I'm tired of doin' this shit. I'm tired of lookin' over my shoulder every fuckin' day. I gotta hear Setchi complainin' all the goddamn time and my mother's broke-ass bitchin' all day…man, I swear! And Ronnie…that's all that fool talk about is money—how he gotta get paid! Money ain't everything! Shit, I'm just seventeen years old, cuz. I'm try'na live! See some shit! Not sit around, try'na outsmart the po-pos all day. I'm try'na invest and have stocks, you know what I'm sayin'? That's why I'm tellin' you, cuz, when you graduate, we need to start our own business. You can be the cook and I can be the money. We can call it something like, *Chancey-Kay's Eatery* or some shit."

"A restaurant?" Kaylin asked, laughing a little at the thought.

"See, why you laughin'? I'm serious! You don't never think about shit like that? You don't dream?" Chancey paused with a deep inhale. "Shit, I dream so much, I be believin' I'm really livin' like that sometimes," he said seriously. "Like I got a dope-ass crib wit' a white picket fence. Shit, nigga, a proper wife, some kids—lil' Jr. and Tianna..."

Kaylin laughed out loud. "Tianna?" he asked, picturing Tia in his mind.

Chancey looked at Kaylin and smiled. "Cuz, I'm serious. I be sittin' in the dark sometimes, just thinkin', you know what I'm sayin'? You know how I get."

"Yeah, I know."

Chancey sighed. "Shit, I guess dreamin' is the closest I'ma ever come to havin' shit."

"I knew it!" Kaylin cut in. "There you go! You been drinkin', huh?"

"Nope! But since you mentioned it, take me by the liquor store."

Kaylin smacked his lips.

"Well, you shouldn't of brought the shit up! Every time I try'da talk about my feelings, you wanna think I'm drunk. So, fuck it!"

"Yeah, 'cause you always start talkin' crazy and feelin' sorry for yourself."

"That's 'cause I'm a sorry-ass nigga!"

"I ain't about to sit here and argue with you," Kaylin said, turning his stereo up.

Chancey turned it down. "I got a headache."

"Fool, I don't give a damn!" Kaylin snapped, turning it back up.

Almost immediately, Chancey extended his arm toward the knob. Kaylin gave him a look of warning.

"I gotta tell you something!" Chancey said.

"What!"

"I seen Tia today."

"So!" Kaylin hesitated a few, then asked, "Where you see 'er at?"

"She was at the store...Grape Supermarket..."

"She talked to you?" Kaylin asked, surprised.

"Yeah...I mean, not really...she just...shit, I don't know." A faint laughter seeped from Chancey's lips. "She weird, cuz...nah, she ain't weird..."

"I know she's a lil' childish," Kaylin said.

"Yeah, I know. You can tell she ain't been around—a virgin, you know what I'm sayin'?"

Just talking about Tia put Chancey in better spirits. He grinned at her presumed pureness and prayed that she would call him tonight before he went on to declare to Kaylin that he was going to marry her one day.

"Not if Ronnie can help it!" Kaylin taunted. His mockery brought Chancey back to reality.

Suddenly, Chancey's cell phone rung. He looked down at it and said, "I bet this is that nigga right now. I bet it's him! I'm tellin' you, man, that fool be on me! Like today...you should'a seen the way he was goin' off! And it wasn't even so much that I was late! He acted like he was mad 'cause I was with Tia!"

"Maybe he's gay," Kaylin said and laughed.

"I don't know what's wrong wit' his ass. He betta' recognize though. Shit, I ain't the one!"

Chancey finished his food. Kaylin was still struggling with his, trying to bite into his cheeseburger, while he drove, signaled, and turned. "Drive while I eat this real quick," he said.

At the next stoplight, he and Chancey quickly swapped seats. Chancey asked, "You ever see Tia at school?" as he re-buckled his seatbelt.

"Sometimes."

"Who she be wit'?"

"I see 'er with Carla's fat-ass most of the time."

"She don't have a boyfriend?"

"Hell, I don't know! I thought you said you talked to her!"

"I did! But we didn't talk about stuff like that," Chancey said. His tongue tied when he spotted the black-and-white gaining on them. He was almost stressed out until he realized his seatbelt was on and he was driving the speed limit. Then another red light, the last light before they could venture off to the back roads leading home, brought them to one more halt.

Kaylin was talking away, not realizing he was being ignored by Chancey, who was glaring out the rearview. As the black-and-white slowed down behind them, Chancey rolled his eyes at the sight of Officer Woods. "Damn! Woody's faggot-ass is behind us."

Kaylin almost turned around in his seat when he looked back.

Chancey said, "Don't look…" but Kaylin's deer-struck eyes were already gleaming out the back window. Chancey could have wrung his neck! "What the fuck you look back for?!"

"Who you yellin' at?! Shit! How was I 'spose to know?"

"I said 'Woody is behind us'! What part of that didn't you hear?"

They were both breathing heavily as they waited on the light to change. Chancey was sweating bullets, thinking about the sack of illegal drugs in Kaylin's trunk. He mused crazily about his foot accidentally slipping off the brake pedal, making him run the red light. He pressed his foot down extra hard on the brake, just in case.

It wasn't easy for Kaylin to sit still. He wanted to look back and see what Officer Woods was doing. He kept looking at Chancey. Chancey finally cut a look from the corner of his eyes, urging him to stop looking so suspicious. The light turned green, and Chancey pulled off slower than normal.

"You need to speed up, before he pulls you over for driving too…"

"Shut up!" Chancey snapped, peeping out the rearview.

Officer Woods was back at the intersection, waiting for a break in traffic so he could make his left turn. Chancey couldn't pull off Century fast enough. He burned rubber as he sped out in front of the nearing cars and made a left on Grape.

*   *   *

"Oh, now *he* was what you call good-looking," Carla said as she eased her way up Grape to the light at 103rd.

"Who?" Tia asked.

"The guy that just passed us in that gold Impala."

Tia looked back and followed the Impala until she saw the brake lights flash in front of Jordan Down's recreation center.

"See! We could'a been chillin' right now," Carla said, glancing back for one last look as she made her left turn. "Dang! We just missed 'em by two minutes. Shoot, it's all kind of niggas over there, huh? That's the hang-out spot. And Ronnie, with his fine ass…that's gon' be my baby daddy."

Tia ignored Carla. She was ticked off and too annoyed to even think about feeding in to her disgusting fairytale.

"I was just about to get his number until you messed everything up! Shoot, me, you, him, and Chancey could'a all went out on a double date."

Now, that comment made Tia smack her lips hard. "Puh-lease! Girl, he was *way* too conceited!" Then, she suddenly remembered Chancey's numbers in her palm. She looked and found the number to his cell phone smeared to the point where it was no longer readable. She made herself conscious not to smudge his home number, and rode the rest of the way with her palm facing up.

"Yeah, but still, he was talking to me," Carla stated.

"Yeah, only when you asked him something!"

"I know! That's why I said I was finna get his number!" Carla said, smiling at her plans.

Tia found Carla's overconfidence incredible. Rondell's attitude even more so. "Unh-unh...I do not like him! And obviously he don't like me either," she said.

"Did you see the way he was looking at you?!"

"Yeah! I was wondering if you caught that!"

"Yeah, I caught it. I was like, dang, if looks could kill..."

"My ass would'a died a thousand deaths!" Tia said. "And you wanted to stay?! Shoot, I was try'na get the hell up outta there! And did you hear him when he said something about us looking like the stuck-up type?"

"No, he was talking about you! He was cool with me. But you...you *was* acting a lil' stuck-up though, Tia."

Tia glared at Carla and thought, *No she didn't take it there.* If only she could tell her what she really thought and still remain friends.

"No, seriously, you was!"

"Why I gotta be stuck-up? 'Cause I ain't lying to kick it like you? Shit, I don't smoke weed! Never have and don't intend to! So, if they can't understand that, then oh well! I don't have to be somebody I'm not just to have fake-ass friends," Tia said. She didn't want to, but Carla had to push her.

"I'm not lying to kick it either! Okay, so you don't smoke weed? Cool! I don't smoke it either! But dang, since we was all kicking it together, why not? It ain't like I smoke it all the time. Shit, I may never smoke it again in my life!" Carla pushed back. "My whole point is, if we supposed to all be kicking it together, I'm not gon' be all quiet and to myself like I can't talk to nobody. That's all I'm saying."

"I wasn't acting all quiet, but I wasn't about to sit up there and talk to somebody who didn't have nothing to say to me. Ronnie wasn't talking to me; he was talking to you, Tomika, and Yolanda! And anyway, all y'all need to be ashamed of y'allself! Out there smoking weed with that lil' girl!"

"No, that was Tomika and Ronnie. You remember, I was like, 'You too young to be out here smoking weed'. Shoot, I don't play that. That's like smoking weed with my lil' sister!"

"Unh. Well, that lil' girl need her ass whipped, I know that!"

"I wonder was that lady in the gym her mother."

"I don't know."

"Yeah, it was, now that I think about it. That's what Tomika said."

"And Tomika was getting on my last nerve wit' her instigating ass, talking about, 'That's Chancey's girlfriend'! She was just trying to be funny. I ain't stupid!"

"And we never did go to Jack in the Box! She just said that so I would take her to Jordan's," Carla said.

"I could'a told you that! All she wanted was a free ride. She see you got a car to drive and wanna use you for a taxi. The least she could'a did was offer you some gas money. Shoot, everywhere we went was for her! I can't stand people like that."

*   *   *

Chancey parked Kaylin's car in the last available parking space out in front of the gym. He opened the trunk and tossed Kaylin his keys. Then, he checked the number on his pager when he felt it vibrate; it was his home number.

"What's up," Kaylin said to everybody he saw before trotting to his house. "'Ey, Chance, I'll be right back," he yelled from a distance.

"Meet me at my house!" Chancey yelled back.

He leaned in the trunk to get his goods and handed them to Rondell when he came over to the car. "I gotta go to the pad for a minute. Somebody just paged me."

"Alright. I'll see you in a minute," Rondell said and headed to Rosie's place.

Chancey walked over to Tomika, who was skewed against the wall of the gym, looking tired by the way her eyelids blinked lazily. "What 'chew doin' over here?" he asked her. "I didn't say you could come out the house."

Tomika blushed.

"Let's go get buck wild," Chancey said, not really expecting to, but just picking her brain to see how she'd react.

Tomika responded by smiling and looking like she was actually giving the question some thought. But when Chancey broke out laughing, she said, "Nigga, move! Shit! You fuckin' up my high!"

Yolanda started to laugh.

"This is an A and B conversation, so what 'chew laughin' at?" Chancey said and playfully popped Yolanda in the head. She was squatted on the ground next to Tomika.

"Stop, trick!"

"What! Oh, okay, I'm finna go tell Jackie you out here high as a kite."

"No!" Yolanda yelled, locking her arms around Chancey's legs. They laughed and tussled a bit, with Tomika watching and giggling from the side.

"There go BMW again," Rondell said, pointing out the black BMW cruising pass as he walked up to Chancey and the girls. He had already dropped the cocaine off to Rosie and gave her the usual instructions on what to do.

Tomika looked, then yelled, "That's what's-his-name!" She started popping her fingers as if it helped her think. "Curtis Moore! He's married to my cousin's baby mama, Tiffany. They got a house over on Crenshaw…" Tomika stopped and stared oddly at Rondell. "What's he doin' way over here, I wonder?"

"I don't know, but cuz, if he roll up on the set one more time…"

The BMW drove all the way to the end of the block and parked. Rondell walked out in the street, but still, he had a hard time seeing what was going on. He had a hard time seeing the car for that matter. He squinted, ducked, strained. Nothing! "'Ey, I should drive down there, huh?"

"Yeah, let's go drive down there, then you can take me home," Tomika said.

"How you get over here, 'Mik?" Chancey asked. Before Tomika answered, she stalled to see what Rondell was going to do.

"Uh-oh!" Yolanda yelled as she spied Rondell's moves.

Rondell limped coolly toward Chancey with a roguish grin. Both Tomika and Yolanda knew he was getting ready to clown, and the anticipation made them laugh ahead of time.

Rondell said, "Oh yeah, I almost forgot. I finally got to meet that...yo' lil' girlfriend."

Chancey looked at Tomika and wondered what was funny. If he didn't know any better, he'd swear there was a comedian around by the way she fell to her knees laughing. "Who's my girlfriend?" he turned back to Rondell and asked, thinking the answer better be good.

"Tia!" Rondell said.

"Tia?!"

"Yep! Over here lookin' like a lil' boy wit' 'er lil'-ass titties!"

Tomika and Yolanda grabbed each other and ran in the gym so Chancey wouldn't see them dying with laughter.

"That's fucked up."

"What? She *do* look like a boy!" Rondell said, then shook his head at Chancey. "You fucked our money off for that? I mean, I didn't have a chance to see her body 'cause she was in the car the whole time, you feel? Do she got ass? Hips or somethin'? Shit, somethin'?!" Rondell let out one of his sarcastic chuckles and said, "Maybe you should tell 'er she needs a perm. What do you think? I mean, 'cause she was looking just a *little* outta context, you feel? I mean, you *do* care about her, right? This is the girl you always speaking highly of, right? So, I'm sayin', you know, you should try'da keep her up to date on clothes, hairstyles, nails—shit like that, you feel me? 'Cause she was over here lookin' tore up from the floor up."

"Fuck you!"

"Fuck me? Nigga, I'm try'na help you out. I'm just saying, she representin' you! If she lookin' to the curb, then you lookin' to the curb! Shit, don't get mad at me. I'm just callin' it how I see it." Rondell rolled his eyes away. He had more to say, but couldn't remember what it was. He fiddled around in his pockets and played with his keys and some change, then started up again. "And that other one...what's her name, 'Mik?"

It took a minute for Tomika to get Carla's name out. She was too busy in the doorway laughing hard at Rondell's entertainment.

"Yeah, Carla!" Rondell yelled. "That's it. Carla. Lookin' like a big-ass potato!" He stopped to laugh at his own joke.

Tomika and Yolanda were in tears.

"I'ma name 'er big ass, Ms. Potato! Yeah, that's what I'ma call 'er!"

"'Ey, I can't even lie...she is shaped like a potato!" Tomika managed to utter through all of her intense laughter.

"Y'all stupid as hell," Chancey said. He overlooked most of the disrespect, especially coming from Rondell. He knew Rondell turned Setchi's age when he got high.

Chancey felt his pager vibrating again and started walking home before he pulled it from his pocket.

"Where you goin'?" Rondell asked.

"Home!"

Rondell ran to catch up with Chancey. "You know we gotta go drop this shit off in a few hours, right?"

"Yeah, nigga! Damn!"

"I know you ain't trippin' off what I said about Tia."

Chancey stopped. "Nah, I ain't trippin', 'cause I know you lyin'! Tia didn't come over here."

"Yes she did! I ain't lyin', she did! Ask Jackie, she'll tell you. She was smokin' herb wit' us and everything!"

"Tia?"

"Yeah! You don't believe me, call 'er and ask her. Oh, that's right, I forgot...she never gave you her number. See, you like her, but she ain't feelin' you, right?"

"Man..."

"That's what she told us!" Rondell said persuasively. "She said you wasn't her type."

Chancey couldn't deny nor hide the anger that was building up inside. He stared at Rondell in a huff, wondering if he was telling the truth.

"She told us she didn't like drug dealers."

"How she know I sell drugs?"

"Tomika! How else? They're potnas! You didn't know that?"

"Tia?"

"Yes, nigga, Tia! And you said she was a good girl…" Rondell laughed. "What you need to do is…"

"Why the fuck you keep tellin' me what I need to do?! Stop worrying about what I need and stay the fuck out my business!"

"Nigga, fuck you, then!"

"Fuck you! Stop tellin' me what the fuck I need to do! You gettin' on my nerves wit' that shit!"

"I'm just try'na keep yo' ass from looking stupid! Runnin' 'round here worried about a bitch that don't give a fuck about you…"

"What's it to you? You all up in my business like it's the fuckin' thing to do! I see who the fuck I wanna see! You don't tell me who the fuck I can talk to…"

Rondell remained quiet. He listened to Chancey carry on until he realized he was arguing by himself. When Chancey quieted down, Rondell said, "Look how that bitch got you actin'! Look!"

"Man, I ain't try'na hear that bullshit…" Chancey said, mumbling the rest of his sentence as he walked off and continued home.

Rondell followed. "Nigga, you got a hot-ass temper. You need to calm the fuck down."

"There you go tellin' me what I need again."

"Chancey, I'm serious now. All BS to the side…"

"I'm serious, too!"

"We 'spose to be a team, cuz! You ain't 'spose to *never* let a bitch come between us!" Rondell said. He always knew what to say to get Chancey's attention. "You never see me lettin' a bitch stop my cash flow. Or yours!"

Chancey stopped and made eye contact with Rondell. "Ronnie, you act like we didn't get the shit! The shit is in there with Rosie right now, so what's the problem?"

"Yeah, but you was still late!"

"Okay! I was late! Now what?"

"See, there you go flarin' up again…"

"I'm sayin', how many times you gon' say the shit? It's over! And you blowin' shit all outta proportion about Tia! It ain't that serious! I saw her one time, nigga. Once!"

"And look what happened," Rondell said. "She already got shit fucked up! You ain't even focused no more! Right when shit is startin' to take off for us! We ain't out there grindin' in front of the gym no more! We gettin' rid of ounces now! Makin' real money! And I ain't try'na let nobody fuck that off! Nobody!"

Chancey stared at Rondell mesmerized. He didn't know what else to say. What do you say after hearing something like that? "I'ma catch up to you in a minute. I gotta go in here and see what's up real quick," he said, pulling his keys from his pocket. Rondell stuck out his fist. Chancey reluctantly stuck out his and they both gave each other a pound.

"I'm 'bout to go take Mika home, then I'll be back," Rondell said. "When you finish, come over Rosie's house. Oh! Here, take this..." He pulled a white rock from his pocket. "It's the last one left. Go put it up for me. I don't wanna drive with it."

Chancey stuck the rock in his pocket and walked in the house.

12

Setchi dried off, lotioned up, and sprayed herself down with Liz Claiborne perfume. She was on her way to meet Curt, but first, she had to talk to her brother. She paged him twice, but he hadn't called back. She knew she couldn't leave without talking to him.

She picked her sleeveless, summer dress up from her bed and held it up to her body. She was ready to slip into it, just dying to see how sexy it made her look. She thought about paging Chancey again, then thought about his cell phone. "What was the purpose of having one if he never answered it?" she thought out loud.

Time was winding down. The boxed clock on the dresser told her she only had fifteen minutes left. Frustration was starting to kick in. She threw her dress down and walked out in the hall. "Ma! Chance hasn't called back yet?"

Nikki was lying on the couch, flipping through the channels with her remote. She yelled, "Nope!" then turned the TV off. She got up and walked back to the room. "Just get dressed," she said. "And you better hurry up! You don't want him popping in on you."

"I know," Setchi said. "Okay, I'm gettin' dressed right now. What shoes you think look better, the heels or the flats?"

"What dress are you wearing?"

"This one," Setchi said, showing the inside of her palm when she presented her beautiful summer-dress with pink floral designs.

"Oh, that's cute." Nikki lifted the dress and held it up close to her. "When you get this?"

"Last week. I got it from the Fashion Posh. It was on sale for nine dollars."

"Oh yes, I wanna sport this."

"I don't care. It's a size four though."

"I ain't trippin'. It'll just be a lil' tight," Nikki said, hugging the dress and swaying from side to side with it. She passed it to Setchi and said, "Here, put it on and let me see how it looks."

Setchi gladly slipped her lean physique in it, then gave her mother a pose that you'd see inside of a Vogue Magazine.

"Hey now! Shake what your mama gave you!"

Setchi started pumping her butt.

Nikki started pumping hers, too. "Girl, when he see you, he ain't gon' know how to act!"

"Oh God, I better hurry up! He's prolly out there waitin'." Setchi quickly put on her high-heeled scandals, took the black eyeliner and lined her lips, then coated them with Vaseline.

"Want me to go out there and see if I see Chancey?"

"Oooh yeah, yeah! Please!"

Nikki was on her way.

"Thank you, Mama!" Setchi yelled.

Nikki slid her feet in her house shoes and went to open the front door. Shockingly, Chancey was opening it from the outside.

"What are you doing here?" Nikki asked loud enough to alert Setchi.

"Last time I checked, I was livin' here. Did 'ju kick me out and forget to tell me or somethin'?" Chancey asked as he passed his mother. He stopped short, puzzled that she was still standing in the doorway staring at him. "What?"

"Nothing…"

"Where's Setchi? Who paged me?"

"Uh…"

"I did," Setchi said, coming from the room with her bathrobe nuzzled around her and her summer dress.

"What's up?"

"Never mind now! You took so long to call back, shoot, I forgot what I wanted."

"Did anybody call me?"

"Yeah, a lotta people."

"Did Tia call?"

"I don't think so," Setchi said, following Chancey to the room. Nikki followed behind Setchi.

Chancey stepped into a sweet aroma when he walked through the bedroom door. "What's that smell?"

"Perfume," Setchi said.

"Where you goin'?"

Setchi huffed, puffed, then said, "Over Kashaun's, Chancey." She prayed that he would leave now that he had discovered everything was okay.

Chancey copped a seat on his bed, leaned back, and looked up at his sister and mother. He knew they were up to something by the way they hovered over him. "This late?" he asked, keying in on Setchi.

"It ain't hardly late, Chance!" Setchi yelled, almost pouting. "See, Ma!"

"See, Ma, what? It's goin' on nine o'clock."

"Ma, would you please tell him that I'm goin' over Kashaun's house…that you said I could go."

Nikki hesitated before attempting to come up with a good story. She was calm, her voice low. "Chance, Kashaun is having a get-together at her house and I told Setchi she could go."

"And how's she gettin' there?" Chancey turned to his sister. "How you gettin' there, Setchi?"

"I'm walkin'! It's just right…"

"You not about to walk through these projects!" Chancey roared.

"I'll walk with her, Chancey," Nikki interjected.

"Setchi's not walkin' through these projects *at all* this time of night!" Chancey got up and walked out. He was going to the bathroom, but did a 360 when he heard the knock at the door. On his way to answer it, he stopped at the bedroom where Setchi and Nikki were standing around in a frenzy. "I don't know what's goin' on, but

Setchi, you bet not leave this house. And I ain't goin' nowhere, either! I'm in for the rest of the night!"

After hearing that, Setchi broke out in tears.

"Well, you know how your brother is," Nikki said, wiping Setchi's eyes. "Just have him take you to Kashaun's and tell Curt to meet you over there. That's all you gotta do."

"He ain't gon' take me!" Setchi cried.

"I'll make him!"

"Yeah, but then I gotta change my clothes and try'da sneak my dress…just forget it!"

"Setchi, get undressed," Nikki said and closed the door. Setchi unzipped her dress and let it fall to her feet before she angrily stepped out of it.

Nikki grabbed the dress and balled it up in her hand. "All you gotta do is take this shit and stick it in your purse. Where's your purse at?" When she laid eyes on Setchi's purse, she shoved the dress down in it. "Now, put on one of your sweat suits or something. I'ma go tell him you're ready to go…"

"I gotta call Curt real quick…"

"And call Kashaun, too, so she'll know what's up," Nikki whispered as she exited the room.

She walked in the living room, then the kitchen. Chancey was sitting at the table with his back turned talking to Kaylin.

"What's up, Nik?" Kaylin said.

Chancey turned around and saw his mother looking just as mistrustful as she did in the room.

"Hey, Kay-Kay," Nikki said and kissed Kaylin's cheek. "How's Niecy?"

"Fine."

Nikki looked at Chancey and said, "Drop your sister off at Kashaun's, Chancey."

"I ain't droppin' her off nowhere."

"Come on! I don't want Kashaun's mother to haf' to come and get her."

Chancey looked Nikki right in the eyes. "Why you in here lyin' for her?"

"Lying about what, Chancey?"

"Setchi ain't goin' to no Kashaun's house! That room smell like a fuckin' flower shop, where she don' poured that shit all over her! Talkin' about she's goin' to Kashaun's house! Smellin' like that?"

"Kashaun is having a party at her house…"

"Yeah, let 'chew tell it!"

"I don't have to lie to you! Shit, I'm grown, remember?"

"Whateva," Chancey said. He started punching in numbers on his cell phone.

Kaylin was watching and wishing he had some popcorn. He loved when Nikki and Chancey went at it. He found it amusing and humorous, although Chancey hated when he laughed. But Kaylin laughed, not because they were both upset, but because the relationship between he and Niecy was so serious and strict that he knew he could never stand up to her, even when she was wrong. Therefore, he released his frustrations through Chancey's guts and ill-mannerism.

"Do you hear me, Chancey?" Nikki asked.

Chancey heard her, but proceeded with his phone call. "What's up, cuz? Where you at?"

Kaylin was tickled.

Nikki sighed, then yelled, "Chancey!"

"Bring me back a 40 oz," Chancey said into the phone. When he hung up, he irritably rolled his eyes up to look at his mother. "What?!"

"You heard me! You heard every word I said! Now, quit acting stupid and take Setchi to Kashaun's house!"

It was getting heated just the way Kaylin liked it. He positioned himself comfortably and eyed them both closely, intending not to miss a thing.

"I can't take her right now. She gotta wait," Chancey said, cooling down the temperature and putting a damper on Kaylin's silly mood.

"She said take her now!" Kaylin said, instigating.

"Yeah, Chancey! Don't nobody got all night!" Nikki yelled.

"Please don't get her started," Chancey told Kaylin, not realizing her rage was already in progress. "I don't even feel like trippin' wit' her today."

"You gon' be doin' more than just trippin' if you don't take Setchi to Kashaun's house!" Nikki warned.

"Damn! What's in it for you? You *must* be gettin' somethin', 'cause you doin' way too much," Chancey said as he got up to search through the refrigerator.

"Nigga, you kiss my ass! I ain't gettin' a damn thing! And if I was, that's my business! Lil' fucker!" Nikki yelled. She needed a cigarette after that. She reached up to the top of the refrigerator and felt around for her pack. On the way down, her arm accidentally grazed the side of Chancey's head. He leaned over and the reflexes in his arm made him lightly shove Nikki back a step.

Nikki, already mad and looking for an excuse to knock fire from her son, got just the break she needed. She grabbed a decent amount of his T-shirt and slung him into the refrigerator door; she was strong for a petite woman. The door flew wide open and jolted the refrigerator a few inches. A bottle of mustard popped out and rolled around on the floor.

"What the hell you doin'?" Chancey yelled, rubbing the side of his arm.

Nikki regained her composure. "I told you once before not to put your hands on me." She calmly lit her cigarette and took in some smoke.

"Oh my God! Kaylin! Did you see me put my hands on her? I didn't touch her, huh?"

Kaylin was laughing too hard to answer.

"Kaylin!" Chancey yelled, then sighed when he couldn't get his attention. He looked at Nikki and said, "You...see, you...you got a problem!"

"You would wanna take Setchi to Kashaun's, Chancey," Nikki said, still well composed, yet sounding threatening at the same time.

"I ain't takin' 'er nowhere! Shit! Let 'er ass walk!" Chancey pulled out a chair and sat at the table.

Setchi came storming from the room, pissed that all her plans were ruined. "Kaylin, can you please take me to my friend's house?"

"He ain't takin' you either! Make your mother walk with you!"

Setchi evil-eyed Chancey and ran back to the room, returning not a minute later with an oversized purse.

"Where you think you goin'?" Chancey asked, frowning up and down at his sister.

"Come on, Setchi," Nikki said, pulling Setchi by the arm. They both ignored Chancey and barged out the front door.

"Setchi!" Chancey yelled.

Setchi stuck her head in the door. "What!"

"I said where the hell you goin'?"

"The same place I was going before!"

"Is your homework done?" Chancey was looking for something to fuss about now.

"YEAH!" Setchi hollered.

Chancey rose from his seat and got in his sister's face. "Who the hell you yellin' at?"

"Well, you could'a asked me that earlier! I'm already late for…"

"Do I look like I give a fuck?"

"Well, you…"

"Shut up, Setchi! Say one more word and I'm slappin' the shit outta you!"

Chancey yanked his chair back and plopped down in it. Things weren't so funny to Kaylin anymore. It never was when he saw Chancey chastise his sister. He knew Chancey was serious to the core when it came to Setchi, and didn't dare laugh.

Chancey looked at Setchi. "It's mighty funny you breakin' your neck to get outta here tonight." Then he turned to Kaylin and added, "And when the morning time come, I gotta drag 'er ass outta bed and make her go to school."

"Tomorrow's Sunday!" Setchi said, balling her heart out. Nikki wasn't there to back her up anymore. She had wandered off with some of the neighbors.

"I know! I'm talkin' about through the week!"

"Well, it's the weekend now! God! I can't do nothing!"

Rondell walked through the door. He stared at Setchi as he passed her, curious to know why she was crying. He sat Chancey's beer on the table, then went in the living room and stood in front of the TV. "Who rented New Jack City, Setchi?"

Setchi gave Rondell a look that told him not to talk to her.

Chancey stepped in and said, "My mother, I think."

Kaylin watched Rondell stand in front of the television and stare at the glass like he was trying to learn something. "This fool love New Jack City!" he commented.

Chancey unscrewed the top to his beer and took a swig. He eyed the bottle for a minute, then looked at Setchi. "You better have yo' ass home by twelve!"

Setchi almost ran out the door.

"I'ma be here waitin' on you, too!" Chancey yelled.

"I'ma go drop 'er off," Kaylin said.

"Cool! And make sure her ass go in, too."

*   *   *

Setchi ran out to Grape and looked up the street. Nikki left her group of associates and ran after her. "Is he still down there?" she asked.

Setchi smacked her lips. "I don't see him. Guess he must be on his way to Kashaun's house. See, Chance just messed me all up!"

"You want me to still walk you?"

"Yeah, if you want to."

"You got about twenty dollars I can borrow?"

"Twenty? I thought you said ten!"

"I'm tacking on another ten for all the extra work I had to do," Nikki joked. "Just get some more money from Curt..."

"I don't wanna keep asking him for money every time I see him, Ma!"

"Girl, you better get that money! Shit, make his ass pay for the cooch! Yo' shit ain't free! I *know* I taught you better than that!"

Setchi sadly pulled a ten and two fives from her purse. Just as she thought her night couldn't get any worse, she turned toward the footsteps running her way and saw Kaylin.

"Come on, I'm takin' you to Kashaun's house."

"See there!" Nikki said and smiled. "Now, you don't have to walk."

"Yeah, whatever," Setchi pouted and stomped over to Kaylin's car. She didn't talk to him the whole way. And when he asked her a question, she made it a point to be short and snappy when she answered.

Kaylin pulled in front of Kashaun's house. Setchi opened the door before the car stopped. When she got out, she slammed it. "Don't be slammin' my door!" Kaylin yelled. Then he pulled off and almost immediately hit the brakes.

Setchi watched him with irritation in her eyes as he backed up. She walked up to Kashaun's door and rung the bell. "It's me,

Shaun!"

Kashaun opened the door with a big, cheesy grin. She stepped on her porch and tried to focus past the tint on Kaylin's windows. "Is that him?"

"No, that's Kaylin!" Setchi said and snarled as she walked in.

"Oh, hi, Kay-Kay!" Kashaun yelled and waved before going in after her.

Kaylin blew and drove off.

"His car is tight! When he get that?" Kashaun asked.

Setchi was quickly peeling off her blue sweat suit. "I don't remember," she said, then slipped her dress over her head. "Did Curt come by?"

"If he did, he didn't ring the doorbell."

Setchi sucked her teeth and walked outside to look for him. She looked up one end of the street, then the other. Soon as she was ready to give up, a black BMW was gliding her way.

Curt let his window down with a press of a button. "Hey, beautiful," he said in a clichéd way.

Setchi thought that line was the oldest line in the book. But hey, it was coming from Curt, so, quite naturally she blushed. "Let me grab my stuff. I'll be right back!" She hurtled in and hurtled out with Kashaun racing behind her. "Curt, this is my friend, Kashaun."

Kashaun eagerly extended her arm. "Nice to meet you," she said and smiled, but couldn't help her eyebrows from puckering as she examined his white-collared shirt and black slacks, thinking all he needed was a briefcase. She saw his facial hairs looking extremely thick—full mustache and beard. She suspected he was around twenty-something. She looked at Setchi, and right away, Setchi read her mind.

"I'll call you later," Setchi said, fixing her eyes in a way that let Kashaun know now was not the time to pass judgment. Kashaun backed off and went in the house with a load of gossip to spill.

"You look appealing tonight," Curt told Setchi when she got in and relaxed.

"Thank you," she blushed.

"What have you done to me, girl? You got a brother wanting to see you so bad, he can't even go home and change his clothes when he get off from work!" Curt said when he saw Setchi looking over his clothing.

Setchi was on cloud ten.

"So, is everything okay at home?"

"Yeah," Setchi said with a sigh. "My brother was just tripping, that's all."

"Protective, huh?"

"Very!"

"Just think, in a few weeks, you'll be graduating from high school and on your own!" he said, smiling. "Nobody can say shit, then!"

Setchi sighed fretfully.

Curt stopped at the stop sign on the corner of Kalmia. "Oh, by the way, the next showing for Forrest Gump doesn't start for another two hours. You wanna go kick back at a room or something to kill some time? I know you're drained from all the chaos you went through tonight." He saw the fret on Setchi's face and caressed her hair. "You okay, beautiful?"

"Yeah, I'm okay. I just didn't realize how late it was. And my mother...she, um, had wanted me to be back by twelve, right? 'Cause she was saying she needed me to do some stuff for her..."

Curt frowned at Setchi first, then looked down at his watch. He looked at Setchi again, this time chuckling. "Since when did Nikki need you home?"

Curt's question hurt Setchi's feelings a little. What was he trying to say? That her mother didn't care about her?

"Why do I get the feeling it's your brother who wants you home by twelve?"

Setchi's mouth formed an unintentional grin. She fluttered her eyes bashfully at Curt and said, "It is, Curt. I'm sorry."

"So, you still haven't told him about us?"

"No, not yet..."

"What are you waiting on, Setchi?"

"You don't know my brother!"

"Yeah, but I've already met your mother, so what's the problem?" Curt asked with a touch of edginess in his voice.

Setchi began to sigh. "Just don't worry about it, okay?"

"I am worried about it! Every time I come to get you, I have to drive all around the fucking neighborhood until you finally decide to come out! And this time..." Curt chuckled sarcastically, "you had me waiting on you for almost an hour!" he yelled. "I used to be able to come to your house, but now that your brother's home, you got me sneaking around like a lil' schoolboy! All because you're not ready to put things out in the open!"

"I am ready! It's just that...it's not that easy! My brother won't..." Setchi was getting choked up.

"Setchi, beautiful, I'm starting to really care for you...and I know I'm a lot older, but your mother doesn't seem to have a problem wit' it. And she's the only one I'm concerned with. As long as she accepts me and allows me to see you, then I'm happy."

"I know, but..."

"But, what? She only lets me see you 'cause I give her money? You've told me that before, you know."

"Why you keep throwing that up in my face?"

"Hey, those were your words, not mine!"

"Curt, when I said that, I was just playing!" Setchi lied. "God! How many times do I have to keep telling you that?"

Curt was ready to give Setchi an answer that would have probably pissed her off, but when the car from behind blew at them, it knocked his whole train of thought off-track. He pulled over to let the car pass. When the car rolled up and stopped beside them, he dropped his window.

"Is everything okay?" Officer Woods asked.

Setchi quickly hid her face. She moved her purse to the side, just enough to let one eyeball show when she peeped at Officer Woods; he was looking her dead in the face.

"Everything's just fine, officer," Curt assured.

"Well, you can't be blocking traffic..."

"Yeah, I know. I just didn't see you behind me or else I would have moved."

"Maybe if you lighten the tint on your windows, you'd be able to see, don't you think?"

Curt gave Officer Woods a pleading look as he stammered over some excuses.

"Well, just take care of it. The next officer might not be so nice." He drove off, but only out of Curt and Setchi's sight. When they pulled off, he cruised a few cars behind them, mulling over the fact that Setchi tried to hide from him. Then he thought about Chancey and came to the brilliant conclusion: Chancey didn't know where his sister was! He laughed at his intellectual gift. He couldn't help but feel for Chancey though, wondering where was he now. He knew how much he loved his sister. He saw the way he tried to discipline and protect her. He knew he would hit the roof if he saw her now, with this man who was sure to be twice her age.

He hit Imperial Highway, still snooping to see where the black BMW was headed. His bottom lip dropped almost to his chest when he saw the car pull into the parking lot of a rickety motel.

*   *   *

Rondell was sitting on the floor with his back against the couch, praising Wesley Snipes for punishing Christopher Williams when he thought he was working with the cops. He sprinkled some marijuana flakes into a cigar he had sliced open. He re-sealed it, then looked it over, pleased at how perfect it was rolled. He was just about to fire it up when his cell phone rang. He answered it. The conversation was quick. When he disconnected, he yelled, "Alright, cuz, come on, let's go!" to Chancey. "That was Rosie!"

Chancey was in the bathroom taking a dump and had no plans of getting up any time soon. "Go 'head! I'll be over there in a minute!" he yelled back.

Rondell stuck his joint behind his ear and headed out. His feet created a rhythm as he practically ran down the steps. He started to acknowledge the old lady rocking in her unstable chair, but didn't stop. He didn't have time to talk; he had money to make.

Chancey sprayed what was left of the powder-scented air freshener, then tossed it in the garbage. He walked out the bathroom and discovered he was home alone. The peaceful atmosphere was soothing. He walked out in the living room and sat on the couch. If he didn't have anything to do, he would have let his body fall into a deep coma. The stillness made him realize how tired he was. It also allowed his brain to think clearly. Tia was the first in mind. He looked at the phone and checked all the plugs. Then, he lifted the handle, heard the tone, and hung up.

He submerged down in the couch and closed his eyes. Setchi crossed his mind briefly. He told himself he needed to be home more to monitor her. Then he thought about Kashaun and wondered if Setchi had her number lying around somewhere.

Just then, the phone rang. He jumped up and answered it on the first ring. He didn't mean to; he was just overanxious, he supposed. Just as he said hello, the party on the other end disconnected.

Annoyed, he slammed the phone down and looked around for his keys. He felt his pockets and headed out the door when he felt the hard mass of his key ring. He walked down the stairs like he had nowhere to go. His stride was slow and unanimated. When he reached the bottom, he said, "What's up, Ms. Doris," to the old lady sitting in a daze in her wobbly chair.

Ms. Doris looked at Chancey like she could barely see him. "Is that you, Chancey?" she asked. Her shrill voice was slow, slurred, and had a slight tremble to it. Her breathing was irregular and heavy, mainly when she spoke, as if it took a lot of effort to breathe and talk at the same time.

"Yeah, Ms. Doris, it's me. Why you not in the house? It's chilly out here tonight."

"Oh," Ms. Doris sighed. "I don't know, baby. I guess I just got tired of looking at the walls and came out here to get some air."

"Well, it's cold out here, and you don't have on a jacket..." Chancey reached to help Ms. Doris up. "Come on, let's get you back in the house," he said. "You take your medicine today?"

"I don't remember if I took it today or not..." She stopped to try and think. "I don't know where my mind is these days. I'm just a little old lady, I guess."

Little was something Ms. Doris was not. She fought to lift her overweight body out her chair. Chancey palmed her elbows to guide her.

For as long as he could remember, Ms. Doris lived downstairs from him. For thirteen some odd years, Chancey recalled her wearing the same old ruffled gown with an apron tied around her waist and wig cocked to the side on her head.

She was known for being the neighborhood watchdog. She was always home and could tell you who came by, who just left, and what they were wearing. And if she felt up to it, she'd follow them to the parking lot to report what kind of car they were driving. Everyone in the unit loved her for that.

After Chancey finally got Ms. Doris to stand on her swollen feet, she started telling him how her legs were bothering her.

"Oh yeah?" he said, not really paying much attention. He was trying to tune in to the familiar marching sounds approaching.

Officer Woods and his entourage showed up on the scene, galloping forcefully through Chancey's unit on their way to handle a domestic call. Their steps were loud and organized, stopping at the victim's doorstep across from Ms. Doris.

Chancey laid his eyes on Officer Woods and kept them there. No one else in the group mattered. He stared to the point where Ms. Doris had left him standing outside when she went in.

"Baby, you coming in?"

"No, no, I gotta go do something for my mother."

Officer Woods looked over. He saw Chancey and returned the same face of stone as one of his colleagues tapped on the door with his club.

Ms. Doris hobbled back outside. "Okay, well you be careful out there," she said. "Don't be speeding down these streets."

"Oh, never that!"

"Okay now, 'cause they're cracking down on these hardheads out here. I saw on the news just the other day…"

Chancey hated when Ms. Doris couldn't take a hint. There he was backing up to leave, and she kept right on talking.

"So you better be careful, 'cause night don't have no eyes. And I appreciate all you do for me, but I'm okay. You just take care of *you*. 'Cause me? Hey, I'm here!"

"Still gettin' your groove on," Chancey said and giggled.

"Hey, that's right!" she boasted, wiggling her hips. "I still got it! I may not be as fast, but I still got it."

Chancey laughed. He walked up to her and gave her hug. "Now, don't forget your age, okay? I don't wanna haf' to call the ambulance over here," he said, making Ms. Doris turn red in the face.

"Chancey, you're just as nutty as fruitcake, you know that? Get on outta here," she said and released jolly laughter. Chancey was good for always bringing a smile to Ms. Doris' face.

When he turned to leave, he frowned in the eyes of Officer Woods staring and being nosy. *Ugh!* he thought and rolled his eyes away, wishing he could take that billy and go upside his head with it.

He walked up 99th Place to Rosie's, but didn't knock. He wanted another drink first before dealing with Rondell. He walked over to both his cars, thought a minute, and decided to take the Monte Carlo.

Chancey had his music thumping like always when he pulled up at Grape Supermarket. The place was like a ghost town, which was cool. He was able to go straight in with his money and come straight out with his 40 oz of Old English Malt Liquor.

As he wheeled off, he hit the hydraulics that put his car in three-wheel motion, with the right front tire floating in air as he turned on Grape. Out of nowhere, Officer Woods flew up behind him, flashing his reds and blues. Chancey drifted to the side. Boy, did he hate Officer Woods!

He tried to keep his racing heart in check as he thought of a reason for not having a license. He almost cried over the fact that next week he was really going to the DMV. Boy, did he hate Officer Woods!

Officer Woods brought his tall, husky frame forward, holding on to his gun like he had clout. "License and registration," he said, knowing chances were Chancey didn't possess either of the two. He waited eagerly to see what lame excuse he would come up with.

Chancey was at a standstill, thinking how could he outfox Officer Woods. Then, he had to remember this *was* Officer Woods, the dummy who didn't have a clue about upholding the law! He didn't scare anybody! He couldn't even control his own territory! If he could, guys like he and Rondell, and anyone else who didn't play by the rules, wouldn't regulate it the way they did. And anyway, *what's the worst that could happen?* Chancey asked himself, hoping he'd get a measly citation and be on his way.

He snapped out of his thoughts and looked at Officer Woods with ease. "I don't have a license yet. I'm goin' next week…"

"Chancey Walker, right?" Officer Woods cut in. He knew who he was, but it was just part of the job. He radioed Chancey's name in to the dispatcher down at the station and tried to pick an argument while he waited on the comeback. "One of the lil' dope dealers over here at the Jordan's, right?"

"What?"

"Oh, yeah, I know your mother," Officer Woods said.

Aw hell, Chancey thought. "'Ey, cuz, I don't know what she told you, but I don't sell drugs."

"Who said she told me anything. Did I say that?"

Chancey was starting to get uncomfortable, feeling things weren't supposed to go this way. He knew what he was pulled over for, so where was his ticket? What was up with all the drug talk? "Well..." he said.

But Officer Woods cut in again. "Probation, right?" he asked.

Chancey wasn't ready for that question. "Huh?"

"You on probation?"

"Noooyea...I mean, I..."

"Don't lie to me, son. It's not like I won't find out," Officer Woods said, waving his walkie-talkie.

"Check this out, cuz," Chancey said, chuckling nervously. "Am I gettin' a ticket or what? 'Cause..."

"Hold on, homie! Stop! I asked you if you were on probation..."

"Yes! Alright? Yeah, I believe so..."

"'Cause if you are, you've just violated it," Officer Woods stated with a smile on his brown face that said he loved his job. It was the same smile he held five years ago when he located the gun Chancey tossed over the wall in Security Pacific's parking lot. "Know what it means to violate your probation?"

Of course Chancey knew what it meant. "No, but I'm sure you gon' tell me, right?"

"It means you're under arrest. What do you think about that?"

Chancey was straight-out frightened, but too heroic to show it. The thought of going back to jail was so tormenting that he wanted to put his car in drive and skid off.

Sensing Chancey's actions, Officer Woods said, "Turn your car off for me, will you?" Then he positioned himself to ruff him up if he tried anything funny.

Chancey shut off his ignition and got out, practically being pulled by the arm. He turned around and placed his hands on the car; he knew the routine.

Officer Woods helped spread his legs apart. "Don't you get tired of this, son?" he asked, while at the same time feeling the rock in Chancey's pocket. "What do we have here?"

Chancey's heart skipped ten beats. "That ain't mine!"

"Whose is it then?"

Chancey didn't say anything. Nor, did he have the guts to reveal his watery eyes. He turned away.

Officer Woods put his face in Chancey's. "Wanna tell me who it belongs to, since it's not yours?"

Chancey turned his head in the other direction. His eyes needed to blink, but he knew the smallest bat of their lids would squeeze out a tear, so he tried to hold them open, even when they burned. "Just arrest me, man!"

Officer Woods had to admit that it was weird standing before Chancey, the young man he's been studying for about a year now. Night after night, he thought about this day; the day he'd bust him and take him down for a second time. He thought about how it would be, what he would say, and how he would manhandle him to prove who the strongest *really* was. However, looking at Chancey now, he saw nothing more than a scared little boy living a grown man's life.

"Whose car is this?" Officer Woods asked.

"Mine," Chancey murmured.

"This is a pretty nice ride! I don't see you going to work everyday. How you manage to afford something like this?"

"Somebody helped me get it."

"Oh yeah? Who, Rondell?" Officer Woods smiled another I-love-my-job smile. "You young cats today are something else, you know that? You think you're the smartest thing walking, not realizing you're a bunch of fools! Now, son, if you honestly think I don't know you sell drugs…"

"What do you want me to say…that I slang rocks? Huh? Is that what you wanna hear?"

"I want you to tell the truth…"

"Yeah, well, I got the right to remain silent…"

Officer Woods laughed at Chancey.

Chancey looked at him like he didn't have good sense. "Look, man," he said, "am I under arrest or what?"

Officer Woods sighed deeply and sincerely. "I don't wanna arrest you, lil' brotha'. You don't deserve that." He was serious!

Chancey's eyes almost popped out the sockets.

"Yes, you heard me right!" the officer pledged. "See, when I was your age, I was just like you. Only, I was prettier..." When Chancey didn't crack a smile on his puzzled face, Officer Woods turned serious again. "I was on the streets with no direction in life! Fatherless! And stuck with a sister, just like you, that I felt obligated to raise. My mother was out trickin', son. Understand? You're better than I was though. See, I was selfish! My sister needed me to step up and be the mother, the father, *and* the big brother...I'm guessing like Shelly needs you to be."

Chancey was too bowled over from the words the officer spoke to even think to correct him on Setchi's name.

"We were living in poverty right here in Watts! I was involved in more shit than you could ever imagine! My sister was out trickin' in my mother's footsteps. Sixteen years old! I knew it. But I didn't care. I was too busy running wild my damn self. Probably out somewhere gettin' high and chasing all the honies!" Officer Woods started laughing at his past.

Chancey gave him a strange look, then glanced around on the sly, peeping to see if anyone was watching.

The officer continued. "By the age of nineteen, my sister was having my third nephew. And by the age of twenty-two, she was strung out on drugs..." Releasing a mournful sigh, "At the age of twenty-five, she was being buried, son! Listen to what I'm saying! Some lil' hoodlum beat 'er to death for cheating him out of five bucks! For a long time, I blamed myself for letting her down. For not being there like I should. It only took one month after she was laid to rest for me to wake up and realize the streets ain't where it's at. I went out, got my GED, then I signed up with the LAPD, *just* so I could take down all the lowlifes like the hoodlum who killed my sister..."

Chancey was stuck to the point where he couldn't take his eyes off the grief-stricken officer. Still, at the same time, he couldn't help but wonder where he was going with his sad story. Wondering what would happen next. Would he be cited? Should he say something? Give his condolences?

"If I take you in right now, son, it'll be just like letting my sister down all over again. 'Cause see, unlike me, you looks out for Shelly, seeing her off to school and whatnot...oh yeah, I see you. And I commend you for that! But now, what about you? What's it gonna take for you to wake up and realize you're traveling down a dead-end road?"

Chancey kept seeing Niecy's face. He couldn't throw her out of his mind. Officer Woods sounded a lot like her. The way he tried to school him and put him on the right track reminded him of her. He knew it was time to stop avoiding her and go see her. Then the thought of her lengthy lectures made him change his mind.

Officer Woods started talking again, but by then, Chancey's pager and cell phone was going off like mad. "I don't mean to cut you off, 'cause you know that's good how you try'da clean up the streets and everything, you know what I'm sayin'? And I'm right here wit' 'chew, man! I feel you!" He looked back at his car, keen to jump inside and drive off.

"Consider this your lucky night," Officer Woods said sternly. "But I want you to keep in mind that I see everything, Chancey. And I know everything! Matter fact, from now on, think of me as Officer God! You can't hide from me. I know about you, Rosario, Rondell…I know about all of you! How you sell your drugs out in front of the gym…right in front of those innocent kids!"

Chancey got defensive again and said something to the affect of being locked behind bars if he was really a drug dealer. He called himself being a smart-ass.

"Oh, you will be! Trust me on this one! It's just a matter of time," Officer Woods promised, chuckling. "So, with that said, and you being aware that I'm aware, I want you to see my face the next time you place another one of these in your hands." He showed Chancey the rock he took from him, threw it on the ground, and crushed it with his monster-sized black shoe. "Because I'm coming for you! You and your whole damn crew! And when I do, I want you to see Shelly's face, 'cause she's the one you'll be leaving behind to end up just like my sister did!" Officer Woods' powerful advice finally tapered off with, "Let me leave you with this here, I'm not your enemy, son. I'd rather put some knowledge in your head than put you in jail. Understand me?"

"'Preciate it."

"I hope so, because like I said, I'm not the enemy!"

Chancey started backing up.

Officer Woods starting walking forward. "Now, I want you to do yourself a favor and go get your license..."

"Yeah, yeah, for sure. I promise."

"Okay now, 'cause if I pull you over again and you don't have a license, I want you to just get out of your car and get into mine, 'cause you're going to jail, understand?"

"Understand," Chancey said. He hurried up and got in his car, taken aback by all that had happened.

"Chancey!" Officer Woods called out. He walked up and bent down at the window. "Where's Shelly now?"

"SETCHI is at her friend's house..."

"Oh, Seshi?"

"SeT-chi..."

"Oh, Setchi? Okay, I apologize..."

"Don't trip. But uh, yeah, she went to a party or somethin' at one of her lil' friends house."

"Oh, okay," Officer Woods said. He thought to tell Chancey what he saw, but wasn't sure of the level of aggression it would lead to. "You keep a close eye on her. She needs you to be there for her. And the only way to do that is to start being there for yourself!"

"You right..."

"Don't just say I'm right, son, then tomorrow I see you back on the streets."

"You won't!"

"Oh yeah, and keep all four of these tires on the ground when this car is in motion, understand?"

"No problem," Chancey said. He scurried to Rosie's house and knocked fiercely on her door. When she answered, he barged right passed her and asked, "Where's Ronnie?"

"He's gone already."

"Shit!" Chancey snapped. "I know his ass is pissed, huh?"

"Hot!"

"I bet his ass was talkin' a gang'a shit, too!"

"Where'd you go?" Rosie asked, giggling.

"Cuz! You won't believe what just happened to me."

Ronda totted in the living room. Chancey smiled and leaned toward her. She responded by reaching up for him to pick her up, which he did. He squeezed her tight, then put her back down and went in the kitchen. As he pulled his malt liquor from the bag, he started explaining his dilemma without being too explicit in front of the little one. "I'm tellin' you, Rosie, that fool knows everything!"

13

This was not his day, Rondell thought as he twirled his steering wheel to the right and entered Jordan Downs. After coasting over a speed bump or two, he twirled the wheel to the left and parked next to Chancey's Monte Carlo slanted wildly in one of the spaces.

Chancey's disappearing acts were getting old, he thought. He jumped out of his ride with a spark, placing his palm on Chancey's hood; it was warm. Mad, he called him every name in the book, figuring he had just made it back as he unlocked the trunk to his Impala and removed his satchel.

He set the alarm and walked away from his car with his eyes glued to it as if he would never see it again. He thought it was time he called his main squeeze—the woman with the four-bedroom house in Southgate, to check on his Lexus. Plus, he thought she was due for another night of his pleasure. Or maybe he was due for another night of hers. With all the stress bordering him, he was due in a major way, he thought.

He saw Stan roaming around like he was lost and called out his name.

Stan woke from his daze. "Ron, my man," he said, moving vividly as he approached him.

"Watch my car for me. I'll be right out," Rondell said.

"No problem, man, but man…" Stan's eyes turned puppy-doggish as he followed behind Rondell. He started holding himself like he was in pain.

"I know!" Rondell said. "I'ma take care of you. Just let me run in here real quick." He tapped on Rosie's door. Speaking of stress, his whole neck stiffened when Chancey unlocked it.

"I know what 'chew thinkin', but no, I was not wit' Tia!" He was all hyped up and ready to enlighten Rondell on the Officer Woods' incident.

"Let me guess. You didn't get my page, right? No, no, here it is…you was just about to call and then your phone went dead, right? That's what happened."

"Cuz, Officer Woods…"

"I don't wanna hear it!" Rondell said. He sat down on the couch and sat his bag at his feet.

Rosie said, "No, for real, Ronnie, Officer Woods…"

"Fuck it!" Chancey snapped. "Don't tell his ass shit!" He sat on the couch and continued playing one of Rosie's video games.

"That's right, fuck it! Fuck Officer Woods and fuck you, too! Shit, I'm tired of always havin' to be the one to go get the shit, drop the shit off…"

"So, you sayin' you the only one?"

"Nigga, I'm the only one! I'm doin' all this shit by myself! Droppin' shit off here, there…you ain't doin' a mothafuckin' thing, but runnin' behind that bitch!"

Chancey handled the joystick with aggression, forcing Ms. Pac Man to gobble up her pellets, while Rondell ran off at the mouth talking what Chancey thought was a bunch of nonsense. He even laughed at some of the garbage, thinking Rondell was out of his wits.

"I shouldn't give yo' ass shit! Matter fact, I ain't!" He saw the expression on Chancey's face and said, "Look who's laughin' now!"

"Don't let New Jack City get you fucked up, thinkin' you Nino Brown, nigga!"

Rondell had to smile—just a little. "Nah, I ain't playin' now! I'm serious, cuz," he said, making himself get serious.

"I am too!" Chancey yelled. He tossed the video controller aside and got up. "Matter fact, come on, let's split this shit so I can go," he said, beckoning for the bag.

Rosie saw it coming when Rondell grabbed the bag and held it away from Chancey. "Come on, y'all, please don't start! Ronda is back there sleep!"

"Nah," Rondell said, "fuck that!"

"Quit playin' wit' me about my chips, cuz!" Chancey said.

"Yo' chips?! Negro, please!" Rondell said. Really, he was going to give Chancey his portion of the money, but he wanted to teach him a lesson first. "Why should you get a penny, nigga? You ain't did shit! I was blowin' your pager *and* cell phone up! Once again, yo' ass was nowhere to be found! You supposed to be watchin' my back! But nah, you too busy watchin' that bitch's back! I'm sure you watchin' the back, 'cause ain't shit in the front!"

"He was gettin' jacked by Officer Woods, Ronnie!" Rosie yelled, stepping in.

"Don't believe his ass, Rosie!" Rondell yelled back.

"Man, I'ma tell you one more time...stop playin' wit' my mothafuckin' money!"

"I wouldn't give a fuck if you told me two more times! Shit, nigga, twenty more times! You ain't gettin'..."

Before Rondell could finish, Chancey rushed him; the bag flew from his hand.

"Stop! STOP! Y'all gon' break something! Chancey! Ronnie!" Rosie tried to part the two until she almost caught one of Chancey's swinging elbows. It barely missed her and hit the lamp by the television.

"Watch out before y'all break my lamp!" Rosie screeched.

Rondell wrestled with Chancey until he seized him up nicely and slammed him down. Chancey's back hit the hardness of the floor. He was quick when he hopped to his feet, but Rondell was quicker when he seized him up again. He lifted him and went to slam him once more. Chancey made sure he wasn't the only one tumbling this time though. He held on tight and brought Rondell with him. They both plunged hard. It sounded like a big explosion when they crashed. They rolled around and scuffled. All that was heard was heavy breathing, loud grunts, and popping sounds the floor made.

Rondell ended up on top. He had Chancey pinned to where he couldn't move. Chancey tried hard as he wiggled, growled, and pushed Rondell nowhere.

"You think you stronger than me, punk?" Rondell asked, out of breath. "You ain't stronger than me! Look at 'chew! Look! You can't even move!"

After a long struggle, Chancey boosted Rondell off—Rondell, however, will tell you he backed off. All Rosie knew was they both looked pretty exhausted.

Rondell stood up with no problems; he hid his fatigue well. Chancey worked his way up and staggered when he stood on his feet.

Rondell stayed alert. He knew he was in for a long-lasting battle; Chancey never knew when to quit. He watched Chancey bend over and rest his arms on his knees. He saw his eyes look up to meet his. Then, BAM! Chancey rushed him into the wall.

When Rondell forced Chancey down again, Rosie ran over to inspect the deepness of the hole from the impact. Her mouth opened wide, and so did her eyes. "Look what you guys did!" she yelled.

"I don't know why you keep thinkin' you stronger than me, cuz! Look at 'chew!" Rondell was telling Chancey.

"Fuck you," Chancey said, trying to, once again, raise Rondell off of him.

This went on for almost an hour. Chancey wouldn't renounce! Whenever Rondell let him up, he'd charge Rondell again. Rondell admired his bravery, though—almost to the point where he wanted to let him win. He was dead tired anyway, and ready to quit.

"What's up wit' it, cuz? We can go at this shit all night," he lied, panting and wishing Chancey would give up.

"You ain't sayin' nothin' but a word!"

"What's up, then," Rondell locked Chancey down harder with what little strength he had left. Chancey fought just as hard to break free.

Rondell pushed himself off of Chancey. They both sat on the floor, winded. Rosie stood back and observed them with her inquisitive eyes flipping from Chancey to Rondell...more so Chancey.

As Chancey started to slowly creep up, Rondell jumped up and said, "Come on, so I can drop yo' ass again. Come on!" He bobbed and weaved with his fists in a boxer's position, praying Chancey wouldn't listen to him.

Chancey practically fell on the couch. "You better be glad I'm drunk!" He laid his head back and took a couple of deep breaths to calm down.

Rondell thanked the heavens above, happy that he had to no longer fake his worn-out demeanor.

There was a knock at the door, and Rondell shuffled off to answer it. "Oh, man, I forgot…" he said when he saw Stan's face. He had to stop and catch his breath before continuing. "I forgot…hold up…I'll be out in a minute," he added, breathing erratically.

Before Stan went back to being a surveillance for Rondell's car, he peeked his head inside and threw his probing eyes around Rosie's living room. Things began to add up when he saw Chancey fighting for air on the couch. "What's going on in there?"

"Come on, Stan, not now," Rondell told him, blocking the doorway.

"Y'all can't be fighting! You guys are boys!"

"Okay, man. Okay. Point well taken…"

"I'm an O.G., man! I've been around the block a few times…"

"Okay, man…"

"Ain't nothing in the world worth losing your friendship over, ya' hear me?"

That was all Rondell needed to hear. He opened the door and welcomed Stan inside. "Tell that to this nigga!" he said.

Stan was happy to come in and share his wisdom. Before shedding some light on their situation, he started out by letting them all know he was a smart drug addict. "A woman is dangerous to a man on his paper trail," he said to Chancey.

"Thank you!" Rondell yelled.

"Especially at your age! You need to listen to that rapper…the Doggy Dog guy," Stan said.

"Snoop Doggy Dog," Rondell said.

"Yeah, Snoop Doggy Dog'll tell you…you know how it go…'I don't love…'"

"Them hoes!" Rondell chanted with Stan. He and Stan laughed

and slapped fives.

"*Aaaw…*" Rosie pouted, "y'all need to leave Chance alone." She walked over to Chancey and pinched his cheeks. "He's just in love."

Chancey frowned at her. "What?"

"That fool don't know what love is. He still wet behind the ears," Rondell interjected.

"Have you hit the skins yet?" Stan asked Chancey.

"Hell nah!" Rondell yelled. "She don't even like his ass!"

"Well, she must like something, 'cause he keeps sneaking to be with 'er," Stan said.

"Here we go with the sneakin' off shit again!" Chancey cut in.

"What else do you call it?" Rondell asked. "You didn't tell me you was leavin'…"

"Yeah, Chancey! You could of at least called and told the man. That's all we're saying," Stan said.

"I TOLD YOU I GOT PULLED THE FUCK OVER BY OFFICER WOODS!"

"Where's your ticket, then?" Rondell asked.

"He didn't give me one!"

"You been wit' his ass all this time and didn't get no ticket?" Rondell asked, doubtfully.

Stan broke in. "Maybe he…"

"Now that I think about it," Rondell interrupted, "this nigga's on probation!" Looking at Chancey, "Yo' ass would be in jail right now 'cause you don't have a license, and that's a violation!"

"Yep, that *is* true," Stan said.

"So why you sittin' up here lyin' to people?" Rondell asked.

"Man, I don't need this shit," Chancey said, patting his pockets for his keys.

"There he go, runnin' again like a lil' bitch," Rondell said.

Chancey walked out the door, heated! His face was bloodshot red. His head, pounding!

Rondell pulled some chump-change from his pocket and gave it to Stan.

"Thank you, man," Stan said and fled happily as usual.

Rondell picked up his bag, told Rosie he'd get with her later, then hurried to catch Chancey.

"What about this hole in my wall!" Rosie yelled.

Chancey was cursing to himself about Rondell, Stan, and Tia, thinking she wasn't worth the headache. At the same time, he wondered why she hadn't called him.

"Where you goin'?" Rondell asked.

Chancey ran up the stairs.

Rondell stayed below. "You know I'ma give you your money, right?"

Chancey's eyes bucked. "Oh, I know! Trust me!"

"You comin' to the crib, or stayin' here?"

"Stayin' here!" Chancey snapped. He pulled out his keys, then remembered he no longer had a key to the house; Nikki got mad at him one night and changed the locks. He banged on the door and waited. He banged again and again. "Setchi!"

Rondell smiled when no one answered.

Chancey dialed his house number on his cell phone. "I pay the rent around this mothafucka and ain't even got a fuckin' key!" He let the phone ring for a long time. "This shit don't make no fuckin' sense," he said and finally hung up.

Chancey was fuming and ready to hurt somebody as he ran back down the stairs.

Rondell moved swiftly to the side so he wouldn't get ran over. "Where you goin' now?"

"Don't worry about it!"

"Humph," Rondell grunted and rolled his eyes. He watched Chancey rave as he paced toward Kaylin's unit.

Chancey told himself not to look back, sure to see Rondell's pathetic face if he did. Soon as he hit the corner that parted Kaylin's unit from the rest, he glanced out the corner of his eye. Rondell was walking away…going back to Rosie's, he assumed.

Chancey went around to Kaylin's window and tapped lightly. It took a while for Kaylin to register the strikes, but when he did, he got out of bed, leaped over to the window, and pulled the blinds back.

"You sleep?" Chancey asked.

"Nah, I'm havin' a party! What 'chew think?" He opened his window and stood back so Chancey could climb in, then almost knocked him back outside when he heard his mother at his bedroom door. "That's Ma!" he warned in a loud whisper.

Chancey hopped down from the pane and quickly got out of dodge.

"Who are you talking to, Kaylin?" Niecy asked when she entered her son's room.

Kaylin was closing his blinds. "That was the window you heard. I opened it to get some air."

*   *   *

Chancey went back to his house and tried his luck again, thinking Niecy and her third-degree was the last thing he needed right now. He banged on the door, called out his mother's name, and then his sister's. He looked through a small opening of the drapes. Everything was still. "Shit!" he snapped, and moped back down the steps in need of a place to stay for the night.

He walked slowly toward his car with nowhere to go. He had a pocket full of money—that wasn't the problem. The problem was he had no identification, and even if he did, it would prove him to be under age and unauthorized to get a room for the night. With nothing left to do, he started up his Monte Carlo and took a ride.

*   *   *

Rondell sat his bag down and turned his heater on to warm up his place. It was chilly for a summer night, he thought. He screened through the calls on his answering machine—all nine of them. One message after another relayed a female's voice, trying to be overly erotic as she revealed her needs and wants. *Damn, bitch!* he thought, annoyed after hearing the sixth message. The last three calls were from clients talking about money, appointments—things of that nature.

He went in the kitchen, poured a glass of cherry-flavored Kool-Aid that Chancey made, took it in the living room, and turned on the TV. He moved Chancey's clothes and other belongings on the couch when he descended into his plush, black leather. No Chancey to clown around with tonight, he miserably thought and sighed, jealous that Chancey was in Kaylin's comfort zone. That's where he always ran whenever Rondell pissed him off. Sometimes, Rondell wished Kaylin didn't exist. *Who would that nigga run to then?* he wondered. To Rondell, it was all about power. And he thrived off the fact that he had more of it. *That nigga needs me! He can't even buy his own beer!* Rondell smacked his lips grudgingly over the fact that Chancey somehow established a good rapport with Hasan down at Grape Supermarket. *I should turn Hasan's faggot-ass in for sellin' alcohol to minors!*

After flipping from channel to channel, he discovered there was nothing on cable. He took the remote and zapped the power off to his big screen, then unzipped his satchel. He took out all the money, set aside a small amount for Rosie, then split the rest down the middle. *Lil' crybaby,* he thought as he stuck Chancey's half under the pillows of the couch. *Up there actin' like somebody want his money! I don't need his money! I shouldn't give his ass shit though, just on G.P.! Runnin' up on somebody like he doin' somethin'. I see what I'ma haf' to do—I'ma haf' to start knockin' fools out and lettin' niggas know! Everybody wanna think I'm a busta, but they just don't know! I don't fight 'cause I don't like to get my hands dirty! Not because I'm scared of a nigga! I don't fear no man! And Chance walkin' around like he hard...somebody gon' bust a cap in his ass one of these days, watch!* Rondell put the brakes on his thoughts. Then, *I should call over there.* He got his cordless and started to dial Kaylin's number. *I ain't callin' over there, fuck it! Lil' mama's boy'll prolly get in trouble if the phone rings this late!*

Rondell knew Chancey was mad at him and more than likely wouldn't answer his cell phone, so the thought to try and call it didn't even cross his mind. He sat his phone on the coffee table. *What time is it?* he wondered. *I should call Trina and see about my car. I hope she parked my shit in the garage. Damn, Anita called me six times tonight! That bitch is sprung! I should'a never let her taste my shit.* Rondell smiled and gripped his crouch. *Bitches be goin' crazy!* he boasted. *Chancey's stupid! That nigga got bitches, too. Fine bitches! Not as fine as mine though. But still, they cool. And he runnin' around after this ol' frail, funny-lookin'-ass, bitch! She skinny, got big lips...she got some nice lips though.* Rondell pictured the fullness of Tia's lips. *Man, fuck that bitch! She startin' to fuck wit' my money, and I ain't havin' that shit!*

Rondell thought of a way he could get rid of Tia. Just as he came up with his master plan, he heard the locks on his front door being unlatched.

*   *   *

Setchi always felt dirty when Curt took her to the Magic Carpet Motel. Its name fit to a "T", she thought—the fine particles extracting from the carpet whenever something made contact with it, *was* magical, she thought! And soon as they got there, she made Curt take his socks off for her to put on, so her feet wouldn't touch the dusty, blue rug.

As she got out the shower, she wished he would take her somewhere decent for a change. Somewhere that at least had a complimentary bottle of lotion in the bathroom. "I'ma be ashy!" she yelled.

Curt walked to the bathroom and stood in the doorway. "What's wrong, beautiful?"

"I need some lotion!" Setchi said, frowning at the paleness of her bright skin. She took her towel and secured it around her body when Curt began to step toward her.

Curt pulled her in his arms. "You don't need a thing, baby-girl. Absolutely nothing!" He went to undo the knot in Setchi's towel and she reacted quickly.

"You are one of the most shyest eighteen-year-olds I've ever met in my life," Curt said when Setchi clutched her towel and withdrew from him. "Come in here and lay down. I'm going to see if I have some lotion in my car."

Setchi was an emotional wreck. She bubbled with excitement. Yet, at the same time, fear raced through her veins, dreading what Chancey would do if he ever found out where she was. She'd been calling home all night, but there was never an answer, which was a good indication that he wasn't there. She figured he wouldn't be. He was just talking a bunch of baloney as always. The only time she really saw him was when he came home in the mornings to see her off to school. Other than that, most of his nights were spent over Rondell's house.

She reached over to the nightstand and picked up the phone to dial home again. Still, no answer. *Yes*, she happily thought. It was almost two in the morning. If he wasn't home by now, he wasn't coming home, she thought.

She wondered what was taking Curt so long. Her skin was beginning to shrivel up like a prune. He was just going to his car, which was only a couple of rooms down, for crying out loud! She wrapped the tasteless, white towel around her, covering as many important parts as she could, then stepped outside of the motel room.

"Curtis Moore! Why, you son-of-a-bitch!" Setchi heard a woman shout.

She looked approximately two rooms down and saw Curt holding off a mature-looking woman by the shoulders.

"Is that her, Curtis? Tell me! Is it? Say something, you son-of-a-bitch!"

Curtis Moore? Setchi thought his name was Curt Jackson.

"Go back inside, Setchi," Curt said.

Setchi slowly backed her way through the door of her motel room as she stared in the woman's face. The woman was crying. Her face was full of hurt. Her attire was scraggly as if it were pieced together. Setchi thought her hat, sweatshirt, pajama pants, and slippers were something she would throw on when she had to make a quick run somewhere.

Setchi didn't too much concern herself with the unknown woman's clothing though. It was the anguish in her eyes that had her wedged. Who was she? And why was Curt's face and neck scratched up?

She poked her head outside. She was scared to death, but too involved to close the door.

"Go back inside, Setchi!" Curt said. This time he yelled.

"Naw," the woman said, "you come on back out here!" She started kicking off her slippers.

Setchi quickly slammed the door and locked it.

"Come on, baby, calm down," she heard Curt tell the woman.

Baby! That word brought tears to Setchi's eyes, along with a shaking spell that she couldn't control. She lifted one of her trembling hands to steal a peek through the curtains and watched it all unfold right in front of her eyes. There Curt was begging to save his marriage!

"I don't believe you!" the woman yelled. "That's the girl on the picture I found in your wallet! Why, you son-of-a-bitch!" She started hitting and scratching Curt again. "We have a home, Curtis! A marriage! What about our kids? Huh? Did you stop and think about them while you were out with this little girl? How old is she anyway, Curtis? Answer me, you son-of-a-bitch!"

"Baby...beautiful..."

"Don't beautiful me!"

Setchi pushed the curtains back, just slightly, to get a wider view when she saw the wife of the motel owner, an Hispanic lady, run out. The Hispanic lady was enraged and threatening to call the police if the fighting didn't stop.

"Call 'em!" Curt's wife yelled. "And while you're at it, tell 'em there's a kid occupying one of your rooms!"

"Come on, Tif'. Now, baby, listen..."

"You get away from me! You're one sick bastard, you know that?" Curt's wife turned to the wife of the motel owner and said, "He's a sick son-of-a-bitch! A child molester! There's a young girl in your motel room! Do you understand what I'm saying? Do you speak English?"

Setchi thought the lady couldn't have, because she kept standing there yelling, "Llamada a policía! Llamada a policía!"

"Don't be ridiculous, honey," Curt said, still trying to reason with his wife.

"Oh, you close your mouth! Don't say shit! You can't even please a real woman! You have to go out and get a kid to try and satisfy with your two-inch thriller! That was real smart, Curtis!"

"Baby, please let me explain."

"The only thing you'll be explaining is why your twenty-seven-year-old ass is broke, busted, and disgusted to your little fling in there, 'cause when I get back home, I'm throwing all your shit OUT, son-of-a-bitch! I'm gonna get me a good lawyer..."

"Baby, please! Wait!" Curt watched helplessly as his wife sped off in her gray Ford Taurus. He pitifully walked up to the window where Setchi was. She watched him with tears flooding her eyes. When he put his hands on the glass, she rammed the curtains shut.

"Salga de aquí!" the owner's wife yelled. She was telling Curt to get away from her motel.

"Back to you!" Curt told her as he got in his car.

"Ándale!"

Curt started his ignition. "Andalay yourself!" he said, burning rubber as he drove off.

Setchi pulled the curtains back once more. Everyone was gone. "What now?" she asked herself, boohooing like a baby. She didn't have a dime to her name. All the money she had was turned over to Nikki. *And for what?* she angrily thought. To find out the man she was going to marry was already married? She snatched up the phone and called her house again. "Please, God!" she prayed while she waited. After the fourth ring, there was silence. Someone picked up the phone. She could tell by all the fumbling noise she heard in the background. She was scared to say anything just in case it was her brother trying to trick her. So, she hung up. Minutes later, she called back to find the line busy. She hung up, waited a minute or two, called back—the line was still busy.

Setchi's tears began to outrun each other down her face. She was stranded at a crummy motel with no money. What's worst, Curt only paid for a two-hour stay, which meant she had to vacate in less than twenty minutes. She picked up the phone to call Kashaun, then thought it was too late and hung up. She tried her house again—still busy. *Damn*, she thought.

Setchi walked over to the window and looked out of it, praying long and hard that maybe, just maybe, the folks at the front desk wouldn't remember the remaining balance owed on the room. Just as she said, "Amen," the phone rang. The ringing made her almost jump out of her towel.

She was hesitant on answering it, thinking something crazy like, *What if that's Chancey?* She let the phone ring almost ten times before she picked it up and said, "Hello."

"Your time is up," a male's voice told her. He was firm and to the point.

Setchi started to panic until she detected his Spanish accent. "Excuse me?" she asked.

"Either you pay for whole night, or you go!"

"Is there any way I can pay you in the morning?"

"No, we can not do that!"

"I don't have any money and I don't have a car," Setchi cried.

"You don't get out, I call 'de police!"

"No! Okay? No. I'm packing up now."

Setchi took the front of her wild hair and tied it toward the back, out of her face. She threw on her sweat suit, grabbed her things, and left the key on the bed. As she was leaving, the owner was coming to inspect the cleanliness of his room. She didn't give him the pleasure of looking his way.

Outside it was freezing. The cold air blew goose bumps all over her body. Her nose was red and now, running. She sped up her stride to warm up. She walked a few blocks up Imperial and darted across the street before the light changed. She didn't see Officer Woods pass her until she heard his brakes squeak when he stopped. She looked back and saw him swerve a "U" at the light. Before she could think, he had swung up on the side of her.

Officer Woods shone his spotlight in Setchi's face. All she could do was stand still and listen to her pounding heartbeat.

"Where you headed?"

"Home," Setchi said. The coldness made her voice quiver. Her body shuddered like a leaf.

"Need a lift?"

"Uh…" she muttered, looking around.

"Hop in," Officer Woods said. "It's not a good idea for you to walk around out here like this."

Setchi got in.

"Where's your friend? The gentleman you was with earlier?"

Setchi gave the officer a surprised look. She was too afraid to answer him. Fortunately, he didn't press the issue.

The ride home was a smooth one up until Officer Woods made a right onto 99th Place. Setchi liked to have grabbed his steering wheel when she said, "I can get out here!"

"Oh no, it's okay. I'll drop you off in front. What building are you in?"

"Thirty-seven," she lied. It was funny how Officer Woods pulled up at building thirty-six—he was the only one amused though.

Setchi looked around nervously, then quickly jumped from the police car. She started running toward building thirty-six.

"You're forgetting your purse!"

Setchi hysterically turned to approach Officer Woods' car.

"I thought you were in building thirty-seven."

"Oh, did I say that? I meant thirty-six," Setchi said as she grabbed her purse.

Officer Woods smiled and shook his head. *What a shame*, he thought. "Have a good night," he said.

Setchi ran to her residence like an escapee. She must have dropped her purse at least three times. Officer Woods laughed at her. She rushed up the stairs, said a quick prayer, and begged the Lord to listen this time before she unlocked the door and entered.

She moved stealthily toward her mother extended across the couch; Nikki was so out of it that she looked dead. Setchi took the phone out of her hand without waking her, and hung it up. She was clever, showing her true talent when she went into the room, moving about silently and artfully. She did a double take to look at Chancey's bed, and cried out, "Thank you, Jesus!" at its emptiness.

14

Man, if this fool get up and say somethin' to me this morning... Chancey stretched out, then turned to lie on his side. *I wasn't gon' even come here, but shit, Nikki's punk-ass wouldn't get up and open the door! I know she was home! Prolly in there fucked up! That's why I'll be glad when I get eighteen,* Chancey thought. *The first thing I'ma do is get my own place!*

Chancey paused and scratched his scalp. *I gotta wash my hair today,* he said to himself, wondering what time it was. He strained to see the clock across the room, but couldn't really make out which numbers the hands were pointing to. He smelled the marijuana blazing in the back and figured it must be around seven—the time Rondell usually got out of bed.

Chancey sat up on the couch, then took his money from under the pillows and counted it; it was the right amount. *It better be the right amount! Talkin' about 'I ain't givin' you shit'. I wish that fool would! I'll beat his ass like Ice T beat Wesley Snipes in New Jack City! That's why his ass bowed down when I walked in last night. He know what time it is! Busta-ass nigga!*

His pager kept alerting him with a single beep that someone had paged him. He finally picked it up from the coffee table and saw he had four pages, all of which were from Kaylin.

"Want a grilled cheese sandwich?" Rondell asked as he went into the kitchen.

Chancey ignored him and made a call to Kaylin, explaining why he didn't come back last night. "I didn't feel like waitin' on Ma to go to sleep. Shit, it was cold out there," he said. He cut their conversation short and told Kaylin he would be over before Niecy got out of church. Then he went in the kitchen. The smell of the grilled cheese sautéing was alluring. He stood over the stove and watched hungrily as Rondell flipped the sandwich over and over.

"You want one?" Rondell asked.

"Is it some syrup left?"

"Should be. I just bought some," Rondell said, checking through the cabinets. He sat a bottle of Mrs. Butterworth on the table.

"Yeah, make me one," Chancey said, walking over to the table and sitting down. "Please," he added when Rondell gave him that look—the make-your-own look!

"Byrd called last night," Rondell said, giving Chancey the sandwich he was fixing when it was done. "I hope you got your money ready, 'cause he said he was able to get the kilo for us after all," he told Chancey as he put some more butter in his skillet and prepared a new sandwich to fry.

"How much he lettin' it go for?"

"Sixteen."

"Damn! He can't work wit' us?"

"It's drought season, cuz. That's just how it is sometimes," Rondell said. "It's only, what, eight a piece, right?"

Chancey was wordless. He poured Mrs. Butterworth in a bowl and dipped the corner of his sandwich in it.

"Why you so quiet?" Rondell asked. "Ah hell, don't tell me you let Tito take you all in, nigga!"

"You real funny," Chancey said, holding a straight face. "On the real though, I don't know if I'm goin' in with you this time."

Rondell immediately withdrew from the food he was cooking and walked over to the table. "What!" he said with a conduct that showed signs of violence if Chancey didn't change his answer.

"I ain't drunk now, cuz! I will have you touching everythang up in this mothafucka!" Chancey responded.

"Yeah, you prolly believe that shit, too! You know what…I was just thinkin' about this shit last night—you don't see me checkin' enough fools! I've been too soft with niggas lately—you prolly think I'm a punk or somethin'…"

"You *are* a punk."

"Fuck you, nigga! I ain't no punk! You got me mixed up with the next fool! Don't think you can say whatever the fuck you wanna say to me, and I'ma just walk away with my tail between my legs!"

Chancey saw Rondell was more hurt than anything. They've argued like this for as long as they've known each other, and never has Chancey seen Rondell this defensive. "Why you takin' the shit all personal like you never said nothing fowl to me before? You say shit to me, too…"

"Nah, fuck that! I look out for you, cuz! And you wanna talk to me like I'm a stepchild or somethin'! I let you have a key to my house! I'm the one that got you that jeep! That shit is in my name!"

"I could'a got it in my name! You wanted to get it in your name!"

"Nigga, you can't do shit without me! You just a teenager! How you gon' get a twenty-somethin'-thousand-dollar car in your name? With no job at that!"

"You ain't got a job either, nigga!"

"So what! They don't know that! As far as they know, I'm fully legit."

"You mean Trina's fully legit! If it wasn't for her lyin' for you, you wouldn't have shit in yo' name either!"

"That's okay though. Quit bein' a hater, nigga! You wish you did have a woman that was a supervisor! At least I *am* over eighteen! Shit, Trina can give me a verification slip sayin' I make twenty dollars an hour if she wanted to. It ain't like people won't believe 'er! The most she can say you make is minimum wage!"

Chancey was silenced.

"Yeah, yo' ass is quiet now, huh? You can't even buy no alcohol without me! You can't gamble! You can't do shit!"

"How you gon' act like I'm just needin' you so much? You need me, too!"

"What I need you for?" Rondell asked as if the world was already his.

"You need me to have your back! Bring you clients..."

"I don't need you to bring me clients."

"Whatever, cuz! You ain't *never* had this much business before! Now you wanna sit up here and act like you don't need me!"

"I had people buyin' from me before you even got out."

"You didn't have *half* the people you got now! Wasn't nobody fuckin' with you! You too funny-style! And if it wasn't for me, they *still* wouldn't be fuckin' with you!"

"Ah, whatever!" Rondell said, fanning Chancey away. Then, he almost broke his neck to get to the burning grilled cheese sandwich. He snatched the scorching skillet from the stove. His sandwich was fried to a pitch-black crisp. He went to grab some more bread, but the plastic only had hulls in it. He looked over at Chancey, and Chancey shoved the last bit of his sandwich down his throat.

Rondell took his overcooked food to the wastebasket and scraped off the burnt parts with a butter knife.

"Ugh! I know you not finna eat that."

"*Shid*...nigga, I'm 'bout to tear this shit up!" Rondell said. He wasn't lying either. He ate the sandwich up like it was going out of style.

*   *   *

Tia lost hours of sleep last night from thinking about Chancey. It wasn't even quite eight o'clock in the morning yet, and there she was wide-awake with Chancey still roving around in her head. She could see his beautiful features just as clear as day. His eyes were staring her down. *How gorgeous*, she thought as she lied in her bed, reminiscing on yesterday.

She didn't mean to hang up in his face last night, but the sound of his strong voice made her freak out. And anyway, she only called to see if she had the right number.

She looked down at the phone beside her bed and smiled. Then she thought, *Hmmm...should I?* Feeling prankish, she picked up the phone and dialed Chancey's number, intending to hear his voice and then hang up.

"Hello," a sleepy voice answered.

"Hi. Who am I speaking with?" Tia asked.

"Setchi," Setchi said, sounding gullible.

She's young, Tia thought and began to prey off her immaturity. "Is Chancey there?"

"Unh-unh. He's over Rondell's."

"Do you know what time he left?"

"He been there since last night—that's where he stay! Who's this?"

"Ti...ammy...Tammy. I'm just a good friend of his. Do you know how I can get in touch with him?" Tia asked, then kicked herself for sounding so stupid. *If I'm such a good friend, I should know how to get in touch with him. That was stupid, Tia,* she thought.

"You can call over Rondell's house, or call him on his cell phone...that's if he'll answer it. You got his cell number?"

"Uh...I got it written down somewhere. Can you just give it to me so I won't have to look for it?"

Setchi started reading off Chancey's mobile number. "You want Rondell's, too?"

"Yeah, that's fine."

Setchi started reading off Rondell's home number, then the number to his cellular.

By the time Tia hung up with Setchi, she had all of Rondell's numbers, along with Kaylin's home number, and the best time to call for Chancey. She knew Chancey's mother's name, how many siblings he had, his date of birth, and all his hangout spots. *That was like stealing candy from a baby,* Tia thought as she dialed the number to Rondell's home. When a male's voice answered, she quickly hung up.

Tia knew right off the voice belonged to Rondell by the way he said hello. His tone was so smooth and even—the only thing she really liked about him, besides his gray eyes. Okay, he was handsome all across the board, Tia felt, but his personality was about as boring as her history class. And it took more than just good looks to woo her.

Getting up the nerve to call and talk to Chancey was becoming a pain in Tia's rear. She wanted to hear his voice so bad that she would pay somebody to get her digits to him. He would have called her by now, she figured, wishing she had given him her number when he asked for it.

Suddenly, Tia was struck with a bright idea. She picked up the phone and called Setchi back.

"Hello."

"Can I speak to Chancey?" Tia asked in a camouflaged voice.

"He's not here," Setchi said.

"Can you tell him Tia called?"

"Tammy?"

"No, Tee-ya."

"Oh, okay."

"Let me give you my number," Tia said and smiled.

Setchi lugged herself out of bed for a pen and some paper. "Okay, what is it?"

Tia began calling off her telephone number.

*   *   *

Chancey and Rondell's conversation was rudely interrupted when Chancey's cell phone started to ring. He answered it and got hung up on.

"Who keep playin' on the phone?" Rondell asked.

"It gotta be somebody we both know, 'cause they call you one minute, then me, the next," Chancey said.

They sat still and waited on Rondell's phone to ring. Sure enough, his cordless started to chime. "Don't answer it," Chancey said.

"I ain't."

"That's prolly Setchi's ass actin' stupid!"

"Anyway, back to what you was sayin," Rondell said.

"I'm sayin', people like fuckin' wit' me 'cause I'm cool! You, though? You too stuck up. That's what *errrrbody* be sayin'!"

"Mothafuckas just jealous, that's all! I don't trip off shit like that, cuz. That's petty shit to me! Nigga's prolly mad 'cause I fucked they bitch," Rondell said, smiling. "And don't act like you don't know what I'm talkin' about!"

"What? If you try'na be funny 'cause you fucked Tomika…"

Rondell laughed like he was out of his mind.

"You ain't hurtin' nobody! Fuck Tomika! Shit, she prolly gave you somethin'!"

"And Pam prolly gave you somethin'!" Rondell retorted.

"I never fucked Pam," Chancey said seriously.

"That ain't what 'Mik said."

"Man, fuck Tomika! How you gon' listen to what her black ass gotta say?"

Just then, Chancey's cell phone rang. "Hello. Alright, I'll be there in a minute," he said and hung up.

"Who was that? Kaylin?"

"Yeah," Chancey said, rinsing the syrup out of his bowl before setting it in the sink with all the other piled-up dishes.

"So, we gon' do this, right?"

"I'll think about it," Chancey said as he gathered up his things.

"Cuz, I'm tellin' you, Officer Woods don't have shit on us! Trust me! If he did, he damn sho' wouldn't be tellin' you about it! You can believe all that 'I know everything' bullshit if you want to. But me? I ain't worried at all! Nigga, I'm chillin' like a villain!"

"What about my license? I gotta get that with the quickness!"

"I know! I said I'ma take you down there on Monday. I'ma help you study and everything!"

Chancey looked at Rondell and stroked his chin as he thought about some things.

"Now what?" Rondell asked.

"Nothing. I'm just thinkin' about...shit...about Officer Woo..."

"Cuz, fuck that nigga! Don't even worry about him! Alright? His ass ain't gon' do shit! If he was, he would'a already did it by now! He's just try'na scare you, that's all! He don't never say nothin' to me, 'cause he know!"

"Well, all I wanna do is get my license, then I'm straight. 'Cause at least that way, I'll feel comfortable when I'm drivin', you know what I'm sayin'?"

"Yeah, and quit ridin' dirty," Rondell said.

"I know. That was an accident though."

"Yeah, but look what that accident almost cost you!"

"Yeah, you right."

"I'm always right!"

"I don't know about all that," Chancey said and smiled.

"Serious though, you need to start listenin' to me, cuz. I won't tell you nothin' wrong. Like when I try'da tell you about Tito..."

"Her name is Tia, nigga!"

"Whatever. She ain't for you, cuz...not right now. We try'na make it to the top, not fall in love. And I don't know about you, but I'm try'na touch the fuckin' sky! Remember what I told you last year? I said, 'give us a year', remember? It's been a lil' over a year, and look! We went from slangin' rocks in front of the gym, to sellin' ounces! Now, we're about to get this key...that's the most we ever got! You can't tell me we not finna blow up! *Shid*, nigga, I'm try'na get the fuck up out the ghetto! And you comin' wit' me, if I gotta drag yo' ass like this..." Rondell started moving around like he was dragging someone by the feet.

Chancey laughed. He didn't know how to explain it, but in a strange way, Rondell gave him something to believe in. He gave him guidance and financial assurance. He was the icon of his success...a father figure.

Maybe one more sell wouldn't hurt, Chancey thought as he looked for his keys. "Alright, then, I'ma hook up with you later."

"Alright," Rondell said and opened his palm to Chancey. Chancey gave him a firm handshake. Then they both gave each other a male hug—the kind where you lean in at the shoulder and give each other a ruff embrace.

"So, I'ma see you back here at five, right?" Rondell asked.

"Yeah," Chancey said.

"FIVE O'CLOCK!"

"Five o'clock!"

"Alright," Rondell said. "I'ma go call Byrd and let 'em know what's up."

*   *   *

Sundays were always dull to Tia. Nothing exciting going on, just all the inquiring about what to wear to school on Monday. Had she known Chancey wasn't going to return her call, she would have gone to church with her mother.

Setchi told Tia that Chancey usually came home in the morning for a quick check-in, before he was off again. If this were true, Tia's phone should have been ringing off the hook three hours ago. It was already noon by her time. She was beginning to assume that his sister didn't give him the number.

Tia had hoped to be engaged in a deep conversation with Chancey by then, while she had some privacy. Why did she have to be an only child, she thought, feeling like her mother needed to spread some of her attention elsewhere. *Do this, Tia! Do that! Sit up straight! It's no such thing as 'ain't'!*

Tia began straightening up her room to release her frustrations. She thought with her luck, Chancey would probably call as soon as her mother walked through the door. She glanced at her mirrored-clock nailed across her wall and frowned at the big hand on the twelve and little hand on the one. "Welp, she's outta church," she sighed. "At least she can't say nothing about my room being dirty!"

Tia's stuffed animals were sitting neatly at the head of her pink canopy bed. She popped a Whitney Houston tape in her cassette player and started singing "Saving All My Love for You" with the gifted songstress. She was into it, out-singing Whitney on the high notes. Her phone was practically screaming in the background. She thought she heard it, but wasn't sure. After the fourth ring, she turned her radio down and stood still. On the fifth ring, she answered delightfully. "Hello."

"Tia?"

"Oh, hey, Carla," Tia said, sounding down. She flopped on her bed and asked, "What's up?"

"Nothing. What are you doing?"

"Nothing."

"Mmm. You goin' to school tomorrow?"

Tia was bored with Carla's dialogue already. Any other time, the small talk would have been okay, but now, Tia's mind was somewhere on a secluded island with a man named Chancey. "Yep," Tia said stiffly.

"What are you wearing?"

There was a loud tick. "Was that your phone or mine?"

"I think it was yours," Carla said.

Tia enforced her two-way feature when she clicked her phone over to answer her other call. The nervous energy was trying to creep up on her, but she wouldn't let it. There was no time for that, she thought. All morning long, she'd been waiting on this moment, the moment she would prove to Chancey once and for all that she wasn't goofy and silly. There was no way she was going to let a bunch of obnoxious giggling, stupid questions, and childlike answers make a fool out of her twice!

"Hello."

"Can I speak to Tia?" Chancey asked.

Oh my God! Tia thought, standing up with inflated eyes. She started hyperventilating to the point where she felt dizzy. She gripped the phone with both hands and raised it toward the ceiling to silently give praise before opening her mouth. Cautious not to let him hear the tremor in her voice, she said, "This is her."

"What's up?"

"What's up?"

"You," Chancey said. "What took you so long to call me? You had a nigga waitin' all day yesterday!"

Tia giggled femininely and in her sweetest baby-talk voice, she said, "I'm sorry."

"Oh, so you think I'm supposed to bow down 'cause you talkin' all sweet 'n shit?"

Tia tried not to overdo it when she let out another womanly giggle. "I know you're not try'na be hard! Don't get yo' cap peeled, okay?"

Chancey laughed at Tia's slang talk. "Cap peeled, huh?"

Again, Tia giggled. She couldn't help it!

"So what's up though? Is it cool to come see you?"

"Why you wanna come see me?" Tia asked, then frowned. *Stupid question number one!*

"Go on wit' that," Chancey said and giggled. "We not finna go through this again."

"Go through what?" Tia asked in a sexy tone. "You can't tell me why you wanna come see me?"

"I don't know why," Chancey said. "You always givin' a nigga a hard time, you sassy as hell, and you talk a lotta shit..."

Tia roared with laughter.

"'Ey," Chancey said, quieting her hilarity, "you still stay on Kalmia?"

"Yeah, why?" Tia asked.

"'Cause, I'm finna come take you to lunch."

Pushy, Tia thought, loving every bit of his assertiveness.

"Yellow house, right?"

"Yeah, but I'll be over my friend's house. She lives a few houses down." Tia started reading off Carla's address. "I'll be standing outside so you can see me. Just call me here at my house before you leave."

"Alright, T."

He called me T! How cute, Tia thought, smiling as she hung the phone up.

Talk about "jump for joy"—Tia was jumping so high, she could lay hands on the ceiling. She ran to her closet and threw things around like a madwoman.

* * *

"Tell me again, Setchi!" Chancey demanded.

"I told you three times already, dang! How many times you want me to say it?"

"Just tell me one last time."

Setchi sighed, looked at her brother with provoked eyes, then said, "I said, 'Hello', and she was like, 'Is Chancey there?' I said, 'No, may I take a message?' She was like, 'Can you tell him Tammy'…I mean, 'Tia called?'…Somebody name Tammy called, too!"

"Tammy?" Chancey frowned. "Who the hell is Tammy?"

"I don't know! She said she was your friend."

"How did she sound?"

Setchi screamed out her frustrations.

"Well, you sure she said Tammy?"

"Chancey," Setchi said, annoyed to death, "you gettin' on my nerves."

Chancey didn't say anything else for a minute. Then, "So, Tia was like, 'Give 'em my number'?" he asked, smiling at the paper with Tia's number on it.

Setchi almost cursed. "You just called her, didn't you?! Where else you think I got the number from?"

Chancey smiled, showing all his teeth. "I knew she liked a nigga! She was just try'na play hard to get."

Whatever, Setchi thought. She was in a bad mood.

"That's about to be Mrs. Walker, watch and see."

"What happened to the other girl? I thought she was gon' be Mrs.

Walker."

"Nah, I was only out for one thang wit' her. You talkin' about Monique, right?"

"Whatever her name was," Setchi said.

"Yeah, Monique." Chancey started chuckling. "I was messin' wit' her when I was wit' Tomika."

Setchi's heart shattered. Her nose expanded five inches in width. "So, you used her? Had her thinking you really liked her, when all you wanted to do was to get in her pants?"

"Yep!" Chancey said, smiling boastfully. "It only took one week, too, then I was tearin' that shit up!" He was laughing until he saw Setchi's opposition. "I mean, not like that, but, you know..."

"No, I *don't* know."

"Monique was just a quick hit. You know, a wham-bam-thank you-ma'am!"

Setchi held a look of blankness on her face. Her inner voice was asking lots of questions. She was thinking so much, her brain ached. She sighed, inaudibly wondered, and then asked, "Chancey, why do guys cheat?"

Chancey was brushing his hair in the mirror at the time. He had just washed it and moisturized it with some Blue Magic hair grease. "I can't be goin' nowhere lookin' to the curb," he said, molding his tiny curls close to his scalp.

"What makes a guy cheat on a girl, Chancey?"

"I don't know," Chancey said quickly and uncaringly as he sat down and commenced to tying his shoelaces.

Setchi knew he knew. He just wasn't paying attention to her. "You don't know what?" she asked, knowing that would make him take heed.

Chancey's expression showed how clueless he was when he looked at Setchi and waited for her to fill him in.

"*I said*," she sighed, "why do men cheat?!"

Chancey still didn't get it. Well, he got it, but he wondered why she was asking.

"If a guy cheats on you, then he don't love you, huh?"

"Right. I mean, not always. Why?" Chancey asked, concerned. Very concerned!

"I just wanna know."

"Some guys just cheat to be cheatin', you know what I'm sayin'? Others just...shit...I don't know..."Chancey attended to his shoes again.

This isn't going anywhere, Setchi thought. "You not makin' sense, Chance."

"Well, shit, I can't speak for the next man." He could, but his mind was too occupied with what restaurant he would take Tia to.

"How do you know when a guy really likes you, then?"

"You should know that, shouldn't you? Shit, let 'chew tell it, Curt's punk-ass really likes you, don't he?"

"Chancey," Setchi said, warning him not to get started. "I'm not asking for me. I'm asking for Kashaun!"

"What time you leave Kashaun's house last night, Setchi? And who brought you home?"

"*See*," Setchi whined. "When you ask me something, I answer it, but when I ask you something, you can't never give me a straight answer. That ain't even right!"

Shit, Chancey thought as he got up and went over to sit next to Setchi on her bed. "When a dude likes a girl, he'll be open wit' 'er, you know? Like, he won't just give her his beeper number. She'll have the beeper, house, cell, work...he'll bring her to his crib, meet her parents, shit like that..."

Chancey was putting it out there for Setchi. And although she had asked for it, she was wishing now that he would close his mouth. She sighed and held her pillow tight, relating to what the old people say about the truth; hurt was an understatement—the truth was kicking her ass!

*   *   *

It's a good thing Tia couldn't find anything to wear in a hurry. She would have been pretty upset, being dressed and having to wait on Chancey forever. She stood and stared at herself in the framed mirror on her bedroom door. She loved that mirror! It emulated her from head to toe, not like the one on her dresser, where the lower part of her body was always cut off.

She didn't have time to stand there and wonder if she should wear the black and white shirt in place of the all-black one she had on with her white Guess jeans. It was going on two o'clock, and her mother would be home any minute.

Tia thought to call and let Carla in on the game plan—Chancey would pick her up from Carla's house instead of hers. "Carla!!" she yelled as she worriedly dialed Carla's number. When Carla picked up, Tia let loose. "I forgot about you, girl! Sorry 'bout that, but guess who that was? Chancey! He's on his way over here. I'ma have him meet me at your house, okay? Girl, I am so nervous! I got on my white Guess jeans and a black top. You think that will look okay? Tell me how you think these pants look when you see 'em, too. Girl, I am so nervous! You finally get to meet him! And I want you to be honest and tell me what you think about him…"

"When's he coming?" Carla asked, dominating her way into the conversation.

"Should be on his way. He said he would call me when he was leaving out the door." Tia's phone clicked. "I hope that's him. Hold on." She answered her other line and returned seconds later. "Girl, that was him! I'm on my way!"

Tia hung up as Carla was saying goodbye. She grabbed her purse, turned off Whitney, and wrote her mother an I'll-be-home-soon note before spurting out the door. She crossed the street and ran south on Kalmia to the third house down from hers. Carla was waiting in the doorway.

"Those jeans fit cute," Carla said.

"What about my hair? Does it look okay like this?" Tia asked, referring to the French roll she had secured neatly with hairpins. "Maybe I should'a put some bangs in the front, huh?"

"Yeah, to hide that fo'head!" Carla laughed. "Nah, I'm just playin'. It's cute."

Tia stepped up the steps to Carla's porch and stood in the doorway with her. They talked about Chancey, of course. Carla was asking a bunch of questions about their plans for the day.

Then, the sounds of an approaching car hushed them. Tia hid behind Carla. "Is it him? Is it him?"

Carla's eyes narrowed as she observed the black jeep coming their way. "Does he have a black jeep?"

"Yep!" Tia smiled.

The black jeep slowed in front of Carla's house. Tia stepped around Carla so Chancey could see her.

"Standin' outside, huh?" Chancey said with a grin. He placed his jeep in park and turned the motor off before stepping out like he owned everything around him.

"I am outside," Tia said, smiling as she and Carla emerged from the front door.

"Hurry up and introduce me," Carla kept whispering and nudging Tia's shoulder as they made their way to Chancey.

"You look cute," Chancey said, turning Tia around by the hips to get an overall view. "Guess? You think you doin' somethin', huh?"

Tia laughed embarrassingly. "Forget 'chew!"

Chancey flipped his impressive eyes over at Carla. "What's up, Carla?"

Carla was baffled. "How'd you know my name?"

"'Cause Tia said she was goin' to Carla's house," Chancey said, coming across as being very outgoing and charming when he smiled at her.

Why did he have to go and make Carla cream in her panties like that? Hypnotizing her with his eyes like that? He had her so engrossed that she couldn't turn away. She hoped no one noticed.

Rondell was good-looking, Carla thought, but he knew it, which made him, well, still good-looking to her. However, Tia was right; his arrogant personality did take away from his attractiveness. Chancey, though? Now he was breathtaking! Carla could see why his presence kept Tia spinning out of control. Just looking at him now, in his black Raiders shirt, black jeans, and boots, had *her* head whirling! And if he gazed at her one more time with those tempting eyes of his, she was going to fall to the ground!

"I like your jeep," Tia said, walking around it to inspect its perfection. "This is nice."

"Thank you," Chancey said.

"Don't think you got it going on," Tia told Chancey, smiling.

"You got any brothers?" Carla hinted.

Chancey laughed. "Nah, but I might have a couple of homeboys I could hook you up with."

"Well, hook me up, then!" Carla said excitedly.

"What's in it for me?"

Carla's eyebrows rose. "What 'chew want?"

Tia blushed when he looked at her and smiled.

Carla pushed Tia into Chancey and said, "She's all yours!"

"Carla!" Tia yelled and tried to back away from Chancey, but he held her in his arms.

"Stay right here," he said in a low, persuasive tone.

"Move in closer, girl. Don't be shy," Carla joked.

"Yeah, don't be shy," Chancey said. He leaned back against his jeep and brought Tia with him. He squeezed her waist and boldly looked her in the eyes. Unaware of her actions, Tia boldly looked back. Their gaze was strong before Carla broke in and told them to get a room.

Chancey looked at his watch. *Damn! Three o'clock already!*

"You ready to go?" Tia asked.

"Yeah, let's go get something to eat." He turned to Carla and asked if she wanted to come, too.

Yeah, Carla thought, smiling at Tia for her approval.

Chancey smiled and said, "I know you hungry, Carla! So you might as well come on and quit frontin'."

Embarrassed, Carla laughed. "No you didn't," she said and punched Chancey in the arm.

"Nah, I'm just playin'. For real though, come wit' us."

Carla, you bet' not! Tia thought, looking at Chancey disdainfully for his unwanted generosity.

"Where y'all going?" Carla asked.

"Where you wanna go, T?" Chancey asked Tia.

"I don't care," Tia said, almost snapping.

"Well, I'll go as long as it's not Chinese food. I hate Chinese food."

Tia looked at Chancey. *Let's get Chinese. PLEASE!*

"I hate Chinese food, too," Chancey said and got in his jeep.

Tia could have slapped them both!

Chancey unlocked his doors and started the engine. "You like Mexican food?"

"I love Mexican food," Carla said, grinning immensely.

"What about you, T?" Chancey asked.

"It's aw'ight," Tia said and snarled.

"Cool," Chancey said. "Let's go get some Mexican food, then."

"Okay!" Carla said and ran in the house to tie up some loose ends before returning with her purse and a fresh outfit on.

UGH! Tia thought resentfully. *I don't wanna go now!*

15

"Did he call yet?"

"Not yet."

"Girl, I had so much fun! Chancey is hella cool! I hope you don't run him off like you did all the others!"

Tia started laughing. "Forget 'chew, Carla!"

Carla was laughing with Tia before settling down to say, "'Cause if you do, I'ma be right there waiting!"

"Girl, please!"

"Girl, please, nothing! I'ma be like that "Clean-up Woman" song, and sweep him off his feet."

"You so crazy, Carla," Tia said and softly chuckled. "I had so much fun today..."

"Me too! And did you see how much the bill was?! Girl, it was over fifty bucks! Did you see that?"

"I know! He got money!"

"He got BANK! And he is *so* freehearted. Most guys are stingy!"

"Tell me about it," Tia said.

"That was sweet of him," Carla sighed happily.

After everything was said and done, Tia realized that *was* sweet of Chancey. She had her doubts about Carla going in the beginning, but as she lay across her bed nibbling on a leftover enchilada, she wouldn't change a thing about their outing.

Chancey treated them to one of Los Angeles' many Mexican restaurants. It was small, cozy, and surrounded by lots of palm trees. The weather was beautiful. Chancey suggested they eat outside, and had the host seat them right in front of a sparkling water fountain. The setting was perfect to Tia. She couldn't tell you how to get there. She didn't even remember the name of the place. All she knew was it was somewhere downtown and it was "the bomb", as she put it.

Chancey was spending money like it fell from the sky. He paid for their meals, dessert, and introduced them both to a Strawberry Daiquiri—a virgin daiquiri, that is. The waitress didn't think for one second that any of the three were twenty-one or above.

The entire time was spent sitting around the table laughing about a bunch of nothing. Carla was the life of the party. She and Chancey went back and forth trying to out-rap each other. Chancey had skills, Tia thought, while she laughed at Carla, thinking she couldn't have been serious from some of the lyrics she made rhyme. *And since when did she start calling herself "Lady C"?* Tia wondered.

Chancey had Tia's head in the clouds. The only thing she lacked from him was that deep conversation she wanted to get into. She figured Carla would stop their intimacy, which is why she didn't want her tagging along in the first place. Chancey, though, promised he would call her later that night so they could take care of some unfinished business. Thank God she had Carla to keep her company while she waited impatiently on his call.

"What time did he say he was gon' call?" Carla asked.

"Around seven."

"What did he have to do?"

"He said he had to take care of something at five o'clock. She could tell Carla was ready to hang up by the way she kept talking about the time and how she had to get ready for school, and so, without further ado, she released Carla of her babysitting duties.

Seven o'clock was close at hand. Tia had already taken her shower, had her school clothes out for tomorrow, and had her homework done. So far, everything was running smoothly. Her mother had just left for the night service at her church and wouldn't be home for another two hours. Now it was up to Chancey to call on time so they could enjoy each other up until the last minute.

She sat on her bed with the phone by her side. She tore off a sheet of paper from one of her notebooks and started jotting down all the questions she would ask him. "Did you use to go with Tomika?" she asked out loud as she wrote. "Question number two," she said, jumping at the ringing phone. Before answering, she looked at the clock and smiled. "Six-fifty," she said, and gave Chancey another point to add on to the other million he had already earned from earlier. "Hello."

"What's up, T?"

"You," Tia said, imitating him from earlier.

Chancey laughed. "Nah, it's all about you."

How sweet! Tia giggled as usual.

"Did your mother go to church yet?"

"Yeah, she just left."

"Are you still dressed?"

"I got my pajamas on, why?"

"'Cause, I wanna come get you for a little while."

Tia's eyes bucked. She started stuttering something about her mother.

"I'll have you back before she even gets home. I promise," Chancey said.

"Uh…"

"Come on, T."

"But I gotta get ready for school though."

There was silence on Chancey's end.

"You mad?" Tia asked.

"Nah," Chancey lied.

Tia sighed. "Boy, where you try'na take me to?"

"I just wanna see you! And I know I can't come chill over there. You showed me that when you had me pick you up at Carla's house."

Tia was humiliated. "No, no, that's not why I had you pick me up over there. I just…"

"Quit lyin'! You know you can't have boyfriends."

Now, Chancey was going too far, she thought. Then, he had to go over the edge. "You a virgin, Tia?"

"What! That's none of your business!"

"I'm sorry," he apologized sincerely.

There was silence on Tia's end.

"You mad at me?" Chancey asked.

"Nope," Tia lied.

"Tia?"

No answer.

"Tia!"

"What!"

"Can I come get you for a little while...*pleeeeeze*?"

Tia smiled. She was a sucker when he begged. "Where we goin'?"

"Just get dressed. I'm on my way."

*   *   *

Chancey called to touch base with Rondell so his cell phone and pager wouldn't buzz like crazy for the next two hours—the time he had with Tia before her mother came home. Just like expected, Rondell asked a trillion questions, finding it suspicious that Chancey was staying at his mother's house all of a sudden. And, just like expected, he began throwing in all the "You're going to see Tia" assumptions.

There was only so much accusing Chancey could take before he'd cut Rondell off completely. Like tonight, he slammed the phone down in Rondell's face and quickly turned his cell and pager off, knowing it was just a matter of time before the two sounded.

On his way to get Tia, he smiled, thinking it was time he popped the question. *Tia, I've been likin' you for a long time, and I was wondering...would you be my girlfriend?* "Hell nah!" he yelled. "I'm not sayin' that phony-ass shit!" He made a left on to Kalmia's murky road. Kalmia was always dark right at the corner house and until a few houses down from the corner house. It was almost like going through a tunnel by the way the street started to light up at about the middle of the block. A lot of women hated to drive down Kalmia at night, because not only was it gloomy, but as soon as they hit the corner, they ran into a squad of men doing illicit things. What really got their feathers ruffled was how they'd have to sit and wait until some bully or another decided he was ready to get out of the street and let them pass. Chancey didn't have those kinds of problems though. In fact, when he turned on Kalmia, he was saluted, if you will, by a couple of young men who flagged him down to chitchat.

Once he overcame the obstacles at the corner, his face lit up when he reached his destination. The yard was well manicured with a colorful flower bin to give it that extra touch. He couldn't bring himself to ring the doorbell fast enough, feeling awfully curious about her home life. "Your street is dark down there at the corner," he said when she opened the door.

"For real? Lamar prolly shot the streetlight out again," Tia said, acting as if she was in a hurry to get going.

"Hold up," Chancey told her and tenderly pushed her back inside. "I wanna see your house."

Tia started to sweat. She threw her expanded eyes around outside, especially across the street at Ms. Johnson's house before closing the door. All of Ms. Johnson's lights were out, which was relieving. Then again, what if they were out so Ms. Johnson could see her better? *Oooh,* Tia cried worriedly, *let's hurry up and go!*

Chancey was taking his time to see how Tia was living. He eyed around the living room, nodding and holding an expression that said he liked what he saw. They weren't doing it leather-style like Rondell, but the matching cloth couch and love seat was just as stylish. Then, on the other hand, maybe not.

"Where's your father?" Chancey asked.

"He don't live here."

Chancey could tell by the flower-patterned print the furniture contained; *NO* man would go for that, he thought. Still, he supposed it was tasteful in its own right as he worked his way from the living room to the back. "How many rooms is this?"

"Two," Tia said, trailing him nervously.

"You got any brothers and sisters?"

"Nope, it's just me."

"Where does your father stay?" Chancey asked, peeping in the bathroom filled with seashell decorations.

"Wit' some lady outta state. Him and my mother got a divorce a long time ago."

Thank God, Chancey thought as he continued to spearhead them down the hall. He opened the door to a bigger-than-average-sized room packed with the smell of cigarette smoke. "Mother's room?" he asked, seeing it had the look of an older person by the pastel-purple drapes and matching quilt.

"Yeah," Tia said. "Old fashion, huh?"

Chancey chucked. "I thought you said she was into church."

"She is!"

"Smokin' cigarettes?"

Tia laughed.

Chancey did, too. "Oh, she's one of them hypocritical church folk, huh? I bet she wear make-up, mini skirts, the whole nine, huh?"

Laughing, "Boy, don't be talkin' about my mother," Tia said and gave Chancey a soft love tap.

Chancey proceeded with his tour. "This is the room I wanna see," he said, walking into Tia's space.

She was blushing.

Chancey looked around quietly at first. Things looked so innocent and pure from the crimson-colored walls and carpet. He looked at Tia and smiled, loving the way her room fit her. She looked just like an angel to him, standing there just as kind as she wanted to be. He softly pinched her cheek and said, "Pretty in pink." Then, he was hit with a meddling streak. He started inspecting Tia's wardrobe, then the items on her dresser.

"Why you being nosy?" she asked, delivering another love tap.

"I just wanna see what kind'a taste my future wife got!"

Future wife? That's so sweet, Tia blushed.

Chancey started thumbing through the cassette tapes she had stacked neatly by the stereo on her dresser. "Whitney Houston, Boyz II Men, Mariah Carey, Michael…what 'chew doin' wit' some Michael Jackson?!" he asked and laughed.

"I like Michael Jackson!" Tia said, feeling no shame.

"I'm messin' with you. I like 'em, too," Chancey said, and started singing, "Do you remember the *tiiiiiime* we fell in love…do you remember the *tiiiiiime* when *weeee* first met, *girrrl*…" He kicked up one of his legs, then grabbed his crouch and started pumping the air. What had Tia rolling on the floor in laughter was when he spun around and landed on his toes. "'Ey, "Remember the Time" was tight!"

"I know! That's one of my favorite songs," Tia said.

"And what about this one?" Chancey cleared his throat.

"*Girrrlfriend…*I'm gonna tell your *boooyfriend…YEAH…*"

"*Tell* him…" Tia sang excitedly, "exactly what we're

doooing…YEAH…" Tia was having a ball. She laughed, sang, danced, and felt awkward when he went to kiss her. She didn't shy away from his signal though. She just didn't act on it. She stood still, watching his lips pull together to meet hers.

Chancey moved in close, and swore he was struck by a bolt of lightening when his lips made contact. He heard the thunder and everything! He frightfully looked around the pink room filled with teddy bears and Boyz II Men posters, and felt like a vampire faced with a clove of garlic. "Let's go to my house for a lil' while," he said, nearly jogging toward the front.

And by the look of things, Tia was trying to beat him out, knowing she shouldn't have had him there to begin with.

*   *   *

Back at home, Setchi was waiting at the foot of her bed for her brother's arrival. When she heard the door opening, she jumped up and walked in the living room to meet him. "Ronnie just left," she said, looking like something was wrong.

Chancey returned the same look before rolling his eyes away with a detesting sigh. He changed his mode when he saw Tia's apprehension. "Come on in," he told her, lightly guiding her with his palm on her back. "You have to excuse this house. It ain't all pretty wit' flowers 'n shit everywhere like yours."

"Boy, please! Ain't nothing wrong with this house," she said, trying to shake the spine-chilling feeling when she sat on the couch and searched out all the dirt around the living room.

Chancey pushed Setchi to the back. "Now, what 'chew say?" he asked with an attitude.

"Ronnie came by! I told 'em you went to get Tia," Setchi said.

Chancey blew up! "Why you all in my business!" he yelled, then shut the bedroom door.

"I didn't know it was a secret!"

"Shhh! It ain't a secret," Chancey whispered, then yelled, "It ain't a secret!" loud enough for Tia to hear before lowering his voice again. "I'm sayin' though, how you know I was goin' to get her?"

"'Cause I heard you on the phone," Setchi said.

Chancey rolled his eyes at his sister. "You get on my nerves, Setchi!"

"You get on mine, too, trick! Shoot, you should'a told me not to say nothin'."

"I would'a if I had'a known yo' ass was up in my conversation!"

"Well, you was talking loud enough!"

"Shut up, punk!" Chancey insisted, then asked, "What he say?"

"He told me to tell you he was comin' back."

Chancey rolled his eyes again. "Man, you get on my nerves!"

"Well, how was I suppose…"

"Shut the hell up!" he yelled as he left the room.

"You shut up!" Setchi yelled back, then lowered her voice and whispered, "Bitch-ass." She was still seething over Curt and what he put her through earlier that day.

"Is everything okay?" Tia asked when Chancey came in the living room.

Hell no! Chancey thought. "Yeah, it's cool," he said. He bent down and flicked the knob to the radio on his mother's clock sitting on the floor next to the couch. He tuned it to KJLH, where they played everything from Keith Sweat's "Make it Last Forever" to "Never Too Much" by Luther Vandross. Right now, they were broadcasting Teena Marie's "Out on a Limb".

The atmosphere was very relaxing to Tia. She didn't have to worry about her mother unexpectedly appearing. And Teena Marie had her feeling sensual to the point where she was longing for Chancey to try and kiss her again. Touch her. Do something!

Chancey sat on the couch next to Tia, looking like a crash dummy as if he couldn't move. The only time he did budge was when he flinched at the sound of the sporadic noise outside.

"So, where are your parents?" Tia asked, trying to spark up a conversation.

Chancey was deep in thought, thinking, *I know that nigga's 'bout to come here clownin'…* He leaned back on the couch and looked at Tia. "You feel alright?" he asked.

Tia was mystified. "Yes," she answered with a frown. "I said, where's your parents? What did you think I said?" she asked, chuckling.

Let 'em come back...and I'ma leave his ass standin' outside! Chancey was thinking. *Then again, I should just introduce 'em. Shit. Fuck it! What he gon' say? Tia, you gotta leave? I wish that nigga would! Matter fact, if he say anything fowl to 'er, I'm sockin' his ass! Yep!* Chancey looked over at Tia again. "You cool?" he asked.

"CHANCEY!" Tia yelled and popped him. "Yeah, I'm cool! Why you keep asking me that?"

Chancey laughed, easing some of his tension. "Don't trip off me. "I'm just..."

"CRAZY!" Tia yelled, finishing his sentence for him.

"Who you callin' crazy?" he asked as he slowly stuck his face in hers.

"You," she said, welcoming his lips by opening her mouth when he kissed her.

Chancey's bodyweight forced her back as he leaned into her. She felt a tickling sensation from her belly down to her toes when he slithered on top of her and started to grind. He was crushing hard against her pelvic bone. Tia couldn't believe her hands rubbing up and down his back. The mood couldn't have been more right, she thought. There Chancey was trying to smash himself through the crouch of her jeans, while Prince screamed, "Do me baby," through the tiny speaker of his mother's alarm clock.

"Can I make love to you?" Chancey whispered.

Tia clammed up. "Now?!"

"No, not now!" Chancey said as if she was being ridiculous. "One day...when the time is right...and it ain't some nosy ears in the background listenin'..."

"Ain't nobody listening to y'all!" Setchi angrily yelled from the room.

Both Tia and Chancey started to laugh.

"See what I mean?" Chancey said as he eased himself up. "'Ey, I'm sorry. I didn't introduce you to my sister, huh? You wanna meet 'er?"

Yeah, later, Tia thought, aching to have his body still on top of hers. "I was wondering why you didn't introduce us."

Chancey called Setchi out. Setchi waited a long time, then came shuffling into the living room like she'd rather be back in her bed.

Tia greeted her with a smile. "She's so pretty!" she looked at Chancey and said. "I bet you got a lotta of boyfriends, huh?" she turned to Setchi and asked.

"No, she don't," Chancey said seriously. "She got a lotta school work though!"

"Ugh!" Setchi smacked her lips and pouted.

"Don't pay him no attention, girl," Tia said, smiling. "We'll get together later and talk about girl stuff, okay?"

"Okay," Setchi said. Then she asked, "Don't you go to Jordan High?"

"Yeah."

"She goes there, too," Chancey said.

"Yeah, I saw you at lunch one day," Setchi said.

"Who was she with?!" Chancey jumped in and asked.

"I don't know, but he was fine as I don't know what!"

Chancey looked at Tia. Tia started snickering.

Setchi asked her was she a sophomore, too. Tia told her she was a senior. Setchi was ready to ask something else, but Chancey jumped in again.

"Okay, Setchi, goodbye," he said.

Setchi turned up her nose and went back to the room.

"Nice meeting you!" Tia yelled, then turned to Chancey and asked, "What are you guys mixed with?"

"Black and black," Chancey said.

"No, I'm serious!"

"Me too!"

"Come on, Chancey, you gotta be mixed with something," Tia said, grazing her fingers through his curls. "What about your parents? Does your mother have good hair, too?"

"It's alright."

"What about your father?"

"I don't know. I never seen my father before. Couldn't even tell you what his ass look like."

Tia's face was full of concern as he explained the story of his disordered life to her. The honesty in his voice made her want to cry. Reach out and hold him. Fix all his problems. She listened to his hardship and nodded from time to time. When he paused, she said,

"That is so fucked up."

Chancey looked at Tia and said, "*Whud*! You cursin'?!"

"No, I'm serious, Chancey. I hate that! That's just like my mother, right? She's so quick to down me about something, but look at her! She ain't right her own self! She smokes and curse worse than a sailor! Then on Sunday, hollering Jesus!"

Chancey giggled. "Is that right?"

"Yes! I mean, don't get me wrong, she does try, okay? And she looks out for my best interest, but..."

"Then, that's all that matters," Chancey said. "'Cause, shit, my mother just don't give a fuck! She's out there doin' her own thing, you know what I'm sayin'? Like right now! I don't know where the hell she is! You would think she would be here with her daughter havin' girl talk wit' 'er 'n shit like that, but nah, not Nikole Evans..."

"That's your mother's name?"

Chancey nodded.

"You got any pictures of her?" Tia asked.

"Hold on, let me see." Chancey went to his room and came back with a snapshot of Nikki in her early days.

Tia looked at the picture and saw where Chancey's looks came from. She studied Nikki's young-looking face and couldn't imagine her being anywhere near the person Chancey said she was. "How old is she?"

"I don't know how old she was right there, but she's thirty-five now."

"She's young, huh?" Before Chancey could respond, she added, "Yeah, but still, she's old enough to know she needs to look after her daughter."

"Right! I mean, damn! At least talk to her about her period and shit like that, you know what I'm saying? 'Cause I don't know about all that shit...cramps and yeast infections 'n shit!"

Tia laughed at Chancey's aggravated expressions.

"Man, you laughin', but you just don't know..."

"I'm laughing 'cause it's a trip hearing you talk like this!"

"Like what?"

"You seem so...so...I don't know...mature or something," Tia tried to explain. "You don't talk like a seventeen-year-old."

"Yeah, well, when you come from where I came from, you learn how to grow up quick."

"You mean, living in the projects?"

"That and everything that comes wit' it."

"So, what's it like living in the projects, anyway?"

"Well, see, Oprah, it's like this…"

Tia slapped Chancey in his back. "Boy, forget 'chew!"

"Boy, forget 'chew!" he teased, copying Tia. "That's all you know how'da say!"

"Forget…" Tia stopped herself and laughed loud and hard.

"See! Just that fast, you was gettin' ready to say it again!"

"So what!"

"I know. It's all good," Chancey said, pecking Tia on the lips.

"I'm for real though," she whined. "I wanna know."

"Alright, what do you wanna know?"

"Okay…" Tia got comfy. "Was it hard for you growing up?"

"Yeah! I mean, shit…take a look around…" Chancey showcased their tiny apartment. "This is what I grew up in. I came from the slumps. You know what I'm sayin'? No food! No PG&E! No school clothes!"

"You didn't have school clothes, Chancey?"

"Man, I used to have to pull clothes out the dirty clothes hamper, 'cause I didn't have nothin' to wear. I couldn't even afford to go to the laundry mat…that's how broke I was," Chancey said. "See, that's why I try to look out for my lil' sister so she won't have to go through that."

Tia's eyes were drawn to Chancey's as he spoke deeply and passionately about his hopes and dreams, like where he saw himself in five years and how he felt about marriage and kids.

"I had to do everything for myself, by myself! I didn't have nobody to look out for me like I do Setchi. Wait a minute. I take that back…I gotta give Ronnie his, 'cause if it wasn't for him, shit, I don't know what I would'a did when I got outta jail."

"He was there for you?" Tia asked.

Chancey nodded.

"How?"

Chancey ran down his and Rondell's friendship to her, then his and Kaylin's. "Now Kaylin, that's my dog! I love him to death! He's like my brother," he told her.

"Really? I didn't know that."

"We've been through everything together! Shit, even cried together! Now look at 'em...gettin' ready to graduate and thangs..." Pausing, "I'm proud of 'em," Chancey said and smiled.

"Listen at you! What do you know about being proud of somebody? I swear you talk like a grown man."

"I'm serious! Shit, I am proud of 'em! It's almost like I would hate to see him fail, you know what I'm sayin'? 'Cause, see, technically, he's not supposed to be graduating. He's a nigga from the projects! He's supposed to be either dead or in jail, you know? But he's not! He's one of the few that beat the odds! How could you not be proud of that?!"

"Chancey," Tia said and wrapped her arms around his neck, "when you first tried to talk to me, I was skeptical because I thought you was just like everybody else...you know, only out for one thing. And if that's the case, you're a damn good actor! I don't know...I can't explain it. You just don't seem like all the other guys I know. You seem more real and honest...and intelligent!"

"*And* more handsome," he said and chuckled coolly.

Tia laughed out loud as she held him tight in her arms. "Don't *even* go there, boy!"

Chancey loved making Tia laugh. Just seeing how the littlest things brought her joy, let him know that she didn't want for much. He didn't have to buy her smiles. She gave them willingly. Her hands were comforting. Her eyes were caring. And above all, her heart was sincere. Although, he couldn't forget about her baby face, her pureness, sharpness, her sexy lips, pop-booty... "I want you to be my girl," he said. "I've been likin' you for a long time and I *know* you know that!" he said.

Tia looked at Chancey with serious eyes. "I'll be honest, Chancey. I haven't really been with anybody before..."

Tell me something I don't know!

"And I've always told myself that when I do get with someone, he wasn't gon' be a drug dealer..."

Damn! Chancey thought, this time looking at Tia with anguished eyes.

Tia grasped his face. "OR a guy that sleeps around..."

Where did that come from? he wondered, frowning.

"Tomika told me how you…"

"Oh, hell nah!" Chancey yelled, jumping to his feet. "I was waitin' for you to bring her ass up! Look, I don't know what all she said about me, but I'ma tell you just like this…" he stopped to think of a way to explain their relationship without telling too much.

"She said all you wanted to do was do *it* to her," Tia threw out.

Chancey was embarrassed. He smiled and put his head down. "Nah, mm-mm," he faltered, shaking his head.

Tia had been holding out on bringing up his and Tomika's sex affairs since the day she found out about it, and smiled at the fact that she had him cornered.

"No, don't smile like you just busted me or somethin'! That shit was a long time ago!"

"Yeah, but if you used her, what makes me think you won't use me?"

"Wait, hold up, hold up, you got it wrong! Tomika wasn't just somebody I was fuckin'…I mean, doin' it to. We was together for a long time!" Chancey went on to tell Tia that he really cared for Tomika, but he had to leave her alone because she kept cheating on him.

"Did you ever cheat on her?" Tia asked.

"I mean, not…not like she did. She was the one who cheated on me!"

"Chancey," Tia said, giving him a be-honest look, "did you cheat on her, too?"

"I don't even know why we havin' this conversation!" Chancey snapped. "But since you wanna know…YEAH!"

"See," Tia said and shook her head.

"Tia, all bullshit to the side…when me and Tomika broke up, I was hurt…I mean, not really hurt…I just liked her a lot…fuck it, I'ma just be honest…I was in love wit' Tomika! She broke my heart!"

The knife went straight through Tia's chest.

"We was goin' through a lot of the same things at the time with our mothers and shit like that, you now what I'm sayin'? We would sit up and talk all night about how we was gon' buy us a big house in Beverly Hills one day. We was just dreamin', you know, 'cause ain't neither one of us had shit!" Chancey chuckled. "But that was okay though, we was broke together. I would bring her over here and not haf' to worry about her feelin' outta place 'n shit, 'cause her house was just as fucked up as mine. Then I started sellin' drugs and makin' a lil' money..." He sighed. "And I stopped spendin' that quality time wit' 'er. I didn't stop to think that she was out there fuckin' around, 'cause she was always at home. Then one night, my homeboy came over here..."

Chancey's narrative was touching. Some of the things he said about Tomika were so gripping, it almost seemed unreal. But again, the authenticity was there—either that, or he was a damn good actor, Tia thought. "Do you miss her?" she asked.

"Not at all!" Chancey said.

Tia twisted her lips and looked at him with doubt. "You know you miss her."

"Nah, bruh! Not at all! If she was the last girl on this earth, we'll just be two horny individuals!"

"Yeah, right!"

"I'm serious! She's too triflin' for me."

"Whatever!"

"Let me tell you what she did," Chancey said. "She fucked Ronnie behind my back!"

Tia's eyes widened. She inhaled deeply like she was being injected with helium. "*Foreeeeal?*"

Chancey smacked his lips. "Man, you betta' ask somebody. That's why I don't really fool wit' 'er no more. I mean, we prolly could'a made things work if she had'na did that."

"Ronnie was wrong, too, Chancey," Tia said.

"Oh, I know! That nigga ain't cool either. But you know, I'm like this...if a bitch...I mean, girl ain't woman enough to keep her legs closed, then..."

"What about the guy being man enough to keep his thing in his pants?!"

"*Noooo*...a man will go as far as the woman lets him. See, so it's on her to..."

"Why it gotta be on her?! Shoot, it takes two to tango!"

"Yeah, but a man's gon' be a man regardless, so..."

"What's that supposed to mean?"

"IT MEANS THEY'RE DOGS!" Setchi yelled from the room. She had Tia in tears.

"Take yo' ass to sleep, Setchi!" Chancey yelled.

"She can talk if she wants to!" Tia said, still laughing, and jumping in Chancey's face with her chest out.

"You little..."

"Little what?" Tia asked and started playfully pushing him around. "What 'chew gon' do?"

"Girl, I will break you in half."

"Bring it on then, nigga!"

"What did you call me?!" Chancey asked, frowning and smiling at the same time. "Girl, you better watch yo' mouth!"

"Make me watch my mouth!" Tia said, holding her leg up with her hands facing outward like Jamie Foxx when he portrays "Ugly Girl" on the sitcom, "In Living Color".

That was one of the cutest things Chancey had ever seen. He couldn't stop laughing at Tia bouncing around on one leg. He was laughing so hard, Setchi had to run out and take a look, which she, too, started giggling at Tia's funny-looking pose.

"Setchi, you get 'em from the back and I'll get 'em from the front."

"Setchi, you bet not!" Chancey warned.

And she didn't. She just called him a couple of names and went back to the room and climbed back in bed. She needed that second's worth of laughs to help take her mind off Curt.

"Aw, why you make her leave?" Tia asked with sad eyes.

"'Cause she gotta go to sleep so she can get up for school in the morning," Chancey said, alerting Tia.

"I better get ready to go so I can get ready for school tomorrow, too," she said.

"Nah, you leavin' so you can beat your mother home!"

There was nothing Tia could say. All she could do was smile.

"So, when do I get to meet 'er?" Chancey asked.

Tia's eyes grew big. "You wanna meet my mother?"

"Nah, on second thought, I better wait 'til I get a job, 'cause I know that's gon' be the first question out her mouth."

Tia got offended. "Yeah, you right. And after you get a job is when I'ma be your girlfriend!"

"Here *you* go," Chancey said, reaching out for her waist.

Tia slapped his hands away. She was really insulted. "I'm not playing, shoot!"

"Why you gettin' mad?"

"'Cause you actin' like you can't meet my mother or something!"

"Don't you want me to get a job first?"

"When is that gon' be, Chancey? Don't think I'ma be waiting forever, 'cause I ain't! The last thing I wanna do is be sitting up somewhere worried about my man going to jail. I don't have time for stuff like that."

"That's my girl!" Chancey yelled. "You puttin' it down, huh?"

Tia blushed embarrassingly.

Chancey put his arms around her and said, "I know you don't, T. That's why I'm 'bout to get a job."

"When?"

"Soon."

"How soon?"

"I'ma start lookin' next week," Chancey lied.

"Do you have a résumé?"

"Nope."

"How you goin' to look for a job with no résumé, Chancey?"

He shrugged his shoulders.

Tia took him by the hand and pulled him into the kitchen. When they sat down at the table, she removed a pen from her pocketbook. "Give me all your information, like your full name, address, phone, education, and job history. I'ma type up a résumé for you in my typing class tomorrow."

Chancey started writing down everything Tia asked for. He was stuck on the education part, even more so on the job history part.

Tia saw his hesitation. "Just put Jordan High School down, because that's where you was going before you went to juvenile, right?"

"Right," Chancey said. "What about job history?"

"Did you work any...like, summer jobs or something before?"

"No, but I know this girl that can say I did. She's a supervisor at the Post Office on Century. I can say I work for her in the mail room or somethin'."

"Cool, put that down, then."

Chancey wrote down some lies and slid the paper across the table to Tia.

Tia reviewed the information carefully. "Trina Withers," she said aloud, referring to the woman at the Post Office. "You got her number?"

"I have to get it from Ronnie. It's his girlfriend."

"Oh, it is?" Tia asked. "He's mean, huh?" she bolted out. "He don't like me for some reason."

"Don't trip. Shit, Ronnie don't like nobody," Chancey said.

Tia smiled as she folded his information and stuck it in her purse. They both got up from the table and slowly walked each other back to the living room. Tia saw the big, red numbers showing eight-fifty on Nikki's alarm clock and began moving like someone threw a firecracker her way. "I gotta hurry up and go," she said. "My mother gets home around nine-ten exactly!"

Chancey made sure he had his keys and leaped to the back to tell Setchi he was leaving. When he saw Setchi passed out with her mouth open, he turned the TV off and closed the door.

"Bye, Setchi!" Tia yelled.

"She's sleep." He wrapped his arms around Tia and said, "So, can I go to bed tonight knowing I have you as my girl?"

Something almost exploded in Tia's panties when she felt his private part press against hers. "Can I go to bed tonight knowing you're about to stop selling drugs and get a job?" she asked, batting her eyes sexily.

"Yep," Chancey promised in a soft undertone before passionately kissing her again.

Her head automatically tilted backward, her lips parted, and her tongue rolled around with his.

"Don't leave me," he whispered, pushing Tia's back against the front door. He moved his lips from hers and traced them down her chin, then behind her ear.

"Don't put a hickey on me," she moaned, but gripped the back of his head and cocked hers to the side. He was sucking hard all across her neck, trying to push his face in it. She opened her thighs so he could have a better aim when he applied pressure between her legs. She wanted him to dig deeper.

"Spend the night wit' me," Chancey murmured through heavy breathing.

"I want to, but I can't," she whined, glancing at the clock.

Chancey sighed as he opened the door. "The rest of my night is gon' be fucked up!" he yelled.

"Why?"

"'Cause! After I take you home, all I'ma do is be wishin' you was here," he said, holding Tia's hand as they walked to his car.

16

Tia locked the front door to her house and turned around to find herself facing her mother standing with her arms folded in her white, high-collared blouse and black respectable-length skirt. Her pantyhose were still on, covering her legs and bare feet. Tia knew she was beat by only a matter of seconds. She greeted her mother, then made her way around her and headed straight for her room.

"Tia!" her mother yelled. She didn't even look back. "Get your five-dollar ass back over here before I make change!"

Yeah, okay Wesley Snipes! Tia hated when her mother took pieces of a movie script and ran with it as if they were her lines.

"Who was that that dropped you off?"

"Oh, that was uh…um, Carla!"

"Carla? Do I look like Boo-Boo the Fool?"

"No, Mother Dearest…"

"Keep gettin' smart so I can slap yo' ass into the middle of next week!"

Tia couldn't hold in her giggles.

"I'm not playing with you, Tia Renee Arnold!"

Uh-oh! Tia thought. It was time to do some explaining; her full name had been stated. "Okay, Mama, it wasn't Carla..."

"I know it wasn't!"

"It was my friend from school. He just took me to Barnes and Nobles real quick so I could get this *"Spanish for Dummies"* book for my Spanish class tomorrow."

"I thought you were taking French," her mother said, glaring in her daughter's eyes.

Again, a faint chuckle seeped from Tia's lips.

"Look, hefa, stop playing with me, okay? 'Cause I am not in a laughing mood, Miss Thang! I'm already ticked off with Sister Turner's shit-startin' ass! I had to tell her ass three times tonight that I already paid my damn tithes! But no...her ass wanna keep playin' wit' me, sendin' that goddamn basket my way...forgive me, Lord!" she said and waved her right hand in the air before continuing. "She's lucky I didn't slap her old, wrinkled-up ass! Shit. She need Jesus! Coming to church on Sunday and sinning the rest of the damn week! See, that's a Christian for you!" Tia's mother started pulling her pantyhose down before she went on again. "And you, with your good, lying ass...oh yeah, hefa, Ms. Johnson told me she saw you sneaking some ol' nigga in my house while I was gone..."

"No, see, what happened was...see, he...he had to use the bathroom, right? And I told him I couldn't have boys in here while my mother was gone, right? But he had to use it really bad..."

"Mmm-humph..." Tia's mom grunted with her lips curled to the side. She looked at her offspring for a minute, thinking to herself, *What do I have here?* A daughter who clearly knew she was in trouble, but her cheerfulness wouldn't let the distress show. Finally, *She's in love,* Tia's mom concluded, easing up a little. "So, does this boy have a name?" she asked.

"Chancey," Tia said in her shy voice.

Her mother's face soured. "Chancey? What the hell kind'a name is that?!"

Tia stifled a smile and pretended she didn't hear her.

"How old is he?"

"Seventeen, like me..."

"And does he work?"

"He..."

"Or is he one of them street pharmacist?"

"He…"

"How long y'all been courting, Miss Thang?"

"Mama, we're just…"

"Don't be lettin' no bums from the streets have you sneaking around like some lil' tramp…I'm telling you that right now! That shit is for the birds! If he can't think enough of you to come in here and meet me, you don't need 'em! You better listen! I'm try'na tell your narrow ass something."

"I know, Mama," Tia said, smiling unwillingly at her mother. Any other time, she would have been annoyed to death with her bullheadedness and loud, intimidating voice, but now, she must admit, Chancey had helped her look past the rough surface and see the funny side to her mother; she was a true comedian, Tia discovered.

"Oh, you know, huh? Lord, have mercy! You don't know your ass from a hole in the ground! Out there courtin' wit' some nigga…"

Just keep cool, T! Just keep cool! Tia kept smiling.

"I guess you try'na to be like Carla's dick-hungry ass, right? Guess you havin' sex, too, huh?"

"No, I'm…"

"I keep telling your narrow ass that a man ain't buyin' the cow if he can get the milk free! But see, you can't tell yo' ass nothing. You the type of person that don't believe shit is shit!"

"Barbara Arnold!" Tia yelled, laughing. "Can I say something? Please?"

"You're laughing, Tia, but I'm not playing! Shit! You know I don't like nobody in my house when I'm not here. You *know* that!"

"Mama, it was only for one lil' minute! See, Ms. Johnson's forever try'na tell on somebody. You know I wouldn't even disrespect you like that," Tia said and playfully walked up to her mother, placing her arms around her.

"Move back, girl," Barbara said, not wanting to smile with her daughter.

"And no, I'm not out there having sex either!"

Barbara threw her eyes at Tia and looked her up and down, marveling over whether she was telling the truth or not.

"Come on, Ma, you don't even have to look at me like that. You raised me to be a very respectable young lady, see..." Tia started giving her mother one model pose after another.

"Aw shit," Barbara said, snickering. "You try'na jive somebody now!"

"Unh-unh, Mama, I'm serious!" Tia declared. "He said that's why he likes me."

"That's what they all say!"

Tia's eyes saddened. "You told me that daddy liked you because you were respectable. And you guys stayed married for twenty years..."

"And look at his ass now! All wrapped up with the next hefa!"

"Yeah, but you even said yourself, it's better her than you."

"You damn right! I ain't got no time to be bothered with an ol' alcoholic! And now look at 'em...they don' lost everything! You hear me? Everything!"

"That doesn't mean Chancey's gon' turn out like daddy, Mama."

Barbara stood firm, wearing a look of unbroken stubbornness on her face.

"He's sincere. Watch, you'll see when you meet 'em."

"I don't wanna meet no nigga..."

"Mama! Didn't you just say he should come over here and meet you?"

"He prolly ain't nothing but an ol' street thug! I bet he wear his pants around the crack of his ass!"

"No, he don't," Tia sighed.

"I bet he got a head full of jheri curl juice, don't he?! You better warn my black ass before you bring 'em over here so I can cover up my couches 'n shit!" Barbara pulled a cigarette from her pack and lit it. "You can't tell 'em they don't look good, dripping that gook and shit all over the damn place! Looking like some damn grease monkeys!"

"He does not have a curl," Tia said despairingly, thinking after going through all of this, she and Chancey better stay together forever!

"Yeah, well, whatever! Shit." Barbara took a couple of puffs, then two streams of smoke cascaded from her nostrils. "What are you gonna do with a boyfriend, anyway, Tia?!" she asked. "You have so many other things to focus on, like SCHOOL!"

"Mama, I'll be graduating…"

"Does he go to school?"

"Ye…yeah," Tia lied. And she had a hard time doing it, too.

"Does he go to school, hefa?!"

"Yes!"

"Well, all I'ma tell you is this…don't be so quick to open your legs—I don't care how good the shit is feeling to you!"

"I know, Mama," Tia said, giggling.

"I'm telling you! You make his ass wait! That's how you'll know he *really* cares! Fuck telling you how respectable you are! A man'll tell you anything when he wants some pussy!"

"MAMA!" Tia yelled with rosy-pink cheeks.

"Well, shit, it's the truth! Your mama ain't no watered-down, salad-eatin' bitch! Shit, I'm up on it," Barbara boasted, holding on to her collar. "I'ma tell you like it is…"

Tia put her head down and shook it as she seconded the notion of having Chancey meet his doom: Barbara!

"I just want what's best for you, little girl," Barbara chuckled. "Okay?"

Still embarrassed, but giving her mother an understanding smile, Tia nodded and said, "I know, Mama."

"If you think you've found a nice guy, then fine. I'm happy for you. Shit, to be quite frank, I was gettin' a lil' worried there for a minute."

Tia started busting up with laughter. "Unh-unh, Mama, don't *even* go there! I ain't hardly gay!"

"Well, shit, tell me something! 'Cause, uh…"

"No, you always acted like you didn't want me to have boyfriends."

Barbara got serious. She pulled the last cigarette from her pack and tossed the empty carton to the side. "Yeah," she said while lighting her cancer stick, "I guess you can say I'm a lil' overprotective, but it's only because I want you to be something in life. Be something in life! Not wasting time, assin' around! Life's too short for that. Like I always tell you, have your own! Don't depend on a nigga for shit!" Barbara paused to take a drag. "I had no problem leaving Howard's ass!" she added, drawing her daughter's full attention. "Thank God I had an education, my own job, my own car, my own money…MY OWN SHIT! When he started fuckin' up, gettin' drunk, and not bringing home his check, I left his ass and didn't look back! See, I didn't have to put up with his shit! And that's not to say, Chaney, Changey…"

Tia laughed.

"…whatever the hell his name is! That's not to say he's gon' turn out like Howard did, BUT…all I'm saying is, prepare yourself as if he will."

17

The auditorium was noisy with sounds of friends and proud family members verbally deciding on which seat would give them the best view of the graduates. The tall, wooden stage was set with beaming lights shinning down on the podium. An African American woman dressed in a colorful dashiki walked up to the microphone carrying a stack of diplomas. Portions of her dreadlocks were accented with small seashells latched around them.

She adjusted the stand where she could speak into the mic without much effort. "Well, hello! How is everyone?" she asked cheerfully, smiling in all the faces in the audience. "Before we get started, let's give a few more minutes to those still trying to find a seat."

Chancey got as close to the stage as he could, finally copping a seat toward the middle of row seven. He rested both of his arms on the back of his chair and moved his legs to the left so Rondell could take the last available seat on his right, next to the huge woman overlapping in his chair.

"Here's one, Rosie. Sit right here," Chancey said, protecting an empty seat in front of him.

"You can have this one," Rondell said, but Rosie was already settling in her seat with Ronda on her lap. He sat down with a frown on his face and wiggled himself back in his chair. "I wish her fat ass scoot over," he leaned in Chancey's ear and whispered.

Chancey sighed hard and jerked his body left. "There! Now you got room!"

"I'm not scootin' over there so my ass can be sittin' on the bar! Look!" Rondell showed Chancey what he was talking about when he pointed to the bar linking their chairs together. "I never did like these chairs…all attached to each other 'n shit!"

"Damn, cuz, you hella loud!" Chancey said just as loud.

"So! Shit, I didn't wanna come to this shit no-way!"

Chancey shook his head and mumbled some belittling things about Rondell.

Rondell said, "Shit, we need to be somewhere talkin' about what we gon' do with this key, while you bullshittin'!"

Chancey cut his eyes at Rondell and grimaced. "Don't talk about that shit up in here! You stupid?"

"Hell nah, I ain't stupid! You stupid?"

Chancey rose to his feet and threw his eyes around for another seat. When he didn't see one, he sat back down and grimaced at Rondell again.

"You keep stallin', nigga," Rondell lowered his voice and said. "We should'a *been* had this shit sold. What the fuck you doin', try'na keep it?"

Chancey looked past Rondell and laid his eyes on the heavy-set woman next to him. She was looking straight ahead, but he could tell she was getting an earful by the way she kept glancing at them out the corner of her eye.

Rondell smacked his lips and said, "Her fat-ass can't hear me!"

"I don't think you know how loud you are."

"Nigga, quit try'na change the subject! Why the fuck you keep stallin' wit' our shit?"

"How the hell am I stallin'?"

"We had the shit for over a week now!"

"You don't haf' to wait on me. Go handle yo' business."

"So, what 'chew sayin'?" Rondell asked. "You know we need to get rid of this shit at the same time so we can re-up together! Stick to the script, nigga!"

Chancey looked at heavy-set again. She was still eyeballing them on the sly.

"*Go handle yo' business,*" Rondell said mockingly. "Ain't that a bitch!" He rolled his eyes to look at Chancey and held them there.

They went back and forth, arguing and disagreeing during African American's college-prep lecture. When she read off the first name in line, Chancey focused all of his attention on the young men and women waiting eagerly on the side in their blue and white caps and gowns.

"Naomi Anderson!"

A puny teenaged girl strutted bashfully across the stage after her diploma. She was quickly congratulated, then hurried along.

"Tia Arnold!"

Chancey's eyes lit up as he rose in his seat to get a better view. Rondell put his elbow on Chancey's shoulder, slouched over, and closed his eyes.

As Tia walked happily across the stage, Chancey heard a loud-mouth woman shout, "Yaaaay Tia!" He looked and saw Tia's mom cheering in the front row. He also spotted Niecy clapping a few seats down.

"Tia! Over here!" Lisa yelled, trying her best to crop Tia's face in her camera.

"Look at Lisa," Chancey said to himself and chuckled. He nudged Rondell's elbow off of him and said, "That's Tia's mama right there. See!"

"Nigga, I see 'er!" Rondell snapped, glimpsing Lisa briefly. He slouched back over in his seat and closed his eyes. "Hell, her mother look better than she do."

Chancey ignored him.

"You still ain't hit that yet, huh?"

Chancey looked at Rondell and frowned.

Rondell snickered scornfully. "Nope! *Sho'* haven't," he said before answering his ringing phone.

Chancey started rocking in his seat, sighing and huffing like he wanted to hurt somebody. He saw Tia and slowly stopped rocking. Her sophisticated appearance had him drawn in like a hooked fish.

She looked radiant in her long, satin gown with her thick pearl necklace to bring out the ivory patterns over its baby-blue background. He lost himself for a minute, staring at her off-white pumps as she toed at a crack in the hardwood floors. Tonight couldn't come soon enough, he thought as her lips were now the spotlight in his eyes. Just thinking of all the freaky things he was going to do to her made his mouth form a lustful smirk.

"Kaylin Rogers!" Chancey thought he heard. He quickly turned to the few remaining graduators who were listening anxiously for their names.

He shouted, "KAY-LUN!" as Kaylin strolled to the podium in his blue two-piece suit.

Kaylin threw his fist up at all of his homeboys. He saw his mother running on the side of him, snapping picture after picture. He stopped to pose for her so she could sit down and quit embarrassing him.

Chancey was mesmerized by the whole event, periodically imagining himself strolling with a limp down the stage as everyone called out his name like he was a star. He watched as the last diploma was being issued. Rondell was also watching since it was almost over.

"Ladies and Gentlemen, I now give you the class of '95!" African American shouted. A roar of applauds and cheers shook the auditorium. Graduation caps filled the air. Camera flashes sparked from every which way. Parents ran up to greet their children as they made their way down from the stage.

"Alright, let's roll," Rondell said, jumping up.

"Man, hold up," Chancey said, more like warned. He eased past the people in his row and stepped out in the aisle to meet Kaylin dashing their way.

"What's up, cuz?" Kaylin said, slapping palms with Chancey.

"Look at my boy!" Chancey said, looking Kaylin over with his fist up to his mouth.

"Congratulations, Kay-Kay," Rosie stepped out in the aisle and said. Rondell was slowly dragging his feet behind her, talking on the phone to another one of his callers.

"Right on," Kaylin said and embraced Rosie. When they let each other go, he kneeled down to Ronda's level. "What's up, lil' mama?"

Tomika emerged from a swarm of people, peeling a light sweater off her shoulders. One dude's eyes sprung forward when he saw her hips bouncing from side to side as she switched down the aisle like a model on a runway. She used her arm as a rack for her sweater and took a handful of her long microscopic braids and tossed them to the back before addressing Chancey from behind.

Chancey jumped when he felt something pinch his butt cheeks. He turned quickly and saw Tomika giggling behind him. "Girl, don't be pinching me on my ass!" Chancey said, backing Tomika up. He looked around the auditorium for Tia.

"Where y'all celebratin' at tonight?" Tomika asked everyone.

Kaylin said, "Shit, nowhere! This fool's gettin' ready to go outta town."

"*Whud?*" Tomika asked, surprised. "You not celebratin' Kaylin's graduation wit' 'em, Chancey?"

Chancey threw his arm around Kaylin and said, "We celebratin' soon as I get back."

Tomika eyed Chancey suspiciously for a minute, then asked, "Where you going?"

*   *   *

Tia finally found Chancey, she hoped, struggling to see through a patch of giggly girls jumping around and clinging to each other joyfully as they celebrated their special day.

She'd been looking all over for him the moment she left the stage, wondering why he wasn't there to welcome her like he said he would be. "Excuse me," she told the girls as she squeezed by them. Sure enough, there he was looking around for her, she assumed, when she saw his eyes maneuvering through the crowds.

*   *   *

Just as Chancey fixed his lips to tell Tomika to mind her business, Tia walked up and hugged him like she had just found her lost child. "I was looking all over for you," she said.

Everybody froze. Tomika stepped back and bounced all of her weight to one side. She tilted her head downward, but kept her eyes in Tia's face. Everything from her nose down was twisted. She was debating on whether to snatch Tia by the hair or throat if she dared to say anything to her.

Rondell rushed his caller off the phone. He walked up and took a look at Tia. "Tito. Right?"

"Tia!" Tia quickly said. She looked at Chancey and frowned.

Chancey was watching Rondell evilly.

Tomika was snickering.

Rondell giggled at Tia. "Yeah. Yeah, that's right. Tia." *Bitch!* he thought as he turned to meet Chancey's wicked eyes. "Anyway, nigga, you ready to go or what?"

Chancey was raving inside. He stared at Rondell for a long time, wishing he would say one more word so he could swing. He finally rolled his eyes Kaylin's way. "Get at me later, cuz," he said, reaching out to shake Kaylin's hand.

Kaylin held on and leaned in. "Alright, man, have fun tonight."

As Chancey and Tia walked away, Tomika yelled, "I'll call you later, Chance!"

Chancey didn't even look back.

"Ol' bitch!" Tomika snapped loud enough to be heard by those around her.

Rondell was snapping a hell-of-a-lot more than that under his breath as he watched them walk off hand-in-hand.

Kaylin left the bunch and went to find his mother.

Rondell looked at Tomika and said, "C'mere 'Mik, let me holla at you for a minute."

*   *   *

"What was that all about?" Tia asked as she and Chancey weaved their way in and out of crowds.

Chancey was stumbling with his words.

Tia stopped. "Where are you and Ronnie going, Chancey?"

"Nowhere."

"Then why did he ask was you ready to go?"

"Tia…"

"That's my name!" she snapped.

Chuckling, "Who you yellin' at?" Chancey asked as he went to put his hands around her.

She pushed him back so hard, you could hear the impact of her palms hitting his chest. "I wanna know what's going on, Chancey. Right now! Why the hell was that girl looking at me like that?"

"Who, 'Mik?"

"And oh, I'm Tito now, right?"

"Man, that's Ronnie just being stupid."

"Why you keep hanging around him if he's so stupid?"

Chancey looked at Tia with exhausted eyes. "Tia…"

"And Tomika wit' her shit-startin' self…*I'll call you later Chancey*…"

"Yeah, I heard 'er! I don't know *what* she meant by that."

Tia's eyes showed doubt.

"Tia…"

"Stop calling my name! You still kickin' it with her, huh?!"

"I have not *seen* Tomika since the last time you was at my house! That was what, two weeks ago?"

Tia's eyes were still showing doubt. "When's the last time you *talked* to her?"

"Oh, I…I talked to 'er, um…"

Tia hit Chancey in the chest. "When's the last time you talked to 'er?!"

"Hold on, let me think!" Chancey thought right past the phone call he received from Tomika last night. The call that landed him at her house until almost one in the morning. "A few days ago."

Tia's eyes were now showing hurt. "You sleepin' wit' 'er, Chancey?"

"Don't be stupid," he said, thoughts of last night flashing before him.

Chancey knew there would be a time when he and Tomika crossed paths again. That's why her call last night didn't come as a surprise.

Tomika wanted him bad! Everything she said to him came with a soft pat of her hands to either his chest or face. "Oh, wait a minute. Don't move," she had told him, dusting off a tiny piece of lint from the side of his mouth. She practically got up on him when she stood on her tippy-toes, straddled his leg, and fingered the corner of his mouth. She had her breast pressed against his chest. And she thought sliding down his thigh when she was done was sure to have them rocking the headboard on her bed.

"Look what you did!" Chancey said, looking down at the swelling in his pants.

A sneaky grin appeared on Tomika's face as she reached for his crouch.

Chancey jumped and grabbed her wrists. "I gotta go," he said.

*   *   *

"Yeah, you sayin' that, but I don't know what you do when I'm not around. Shoot, for all I know, you can be gettin' some from somewhere else!"

"Why you keep holdin' out on a nigga, then?"

Tia let her facial expression respond for her.

"That's not what I meant! I'm not try'na say I'm fuckin' somebody else 'cause you ain't givin' it to me."

"Then what *are* you saying, Chancey?"

"I'm sayin', I'm waitin' for you, okay? No matter how long it takes…"

Tia showed half a smile. "Yeah, you cleanin' it up 'cause you think you gettin' some tonight."

"Oh, I *think*?"

A full smile appeared. "You act like you *know* you gettin' some!"

"I *hope* I'm gettin' some," Chancey said, smiling with Tia.

Tia's look turned sexy. "How bad do you want some?"

"Don't play wit' me," Chancey said seriously.

Tia laughed. "Tell me how bad you want some!"

"I want some so bad, just thinking about you makes my dick hard."

"UGH! You nasty!"

"Well, you asked me and I told you!"

"You want some that bad?"

"Hell yeah!"

"For real?"

"Yep! Tonight? Please?" Chancey pulled Tia close.

"Okay, but you gotta be on your best behavior!"

"Best behavior! I promise."

"You gotta treat me like a queen!"

"F'sho!"

"And you gotta run around this auditorium and bark like a dog!" Tia said, smiling.

"Never!" Chancey snapped and pushed her out of his arms. "Hell, yo' shit gotta be all that *and* a bag of Doritos before I do some shit like that!"

Tia was cracking up. She palmed Chancey's cheeks and kissed his lips.

"Did you tell Lisa about tonight?" he asked.

"Yep!"

"What she say?"

"Nothing. 'Be careful'."

"That's it?"

"Yep! I told you she wasn't gon' say nothing. My mother likes you a lot. Matter fact, she thought you was coming by last night. She made this big seafood dish…"

"I couldn't, 'cause…"

"I know. I told 'er you had to take your mother to the hospital. How's she doing anyway?"

"Fine. It was just gas," Chancey said quickly. "Where's Lisa 'nem at?"

Tia stood on her toes and looked around. "There they go!" she said when she saw Carla's basket weaved hairstyle. Chancey followed Tia's footsteps to her folks.

"There go Tia right there!" Carla said when she saw them coming.

Lisa turned around. "Girl! Where have you been? We were looking all over for you!"

"I was…"

"*Chancey!*" Lisa sang and reached around Tia to greet Chancey with a big hug. "How's your mother doing?"

"Better," Chancey said.

"Just knock me over why don't you," Tia teased her mother.

Everyone laughed.

Lisa smiled and said, "Lori, this is my son-in-law, Chancey."

"Hi Chancey. How are you?" Lori said.

"Cool."

"Lori's my mother, Chancey," Carla said.

"Oh, okay," Chancey said, now able to see the resemblance. He looked at Carla's midriff and then at her mother's, thinking to himself, with genes that strong, Carla couldn't afford the thirty pounds she would eventually be cursed with over the years.

"Tia and Chancey are going to Catalina Island, girl!" Lisa said, sounding extremely excited. The diamond stud in her nose created a light show with sparks firing off every time her head moved.

"I wish *I* was going to Catalina Island," Carla pouted.

Tia thought to whack her diploma over Chancey's head if he invited her along.

Lori's eyes puckered. "Catalina Island? Wow! That place is expensive!"

"Yes, girl! He got him a good job working construction with his..." Lisa turned to Chancey. "Uncle, right?"

Both Tia and Chancey looked at each other and said, "Right!"

"How long have you and Tia been seeing each other?" Lori asked.

"Damn near a year!" Lisa said, cutting her eyes at Chancey and her daughter. "Yeah, girl, they been sneaking around playing house."

Again, everyone laughed.

"He used to go Jordan High, too. He graduated last year though," Lisa added.

Carla smiled when she caught Chancey and Tia nervously peeking at each other.

"Well, Miss Thang, you packed? Ready to go?" Lisa asked Tia.

"Just about," Tia said. "I just gotta go through my things to make sure I got everything."

"Well, what the hell you waitin' on? Jesus to come back? Shit, y'all better get on that highway. I don't want you guys traveling at night," Lisa said.

"Yeah, that traffic is a mess out there," Lori co-signed.

"Okay, mama," Tia said and kissed her mother's cheek.

"Have fun!" Carla said in her most cheery voice, and then hugged Tia and Chancey.

"And don't come back here wit' no babies!"

"Mama!"

Everybody laughed hard at Lisa. Chancey's whole body almost turned red.

"Shit, I'm serious! Hell, I'm too young to be somebody's damn grandmamma!"

18

"Tia, would you hurry up!"

"Okay, okay, here I come," Tia yelled. She had left Chancey sitting in the living room for ten minutes too long with backlogged Essence magazines. Just when he'd finished flipping through the third publication, she was running out with the fourth. "This one has Denzel Washington on the front!"

"Man, fuck Denzel's overrated ass!" Chancey said as he remotely flipped through the pages as he did with all the others.

"Ugh! Stop being mean," Tia whined.

"You told Lisa you was packed!"

"I am! I just gotta make sure..." Tia's words faded as she ran back to her room. "We're gonna be near some water, right?" she yelled.

"Going to a place called Catalina *Island*? I doubt it."

"Boy, quit being a smart aleck!" Tia yelled through laughter. "I'm try'na figure out which swimsuit to take, that's why I asked."

Chancey threw Denzel to the side and got up.

Tia smiled when she heard him coming down the hall. "I thought that would make you change your attitude," she said. "Which one you think..."

"The two-piece, most definitely," Chancey said without question.

"What's wrong with the one-piece?"

"On second thought," Chancey said and leaned back on the bed, "put 'em on so I can see."

Tia hit him and laughed.

"What? I'm serious! Let me see which one looks better!"

"I'm taking the two-piece, Chancey," Tia said while laughing, then threw her bikini in the overnight case. "Okay, let's see...I got my toothpaste, toothbrush, makeup bag...oh, my curling iron!" She darted to the bathroom and unplugged her Gold 'N Hot. She looked in the mirror, then plugged it back in.

"Did you get Lisa's ID?" Chancey asked.

"Yep!"

"She didn't notice it was gone?"

Tia laughed. "Not yet, anyway! That's why I'm try'na hurry up in case she's at a store right now writing a check or something. She'll be calling later, I'm sure. Just don't answer your phone." Tia started to laugh again.

During her chatter, Chancey kept glancing at the doorway, expecting her to come through it. One minute. Two minutes. He was actually watching the clock change time. "What 'chew doin' now?" he asked after smelling her sizzling hair.

"Bumping my ends real fast!"

"Man..." Chancey got up and marched to the bathroom. "You worse than my sister!"

"It's not gon' take long!"

"Whatever, man! I'ma run up here to Food 4 Less and get the chips and stuff."

"Oooh, that's perfect! I promise you I'll be ready when you get back!" Tia said, fluffing a section of her hair that she had just curled.

"Be outside! I want you to be standing on the sidewalk like a hitchhiker!"

"Oh, that's cold-blooded," Tia said, laughing.

*   *   *

Chancey unhooked one of the buggies from the stack of carts lined perfectly between the rails, and rolled it through the sliding doors of Food 4 Less. He moved about quickly up and down the aisles, throwing chips, dip, cookies, and soda in the cart. He read the signs hanging from the ceiling, looking for the candy aisle. Low and behold, when he dropped his eyes, they landed right in the face of Officer Woods who was standing in front of a variety of coffee brands.

Officer Woods was working the late shift tonight and using his free time to run some errands with his wife and kids. Chancey hadn't left his mind since the night on Grape Street. He was wondering what life turned out to be like for him. Did he take his advice? Was he selling his drugs elsewhere? He even went as far as looking for him on occasions while patrolling on his route, but never saw him anywhere.

Officer Woods was cautious with his approach. "Son," he said, dipping his head. That was his way of saying hello.

Chancey's smile was big and bright. He stepped to the officer like he wanted to hug him. Officer Woods' soul was touched. The reaction from Chancey made him reach out first. And although the hug was quick and sort of ill at ease, he felt strangely connected to him, almost as if he was hugging one of his own.

"Look what I got!" Chancey said. He pulled a black, leather wallet from his back pocket and shouted, "BOW!" as he flipped it open and showed his license.

Officer Woods smiled and said, "And got it in a wallet, too, huh? Watch out now!"

"Yeah, my girl bought me this wallet."

"And got a lil' honey, too!" Officer Woods said and smiled at his wife.

His wife giggled pleasantly, then introduced herself to Chancey.

"Yeah, this is my wife, Felicia, and my two kids, Lee and Ashley." Everyone did the meet and greet thing before the officer said, "Bet your girl don't look as good as my wife!"

"Oh Clarence, cut it out," Felicia blushed.

Chancey just laughed.

"Babe, me and the kids are going to get the milk. Wanna meet us over there?"

"Sounds like a plan," Officer Woods told her.

Chancey smiled back and forth at the two lovebirds.

"It was nice meeting you, Chancey," Felicia said. "Now, don't you listen to a word Clarence says, okay?" Felicia smiled at her husband, then kissed his cheek.

"Hey, what can I say? She's the boss," Officer Woods said.

When Felicia walked away, Chancey and Officer Woods stood quietly and watched each other idiotically, as if one was waiting on the other to speak.

Chancey said, "Man, thank..."

"So, how..."

"Oh, I'm sorry," Chancey said.

The officer said, "No, you go 'head."

"Well, I just wanted to say thank you for not arresting me the other night. Since then, a lotta things changed in my life. I got my license now, finally. Got a new girlfriend...one that don't play! She ain't into all that hustling and stuff. She's one of them *you-gotta-have-a-j-o-b-if-you-wanna-be-wit'-me* girls! You know what I'm sayin'?"

Officer Woods wore a smile on his face like it was permanent as he nodded continuously.

"Man, I can't cuss around this girl...I can't even drink a beer if I want to just kick back and watch the Lakers play or something! You know what I'm saying?" Chancey started to laugh.

"Sounds like she's the boss, too!" Officer Woods said and laughed.

"Yep, she's the boss! It's all good though. She's the best thing for me right now, know what I'm saying? She's helping me study for the test, you know, to get my GED..."

"Good for you! That's what I wanna hear! That's good, son!"

"Yeah, she's smart, man. She just graduated from Jordan High..."

"Alright!" Officer Woods cheered.

"Yeah, I'm gettin' ready to take her to Catalina Island. That's where she wanted to go, so..."

"She's the boss!" Officer Woods said, smiling.

"Yeah, she's the boss," Chancey said, giggling.

"Now, you just remember what you do to get her, is what you gotta do to keep her. Be expecting to take a trip to Catalina Island every other weekend, okay?" Officer Woods warned playfully.

"Yeah, okay," Chancey said and smiled.

There that dumbfounded stillness was again. And again, they both went to break the silence at the same time. Officer Woods threw up his hands and gave Chancey the floor.

Chancey looked down at his watch and said, "Man, I'ma let you get back to your family. Plus, I gotta raise up anyway so we can get on the road."

Officer Woods looked down at his watch and said, "Yeah, that traffic's a killer around this time."

Chancey and the officer leaned in at the shoulders, slightly longer than the first time, as they said their goodbyes.

Officer Woods let him get nearly to the center aisle before he called out his name. Chancey looked back. "Ever been fishing?"

"Nah," Chancey said.

"You should try it sometime. It's nothing in the world like reeling in a striped Bass. I take my kids up here to Debs Lake on Montgomery," Officer Woods said and thumbed westward. "You and…"

"Tia," Chancey said.

"Tia should come and let the old man show you a thing or two," Officer Woods said, handing Chancey one of his business cards.

"Cool, man. I'ma holla."

*   *   *

Chancey drove down 103rd like a bat out of hell, already able to hear Tia's mouth yelling at him. He thought twice about running the red light at Grape. All four of his tires screeched when he decided to hit the brakes and stop. "Shit!" He looked at the time on his dashboard and shook his head as waited on the green light. He thought about Officer Woods. It was funny seeing him out of uniform. *Ol' Woody had on some gear.* He chuckled to himself at the officer's black-and-white Nike sweat suit. He got his business card and flicked the corner of it as he grazed over the content. Would he call him? Chancey was almost certain that he wouldn't. As bad as he wanted to step outside of his life and try something different for a change, he knew he would never fall in the hands of a police officer. Not willingly, anyway. He didn't want to be disrespectful and throw the card out the window, so he pushed it in his ashtray and thought to dispose of it later.

He picked up his phone from the passenger's seat and wondered why it hadn't rang. "Oh yeah," he said as he noticed the phone's power was off.

The light turned green.

Chancey sped off and hit Kalmia without letting off the accelerator. He rolled up to the curb and thanked God that Tia was not waiting outside, but pretended to be irritated when she raced out the door, practically dragging her overnight case and yelling, "I'm ready!"

Tia's lengthy preparation was well worth the wait, he thought. He was digging the way her low-cut jeans hugged her hips and the earth-toned tank stopped just above her navel, fitting tightly around her breast and belly like it was a part of her body. Her hair was limp and blew freely in the gentle winds, occasionally sticking to her cherry-flavored lip-gloss.

"You changed clothes?" Chancey got out and asked.

"Yeah. You like what I got on?"

"I love what you got on!" Chancey grabbed Tia from behind and stuck his face in her hair. He could smell the fruity scent of her New West perfume.

"Don't you wanna change into some jeans or something?"

"No, Tia!" Chancey yelled and threw her bags in his jeep.

Tia laughed.

"And don't think you about to have me runnin' up to Catalina Island every other weekend, either!"

Huh? Where did that come from?

*   *   *

Tomika was hesitant at first. But just thinking of the way Tia came and snatched Chancey up like she was Mrs. It, gave her some balls the size of two ruby-red grapefruits. They shrunk to the size of lemons when she stepped to Kaylin's door though.

She held her fist up, but didn't knock. She looked around, then brought her eyes back to the door. She knocked, but only in mid-air. She sighed, then dropped her fist. "Come on, Tomika. You gotta do this shit!" She slowly brought up her fist and tapped lightly on the door with her knuckles. She stood. Waited. Then knocked harder and thought, *I usually don't do this, Kaylin, but I'm...* "No, that won't work," she shook her head and whispered. *Kaylin, I'm sorry to bother you, but...Kaylin, can you please drop me off at...*

Tomika jumped when Kaylin answered his door, wiping his eyes like he had been sleep.

"Oh, did I wake you? I'm sorry."

"That's alright. What's up?"

Okay, here it goes... "Sorry to bother you, Kay-Kay," Tomika said, "but uh, I'm kind'a stranded right now...I can't find where my auntie went..." She shut down suddenly, scared that Kaylin saw right through her lies and sought out the truth. She twiddled her thumbs and said, "Sooo..."

"So, you need a ride?" Kaylin asked in a voice that sounded like he knew she was running a scam.

I can't do this, Tomika concluded, until the money Rondell promised her revealed itself in her head. "Do you mind? Just right over here to my um...cousin's house on um..." *Shit, Tomika! Think!* "On Wilmington. I'll give you some gas money if you need some," she said, knowing she didn't have so much as five dollars on her.

Kaylin didn't suspect foul play; he just didn't want to go. He had not too long ago retaliated against the heat when he tore off his suit and made himself comfortable in front of the fan in some cut-off dickeys with a big bowl of Kellogg's Frosted Flakes.

He jarred the door open for Tomika and went to put on his corduroy house shoes.

Tomika didn't go in. She stood on the porch and looked around neurotically.

*   *   *

Tia showed the enthusiasm of a child on its way to a toy store as she and Chancey hurried to catch the Catalina Express. She felt so independent and free to do whatever. She felt incredibly sensual and ready for this hunk of a man standing next to her, carrying all the bags like a strong, black stallion. If the terminal wasn't busy with people pushing and shoving to get on the ferry, she would have tongued him down right then and there. But every time she went to do something nasty to him, some idiot was knocking her out the way with either his bags or big gut as he passed. It was okay, considering she and Chancey had plenty of touchy-feely time on the 710 freeway. It was fun watching him swerve and panic whenever she put her hands between his legs. One time, he grabbed her wrist and made her touch the lump below his waist.

"Ugh!" she screamed, laughing like someone was tickling her.

"Well, stop playin', then!"

"Ugh! You hard!" Tia said. Then she said, "Let me see," and reached over to touch the lump again. She petted it up and down to inspect its width and length.

"It's big, huh?" Chancey said, smiling.

The freeway experience had Tia's panties damp. She was in such a rush to get to the Catalina Island Hotel that it seemed like everyone else was moving in slow motion. And if the man in front of her with the salt-and-pepper crew cut didn't hurry up and aboard his macho self on the boat, she was going to introduce one of her open-toe sandals to his ass to help him along.

"I see you lookin' at that nigga's muscles," Chancey whispered from behind her.

Please! He looks like a geek! Tia thought, but looked over her shoulder and smiled to make Chancey jealous.

Tia spent the longest hour of her life cruising over wave after wave as they sailed to the Catalina Harbor. She had to admit, the sunset was beautiful! The orange sky was picture perfect! Chancey had his arms wrapped around her most of the way, although it wasn't chilly at all. The warm air was still. Everyone was silent as the swooshing sounds of the ocean calmed them. Even kids sat quietly in bewilderment as all the splashing commotion amused their little eyes.

Tia spotted the Catalina Island Inn on arrival. Its Victorian appeal was nothing to write home to her mother about, she thought. She wasn't impressed with the classic look at all. She could tell Chancey wasn't captivated either as she watched him concentrate on nothing but getting his money together as they entered the lobby.

The inside was just as antique-looking as the outside. Very simple and plain with maybe two art drawings on the wall. "What made you pick this hotel?" Chancey asked, frowning.

"It didn't look nothing like this on the internet," Tia said, also frowning.

The place was packed with long lines and restless children swinging on the ropes leading to the front desk. Tia was getting antsy herself, waiting and not really knowing what to expect from the clerk checking in the guest ahead of her. She looked at Chancey with worrisome eyes and said, "I hope this works."

"It will. Just play it cool," Chancey said, thinking, *Damn, we finna get the boot!*

Tia waited for the lady to get her screaming child under control before moving her and her family along. She felt herself tremble when she heard a man's voice yell, "Next in line, please."

As they walked to the counter, Chancey elbowed Tia softly and said, "Stop looking so nervous."

"May I help you?" the man asked in a staged way. His rude attitude and dry tone complimented each other. No smiles. No small talk. Just his wiggling fingers beckoning for her information.

Whoa, Tia thought, glancing at Chancey with her horror-struck eyes, only to find his just as horrified. "Yes, I would like to check in..."

"See your ID, please?" The man's fingers were still wiggling. He typed in Lisa's name aggressively on his keyboard.

Chancey walked away and pretended to be amazed by one of the paintings on the wall.

Chancey! Get back over here! Tia screamed inside.

"When did you make your reservations?" the hotel clerk asked as if there was a problem.

"I'm sorry?"

"I can't find your name in the system, ma'am. When did you make your reservations?"

"I...I don't have a reser..."

"All rooms have to be pre-paid on a credit card, ma'am," the clerk said, handing the license back to Tia.

Chancey peeked over his shoulder to see what was going on.

"They didn't tell me that over the pho..."

"Who did you talk to, ma'am?"

If this honkey cuts me off one more time... "I don't remember their na..."

"Hold on, ma'am!" The clerk walked off.

What an asshole! Tia turned to find Chancey.

Chancey quickly turned his back.

"What can we do for you, miss?" a nicer man returned with the clerk and asked.

Tia took a deep breath and said, "Me and my husband came all the way out here from the Bay Area…on our honeymoon…"

"How nice," the man said and smiled. He squinted his eyes at the computer screen, then typed something on the keyboard as Tia exaggerated her long journey to Catalina Island. He turned to the unpleasant clerk and said, "Let's go ahead and get 'em checked in a room."

"Without a reservation?"

Yes, you redneck!

"Yeah, we'll make an exception this one time."

"Thank you!" Tia snapped, rolling her eyes at meanie.

"In the future though, we ask that you make your reservations ahead of time. It actually secures a room for you, 'cause we fill up pretty quick on the weekends. You got lucky tonight."

"No problem. Thank you so much!"

"Sure thing. Enjoy your stay," Mr. Nice Guy said, then went to assist another one of his clerks.

Chancey appeared out the blue, faking like he needed an update on the check-in process. "Is everything cool?"

Tia rolled her eyes his way and snarled at him as she tapped her foot repeatedly against the floor. "It is now!"

*   *   *

"You left me standing there in front of that ol' racist…" Tia couldn't think of what else to call the clerk as she pushed the back strap of her sandals over her heels with her toes.

"I asked if you needed me! You just didn't hear me," Chancey lied, undoing the buttons to his formal dress shirt.

"No you didn't!" she yelled, throwing one of the pillows at him as she laughed. She tackled him from behind when he turned to hide his smile.

Chancey laughed as she wrestled him down on the bed. He

ended up on his back with her on top, pinning him down by his wrist. The struggling stopped. His laughter turned into a giggle, then a smile as he palmed her hips and moaned softly. Tia wet her panties again when she felt him get hard between her legs. She moved almost unnoticeably on top of him. He pressed her hips to intensify her thrust. His erect penis was almost painful as it pushed against the flatness of her vagina.

After a few minutes of rolling and bumping, Chancey took Tia's hands and rubbed them across his chest, then brought them up to his mouth and sucked one of her fingers; she felt embarrassed when her body twitched. He pulled her tank over her head and sucked on the cleavage bulging from her bra. Those twitches were becoming more frequent as he started to rub up and down her kitty. She wanted to hump his hand like a dog in heat, but was too ashamed to do it. She laid on top of him and tortured herself, trying hard to be still.

"Can I have some…please?" Chancey whispered, pulling on the crouch of her jeans. He was tugging so hard, her whole body was jerking with him.

"Yeah…but…"

Chancey unbuttoned her hip-huggers and almost tore off the zipper.

"Wait! I wanna get under the covers."

Chancey ripped the covers back and scooted his and Tia's body to the head of the bed. Tia hurried the sheet over her body to hide herself.

Chancey pushed her pants over her butt and pulled each of her legs out. He knew it was her first time and wanted to make it as special as possible. He thought to have them take a shower together, put on something sexy and flimsy, throw on some nice tunes, maybe even open the drapes so the moon could shine in on them as they made passionate love. However, now that she had him worked up and on the verge of cumming all over her, he rolled her on her back without missing a beat as he pulled his pants down and forced his way in.

Tia's immediate reaction was to close her legs, which made the pain more excruciating. "Whoa! Wait a minute! Stop for a second!" she screamed as every muscle in her body tensed.

"Open your legs."

"No! It hurts!"

"That's 'cause you gotta open your legs," Chancey tried to explain.

"Okay, wait…"

Chancey was still poking, vaguely.

"Stop moving!"

He got stiller than a dead man.

Tia's face tightened as she slowly slid her legs apart. "Okay. There," she said, bracing herself.

Chancey started working his penis through the opening of her kitty again. "Ooooh…you feel good as fuck!" He had his lips buried in her ear as he openly yearned for her.

Tia held her breath with each of his strokes, thinking it would be a cold day in hell before he got between her legs again.

"Oooh, unh-unh," Chancey sighed. "I swear'da God, you bet' not let *nobody* have this shit."

You ain't gettin' no more either!

Chancey's penetration suddenly got harder as he speeded up his flow. His moans were getting louder. Sweat was dripping from his face onto hers. The lips of her kitty were burning like the skin was being scraped off. He felt his fluids building up and getting ready to burst right through the tip of him. He stuck his hands underneath Tia's ass and pumped three good times. It felt like all her insides went with him when he quickly yanked out of her.

*   *   *

This was the third house Kaylin sat in front of in his car, waiting for Tomika to find this "auntie" she supposedly couldn't catch up with. The heat was letting up, which he thought was relieving. Finally, he could stop wiping beads of sweat from his forehead, temples, and neck—another way of letting him know he needed air conditioning. He had time to think about everything under the sun as he waited on Tomika. The thought of he and his father playing baseball startled him a little. After all these years, he could still visualize his dad lunging for their floor-model TV, which was first base. *Did you see me today, Pops?* Kaylin was smiling at himself strolling across the stage earlier that morning. *Moms said I looked just like you did on your graduation day. Same smile. Same walk. She said you even threw your fist up at your boys the same way I did. That's a trip!* Kaylin thought and giggled. Then he looked around embarrassingly to see if anyone saw him.

His demeanor sobered as his future slowly played into existence. He was leaning more and more toward the "Chancey-Kay's Eatery" that Chancey talked about, thinking a fast food joint wouldn't be such a bad idea to get into after all. A fat hamburger and fries, or a choice of some homemade fried chicken topped with hot sauce, was sure to have these known food chains eating their hearts out. Kaylin was sure of it!

Everybody knew he wasn't a joke when it came to cooking. With a mother like Niecy, who would be? Niecy taught Kaylin how to cook at an early age. If his cake didn't rise, she'd throw it out and make him bake another one. Same with his pot of rice—if it came out sticky, she would spoon it down the sink one scoop at a time. Kaylin hated cooking while growing up. Cooking was for girls, he thought.

Kaylin didn't realize he had skills until he had to help prepare Thanksgiving dinner one year. The spread consisted of macaroni and cheese, yams covered with melted marshmallows, collards, sweet potato pies, rolls with squares of butter stuffed in the center of them, and a goose—not turkey. Kaylin thought turkeys were too traditional, and wanted to kick it up a notch with some juicy dark meat. At nine years old, he was walking plates over to Ms. Doris' house, Nikki and her bunch, Rondell and his mother, and whoever else he could feed without taking food out of his and Niecy's mouth. He knew his dinner was more than just good by the way Chancey came running over, declaring how Christmas was on him.

Kaylin smiled as he thought back to when Chancey stood at his door, pulling up his dirty pants with one hand and wiping his snotty nose with the other.

"I-I-I'ma make a Christmas dinner!" Chancey said. His little self was so excited, he forgot to say hi to Niecy and Kaylin when he barged in.

"He's just try'na copy off me, huh, Mama?" Kaylin said.

"Be nice, Kay-Kay," Niecy said.

"Yeah! Quit being jealous!" Chancey shouted, standing in the middle of the living room floor, holding up his pants, and wiping away a sticky string of mucus sliming down his nose like lava.

"Jealous of what, fool? You can't even cook!" Kaylin shouted back.

"Chancey, go bring me some tissue," Niecy said.

Of course, Chancey returned with only a small square of toilet tissue he had torn off. He was walking up to Niecy with it, but his eyes were glaring at Kaylin.

Kaylin was still teasing him about how he couldn't cook. Chancey was ready to strike back, but Niecy made him shut up and bring her more toilet paper, which this time he returned flying a long line of the tissue like a kite. Again, he walked up to Niecy, glaring at Kaylin.

Kaylin laughed and asked Chancey what he was making on Christmas.

"I'ma make a chicken like you did!"

Kaylin fell out on the floor. He rolled around on the carpet and laughed so hard, he snorted. When his amusement decreased, he sat up and yelled, "He said, 'I'ma make a chicken'!" then tumbled over and roared with hilarity again.

"Tell Kaylin to stop being jealous!" Chancey yelled, frowning so hard that his eyebrows were almost touching each other.

"Stop teasing, Kaylin! I mean it! You stop it right now!" Niecy said, standing over her son until he settled down. When he did, she took Chancey's kite, crumbled it up, held it under his nose, and told him to blow.

Memories of Chancey had Kaylin enjoying himself all by his lonesome at his one-man party in his car. He called Chancey to tease him about the "chicken" incident all over again, but Chancey didn't answer his cell. Still wanting to be humored, he dialed home to remind Niecy of the "chicken" incident. He knew she would be amused, since they laughed about the situation for years after it happened. But Niecy didn't answer either. He looked down at his watch; she was still at work.

He cut a quick glance at the two-story home he was sitting in front of. Then he glanced around the whole area—all the houses were two stories. And each showed pride of ownership. *Nice,* he thought. Very nice. Nothing like Watts! This place had class. He could tell these people had money. From what he could see, there wasn't a driveway that didn't have either a Mercedes Benz, BMW, or Infiniti parked in it. Suddenly, he felt unsuited in his Chevy.

Tomika made Kaylin sorry he had opened his door for her as he leaned toward the passenger's side of his car and widened his eyes to try and see through the blinds in the kitchen window. He has never called a female out of her name before, but tonight, Tomika made him lose his religion. "I wish this broad bring 'er ass on," he mumbled. A broad was the harshest name he could call her without feeling like he had sinned.

Kaylin started honking for Tomika, thinking she was lucky he had home training. When she didn't come out fast enough, he blew like his hand was glued to the horn. Then he stopped and looked around nervously. He knew he was in the wrong neighborhood to be acting niggerish. He opened his car door to get out and go drag Tomika out the house by her braids if he had to. He was ready to go, like two days ago!

Just as he stepped from his vehicle, the front door unbolted. Tomika came out and down the three steps of the porch carefully in her spiked heels. When she reached the bottom, she sprinted up to Kaylin's side of the car. "I'm waiting on a call," she said.

"You waitin' on *what?!*" Kaylin snapped. He jumped back in his car. "Oh, hell no! I'm outta here!"

"Kaylin, wait!"

"Man, you got me all the way out here in Fontana, talking about you waitin' on a phone call! I'm out!" He started his engine.

"I told 'chew my auntie got my keys!"

"What auntie, 'Mik? Where's this auntie you keep talkin' about?" Kaylin asked, looking around sarcastically.

"She lives right here, Kaylin!"

"Well, where's she at, then? Tell 'er ass to give you the damn keys so I can smash!"

"That's what I'm waiting on! She's not here! I just called her cell and left a message..."

Kaylin shook his head. "You crazy as hell if you think I'm finna sit up here and wait on you!" He started revving up his motor.

"Kaylin, just wait five minutes! Please!"

"Have her take you home! Shit, when 'er ass get back, tell 'er you need a ride. Simple as that!"

"She don't have a car, Kaylin!"

"Now she don't have a car," Kaylin mumbled to himself.

"She don't! I ain't lying! She's with the person that gave us a ride to the graduation today. They left me! I put that on everything I love! I thought she was gon' be here. That's the only reason I had you bring me way out here. I wouldn't stand up here and lie to you, Kaylin. I swear I wouldn't!" Tomika said, telling a boldfaced lie.

Kaylin sighed and gritted his teeth.

She could see the shape of his jaw in his cheeks; she knew he was mad. "I can try and get in touch with Chancey," she said. "I think he still got an extra key to my house…"

"Man, I told you fifty times already that Chancey is gone! Damn! And he ain't coming back 'til Sunday!"

"Oh yeah, that's right. Well, let me try and call my auntie again."

Tomika and Kaylin's attention turned to the door when a young girl stuck her head out and yelled, "You got a phone call!"

"Oh good," Tomika said. "That's prolly my auntie right there." Just as soon as Tomika ran in, she was running out with her purse in hand.

"What's up! Was that her or what?" Kaylin asked.

"Yeah! Actually no! It was my mother. She said, um…she's at home, so it's safe for me to come home now so I can get in."

Kaylin frowned. "What the hell did you just say?"

"Never mind! Just take me home."

19

Chancey rolled over on his back, dog-tired. Tia's lovemaking was all that, a bag of Doritos, *and* a Super Big Gulp! He chuckled to himself as he played with the idea of barking to let her know. She saw the grin and asked what was so funny, although the satisfaction written on his face made it pretty obvious. Still, she wanted his raspy voice in her ear again, telling her how good she felt, begging her to never give herself to another.

Chancey turned to Tia and said nothing. He just smiled as he ran his eyes across her lips, then up to her nose, then up to meet her stare.

"What?" she asked, giggling, playing like she couldn't figure him out.

Chancey was still smiling when he shook his head at her. His eyes were marked with pleasure. His mouth was forming a word that wouldn't come out.

"You are so crazy, Chancey," Tia said, laughing at his gratifying sighs and moans.

"You felt *good*, Tia. I swear'da *God* you did!"

Tia smiled. *Tell me more!*

"Yo' shit was warm...and tight...and *oooh*...can I have some more? Please?"

Tia laughed. "Nuh-unh!" she said and held her knees together. "You already wounded it!"

"Did I hurt it?"

"Yes!"

"Let me kiss it and make it better."

"Ugh! No!" Tia thought Chancey was even nastier than before.

"Why not? Shit, it's mine!"

Now she thought he was even nuttier than before.

"It ain't mine?" he asked when he saw her expression.

The cat had Tia's tongue for real. She didn't know what to say or do; this was all new to her. Was that a question men usually asked women after sex? Was it a trick question?

"Is it mine, Tia?" Chancey asked seriously.

"I guess," she said dumbly, too embarrassed to say yes. And she could tell by his reaction that he took it the wrong way.

"You guess?! Man, I wish you *would* let another mothafucka have some of my shit!"

Tia smirked sexily. "What would you do?" she asked.

Chancey got close to her ear and whispered, "I would stick somethin' in it and blow it up!" Then he looked at her with promising eyes.

Tia thought she was sick in the head for allowing that comment to arouse her. And the more he stared in her eyes like there wasn't a playful bone in him, the more she wished he would force her legs apart and try to take it from her right then and there. She almost moaned when she said, "Yeah, but if you do that, then *you* can't have none no more."

"That's aw'ight! I bet 'chew the next nigga won't get no more! Yeah!" Chancey said, nodding authoritatively. He laid back, angered to some extent, and palmed his face, then sighed as he brought his hands down his features.

Tia leaned her elbow right in a puddle of sperm when she went to kiss his rage away. She jumped back and frowned at her arm. "Yuck!"

"Damn, it squirted way over here!" Chancey said, looking around for something to wipe the semen up with. He took off his T-shirt and blotted the spot until it was dry. "There you go. See, I'm lookin' out for you."

Tia popped Chancey and laughed out loud. "Nuh-unh, boy, you looking out for yourself! Shoot, I'm not sleeping on this side, you are!"

"Oh," Chancey said submissively, and threw his T-shirt over his shoulder and onto the floor.

"Yeah! Act like you know!" Tia said and kissed his lips. She climbed on top of him hoping to make him want her again, not that she would make herself available; she would play hard to get all night, of course. She just wanted him to beg, moan, and bite his bottom lip like he was being hurt so good again. "You wanna go walk around on the beach for a lil' while?" she asked, realizing their sexual escapade was done with for the night. His stuff was as soft as hers.

Chancey put his arms around Tia. "Is that what you wanna do?"

"Not really," she answered and giggled. She felt lazy and indolent, and slid down a few inches to put her chin on his chest. "Shoot, we can just lay here and talk all night if you want to."

"I wish we was layin' here like this every night," he said, stroking the back of her hair.

"You mean like getting a place together?"

"I mean like gettin' a place together—just being together! Some permanent shit, you know what I'm sayin'? What 'chew think about that? You think you ready for somethin' like that?"

Hell yes! "You think you ready for it?"

Chancey was staring at Tia's lips as she spoke. When she completed her sentence, he stared into her eyes. "I *know* I'm ready for it," he said. "I've been ready ever since that time I seen you at Grape Supermarket. Remember that?"

Tia laughed. "Don't remind me."

"I'm in love with you, Tia."

Tia's eyes widened. *Dayum!*

"You see I stopped drinkin' for you and everything! Shit, I don't even smoke weed no more! None of that shit! You told me about your father's drinking problem and I respect that. I don't wanna do nothin' that's gon' make you feel uncomfortable…"

Aaaaaaaaaw! Tia reached up and held his cheeks.

"Shit is real, man. You got my head fucked up! I can't stop thinking about you..."

I think about you all the time, too! I go to bed thinking about you. Fall asleep thinking about you. I dream about you when I'm asleep. I wake up thinking about you..."

"I'm sayin', I don't know what I'ma do when Sunday comes. I don't want you to leave. You got me feelin' like I used to feel when I was young and used to spend the night over Kaylin's house. We would try'da stay up all night, scared to go to sleep, 'cause we knew when we woke up the next day, I had to go home. And we only stayed a couple units apart! That was crazy, huh?"

Chancey almost brought tears to Tia's eyes. *Aw, that is so sweet!*

Chancey got very quiet. Thinking, Tia supposed. The fact that she had just lost her virginity wasn't even an issue like she thought it would be. Actually, surprisingly as it seemed, she felt comfortable and at peace. It was like they'd made love many times before. She rubbed his face, massaged her fingers through his curls, and played with his ears. She couldn't stop touching him!

He took her roaming hands and held them tight as he stared at her. She never imagined in a million years that she'd be somewhere gazing into Chancey's eyes this long. She remembered a time when she couldn't look at him more than two seconds.

I love you, Chancey, she wanted to say, but was still questioning his realness in the back of her mind. If, for some reason, he never called her again, at least she didn't say those three words. Then she got mad at herself, thinking, here this man was pouring his heart out to her and all she could seem to do was harp over childish assumptions. "I love you, Chancey," she said, waiting eagerly on his response.

Chancey lifted her chin and whispered, "Marry me."

DAYUM! That one caught Tia by pleasant surprise! She felt her throat tightening. Oh no, she was getting choked up. Her eyes were filling with tears. Her vision was blurring.

"I waited all these years to get with you, and I'm not léttin' you get away."

Now, that's the truth, she thought, teary-eyed as she recollected memories of him that traveled way back to elementary.

"I'm 'bout to get my shit together and get a job, T. I'm serious as a heart attack. My sister was telling me about this trucking school in Arcadia called Dootson or somethin' like that. I'ma find out the exact name when we get back. Once I get my GED, I'm goin' there to get my trucking license. Shit, I heard truck drivers get *paid*, too! And if that don't work out, me and Kaylin been talkin' about opening up a lil' hole in the wall like Jordan's Café. Either way, I'ma do somethin', T. I promise you that."

"Yeah, but I'm just scared that you gon' end up in jail before all this happens," Tia confessed.

"Why would I end up in jail?"

"You said you still got some...you know...left, right?" Tia said it like "drugs" was too dirty of a word to say.

"Okay, *and*?"

"AND I'm just saying...I'm scared something might...that you might get busted or something...I don't know, Chancey. I'm just scared, okay?"

"I told you, T. You don't need to be scared..."

"How long is it gon' take you to get rid of it? And where is it now? You wasn't stupid enough to bring it with you, I *know*!"

Chancey smacked his lips. "You know I wouldn't do no crazy shit like that! I had Kaylin put it up for me," he said. "I got somebody right now that wanna take it off my hands. I just gotta call 'em when I get back..."

"Who's to say he's not a cop?"

"He's not. I dealt wit' him before."

"He's gonna buy all of it?" Tia asked, somewhat confused.

"Yeah."

"How much is it?"

"Half a key."

"What's that?"

"It looks like powder," Chancey said. "You cook it up, make it hard, then break it down."

Tia frowned. *You cook it up, make it hard, then break it down?*

"You stretch it out and make more money that way. I'ma just sell the whole thing though. Fuck it."

"You takin' a lost?"

"Nah, not really. I'm just not makin' a profit. I ain't trippin' though, Tia. None of that shit matters to me! What matters to me is what's layin' right here wit' me," he said and softly pinched the tip of Tia's chin. "Plus, if we got a place together, it ain't like we won't be able to afford it. You 'bout to start workin' at the VA, and…"

"Yeah, that's if I get it," Tia said.

"Have you heard from 'em yet?"

She sighed anxiously. "No. The lady in personnel said I gotta wait 'til the job closes."

"When does it close?"

"The tenth of next month."

"July!"

"Yep," she said disappointedly.

"Well, that's aw'ight, shit, don't worry about it. I got some money to take care of us for a minute," Chancey said, kissing her forehead.

"Where would you wanna live?"

Chancey took a deep breath and thought. "I don't know. We prolly gotta get one of those apartment books. You know which one's I'm talkin' about?"

"Yeah. The apartments in there are too expensive though. We're better off looking in the L.A. Times. I'll get the Sunday paper and look through it."

"Cool."

"Now, don't have me doin' all this, and then you turn around and go to jail on me. I'm kickin' ya' ass if you do!"

"Quit cussin' before I get my belt!"

"Quit cussing? I know you shame! Shoot, you and my mother curse so much, y'all need to go to a rehabilitation center!"

Chancey chuckled a little. "I don't cuss that much."

Tia gasped like she was taking her last breath. "My mother!" she yelled, rolling off Chancey onto her back. "I forgot to call and tell 'er we made it!"

"My cell phone's over there on the table; you can use it."

"Can you get it for me?"

"You get it! Shit, I mean shoot, you closer to it than I am!" Chancey said, frowning.

"You get it. Please…"

"Tia, why can't you get it? You right there!"

"'Cause!" Tia said, snuggling the sheet under her chin. She knew it would be utterly ridiculous to put her clothes on just to walk twelve inches from the bed. She also knew that if she got up, every embarrassing detail of her physique would be exposed. She didn't budge.

"You are so spoiled!" Chancey yelled, then crawled over her, got out of bed, took two steps, grabbed his cell and tossed it next to her before crawling back in bed and laying down.

When Tia turned his phone on, she was alerted with two beeps that sounded more like bells.

"I got a message."

"What's your code so I can see who it's from?" she said in a playful, but serious way.

"It ain't nobody but Ronnie..."

"*Whud-eva*'!" Tia said and proceeded to call her mother up. "Hey sexy," she said, then laughed at Lisa's smart reply. "Yeah, we made it. We're getting situated right now. Prolly go to dinner a little later." Pausing, "Your license? No, I haven't seen it," she said, then smiled at Chancey when he looked at her.

Chancey sat back and watched her role-play.

"Did you check on your dresser? What about in your pockets?" Pausing, "Well, I haven't seen it," she said.

Liar! Chancey thought.

"Okay, Mama. Love you, too. Bye." Tia hung up and smiled as she handed Chancey his phone.

"Liar!"

She giggled.

Chancey dialed the number to his cell and pressed the button that would relay his messages.

"You have four unheard messages," he heard an electronic voice tell him. "To listen to your messages, press 1."

He pressed one.

"Sent today at three-nineteen pm..."

"Chance, it's me, Setchi. Can you call me when you get this message? I need to talk to you about Curt. It's about something I found out. Call me please! As soon as you get this message! I need your advice on what I should do."

Chancey quickly erased Setchi's message, feeling irritated just *thinking* about all the kiddy questions she was going to hit him with.

He pressed one.

"Sent today at four-thirty-five pm…"

"This is Rosie, Chancey. Hey listen, can you call me when you get this message? Okay? I, uh…I…"

Hurry up!

"…uh…just call me when you get a chance, okay? This is like my third time calling you."

So!

"I guess your phone is off."

No shit!

"I really need for you to call me."

Chancey pressed the number to fast-forward Rosie's message, then deleted it. She wasn't talking about nothing, he thought as he pressed one.

"Sent today at seven-seven pm…"

"Hit me when you get this!" It was Kaylin. He sounded angered.

Chancey thought to call him after he retrieved his last message. He pressed one.

"Sent today at eight-twenty pm…"

"Cuz, I've been callin' you all fuckin' night! Won't 'chew turn this shit on!" It was Kaylin again. Sounding *very* upset!

Chancey listened closely.

Kaylin sighed. "Cuz, somebody broke in my mothafuckin' house!"

Chancey sat up, wearing a frown.

"What's wrong?" Tia asked.

"Nothing," he told her, getting up to go to the bathroom.

"They fucked up my room! The kitchen! They pulled all the shit out the freezer and just left the shit on the floor!" Kaylin screamed.

The freezer? "Aw, nah," Chancey whispered, slowly shaking his head as he drew in to Kaylin's voice again.

"They even fucked up my mother's room! The whole house is fucked up! I'm try'na clean this shit up before my mother gets home, but still…the fuckin' front door is kicked in! I don't know *what* I'ma say about *that!*"

"Where's my shit?" Chancey yelled into the phone.

Tia came to the bathroom door asking if everything was all right.

"It's fine, Tia! I'll be out in a minute," he said and locked the door.

She made him miss the end of Kaylin's message. He pressed the button to back it up a bit. He had to find out what happened to his drugs and money!

"I don't know *what* I'ma say about *that!* I'm looking at it right now…it looks like they took the knob off. Oh, okay, that's how they got in. They didn't kick the door in…they took the knob off and came in that way."

Stupid-ass! I kept tellin' that fool to lock his shit up! Chancey leaned against the sink and sighed.

"You kept tellin' me to lock both locks, too! Damn!" There was a brief moment of silence. "Anyway, cuz, that's what's up! Hit me back *as soon* as you get this message."

What about my shit!

"I'm 'bout to clean this shit up and try'da fix this door. Alright, then. Later."

Chancey called Kaylin right away, but there was no answer. He wanted to throw his phone. He closed his eyes to calm down. But he couldn't think. There were too many things going on in his head to concentrate on one theory. He called the number to his cell and listened to Kaylin's message again. He had to get home, he thought. Now! What should he tell Tia? He began to pace the floor.

Chancey put his ear against the bathroom door; it was as quiet as a library on the other side. He paced the floor again to think of something to tell her. *How could you feel like you have everything in the world one minute, then feel like you don't even own your own soul the next?* Chancey asked himself. He stopped pacing and posed with a fist on his hip and the other at his chin as he tried to think about Tia. He didn't want to tell her there was a possibility that every dime he had may have been stolen. Not yet. He started to pray, but didn't know how. And even if he did, his life was so corrupted, he didn't know where to begin.

Tia knocked on the door. "Chancey! You okay?"

Fuck! "Yeah…I'm…hold on, I'ma be out in a minute," Chancey said. He latched on to the knob and leaned his forehead against the door. He waited until he was relaxed enough to at least act like things weren't as bad as they had seemed. He knew that if he had opened the door a moment sooner, he would have bit Tia's head off.

He sighed deeply, then opened the door. Tia was standing in

front of it. She had put her clothes back on. He hadn't even noticed. He was delusional as he walked passed her.

"Chancey, what's wrong?" she grabbed him and asked as if she wanted to cry.

"My mother…she's back in the hospital," he said and frowned. He was too ticked off to try and look sad.

"Oh, Chancey," Tia cried. "I'm sorry…"

"Don't worry about it," he said, cutting her off.

Tia thought he was being a little hard, but blew it off, figuring he was probably uptight because they had to leave sooner than expected. She put her arms around him for comfort. Chancey was huffing so hard, she could feel the air from his nostrils shooting against her forehead. "Don't worry, Chancey, we can come back another time."

Chancey looked at her, puzzled.

"I understand. You have to go so you can see about your mother."
Yeah! See about my mother! That's right!

"When I get this job at the VA, the next trip is on me," she said, giggling to lighten the mood.

Chancey nodded slowly. His face was still long.

"Thank God we didn't unpack," she said, still trying to make him see the brighter side of things.

"Yeah," Chancey said, seeing everything as dark as midnight.

"Don't worry about your mother, Chancey. She's going to be fine, okay? Just think positive," Tia said as she put on her shoes.

Worried? Shit, I wouldn't give a fuck if a diesel crashed into Nikki's punk-ass!

"What hospital is she in?"

"Uh…"

"Duh! I'm sure it's the same one as before," Tia said, chuckling at her stupid question as she quickly fixed her hair. "Can I come with you to see her? I mean, I would hate to meet her in the hospital, but at least that's better than not meeting her at all, you know what I'm saying?"

Chancey wouldn't have been able to come up with an excuse for not wanting Tia to come with him even if he wanted to. His mind was so overloaded with thoughts, suspects, suspicions, accusations, anger, hurt, betrayal, and a billion other notions that he couldn't tell anyone his name at that moment if they asked him.

"Yeah, whatever," he said, vowing to cross that bridge when he came to it.

20

Setchi couldn't conceal her agony any longer. Curt had destroyed everything she was worth! She felt used and already washed up at her tender age of just four days shy of sixteen. All she needed was some reassurance—a simple phone call from him would do. She's been waiting by the phone ever since the day her dream turned into a nightmare, but every time it rang, it was for Chancey. For a person who was hardly ever around, he sure did receive a lot of phone calls, she angrily thought. She stood over the phone and watched it like a hawk, wondering when she would get it through her thick scull: Curt was not going to call!

This is crazy, she thought, and backed away from the phone with an attitude. She dropped on her bed and let the springs in the mattress bounce her. When they stopped flexing, she folded her arms and wept.

She needed to let off some steam. Keeping the pain bottled in like this was healthy for no one, she thought. She didn't want to waste good brain cells explaining her situation to Nikki. Besides, she was never home long enough to hear her out anyway. And now that she was home, she was so tired and out of if, she barely greeted Setchi when she came in.

And no how, no way was she explaining the nitty-gritty to Kashaun. She knew when it came to gossip, Kashaun had a history that was as long as time! And *she*, the laughing stock of Jordan High, never! Besides, the "Curt" conversations she shared with Kashaun usually painted a perfect picture. A picture so flawless, she became the envy of all her classmates! And she wanted to keep it that way, although it was hard maintaining a lavish lifestyle that didn't exist anymore. People at school were already starting to ask questions. Just the other day, she remembered being asked, "You and Curt broke up?" when they saw her walking home from school.

To cover up their split, Setchi said, "No. He had to work late." It didn't make sense to put it out there when he would be calling to try and win her back soon.

Eleven days, fourteen hours, and thirty-three seconds later—no call! Setchi wanted to slice her key right through the black paint of his BMW! She wanted to put the two on the ten when she explained everything to her brother!

She pumped herself up, believing Chancey would hunt Curt down and do God knows what to him once he found out how he has hurt his baby sister. "You just wait," she scowled, dialing Chancey's cell again. "I'm telling him *everything*!" Curt was in trouble now!

Chancey's cell phone didn't ring. The long awaited silence brought a recorded voice that said, "The cellular customer you are trying to reach is unavailable or has traveled outside the calling area. Please try your call again later."

"Shoot!" Setchi hung up.

*   *   *

Rosie got Ronda situated in bed and topped her night off with a bedtime story. The much needed attention had Ronda's little heart bubbling with excitement. She crawled in the burrow of her sheets as her mommy returned the story of Cinderella back to her Disney book holders. She knew what was coming next when Rosie knelt down at her bedside. She wiggled around, thrilled to give the Lord her wish list.

Rosie said, "All tucked in?"

"Yes, Mommy."

"Okay. Now God lay me down to sleep…"

Ronda closed her eyes so tight, her entire face was crunched. "I pray the Lord my soul to keep…"

"If I shall die before I wake…"

"I pray the Lord my soul to take…"

"God bless…"

"Lemme say it! Lemme say it!" Ronda yelled.

Rosie giggled. "Okay, sweetie, go 'head."

"God bless *everyone* in the whole white world!"

"Amen…"

"And God bless Ma, Papa, and my Ti-Ti, Christina…"

"You really miss them, huh?"

"Yes. I wish I can see them. And I miss Auntie Maria, too! And little Jose, and Roberto, and…"

"Okay, sweetie, that's enough."

"But *Mommy*…I'm not finished yet."

"I need you to hurry up, Ronda, so you can go to sleep!"

"And God bless Chancey, Kaylin, and Ronnie. And God please find my daddy and tell 'em I love him and I wish he would come home to me, 'cause I really, really, *really* miss him, God. A-man!" Ronda's innocent expression turned sad when she saw Rosie's eyes. "Why are you crying, Mommy?"

"I'm okay, sweetie…" Rosie's throat was so wedged, it hurt to talk. She wiped her eyes to keep tears from falling in her daughter's face as she nestled the covers around her. She held her soaked cheek against Ronda's and whispered, "I love you," then ran out the room so she wouldn't witness her breakdown.

She held her hands up to her lips and cried out in her palms as she raced down the hall to the living room. She fell on the couch and almost capsized as she broke down, crying a river of hurt. Years of pain was lifted off her back with each drop the fell from her eyes.

She looked back to her daughter's room. That was her *daughter* back there! Her own flesh and blood! How could she overlook her the way she's been doing for the past three years? And how could she sit back and let a man who *she knows* is the father, overlook her?

Rosie's crying subsided long enough to realize she wanted her Ma and Papa just as bad as Ronda did. The life she thought she wanted turned out to be the life she'd wish on no one. She was jobless, penniless, and tired of barely surviving. The only time Rondell helped foot her bills was when she helped *his* to grow. She opened her house to drug attics for him! Prepared his drugs for him! She even went as far as becoming a part-time drug dealer for him—the most she's ever gotten from him was three-hundred-and-fifty dollars to pay her past due rent. Past due rent! Ronda needed clothes, pull-ups, enrollment money for pre-school, love, and affection; he picks and chooses to help out with past due rent! Rosie didn't have to wonder why—if she lost her place, he had nowhere to set up shop. "I got played," she told herself. Need she say more?

She sat alone with nothing but the thumps of her pulse to keep her company. Rondell was the scum of the earth, she reckoned, despising herself for all the times she thought he was cool. She could hear his slick voice laying out his plans to Tomika in her head, and quickly tried to shake his tone from her memory. That was something she wanted no part in! In fact, as he murmured in Tomika's ear, she took Ronda's hands and played patty cake, just so he'd know she didn't want anything to do with it. In fact, if she owned a car and didn't have to wait on him, she would have driven her and her daughter to safety when she first got wind of what he was encouraging Tomika to do.

Darkness was filling the living room as the sun slowly went under. Rosie got scared. Of what, she didn't know. Whatever it was, made her get up and turn on the lights. She sunk down in the couch again, and wondered if Kaylin was okay. She thought of every reason why she shouldn't call and check on him as she dialed his number. She thought about what she would say, then decided to just listen. "Don't say shit, Rosie!" she said, tuning in to one ring after the other.

When Kaylin didn't answer, Rosie terminated the call with a press of a button. Then she browsed over the numbers with the tip of her fingers, pressing slightly harder on the numbers that would reach out and touch Chancey. This would make her fifth time calling him; she just couldn't bring herself to stop dialing! A part of her wished she'd get his answering machine again as she vibrated the phone against her ear and waited.

*   *   *

Tia massaged Chancey's shoulders while he took the rental ten miles over the speed limit down the 710. Something had his mind spinning; she could see it in his eyes. He was so absorbed that she didn't think he realized how fast he was going. "Chancey, you should probably slow down," she said. "Your mother's gonna be fine." Her body jerked forward when he took his foot off the gas.

Chancey sighed with frustration. If Tia said one more thing about his mother, he was going to pull over and put her out!

"Let's talk about something to get your mind off your mother. Oooh, I know! Let's play a game called...I forgot the name of it, but it goes like this: I gotta say something, and then you have to repeat what I said, and say something after that. Then I have to say what I said, repeat what you said, then think of something else to say after it..."

Chancey accelerated twenty miles over the speed limit!

"Okay, I'll go first... It's Friday night," Tia said, smiling elatedly. "It's your turn!"

"And I'm mad as hell," Chancey said.

Tia laughed and said, "Nope! You were supposed to say, 'It's Friday night and I'm mad as hell'..."

"Whoops! I lose," Chancey said and stared off again.

"It's okay. I'll give you another chance."

Damn!

"Okay, you ready? You gotta really pay attention, okay? Okay, here we go..."

Chancey's cell phone rang. His hands moved like the Matrix when he pulled it from his belt buckle. "Hello!"

"Chancey, it's Rosie. I finally caught you..."

"'Ey, Rosie, you s...K..lin?"

"What? You breaking up."

"Can you hear me now?" Chancey asked.

Silence.

"Hello?"

Silence.

"Shit! My phone hung up!" Within seconds, it started to ring again. "Hello?"

"Chancey?"

Aw hell! "What Setchi?"

"I got a problem…"

"Not right now! I'm waitin' on a phone call…"

"But it's important!"

"What is it?" Chancey snapped.

"Alright, tell me what you think about this…"

"Make it quick!"

"Okay, you know my boyfriend, Curt, right…well, he's my x-boyfriend now…"

"Uh-oh…my phone is breaking up…can you hear me?"

"I hear you just fine."

He heard her just fine, too. "Hello? You still there?"

"Yeah, I'm here…"

"Guess I lost you…"

"I'm here!"

"If you can hear me, I'll call you back when I get to a better area." Chancey hung up fast and called Rosie back.

"Hello?" Rosie answered as though she was waiting for the phone to ring.

"Rosie, you seen Kaylin?"

"No…and I've been calling 'em…*and* you…to tell you…are you sitting down?"

Rosie knew what happened, Chancey suspected. By the sound of her voice, she probably knew who did it! "I'm sittin'!"

"Okay, I don't know how you gon' take this, Chance. And I know you're a long ways away…"

"Nah, actually I'm almost at the 110…" Chancey saw Tia trying to surpass Toni Braxton's singing on the radio, and figured his conversation was *his* conversation. Still, he rolled his window down to create a loud, gusty, windstorm in the car, just to be sure.

"Freeway?"

"Yeah. Kaylin left me a message, talkin' about somebody broke in his house…"

"Did they take anything?"

"I don't know! That's what I'm try'na find out! I've been callin' his house, but he ain't answerin'."

"Okay, I'ma ask you this—you don't have to answer if you don't want to…"

"Alright."

"Did you have your stash over there?"

"Yelp."

"Shit, Chance!" Rosie snapped and hit her fist on the coffee table. She sighed and said, "Alright look, you didn't hear this from me, okay?"

"Mmm-humph."

"You know when we was all at the graduation…"

"Mmm-humph."

"And you and Tia left…"

"Mmm-humph."

Rosie paused and sighed. "Okay, promise you didn't hear this from me…and I'm not saying they did it or not, but…"

Chancey was all ears!

"I heard Ronnie and Tomika plottin' to set Kaylin up."

Chancey's adrenaline had him now driving *forty* miles over the speed limit!

"Chancey, slow down!" Tia yelled in a panic. Once again, her body jolted forward when he let off the gas.

Rosie said, "Don't quote me, but Ronnie told Tomika to make Kaylin leave some kind'a way. Then he was supposed to go to the house while they was gone, and get the key that you was holding for 'em…"

"*Holdin'* for 'em? I *know* that ain't what his ass said!"

Chancey's outburst caught Tia's attention.

"Well, don't get me to lying," Rosie said. "Shit, I don't remember all what he said. All I know is they was scheming on poor Kaylin. I felt so bad, too, because Kaylin don't mess with nobody. Every time you see Kay-Kay, he's either on his way to school or to work. Now, am I right or what? And that Tomika's a dirty bitch! She was all gung-ho when she found out she was gettin' some money out the deal."

"Oh, he paid 'er?"

"Well, I heard him say he would give her something when he got it; you had some money there, too, right?"

"Over five G's!"

"Shit!" Rosie said with feeling. "They got you, Chancey. I am so sorry…"

Chancey didn't speak on it. He was too traumatized. Hurt, definitely. Angry, in the worst way!

The stillness made Rosie feel like a masterminded troublemaker! One who has caused the greatest pain that could ever be imposed on someone. She faulted herself for being the Good Samaritan. Wished she could take it all back and mend Chancey's broken heart.

Chancey's heart was broken, without a doubt; he could never imagine himself doing something like this to Rondell. And the thought of Tomika crossing him, made him almost shed a tear. He finally said, "Rosie, let me call you back," in a dry, unnatural tone.

"What 'chew finna do, call 'em?" Rosie asked, strictly out of fear.

"Hell the fuck yeah!" Chancey yelled. His anger was rising. His heart was now racing. His breathing was heavy.

Tia tapped Chancey's leg and whispered, "What's wrong?"

Rosie said, "Please don't tell 'em I told you." She could tell by the way he chuckled that it would be in her best interest to find another place to live. Preferably in another city—in a whole-nother state!

"I'll call you back," Chancey said, positioning his fingers on the "end call" button.

"Chancey…alright, fine," Rosie said, but didn't hang up.

As soon a Chancey heard the pause, he pressed her off the line.

Tia asked, "Who was that?" so fast, she almost bit her tongue.

Chancey looked at Tia and said, "I need to take care of some business, Tia, and I don't want you caught up in it…"

"You not finna take me home!"

Half a smile broke free from his glare.

Tia asked, "What kind of business? And who was that on the phone?"

"Tia, some shit is goin' on right now and I don't want you…"

"We know that! Now, who was that on the phone? And what's this business you taking care of?"

"You a feisty lil' thing, huh?"

Tia blushed for no more than a second before she said, "Boy, you better get to talking!"

Chancey fidgeted while he juggled his thoughts of telling the truth vs. another lie.

A moment passed.

"Chancey."

He cleared his throat and said, "Tia, somebody broke in Kaylin's house," then paused like there was more.

Tia frowned as she waited.

"*Ronnie* broke in Kaylin's house, Tia. My so-called boy! Ain't that some shit?"

Tia's mouth hung open! Chancey could have counted every last one of her teeth if he wanted to.

He said, "Tomika was in on it, too..."

"Tuh-*Meeeka*!"

"They got all my shit—that key I was telling you about...I had that, about five thousand in cash, and a gun in a small gym bag."

"Oh my God! Tuh-*Meeeka*! Five thousand dollars! You had that much money? And what were you doing with a gun?"

"And I've been callin' Kaylin, but he ain't answerin' for some reason..."

"Oh my God, I hope he's okay!"

"He's okay; he left a message on my phone when we was in Catalina," Chancey slipped up and said.

Tia's mind went into mathematical motion. It was all starting to add up. She said, "So, that call wasn't about your mother? That's why you ran to the bathroom..."

"I didn't know how to tell you that I lost just about everything I had, Tia, that's the only reason I lied to you. The *only* reason! Shit, we just finished talkin' about gettin' a place together and damn..." Chancey closed his eyes briefly as he sighed. "I didn't want you to feel like I was lettin' you down already."

"Chancey, I'm not with you because of that stuff."

"I know, Tia, but..."

"Wait a minute. Chancey, I love you for you. Not for what you have! That stuff don't mean nothing to me. I wouldn't care if you was po', broke, and hungry..."

"*Was*? Shit, I am...now!" Chancey said. "It's all good though, 'cause when I see his ass, it's on!"

"Don't go doing nothing stupid. Just pray on it..."

"What? Man, I'm not finna let this nigga get away wit' that shit!"

"Go 'head, then, Chancey. Beat 'em up! Let 'em know you a rider about yours..."

"Why you try'na be funny?"

"'Cause! I'm try'na make you hear how stupid you sound!"

"Tia, you would never understand how I'm feelin' as a man right now! These mothafuckas, excuse my mothafuckin' language, broke in my homeboy's house, took all my shit ..."

"Maybe God is try'na tell you something. You ever stop and think about that?"

"What?"

"You heard me!"

Chancey sighed and mumbled, "Don't come at me wit' all that God shit," under his breath.

"What did you say?"

"Nothin'!"

"Everything happens for a reason, Chancey."

"Mmm," he grunted with a twisted lip.

"And if you ask me, I think God is try'na show you that you don't need all that crap to survive."

Who asked you?

"Whatever they got, let 'em keep it!"

I heard that!

"God has better things in store for you...for us..." Tia took Chancey's hand and held it.

"Yeah, I hear you," he said as if it was just something to say.

He slid his hand out of Tia's and exited off the highway into a neighborhood that she was unfamiliar with; it was still in Watts; she had just never been there. He slowed in front of a house that had the potential of looking nice. Its paint was fairly good—a pretty peach with white trimming. The porch light was made out of brass and glass holding a tiny bulb that was shaped like a burning flame; Tia thought that was cute. She gaped at the lawn though, willing to bet her life the jungle of weeds were taller than she was.

Chancey made a last minute decision to stop, and swerved over in front of the house next to the one he wanted. "I'll be right back," he said and put the Pontiac in park.

Tia grabbed his arm and asked, "Where you going?"

"I'll be right back!"

"No, Chancey," she cried and wrapped her arms around him. She was practically in his seat, holding on for dear life.

"Tia, would you let me go please."

"No! I'm not lettin' you get in no trouble. Tomika lives here. I ain't stupid."

Chancey's nose flared. "Yep! And I'm 'bout to fuck 'er ass up..." Chancey jumped from the car and took Tia with him.

She was glad she was quick on her feet; if she hadn't quickly stepped out of the car, she would have been drugged out.

Tia stood back and watched Chancey head up the long driveway. Soon as he reached the garage, it sounded like ten dogs started barking in the back. She hurried back inside and locked all the doors!

He covered his eyes, briefly, as the security lights practically blinded him when they came on and lit up the entire front yard. He didn't bother to knock; it was clear no one was home. Tomika's grandmother had a house full of three generations—her, her daughter, and her five grandkids; Chancey knew the barking mutts were bound to bring *somebody* to the window by now.

He shuffled his feet backwards down the driveway and kept his eyes locked on the curtains in case they moved.

*   *   *

Rondell passed the cigar of marijuana leaves to Tomika. Tomika took a quick hit, passed it back. She lounged on the baby-soft seats of his leather couch and verbally wondered where Chancey had his goods. "Maybe he took it wit' 'em," she said, while holding in the smoke. She let it marinate until her lungs couldn't take it anymore, and as she coughed, the smoke pushed through each of her nostrils like clouds.

Rondell puffed on the cigar, then passed it on again. He sat on the side of Tomika, quiet, nodding at times, shaking his head at other times as he cursed Chancey in his thoughts.

After Tomika finished choking again, she tried to hand the burning stick back to Rondell.

"Nah, I'm cool," he told her and leaned his forehead on his knuckles.

"Where all did you look?" she asked, sensing his aggravation.

"Everywhere! Shit, I even looked in his mama's room..."

"Maybe he left it with Setchi!"

Rondell shook his head. "Nah, he ain't left shit over there in a while. Not wit' Nikki's smoked-out ass!"

Tomika's eyes bucked. "Yeah! I saw her comin' out a crack-house…I knew that was her! Yep!"

"That ain't nothin' new! Shit, she stay at that mothafucka! How I know? 'Cause that's the house my nigga, Byrd uses to make his money out of! He owns it! That and two other ones!"

"For real?" Tomika said, even though she was sick of Rondell talking about Byrd like he was king of Los Angeles.

"You talkin' about the house on Lou Dillon, right?" Rondell asked.

"Yep! Lookin' tore up!"

"I know. Walkin' around here owin' everybody…"

"She owe you, too?"

"Nikki owe me so much money it ain't even funny. Every time a nigga turn around she askin' to get shit on credit."

"Damn, the whole fam owe you!" Tomika said and laughed.

Rondell didn't find her funny. "Look at this shit!" he said and went over to the hall closet. He started pulling out all of Chancey's clothes, shoes, and grooming utensils. "I bought all this shit! These hundred-dollar-Jordans, these Fubu jeans…all this shit! Look!" He stood over the scattered items and sighed. "All this shit is me!"

"Them is tight right there," Tomika said and went over to the black leather sneaks with a small, red symbol of a man flying in the air, carrying a ball. "These jeans is cute, too. I wonder can I fit 'em." She picked the jeans up and held them at her waist. They looked like they belonged to a child compared to the big hips they were up against.

"Yo' big ass can't get in those!"

"Nigga, fuck you! Shit, yes I can," she said and tried to stretch them out to reach the edges of her hips. "Let me have 'em."

Frowning, "No, I ain't lettin' you take his pants!"

"Why? You said you was puttin' him out anyway…"

"So! That don't mean I'm finna give you his shit!"

"Mmm," Tomika grunted and dropped the jeans at her feet. She rolled her eyes and walked back to the couch with, "Well, when you givin' me my money, then? Shit, a nigga need 'er some clothes," coming from her mouth.

Rondell cut his eyes at Tomika. "I told you I couldn't find the money!"

"I don't understand that type of language."

Rondell mumbled something smart as he raked Chancey's clothes into a neat pile.

"YOU SAID you was givin' me a hu'nid dollars if I got Kaylin to leave the house. You didn't say, ''Mika, if I don't find the money I can't pay you'!" As Tomika spoke, she was waving her finger in the air. Her micros were flapping with her jerking head.

"Quit trippin'! Aw'ight! I'ma give it to you on Sunday when his ass get back."

"Uuuuugh!" Tomika growled and smacked her thigh. She found Rondell's cordless, then called Dame and asked him to come meet her out on 103rd. When she hung up, she looked at Rondell and said, "Niggas!"

Rondell said, "Can't live wit' us..."

"And don't want to!" she said as she slipped on her heels. She stood up and put her hands on her hips.

"Goodbye!"

"Don't rush me!" She rolled her eyes so hard, all you saw were the whites of her eyeballs. "You could at least gimme twenty dollars so I can give Dame some gas money."

Rondell chuckled as he pulled his funds from his pocket. "You know you ain't givin' up nothin' but some ass! Here," he said and slapped a ten, two fives, and some ones in her hand.

"That's alright, it's my ass!" she said and walked outside. As she walked away, she pushed her butt out and spanked it. "I'll be back on Sunday for the rest of my money. And I want it all in big bills, too, busta!"

"Shut up before I have somebody waitin' on that nigga when he get here!"

Tomika walked off smiling and patting her ass.

"And use a condom!" Rondell said and closed his door.

*   *   *

Chancey peered at Tia's long face, wanting to apologize for, as she says, "jeopardizing her life". But since she ignored him from the time they left Tomika's house, until the time they pulled up here at 99th Place, a twenty-five-mile-radius, he lost every desire to do so. "How long am I gettin' the silent treatment?"

"I don't appreciate you putting my life in danger, Chancey," Tia said.

Chancey took her hand and gently squeezed it. "I'm not gon' let nothin' happen to you. Alright? Nothin'."

"What would you had of done if she came out with a butcher knife?"

"Ran like hell! Shit, what 'chew think?"

"Oh, you would'a just left me, huh?"

"If you didn't have enough sense to run, then that's on you."

"Chancey!" Tia yelled and punched him in the shoulder. When she saw it didn't hurt, she punched him again.

"Alright!" he shouted and grabbed his arm.

Tia pouted.

"Don't be mad at me. Alright, Tia? I just wanted to look her black-ass in the face, and ask her why, you know what I'm saying? Why would you let this nigga talk you into some shit like that? You know?"

"Chancey, what's done is done. You gotta put it in the Lord's hands and forget about it. Let him handle it."

"Nah, I think I'ma help 'em out…"

"You not funny!"

"I'm not try'na be!"

"Ugh! You can be an asshole sometimes. I wish I had of known this before I let you take my virginity," Tia said, close to tears.

Chancey closed his eyes and threw his body back against the car seat. "Tia…" he said and ran his fingers through his hair. He stopped and gripped the center of his cranium. "I'm not try'na be mean to you…I'm not a asshole. I'm just frustrated right now. I'm frustrated with life! Seems like every time shit is goin' halfway good, I always get set back some fuckin' kind'a way!"

"I don't look at this as a set back. I look at it as a new beginning. God knows your heart, Chancey. He hears you! That's why he took the drugs away from you. Don't you get it? He knows you want a change…that you tired of selling drugs. This is his way of helping you…by taking it from you. Now, it's up to you to be strong. And fight with this…" Tia tapped on his temples. "Not with violence. Violence ain't gon' do nothing but cause more violence. That's all I'm saying."

Chancey sighed.

Tia looped her arm around his and said, "Come on, I wanna meet your mother. Let's forget about all this nonsense for a while…"

"Tia, me and my mother don't even talk! Alright? That's why I never introduced you to her. Shit, I can't stand her ass! And she can't stand me either!"

Tia looked surprised. "You never told me that."

"It's a lotta things I never told you."

"Like what, you got AIDS?" Tia giggled.

Chancey rolled his eyes to look at her, then rolled them away.

"Oh, baby, I'm sorry," she purred. "Come here…"

Tia took his head, laid it on her breast, and rocked. She twirled a curly strand of his hair around one of her fingers and listened as Chancey opened up to her, telling his inner secrets, fears, wants, dreams, why he hated his mother, and why he thought she hated him.

She was learning his pain. And understood why he felt selling drugs were his only means of survival. Without guidance and support, who wouldn't make bad decisions in life, she thought.

"Still, Chancey," she said, "no matter how you look at it, she's still your mother. And it says in the bible 'He who honors their mother and father, shall live long'."

"Well, I guess I'll just be a short-livin' mothafucka, then!" Chancey said as he rose from her breast and turned the car off.

Tia smiled and said, "Watch yo' mouth, sailor!"

Chancey stepped from the car into a bizarre surrounding. Something just didn't feel right. Like the short trip to Catalina cleansed him from the poverty's filth and now he didn't belong there anymore. He walked around to Tia and waited for her to grab her purse, bag of Frito's, and Essence magazine, then put his arm around her as they walked over to Rosie's apartment.

"How long are we gonna be here?" she asked.

"Not long. I just gotta call Kaylin real quick."

"Why don't you just go to his house?"

"It's a long story."

"You and your long stories are starting to get on my nerves," Tia said.

Chancey tapped on Rosie's door.

Rosie peeked out the window with a frightened face. She saw Chancey and Tia, opened the door and pulled them inside. "Y'all okay? You talked to Ronnie, Chancey? I finally got in touch with Kaylin. Told 'em you was on your way back."

"Oh, you did?" Chancey asked. Then he said, "'Ey, I want you to meet my wife," and lightly pushed Tia toward Rosie.

Rosie clasped Tia's hand in her palms and shook it. "We didn't get to meet earlier. So much mess going on…"

Tia chuckled. "Yeah, tell me about it. I can't believe they broke in Kaylin's house though!"

Rosie raised her eyebrows and nodded.

Chancey said, "Let me use your phone, Rosie. My battery's low," as he dialed Kaylin. Suddenly, he hung up.

Rosie asked what happened.

"Niecy answered."

"You still avoiding her?"

Tia smiled and said, "Oh, so that's why you didn't wanna go over there…"

"The longer you stay away, the harder it is to go back," Rosie said.

"I'ma go see 'er soon as I get my shit together," Chancey said and dialed Kaylin again. "Here Rosie! Ask for 'em…"

Rosie said, "Hello? Kaylin? Hey, it's me. Chancey 'nem are here." Then she hung up.

"What he say?" Chancey asked.

"He's on his way."

Chancey said, "Cool," and sat on the sofa next to Tia, who was reading about a new product line of makeup in her magazine.

"Did you call Ronnie?" Rosie asked.

"Nope!"

Tia said, "I told him he needs to just leave that alone, you know?"

"Yep! That's the same thing I told Kaylin. 'Cause Kaylin's talking about doing something to 'em," Rosie said.

"Chancey, too! But like my mother always said, you need to leave it alone and give it to God. Let him fight your battles."

"I hear you, girl."

Chancey listened to the two chatterboxes go on and on about how a truce should be called as he awaited Kaylin's Arrival.

21

Kaylin was attacked with hugs and concerns when Rosie opened her door. Chancey was behind her looking anxious to get to him. He held Kaylin back by the shoulders and looked him over from head to toe. "You alright?"

"Yeah," Kaylin said and walked in. He noticed Tia sitting on the couch with her legs crossed. "How you doin', Tia?"

She smiled and said, "Hi Kaylin."

"So, what's up, cuz? What happened?" Chancey asked.

Kaylin ran everything down to him.

"Did they get my bag?"

Kaylin had to stop and think where he put it. "I think...no, I don't think so. I don't think I ever took it out my trunk."

Everybody looked at each other with smiles and bucked eyes. Rosie and Tia crossed their fingers.

"Let's go see," Chancey said.

As he and Kaylin exited, Kaylin said, "I know it's there. I forgot to take it out."

Chancey smiled and sighed in relief. He threw his arm around

Kaylin. "See how hardheaded you are! I told you to put my shit up!"

"You know you happy as hell I didn't!" Kaylin said.

"'Ey T, I'll be right back, alright?"

"Don't worry. She'll be fine," Rosie told Chancey.

Kaylin followed Chancey outside and over to his car parked near the gym. He leaned in his trunk and unzipped the Nike duffle for Chancey's eyes to see.

Chancey looked around nervously, quickly peeped out his money, drugs, and the barrel of his .38 snub, then told him to close it up.

"Cuz, you better take this bag! This shit almost got me killed today!"

"Man, wasn't nothin' gon' happen to you. Rosie told you who did it, right?"

"Yeah, she told me Ronnie's crazy ass did it. Cuz, that fool need to have his head checked out. I don't give a damn what you say! His ass ain't playin' wit' a full deck!"

"No, I know! I'm just sayin' he ain't no killer! This was all about money, Kaylin! That's it," Chancey said, walking his bag to the back of the rented vehicle.

Kaylin got in the driver's seat and said, "What is this, a Grand Am?"

"Yeah," Chancey said and sat in the passenger's seat.

"How it ride?"

"It rolls! Shit, I was doing about a hundred and five on the freeway. Mad as hell!"

Kaylin chuckled.

"When I first heard your message, I was like, damn! I didn't know *what* the hell was goin' on! And I kept try'na call you back...how come you didn't answer the phone?"

"That was you? I didn't know *who* that was. I was try'na get all that shit up before my mother came home."

"What she say? Did she notice anything?"

"Nah."

"How's she doin', man? I gotta go see 'er...I gotta get my shit together...I swear, Kaylin, I thought I lost everything! It felt just like when I got outta jail. That same feeling. Like you in this big-ass world with nothing. No money, no food, no place to say..."

"Moms is doin' fine!" Kaylin interrupted. "You should go see 'er sometime. She ask about you all the time."

Chancey's eyes watered, but not enough to form a tear. "I swear to God, Kaylin, I want to so bad. But I wanna go see 'er with something real, like a real job. Not this ol' fairytale bullshit! Like Tia's mama...she thinks I'm a construction worker, building houses and shit. You believe that shit!" Chancey chuckled lightly.

"You can be whatever you wanna be, cuz. It ain't gon' happen over night though. You gotta put in work!"

"I know. I know. I know..."

"Well, then! Shit, you ain't no dummy. You got brains and shit like everybody else! Quit talkin' about what 'chew gon' do and do it!"

Chancey stared at Kaylin, lost in his words of advice.

Kaylin hadn't realized he was sounding scornful until he glanced at Chancey's eyes. "Shit, don't get me started," he said. "'Cause you know I ain't feelin' sorry for you."

"I got five G's, Kay. I'm ready to dump it into something legit. What's up?"

"Like the restaurant?"

"Whatever you think will make us some money," Chancey said.

Kaylin was twisting the steering wheel from side to side as he thought about how to turn five thousand into ten thousand when Tia came from Rosie's apartment, looking around.

Chancey stuck his head out the car and asked if she was ready to leave.

She nodded.

"Alright, here I come."

"Where y'all going?" Kaylin asked.

"I don't know, shit. I'm hungry as hell though."

"Moms made a meatloaf," Kaylin said and frowned. "I ain't eatin' that shit!"

"Come on, let's go to dinner...my treat!" Chancey said, jumping from the car with a fireball of energy.

Kaylin emerged less enthused, complaining about three being a crowd.

"I run this, fool!" Chancey boasted. "Her ass better get in the back seat and shut the fuck up!"

Kaylin smiled as he listened to Chancey blow his own horn, knowing he'd crumble if Tia was to hear him.

"'Ey, gimme about thirty minutes while I run in here and see what the hell Setchi's ass want."

"Aw'ight," Kaylin said and strolled home.

"I'ma call you when I'm ready. Answer the phone!" Chancey yelled.

He secured the locks on the vehicle and stepped a couple of steps away from it, then stopped. He looked toward the units facing 103rd and contemplated what he should do. Should he confront Rondell? Should he just leave it alone like Tia suggested? He backed up to the trunk with his narrowing eyes focused in on the area where Rondell's unit was. As he popped the trunk, he repeatedly called himself stupid for his decision. He took all the cash out of the Nike duffle and put it in the blue suitcase he had packed for the trip. He picked up his revolver, held it down, and checked the chamber loaded with four bullets. He placed it under the cocaine, threw the Nike duffle on his shoulder, closed the trunk, and walked.

He had mixed feelings about facing Rondell. He knew it wouldn't be easy; he could already feel himself shaking as he cut through the grassy field that divided the Jordan Downs into two sections. He didn't shake from fear, but from the immense hurt spurting through his body as he could almost visualize Rondell tearing up Kaylin's house.

He kept a watchful eye out for anyone who might announce his presence and blow his surprised visit as he crept slowly through Rondell's unit.

*   *   *

Rondell was in the middle of stuffing some leftover Shrimp Fried Rice in his mouth when he heard someone knocking at the door. First, he tried to assess the hostility in the knocks. This person was mad, he thought as he slid off his satin comforter. He wondered who he had pissed off as he shuffled down the hall in his blue and green checkered flannel pajama pants and white T-shirt. He went to unlock the door, but the random pounding made him first look out the curtains. When he saw Chancey, he closed his eyes in disbelief, then opened them again; it was still Chancey. He backed away from the window and let his mind run free as he stood with his mouth open until Chancey hammered his door again. He opened it slowly. Very slowly.

Immediately, Chancey walked in and threw the packaged cocaine on the coffee table. "Is this what you was lookin' for?" he asked.

Rondell was caught like a child in the cookie jar. His opened mouth had the audacity to form a smile that soon disappeared when he saw Chancey pull out his black snubby. "What 'chew 'bout to do with that?"

Chancey walked up to Rondell and said, "You's about a dumb nigga, runnin' up in Kaylin's house like nobody would find out it was you! How come you couldn't be a man about yours? Let me know how you was feelin' to my face?"

Rondell was quietly fearing for his life as he backed away from Chancey until the wall brought him to a dead end.

"You a pussy! You wanna do some shit when a nigga ain't around! I should blow yo' fuckin' head off!" Chancey paused for a long time as he stared in the eyes of what was once his closest ally. "But I ain't!" he finally said. "I got too much shit to lose right about now."

Rondell exhaled like he had been holding his breath. He was hot, both literally and mentally. He wanted to throw a right hook to Chancey's jaw followed by an uppercut to the chin. But seeing the metallic peacemaker standing out in his hand like a turd in the punchbowl, he thought to talk his hatred out instead…just as soon as his heart rate slowed.

Chancey went over to the couch not knowing what kind of danger, if any, his threat had put him in, and decided to hold on to the gun just in case he had to find out.

"I can't believe you pulled a gun on me, cuz," Rondell said when he was able to talk.

"I can't believe you tried to rob me! You 'spose to be my boy!"

"I can't believe you pulled a gun on me, cuz…"

"You shouldn't'a tried to take my shit, then, nigga!" Chancey yelled, swinging his hand to express his anger.

Rondell flinched, then moved so he wouldn't catch a stray bullet. "Yo' shit? Nigga, everything you own is me! You rollin' 'cause of me! Takin' trips and shit 'cause of me! Those shoes on yo' feet, nigga, is me! All that jewelry and shit you got on is me! Now that you got a lil' money and a bitch, you wanna act like you don't know a nigga no more!"

*   *   *

"Sure you don't want nothing to drink?" Rosie asked as she sipped the White Zinfandel from her wine glass.

"No, I'm fine, thank you," Tia answered, looking around for a clock.

"Yeah, that Chancey is a fool," Rosie said, smiling. Then she laughed like there was no tomorrow. "Girl, did he tell you he used to have a crush on me?"

Tia was unaware of the frown on her face as she faked a smile.

"Oh, no, no, no, this was a looooooong time ago...before he went to juvie. It was so cute because...well, you know I'm a few years older than he his," Rosie said, leaving no room for a response. "His lil' butt used to ride by my house almost everyday when I lived on Juniper..."

I'ma kill him! He didn't tell me that...

"Him and Rondell. They would always stop in front of my house like they were fixing their chains or something..." Rosie stopped to laugh. "Just phony, girl," she said and sighed. "Yeah, but those were the good ol' days though. Then I had to go and mess around wit' Ronnie..."

Any other time, Tia would have sat patiently while Rosie vented. However, since it had been almost an hour since Chancey said they were leaving, and since she could really give a rat's ass about Rondell, she said, "Excuse me, Rosie, can I please use your phone to call Chancey?"

"Sure," Rosie said, dialing Chancey's cell number and handing the phone to Tia.

"No answer."

"Didn't he go over Kaylin's?"

"I don't know. Let me see. Isn't his number three, five, seven..."
Rosie finished it off.

Tia got the runaround when Kaylin came on the line telling her to call Setchi, who in turn, referred her to Rondell.

Tia hung up concerned. Rosie looked out the door to see if Chancey's car was still parked outside. Seeing that it was had them both assuming he had paid Rondell a visit after all.

"Where does Rondell live?"

"Across the field on the other side."

"Is it walking distance?"

"If you feel like walking!"

Tia got Rosie's hint right away: she didn't feel like walking. She put her hands together like she was praying. "Please, Rosie?"

"It's not that I don't wanna walk—I would walk with you! It's just that I don't wanna see Ronnie right now," Rosie explained. Then she gave Tia directions on how to get there. "It's not far," she said. "See over there?"

Tia looked past the sandbox with swings and slides, analyzing the time it would take to get there.

"You'll be there in less than five minutes. I can stand here and watch you 'til you get over there if you want me to."

*   *   *

"So, *that's* what this is about," Chancey said. "As long as I'm swingin' from yo' nuts, you cool. But the minute you see me doin' my own thang, you got a problem wit' it. Now, you wanna take all yo' shit back..."

"Quit actin' like…"

"I know you helped me get on my feet when I came home. Gave me a lil' money. A place to say. I know that shit! And I appreciate it. But don't stand up here and act like I owe you somethin'! 'Cause let's not forget, I'm the one that let yo' ass go free! Aw'ight! So, if anybody owes anybody somethin', yo' ass should be owin' me! I spent fo' years behind bars and never once mentioned yo' name. Shit, if you wanna get technical about it, all this shit you got is me!" Chancey said, waving his gun around the living room.

Rondell moved constantly so he wouldn't become a target.

"Well, it *was* me! I see you got all my shit piled up, ready to throw a nigga out. It's cool. I ain't trippin', shit. Do what 'chew gotta do."

"I thought you was finna leave…the way you walked off wit'

Tito…"

"I'ma *be* alright! I don't need that lil'-ass half a key. Take that shit! I'ma just take it as a lost. Fuck it! God got somethin' better in store for me. I promise you that!" Chancey said, tucking his gun in the front of his pants.

Rondell saw the whites of his eyes looking glossy and red like he was crying tears that had too much pride to turn into drops as he stood over the pile of his things and sorted through them.

Chancey took the smaller items like his boxers, T-shirts, and grooming utensils, and packed them in his duffle. Then he picked up the bigger items and carried them to the couch. "I gotta go to my mother's house so I can find somethin' to put this shit in."

Rondell never meant to take it this far. He just wanted his friend back, their hustle back! He thought by stealing the drugs, Chancey would have no other choice *but* to come back! Then things would be back to normal, he thought. He didn't know what he thought! But he knew he still had a heart when he felt moisture building up in his eyes. He walked to the bathroom coolly so Chancey wouldn't run after him thinking he had a weapon, only to discover a sensitive side that no one knew he had.

Rondell was just about to turn the water on in the sink just in case he slipped up and sniffled when he heard the sound of his doorbell ring. *Now who the fuck is this?* he wondered, thinking his night couldn't get any worse. He dried his eyes and walked back to the living room. Chancey was in the doorway trying to get Tia to settle down.

Tia was outraged. After every bit of advice she'd given Chancey, he still took it upon himself to do the total opposite. This relationship was going to have problems, she thought. "What the hell are you doing?"

"I'll talk to you about it later," Chancey snapped in a near whisper. "Here. Take the keys and go sit in the car. I'll be out in…"

"I'm not walking way back over there by myself!" Tia yelled. "Nobody told you to bring yo' ass over here anyway! You was so mad at him, remember? Why you over here acting like he's your friend now? He ain't yo' friend! This man don' stole from you, jeopardized your best friend's life, and you over here kissing his ass!"

"You don't know what 'chew talkin' about, alright! I ain't hardly kissin' nobody's ass! I'm over here packin' up my shit, that's what I'm doin'!"

"Well, I'll wait," Tia said, folding her arms.

"Tia, can you please go wait in the car?"

"No, I'ma wait r-i-g-h-t here!" Tia said. Chancey felt her spit spray him in the chin when she exaggerated the pronunciation of the word "right".

"Hi, Tito." Rondell came up from behind Chancey.

Tia put the "G" in ghetto when she gave Rondell a piece of her mind. "Excuse me, but my name is T-yah! O-kay! That's first of all! Second of all, I don't know who the hell you think you are, but you ain't shit to me! Chancey might be over here kissin' ass, but I ain't scared…"

Okay, Chancey thought, *it's time to go.* He held the door with the inside of his leg to keep her from coming in as he reached over the arm of the couch to grab his bag. He looked back at Rondell who was smiling not-so-happily at Tia, and told him he'd be back later for his things.

Tia was still going at it. "Keep playing with me and I'ma call the police and tell 'em you broke in Kaylin's house!" she said. Her wrist and head were rolling in sync with each other.

Chancey hurried up and pushed her away from Rondell's door. "Come on. Let's go to my mother's house."

"Don't push me!"

"C'mon, let's go!"

"Forget him! That's right, forget 'chew! You ain't nothing!"

Rondell stood in the doorway and winked at Tia when she looked back.

"No he didn't!" Tia said and stopped. "You can keep yo' winks and stick 'em up…" She swallowed the rest of her sentence when Chancey jerked her by the neck and pushed her in front of him.

"*Shood*…I don't know who he think he is," Tia said, looking back at what was now a closed door. "And here you are, right back in his face! You scared of him or something?"

"Come on now, you talkin' stupid! I ain't scared of nobody!"

"You could'a fooled me by the way you kept asking me to leave like you was on *his* side or something!"

"I ain't on his side, I just didn't want you making a scene in front of his house. I told you I was handling it! Shit, you makin' matters worse than what…"

"No, I was tellin' him like it is! Something you obviously don't know how to do!" Tia snapped, almost tripping over a hole in the grass.

"That's what you get."

"At least I ain't a sell-out! Over there kissin'…"

"Would you be quiet for a minute? Damn!"

Tia stopped and crossed her arms. "Go 'head! Say what you gotta say!"

"Nobody's kissin' ass, T. I went over there to take 'em the coke. God didn't want me to have it anyway, right?"

Tia grabbed a hold of Chancey's bag and ripped the zipper back. She smiled as she pushed around all of his underclothes.

"Ain't nothin' in there but clothes," he said.

"You really did, huh?" Tia asked, surprised. She reached out and kissed him on every part of his face. "I was praying hard, just asking God to please get all that negativity away from us and He did! Thanks for helping Him out," she said, laughing with tears pouring down her face.

Chancey laid her head on his chest and gently massaged it. He was amazed by the way her spirituality was moving in on him. This girl was special, he thought. So special, he didn't feel deserving of her, but was thankful he had her. His guardian angel! He pledged to do right by her. Always!

"I cry too much," she said and wiped her face.

"It's alright," Chancey said, holding her. "I love you, T. You hear me?"

"Yeah, I hear you. I love you, too, Chancey. I mean, C!"

"Big C!"

"Boy, please!" Tia said, smiling. She and Chancey continued their pace as though they were chained at the ankles.

Chancey's cell rung. "This is Kaylin, I bet," he said and answered it. He told the caller to meet him at the car.

"Kaylin?" Tia asked when he hung up.

"Yeah. We all goin' to get somethin' to eat. You cool wit' that?"

"That's fine with me. Shoot, I'm starvin'!"

"Yeah, me, too!"

Chancey saw Kaylin waiting for them against the bumper of the rental. When they got within hearing range, he said, "Here," and tossed him the keys as he ventured off to building thirty-six.

"Y'all comin' from Ronnie's house?" Kaylin asked, frowning.

Both Chancey and Tia laughed.

"Wait 'til I tell you, cuz!" Chancey said. "I had to keep Mrs. Incredible Hulk over here from beatin' that nigga's ass! Threatenin' to call the police on 'em and shit…"

Tia hit Chancey as usual to show her love. "Nu-uh! You puttin' way too much on it!"

"Don't listen to her, Kay. Listen to me! Watch, when I get back, I'ma have you rollin'!"

"Well, hurry up!" Kaylin said. "The only thing gon' be open in a minute is Denny's!"

*   *   *

Tia was getting more than just her ass whipped tonight if Rondell could help it. Not only did she interrupt the flow of his money, but now she was disrespecting him, too. *Oh hell naw, bitch, yo' ass gotta go!* He furiously felt around for his pistol on the top shelf of his closet; the 9mm made Chancey's gun look like a cheap toy. He packed it away in the inside pocket of his leather coat, slipped into his Adidas open toe flip-flops and hit the block to find Stan.

He knew that Stan would more than likely be walking the streets around this time, and raced up 103rd, running all stoplights that would delay time he didn't have to waste. He drove down Wilmington's long stretch and made a rapid left onto 105th Street. He found Stan like he knew he would, lurking between Hickory Street and Croesus Avenue.

Rondell pulled up on the side of Stan so strong that Stan's sticks for legs almost took off running. He slid the electric window on the passenger's side all the way down, but didn't have to say a word.

Stan saw Rondell's face and immediately his mouth started watering. "Hey, buddy! Good heavens, you scared the shit outta me!" Stan said, giggling nervously.

Rondell was emotionless. "Get in Stan."

"Hey, man, no problem. What's goin' on? Everything alright? I see you got your Lexus back, huh? This mug is clean! I feel like *the shit* just sitting in it!" Stan laughed, exposing all of his rotten teeth. He knew to be quiet when Rondell threw up his palm.

"I need you to do somethin' for me," Rondell said.

"No problem, buddy. What is it?"

"I need you to off Chancey's girlfriend."

Stan gasped. "Whoa! Bud, I...I, uh...I ain't no killer, man! I mean, if you need me to clock the bitch in the back of the head or somethin', I got you covered. But killin' somebody...you askin' for a pretty big favor there."

"A half a key!" Rondell said slowly.

Stan's eyes grew tremendously large. "Get outta here! Serious?!"

Hell no! "Yeah," Rondell said.

Stan looked around, smiling nervously. "Half a key of dope?"

"Straight powder! Ain't even been cooked up yet!"

"And just how am I supposed to do this? I don't own no weapons."

Rondell reached under his seat and brought out his 9mm. He wiped it clean with his T-shirt, then used the shirt as a glove when he handed the piece to Stan.

Stan took the gun cautiously and stared at it as if it was his first time holding one.

"Alright, check it, they at his mother's house right now—building thirty-six," Rondell said and gave Stan the apartment number. "I don't care how you gotta do it, cuz, just do it! When it's done, come see me and I'll take care of you. Deal?"

"Deal!"

*   *   *

Chancey could see Nikki through a gap in the curtains. What an ugly sight, he thought. She was on her back, extended evenly with the length of the sofa, looking comatose with her mouth open. Her hair was tangled like it hadn't been combed since the last time he saw her.

He knocked on the door, then the window; Nikki was lifelessly still with the phone at her side. She must have been guarding it from

Setchi, he thought as he called the house. He could literally hear it ringing through the sill of the window opening. He shook his head, finding it hard to believe the loud rings didn't even make her wince.

He saw the bright fuchsia in the shorts of Setchi's purplish pajama set when she walked from the room to get the phone. He tapped lightly on the door and immediately got her attention.

Setchi let her brother in and greeted him with a frown. "I thought you was gone already."

"I came back," he said and walked over to Nikki. "How long she been layin' here like this."

Setchi rolled her eyes. "All day."

Chancey looked at his mother's stomach to see if she was breathing. "Nikki," he called after seeing movement.

"Don't waste your time; I tried already," Setchi said, walking back to the room.

Chancey went behind her and picked up the McDonalds bag she stepped over. "You just gon' walk right over it, huh?"

Setchi looked back. "That ain't mine! She had that!"

Chancey looked in the bag and saw half of a Big Mac and some fries, and tossed it on the floor by Nikki. "How come y'all don't clean this house up?" he asked, walking into the kitchen to pour himself something to drink. He looked in the cabinets for a clean glass; they were all in the sink, dirty. He curled his nose at the clumps of grease floating on top of the sudless dish water. He stuck two of his fingers in after the beer mug and brought it up by the handle, but didn't feel like scrubbing away the greasy coat that covered it like wax.

He dropped the mug and watched it tumble down pass the greasy ten-inch skillet. He opened the refrigerator and didn't have to look hard for the colorful Pepsi can standing alone on the empty shelf. "Oooh, can I have this?" he asked, popping the top. Then he started searching for something to munch on. "How come y'all don't have no food up in here?"

Setchi walked in the kitchen. "Mama gotta go grocery shopping."

"And who put that pot of grease in the sink like that?"

Setchi smacked her lips. "How long you gon' be here?" she asked.

Chancey started smiling. He got up on her and said, "All night!"

"Dang!" she said and snapped her fingers.

"What's up with you and ol' boy?"

"We broke up," Setchi sighed.

Smiling, "What he do? Start liking one of your lil' friends?" Chancey asked and took a swig of the Pepsi.

"Ha, ha, ha, very funny," Setchi said, rolling her eyes.

"Well, what he do?"

She took a deep breath. "Somebody told me he was married."

This was too much drama for one night, Chancey thought. "How old is he, Setchi?"

"I think like about um…eighteen…"

"Hell nah! You ain't married at eighteen," Chancey said, shaking his head.

"I don't really know. For real! I'm not lying!"

"Who told you he was married?"

"Some friends at school."

Chancey twisted his lips to the side.

"Uh-huh! They did!"

"Setchi."

"What?" Setchi smiled.

"Don't laugh! Ain't nothin' cute about you gettin' with these grown-ass men," Chancey said. "Just because I ain't around that much no more, don't mean you gotta start actin' wild."

Setchi turned sensitive and held a look that showed regret.

"You a pretty girl, Setchi. It's gon' be a lotta men that try'da get at you. That don't mean you get wit' all of 'em. You gotta pick and choose the one that's right for you. But wait, wait, wait, hold up…you shouldn't even be worried about that right now!"

Setchi was looking like there was something she wanted to say.

Chancey was patient. He knew it would come out eventually. "How long y'all been broke up?" he asked to soften her up. He took another swig of Pepsi.

"It's been almost two weeks. He ain't called or nothin'."

"What do you want 'em to say? Hell, he's married! He prolly wit' his wife right now. Chillin'!" He held the Pepsi can to his mouth, tilted his head back, and swallowed.

"I seen 'er, Chancey! She came to the motel and was going off and screaming and hittin' 'em and stuff…" Setchi stopped. "You okay?"

Chancey had unintentionally spit out the Pepsi. He started

frowning and scratching his head as he thought. *Now, I know she didn't just say motel! Nah, she didn't say that...I KNOW she didn't say that!* He chuckled to keep his rage hidden. "When was this?"

"That night you was trippin' about me leaving."

"Uh-huh." Chancey sat his drink down.

"Yeah. Well anyway, his wife was..."

"You talkin' about the night you and Nikki was plottin', right?"

Setchi started smiling.

"Did she know where you was goin'?"

"Yeah! She don't be trippin' off Curt. He be givin' us money, bringin' us food..."

"Drug dealer?"

"No, he works! He work for the City of L.A. He been out there for like seven or eight years..."

"That would mean his ass started at ten or eleven!"

"Huh? No, he...okay, let me see...he..."

"You said his ass is eighteen! So, if he been on his job for seven years, that means he started at eleven! Do the math!"

"No, I said I *think* he was eighteen..."

"And you been to a motel wit' 'em?"

"No!"

"You just finished sayin' the wife saw y'all at the motel!" Chancey's blood was boiling. He had heard enough to slap the taste from Setchi's mouth five sentences ago. But hitting Setchi wouldn't do any good, he thought. She was just young and naïve, and left alone to learn about life the hard way like he did. "You all at a fuckin' motel wit' a nigga at fifteen years old..." He shook his head and walked out the kitchen.

Setchi followed him to the living room.

Nikki was wakening from her lethargic state. She rolled over on her side and adjusted her pillow for comfort. She just so happened to look up at Chancey's argumentative eyes, then at Setchi's fearful ones. She heard Chancey fussing, but her brain wasn't fully functional to where she could make out his words.

"Yeah, I'm talkin' about you!" he said.

Nikki sat upright on the couch. Her eyelids blinked like they wanted to stay closed. As Chancey watched her, he thought about all the times Rondell explained to him what someone on drugs looked like and how they acted; right now, she was looking very familiar.

"Look at 'chew! You ain't even takin' care of yo'self—look how you look!" Chancey hollered.

"Don't worry about how the hell I look! Worry 'bout your own ass!"

"Oh, I ain't worried at all! Trust me!"

"Good!"

"See Setchi," Chancey said, pointing at Nikki, "I don't want you to end up like that. That's why I stay on you…"

"Fuck you, you ol' jail-bird-ass nigga!" Nikki yelled.

"That's the reason right there, Setchi!" Chancey added.

"Aw, nigga, get the fuck outta my house!"

"You wouldn't be in this shit if I didn't pay the rent!"

"Nobody asked you to pay a *mothafuckin'* thing around here!"

"I did it for Setchi! Not for you! For Setchi! But that's okay though, 'cause Setchi's comin' to live with me when I get my own place!"

"Aw, you ain't gon' get shit! And you ain't gon' be shit, either! Yo' fuckin' ass'll be back in jail before you know it! That's yo' home away from home, nigga!"

Those words hurt. Chancey couldn't lie about it. "And who's fault is that?" he asked. "Shit, you ain't never been no type of role model…"

"Don't even try'da blame yo' fucked-up-ass-life on me! Talkin' about Setchi's coming to live with you! Ha! I'd like to see that shit! Yo' ass ain't got a fuckin' pot to piss in! You stayin' wit' Ronnie! How the hell Setchi gon' come live with you? Yo' sorry ass ain't got nothin' to offer nobody!"

"Oh, but you do? Shit, you ain't got shit, either! Nothin' but this dirty-ass, roach-infested apartment!"

"That's alright! It's mine!"

"And if it wasn't for me, you wouldn't have *this* shit! You can't even pay the rent around this mothafucka! You too busy spendin' all yo' money on crack!"

Oooooooooh! Setchi's eyes grew. Her bottom lip dropped.

Nikki had upped her seat on the couch and started yelling vulgar things about her son, threatening to kill him if he didn't leave. The veins in her neck looked like they were pushing through her skin.

Setchi freaked when she saw her mother searching the drawers for a knife. "Chancey, don't say nothing else. Please!" she cried. She turned to Nikki, who was holding up the sharpest knife she had. "He's leaving now, Mama! See! He's leaving!" she said, then turned back to Chancey and begged him to leave.

"Setchi, you don't need to be livin' like this. I don't want you livin' like this…"

"The last time I put yo' ass out, you left walking! This time, nigga, yo' ass is going in a body bag!" Nikki yelled.

"Aw, shut the fuck up! You get on my fuckin' nerves!"

"Chancey, please! Just be quiet," Setchi said as she pushed him out the front door.

"Where does Curt live? And how old is he, Setchi?"

"Don't you fuckin' worry 'bout it!" Nikki screamed.

"Ain't nobody talkin' to you! I'm talkin' to Setchi…"

"I don't give a fuck who you talkin' to!"

"Chancey, just go, please," Setchi begged. She held her fist up to her ear and whispered, "I'll call you."

Chancey stepped down a couple of steps, then stopped to tell Nikki how wrong she was, but Nikki had wandered off to the back somewhere, cursing and declaring how she'd cut a person up for talking crazy to her.

"I'll call you, Chancey," Setchi said.

"Nah, I ain't try'na hear that. Don't let me find out who dude is! That's all I gotta say!" Chancey said, storming down the rest of the steps.

*   *   *

Stan pulled a black beanie over his head to hide his face. He had cut out the eyes so he could see as he prowled quietly through building thirty-six.

Tia and Kaylin were sitting on the hood of the car, listening to the radio and talking about everything from graduation to thieves. Kaylin saw Stan walk toward unit thirty-six, then simultaneously turn to head their way when he saw them.

"Who's that?" Tia asked, jumping down from the Pontiac.

"I don't know," Kaylin said. He put his hand on her back and guided her toward his apartment.

Stan started running after them!

"Oh my God, here he comes!" Tia screamed, jumping in the back of Kaylin.

Kaylin knew they didn't have much of a distance to make a clean getaway, and turned to reason with the gunman. "What 'chew want, cuz? You need a couple of dollars?" He reached in his back pocket for some money in hopes of saving their lives.

Stan was positive Kaylin was reaching for a gun. He reacted outside of his plans and fired a bullet into Kaylin's chest! Kaylin dropped to his knees and fell forward.

Tia wanted to scream, but couldn't. She couldn't run or move. She stood at the mercy of Stan's aim and trembled so hard, you could hear the vibration every time she took a breath. She wanted to beg Stan for her life, but everything inside of her had shut down, including her ability to control her bladder; her urine began to run down her leg like a waterfall.

Stan's confidence was overshadowed by the unfamiliar body lying on the ground in front of him. However, he knew he still had a job to do, and if he didn't do it fast, the person running his way was going to keep him and his cocaine from uniting. He tried hard to keep a steady hand as he ran backwards and fired another shot that blew Tia off her feet.

Chancey pulled his snub from the front of his pants and took a shot that missed Stan by inches as he chased him through the field. He ran after Stan until he got close enough to almost touch him. He stopped, placed his palm under his wrist, and fired off another round that tore straight through Stan's back.

Chancey didn't stick around to see his body fall. He ran to the Pontiac, started it up, and raced off when he heard the rising sounds of sirens. One officer tried to use his car as a rolling road block to keep Chancey from getting away. But he stopped short a minute too soon, and watched helplessly as Chancey swerved his vehicle around him and ran full speed down Grape Street.

Chancey left the officers choking in the dust as he raced down 103rd. All the stop lights made the pursuit torturous. He charged through the intersection at 103rd and Wilmington, thinking he could squeeze between two oncoming cars. Unbelievably, he made it! He was unaware of the officer on the lookout at the corner of Grandee Avenue and 103rd, and spun out of control when he swerved to keep from running over the metal spikes that had been placed in the middle of the road.

The spinning Pontiac finally slingshot to the left and crashed into a light pole. Chancey was dazed, but unharmed. He began to frenetically hunt for his gun as officers closed in on him. When he found it, he pointed it at his temple and closed his eyes.

"HOLD YOUR FIRE! HOLD YOUR FIRE!" one officer hollered at his crew.

Officer Woods crossed Grandee Avenue and veered off to the side on 103rd. He hopped from his car with his gun drawn and ran up to the Pontiac to join the officers surrounding it. "What do we got?" he asked one of the guys.

"Homicide back on 99th Place committed by this kid. Now he's turning the gun on himself."

Officer Woods took one slow step at a time until he maneuvered through the mass of men in blue uniforms. He struggled to see through the cracked windshield at the curly-head kid resembling Chancey. He walked on eggshells around to the driver's side of the vehicle for a better view. Sure enough, Chancey was stooped over the steering wheel, attempting to shoot himself in the head.

"Oh no," Officer Woods whispered to himself. He lowered his gun and asked the officers to step back. "I know this kid!" he told everyone. "Let me talk to 'em! Officer Anderson, step back, man! Officer Jones! Please, man, step back! I believe I can talk him outta this."

Officer Woods put his gun away and asked Chancey if he could talk to him. "You don't wanna do this, son," he said.

Chancey started hitting his head against the steering wheel.

"Now son, I'm gonna open the door…" Officer Woods reached for the handle with caution.

Every officer at the scene stayed on point.

"Now, I just wanna talk to you. That's all…just talk…" Officer Woods said, slowly kneeling down at Chancey's side. "Talk to me…tell me what happened."

Chancey brought his head up from the steering wheel and sat back. His face was drenched from a mixture of sweat and tears. He started rocking in his seat. The gun in his hand was still marking his brain as a target.

"Nothing in the world is worth killing yourself over, son," Officer Woods said.

"Niecy..."

"Okay. Now, who's Niecy?"

"I'm sorry, Niecy..." Chancey said, shaking his head. He looked at Officer Woods and cried. "Man, tell 'er I'm sorry ..."

Officer Woods held out his hand, but was careful not to touch Chancey. "Talk to me, son...tell me what happened...talk to me..."

"I don't know! I heard a shot...I heard a shot...when I got there he was on the ground...I got there too late...he was bleedin'...and he wasn't breathe...he wasn't breathin'..."

"Calm down, son! Just take a deep breath," Officer Woods said. His eyes were now watering. "Who wasn't breathing?"

"And they killed her right in front of me...I was right there!"

"There were two murders?"

Chancey was rocking violently.

"Chancey? Stay with me, son...talk to me..." Officer Woods begged. "Two people were killed tonight?"

"I was goin' back to school...I was finna get my life together..."

"It's not too late! You can't give up! Son, listen to me!"

"We was gettin' married and everything..."

Officer Woods grabbed his chest. "Your girlfriend? Tia?"

"Right in front of me, man! Shot 'er...they shot 'er..."

"Chancey," Officer Woods said. He went to put his hands on Chancey's shoulder, then quickly stopped himself. "You gotta tell me who did this! You tell me who did this! I'm telling you, that person will be history! I give you my word..."

"I already took care of 'em..."

Officer Woods paused. "Okay," he said. "Okay. So you were in fear of your life and you shot 'em! I can...we can fix that...you gotta...please...you gotta trust me..."

One of the officers saw the passenger's door was unlocked. He whispered his plans of going inside to his colleague and asked that he cover him.

Officer Woods said, "All you gotta do is trust me. That's right, son, put the gun down..."

Just as Chancey did, an officer barged in on the passenger's side.

"Anderson!" Officer Woods yelled, "What are you doin'!"

Chancey quickly raised the gun back up to his head and fired!

"NOOOOO!" Officer Woods yelled.

Chancey's body slumped over. Officer Woods grabbed him and checked his neck for a pulse. "Somebody get me an ambulance!" he yelled.

The officers were standing around wondering why he was yelling for the paramedics. It was clear Chancey was already gone by the look of his opened eyes.

Officer Woods held Chancey in his arms. "Somebody call me a fuckin'…"

"Woods!" the sergeant yelled. "He's gone, man! He's gone," he said, pulling the badly shaken officer from Chancey's wilted body.

Officer Anderson was sorrowful to the highest degree when he came up to the sergeant and Officer Woods. "Woods, man," he said, "all I was try'na do was save this kid's life. I was just trying to save his life! I never meant to…I'm sorry, man…"

Everyone was speechless. Officer Woods palmed the back of his head, looked up to the sky, and sighed.

"Woods, I want you to take the rest of the night off. Get you some rest," the sergeant said.

Officer Woods took a deep breath and shook his head. "Thanks Sarg, but uh…I think I'ma just…I don't know, man, just…"

"I understand what you're going through…"

"No, you don't!" Officer Woods snapped. "He wasn't supposed to die! This shit wasn't supposed to happen!"

"I understand that. But unfortunately, this was just one of those situations where it did. I don't know what else to say. Anderson was just try'na do his job…"

Officer Woods walked away from his sergeant. He stopped a foot or two away from him and crossed his fingers at the back of his head.

"Did this kid have a family?" the sergeant asked.

Officer Woods waited a few, sighed, then turned around and said, "He had a mother strung out on drugs and a sister he was try'na raise."

The sergeant closed his eyes and rubbed the brown bald spot on the top of his head. "Aw, man, this is terrible," he said, exhaling deeply. "Do we know where the sister is?"

An eavesdropping officer said, "We were able to pull up an address for..." He paused to eye Chancey's license. "Mr. Walker in the system. No listed number though."

"Okay. Let's go 'head and get the investigators out here..."

"I believe they've already been called, sir."

"Okay. Good deal," the sergeant said before he pulled Officer Woods to the side. "I want you to grab as many of Mr. Walker's belongings as you can and get them to the sister before the big dogs get here. 'Cause when they get here, the car and everything in it becomes their property. Hopefully, he had something she could put to good use, if you know what I mean."

"Yeah," Officer Woods said and nodded. "I appreciate that, man."

"Don't mention it," the sergeant said, patting Officer Woods on the back. He walked off telling his guys to quit standing around and put up the yellow tape.

Officer Woods closed Chancey's eyes and said a quick prayer over his body. He looked on the inside of the car—the windows, seats, dashboard, and front rugs were all sprayed with blood. The gruesome sight was more than his stomach could handle. He quickly popped the latch that would open the trunk and hurried to the back of the car.

The trunk overflowed with luggage and brochures on Catalina Island. Officer Woods snooped in and out of the baggage looking for something of significance. He saw all of Tia's items and left them alone. He wouldn't know where to deliver them if he wanted to. He lifted the flap on the blue suitcase that was unzipped and had to catch his breath when he saw the oodles of money lying on top. He slammed the flap down and looked around with large eyes.

*   *   *

Ninety-ninth Place was lit up like the grand finale of a fireworks show. Red, white, and blue lights were flashing left and right from fire trucks, police cars, an ambulance van, and from a helicopter up above.

Two paramedics jumped from the back of the ambulance with

their emergency kits in hand. One ran to Kaylin's aide, the other to Tia's.

The stubby fellow placed two of his rubber-gloved fingers on the side of Kaylin's neck and sighed at the still flesh.

"I got a pulse!"

Tia was groaning from the pain in her head. "Am I gonna die?" she asked the redhead woman with freckles who was checking her vital signs.

"You're gonna be just fine. Looks like you got shot in the shoulder there. You know who did this to ya'?"

"Why does my head hurt?"

"You took a pretty hard fall when you were hit. You may have even suffered a slight concussion. What's your name?"

"Tia...Arnold...where's Chancey...can I call my mother?"

"Just relax, honey. We're gonna get you to the hospital so we can fix that arm of yours, okay?"

22

"I'm sorry, but there's no way we have enough time for all y'all to speak. We gon' let two more people talk and that's it. You right here," a lady-friend of Nikki's said, pointing out a young man in a blue bandana, blue jeans, and a blue T-shirt. "And you, sir, right here," she said, pointing to Officer Woods.

Whining voices filled the pews.

"We know y'all been waitin' a long time, but we had to go in order. So, we're sorry, and we hope everybody understands. Thank you," she said and stepped down from the mic.

The dude in blue stepped up and took off his scarf. "My homeboy, Chancey, went out like a souljah! That nigga died for his!"

"Watch the language," said a minister.

"I wanna go out just like that when I die! To all my niggas from Grape Street…" He formed a letter C with two of his fingers on one hand and held it in the air. Then he stepped down and placed his head rag in Chancey's casket.

Nikki's friend barged in front of Officer Woods and stepped up to the mic. "I'ma ask y'all one more time: don't put nothin' else in the caskets! Keep your items! Please!" she said and stepped down slightly agitated.

Officer Woods stepped up on the pedestal in a black suit, tan shirt, and a black tie with tan and white stripes. He stood at the mic and studied everyone in the crowded mortuary. Every pew was crammed with bodies. Every side of the building was filled with rows of bodies occupying the walls. Even the door had two or three bodies fighting for spacing in the small opening. He turned to his left to learn some of the faces of the family. He knew a few like Rondell, Nikki, and Setchi. The other twenty or so were unfamiliar to him. He nodded his head to Setchi, then to Nikki. Rondell wouldn't look at him.

Officer Woods turned back to face the crowd head on. "Many of you know me. For those of you that don't, my name is Officer Woods. I work out of the Southeast station. I patrol the Watts area. Now, I know that we're pressed for time, so I'll make this quick. I heard a lot of you bragging and boasting about the way Chancey died. You think that's cool, do you? To go out like a soldier? Well, let me explain to you how this soldier went out," Officer Woods said, adjusting the microphone. "This soldier went out crying! Yes, with tears! I was right at his side! Begging him to put the gun down!"

Nikki ran outside screaming. Setchi stood up to run after her, but some friends and family members beat her to it.

Officer Woods said, "It's nothing cool about blowing your brains out! Not when it's no coming back! Chancey made his last decision! And it was a bad one. A bad one! He'll never be able to play with the kids he may have had. Get that GED he was going after. Get the job he was sure to get. It's over now!"

"Sir, I'ma haf' to ask you to wrap it up. I'm sorry," a spokesman for the family said.

"Before I go, is there someone by the name of Niecy here?"

Niecy was hesitant at first. She finally raised her hand midway past the top of her head. Her eyes were hidden behind a pair of dark sunglasses.

"Ma'am, I don't know who you are," Officer Woods said, "but Chancey asked me to tell you that he was sorry...sorry for letting you down..."

People started boohooing like babies. Setchi was hugging the edge of the pew, crying her heart out. Niecy was also wailing viciously. She held her Kleenex to her mouth to smother the shrieking sounds of her cry. Rondell sat behind Setchi in his beige suit. He loosened the blue and beige tie from around his neck and unbuttoned the first two buttons in his black shirt, thinking it would help him breathe better. Holding back his tears was starting to put a strain on the muscles in his throat. He looked to his left at Rosie and Ronda sitting next to him.

Ronda was making her Barbie doll do the splits when she felt Rondell bounce her Shirley Temple curls in his hand. She looked at him and smiled, then continued to control her doll's acrobatic movements.

Rondell stared at her. He just kept staring. For the first time, he saw himself in her cheekbones. Her eyes were his eyes. Even the complexion in her skin was that of his complexion.

Rosie saw the shadow of Rondell's face from the corner of her eye. She turned to meet his stare; his eyes were apologetic. She assumed for not being a father. She assumed for being such a user. A loser! A conniver! A schemer! Regardless, Ronda was still his. And she pushed her close to him with her hip to let him know it.

His smirk was followed by a chuckle. He put his arm around Ronda to show Rosie that he already knew.

When Officer Woods stepped down from the mic, the spokesperson announced the time for a quick viewing of the bodies. "Please don't stand at the caskets too long. We want to give the family a chance for final viewing as well," she said.

Chancey and Kaylin looked like twins in their black suits, blue shirts, and black brimstone hats with the blue feather stuck in the side. Their caskets were also a matching blue; Rondell picked them out. He coordinated everything. Dressed them and fixed their hair, even. He stood over Kaylin's casket first, said his goodbyes, and explained that he never meant to see him laid to rest so soon. He kissed Kaylin on his forehead and then walked over to Chancey's casket, where his tears began to shed. *Damn, cuz*, he said, shaking his head. *If I could trade places, nigga, you know I would.* He stood and cried over Chancey's body for a long time. *I would, cuz. That's on everything! God wasn't ready for you yet.* Rondell looked back at Setchi and fingered for her to come up.

Setchi buried her face behind the back of Niecy's head. All during the services, she made extra efforts in *not* looking toward the front.

Look at 'er scary ass, Rondell told Chancey.

"Ronnie," the spokesperson said, "I know you sayin' goodbye, but…"

He looked at the lady and said, "Alright, I know…I'ma hurry up…" then looked back at Chancey. At his hair. His features. His hands. His casket. *I don't wanna sound like a broken record, Chancey. I know I apologized to you a thousand times already, but uh, cuz, I…I'm…I know this shit is my fault, cuz, and I'm sorry. And I'm changin' my life…you know a nigga's spooked right now, right?* Rondell chuckled, looking up to the ceiling. *But uh', on the real…I'ma miss you, cuz,* he said and kissed Chancey's forehead. *See you at the crossroads.*

*   *   *

It had been a long day for Setchi. She laid her tired body across her bed and thought about everyone at the funeral. She hoped her brother and Kaylin understood why she didn't want to look at them. She tried not to elaborate on the occasion too long, fearing the nightfall scheduled to take place within less than four hours. To take her mind off of death, she tried to plan out her job search strategy. Focusing on the fact that she was broke didn't help. She sat up and looked out her bedroom window at the innocent kids running and playing, remembering how she and Chancey used to do that. Where did it all go wrong, she thought as the mailman strolled by with his sack of correspondence. She got up from the bed and walked out on the balcony. Nikki was sitting on the steps reading about her son's fate in the L.A. Times. The night of Chancey's death, Nikki swore of a better life for her and Setchi. Setchi sighed quietly, wondering if it was the truth this time.

"Good day to you," the Oriental postman said.

Both Nikki and Setchi reached for the mail at the same time. Setchi didn't know why she was reaching for it; she never received any mail. However, she got to the envelopes first, and again, couldn't understand why she was flipping through the letters like she had something coming. She handed Nikki a stack of bills and kept the one envelope from Bank of America with her name on it. She walked back to her room, frowning and confused. She actually thought about throwing the junk mail in the trash. It had to be junk mail, she figured. Why would she be getting something from Bank of America? Or any bank? She ripped the envelope apart and read the welcome letter inside of it. "Thank you for choosing Bank of America!" she read, frowning. As she read on, the letter stated that a trust fund had been opened for her in the amount of five thousand and twenty-nine dollars, and would not be released to her until her eighteenth birthday.

Setchi looked up to the sky and visualized her brother's face. "Thank you, Chancey," she said. "Thank you."